Praise for *The Deadly Hours*

"What a treat! Everyone loves a good 'curse' story, and here are four of them, all together in one very clever bundle. I was wishing the curse could go on for another decade or two, just so I could read another story about it!"

—Victoria Thompson, *USA Today* bestselling author

"A charming book. Four interconnected visits to a world of danger, wit, beauty, and genuine romance. Treat yourself. Emerge refreshed, and smiling! I did."

—Anne Perry, international bestselling author

"Intriguing, full of suspense, and deliciously satisfying, *The Deadly Hours* is a fantastic read. I've long adored each of these authors' individual work; together, they're an unstoppable force."

—Tasha Alexander, *New York Times* bestselling author

The Deadly Hours

SUSANNA KEARSLEY
C. S. HARRIS
ANNA LEE HUBER
CHRISTINE TRENT

Cover design by Olga Grlic

Published by Poisoned Pen Press, an imprint of Sourcebooks
P.O. Box 4410, Naperville, Illinois 60567-4410
(630) 961-3900
sourcebooks.com

Library of Congress Cataloging-in-Publication Data

Names: Kearsley, Susanna. Weapon of choice. | Huber, Anna Lee. In a fevered hour. | Trent, Christine. Pocketful of death. | Harris, C. S. Siren's call.
Title: The deadly hours / Susanna Kearsley, C.S. Harris, Anna Lee Huber, Christine Trent.
Description: Naperville, Illinois : Poisoned Pen Press, [2020]
Identifiers: LCCN 2020007187 | (trade paperback)
Subjects: LCSH: Detective and mystery stories, American. | Historical fiction, American. | Detective and mystery stories, Canadian. | Historical fiction, Canadian. | Pocket watches--Fiction.
Classification: LCC PS648.D4 D4138 2020 | DDC 813/.087208--dc23
LC record available at https://lccn.loc.gov/2020007187

Printed and bound in the United States of America.
VP 10 9 8 7 6 5 4 3 2 1

"It strikes! one, two,
Three, four… Enough, enough, dear watch,
Thy pulse hath beat enough. Now sleep and rest;
Would thou could'st make the time to do so too;
I'll wind thee up no more."
—Ben Jonson, *The Staple of News*

CONTENTS

Weapon of Choice

Susanna Kearsley

For Diana Gabaldon
who, over dinner, when I told her
what I'd seen Hugh doing,
smiled, and said,
"That sounds like a novella."
And encouraged me to write it.

The Storm

"A fearful eye thou hast…
So foul a sky clears not without a storm."
—Shakespeare, *King John*: act 4, scene 2

February 10, 1733

He never would tire of watching her sleep.

In his boyhood, when he'd still believed in such things, he'd imagined what angels must look like. To his eyes, awake or asleep, that was how Mary looked. Like an angel. *His* angel.

His wife.

If someone had told him a year ago he'd earn the love of a woman like this, he'd have thought them insane.

Before she'd crossed his path, he'd been resigned to going through his life unburdened by entanglements and sentiment, in service to the earl he had protected since the time when they had both been younger men.

He'd done what needed to be done. He'd killed when duty had required it. When duty had required him to guard two women and a man in Paris, he had done as he was ordered, keeping safely out of sight, as was his habit. In the shadows.

He'd been watching from his window when she stepped down from the coach into the Paris street. And from that moment, everything had changed.

She'd brought him back into the light.

She stirred, curled in the berth set in the curved hull of this forward cabin of the ship. They'd shared this cabin once before, when she had neither trusted him nor liked him much, and he had made his bed upon the floor, but now she reached for him, still sleeping, as she often did. Her hand fell on the empty blankets where he had been lying, and he watched her eyes drift open.

"Hugh?"

He'd finished dressing. In its bracket on the wall the lamp was swinging, throwing his tall shadow into motion.

She was only half-awake. "Is something wrong?"

Extinguishing the lamp, he told her, "No. Go back to sleep."

It was a touching measure of her faith in him that, by the time he'd reached the door, her breathing had resettled in its former peaceful rhythm, and he took great care to let the latch fall gently as he left the cabin.

Up on deck, his eyes adjusting to the darkness of a night sky lit by nothing but a crescent moon against a sweep of stars, he found the captain standing by the rail.

Captain Marcos María del Rio Cuerda was Hugh's exact opposite—handsome and cultured and gallant with ladies, his coats made of velvet, his cuffs edged with lace, his dark beard and curling hair trimmed in the fashion of his native Spain. But he'd earned Hugh's respect and, within limits, his trust.

And he didn't miss much. Without looking around from the rail now, Del Rio said, "You have just won me a wager, my friend." He called up to the brown-skinned sailor working to make some adjustment to the rigging, "You see, Juan? It is as I told you."

Whatever Juan answered was carried away by the wind, but Del Rio looked satisfied. "I told him when we changed course, 'Watch now, MacPherson will come up to see what is happening,' but Juan was sure you'd stay sleeping. It was a good wager. Shall I tell you what you've won me?"

Hugh said nothing. Stepped up to the rail. "Tell me why we've changed course."

"Ah. Because of that." Del Rio gave a nod to where the stars were being swallowed by a rising wall of blackness. "It is the time for storms here in these seas of course, but this, to me, does not look like an ordinary storm. And always it is better to prevent than to lament. If it worsens, we may have to change our course again and seek a port for shelter. Portofino is the closest. But that may spoil your plans to be in Genoa in two days' time."

"My plans will also be spoiled if I'm drowned."

Del Rio grinned. "It's true. It's also true, my friend, that you are changed since last I saw you. You now have a sense of humor. I give credit to your lovely wife. A woman most remarkable." His grin broadened. "I can promise you, if you *are* drowned, I will take the best care of her and see she is not lonely."

Hugh reminded him, "You have a wife."

A pause. "Ah, yes, my wife, of course. And now we also have a son. Did I already mention this?"

"No."

"It is a great thing, to have a family. I can recommend it. I would have them with me, but it has not been so safe since this past summer, with so many ships mixed in all the fighting for Oran."

Hugh knew this well, because the war had delayed his own plans to journey with the earl to Spain and build a home with Mary there. Instead, they had been held at Rome.

"Since then," Del Rio said, "the corsairs have been a great annoyance. They have kept me very busy."

Underneath the offhand elegance there lay an iron strength. Del Rio once had been a pirate, before turning those same skills to a more honorable use in hunting pirates for the Spanish crown—specifically the Barbary corsairs who prowled these seas in search of plunder, making slaves of those they captured.

That the Spaniard smiled and joked and was a gallant host did nothing to erase the fact that he was as adept as Hugh at killing when the need arose, and any man who failed to see the ruthless edge concealed within the velvet scabbard did so at his peril.

As did any man who let his guard down when Del Rio asked a question that seemed innocent.

"Your wife's maid and the little dog are still at Rome?"

Hugh answered, not confirming or denying this, "They do not travel well."

"Of course. It's just that I've heard reports you Jacobites have trouble there—that all the court of your King James at Rome is under heavy guard."

He glanced at Hugh, who kept his gaze fixed on the storm, unhelpfully.

"But maybe these reports are wrong," Del Rio said. "The English tell so many lies about your king, to make their own King George seem more legitimate, as though they did not steal your own king's birthright and his crown and put it on a German prince for no more reason than your James was born a Catholic. It's a very great injustice." He sighed, then added, "Still, these things that I have heard about the troubles of your king at Rome—they do not seem like lies. I'm told the pope himself is much concerned, and orders no one is to enter Rome without great scrutiny. As though they fear that someone may be coming who is dangerous."

Hugh kept his face impassive, though he knew it would have no effect.

His silence did not stop Del Rio. "And if your king was sending you to Genoa because of something dangerous, I do not think that you would bring your wife. Unless," he said, "this danger was so great you could trust no one else to keep her safe."

The wind was rising, and more stars had now been lost behind the swiftly spreading blackness. Hugh's eyes narrowed on the swelling waves. "Is that a ship?"

Del Rio looked, and swore.

"Corsairs?" Hugh asked.

The Spaniard raised his spyglass for a better view, and swore again. "No. Something worse."

He handed Hugh the spyglass. From that distance, Hugh could only see the white of sails that caught the pale faint gleam of moonlight, with the dark shape of a running ship beneath it, and small glints of light like those of lanterns near the prow.

Del Rio said, “It is Vautour. We have a long acquaintance.”

“French?”

“I do not think Lambert Vautour claims any country as his own, and I am sure none claims him back.” He called again to Juan, up in the rigging. “Leave that. Go and get the others. I want every man on deck. We make for Portofino. Tell them it is La Sirène.” And with a final quick assessment of the far-off sails now being chased toward them by the ever-growing dark, he turned his back against the rising gale. “At least we know now why there is a storm.”

Hugh frowned. “A ship can’t raise a storm.”

“I would agree,” Del Rio said. There was a grimness to his voice that Hugh had never heard before. “But La Sirène is not a ship.”

First Day

"By accident most strange, bountiful Fortune
...hath mine enemies
Brought to this shore."
—Shakespeare, *The Tempest*: act 1, scene 2

I

February 11, 1733

The innkeeper at Portofino had five rooms—none large, but all were clean. Hugh walked into and out of them until he reached a corner room with windows front and side that overlooked the harbor and the sea and hills surrounding them, and setting down their portmanteau and the long case that held his rifled gun, he told the landlord, "This one."

Mary always found a need to be more friendly. "It's a beautiful room," she said, speaking the Genovese dialect she had been practicing since he'd first told her that they would be going to Genoa, and which apparently they spoke here, too. She liked languages. Since their arrival in Rome at the end of last April, she'd learned to converse in Italian and started a study of his native Gaelic, with help from their Highland-born maid. When he'd pointed out, rightly enough, that her mother was French and her father from Edinburgh, meaning that none of her people had been of the Highlands, she'd answered, "But yours were, and you are, and I want to learn it," and that had been that, though she'd often complained that the Gaelic and he were well matched. "You're both difficult."

She had learned Genovese faster. "That quilt," she said now to their landlord, "is lovely."

His mother had made it. Of course she had. Naturally he had to tell them the story of how it was made, how she'd chosen the fabric, and Mary not only indulged but encouraged him, having a genuine interest in people's small stories.

Hugh caught her eye and motioned they could use a basin and some water, leaving her to ask for it, and when it was delivered—steaming hot, no less, with linen cloths for drying—and she'd thanked their host and shut the door and bolted it, she said, "You see what being nice can do?"

"Aye, waste my time. I could have been asleep already underneath that quilt, without a care for how each stitch was made."

He knew, when they'd first met, she'd feared his size, his face, his tone of voice. But now she only rolled her eyes. "You never lie down in the daytime when you sleep. You're always sitting up. And even then, you're more awake than not."

"I may surprise ye." He had taken off his longer coat and now shrugged free of both the sword belts that he wore crossed one over the other at his chest, and laying those aside moved to the nearest window.

It was raining harder now. The wind flung water at the small glass panes, and although it was midway through the morning any daylight was well hid behind the darker mass of clouds that swirled and shifted shape and seemed alive. Del Rio had been right in one respect, Hugh thought. This was no ordinary storm.

Mary came to stand beside him. "Will they be all right?"

She meant Del Rio and his crew, who had remained aboard their ship moored in the harbor near two smaller vessels that were also sheltering against the coming weather. Hugh glanced once more at the sky, then down again at the small ships and, although unconvinced, said, "Aye."

"Is either of those ships the one you saw last night?" She asked it very casually, and Hugh suppressed a smile.

"What makes ye think I saw a ship?"

"The crew does talk, you know. And I do learn things."

For a fleeting instant he allowed the smile to show, if faintly. "Do ye?"

"Yes. I learned this morning, for example, that the crew seemed most concerned about a captain named Vautour. They also seemed convinced his ship, called *La Sirène*, has caused this storm, which is of course ridiculous, but sailors do sometimes have very curious beliefs."

Hugh said, "*Le Tigre.*"

"Pardon?"

"Vautour's ship," he said, "is called *Le Tigre.*"

"What is La Sirène, then?"

"Not a ship. That's all I know."

"But…surely they weren't speaking of an actual…" She knew, as he did, what "la sirène" meant in French. "They cannot truly think a *mermaid* caused this storm? That's even more ridiculous."

He did not know what they believed, and said as much. "But neither of those ships," he told her, "is the one I saw last night."

"Well then, you do not need to watch them." With her smaller hand in his, she tugged him backward from the window. "Come lie down."

"I never lie down in the daytime when I sleep," he told her dryly.

"Good," she said, and led him to the wide bed covered with the quilt whose history he could quote in detail, intimately. "Because I did not have sleep in mind."

Her smile, just then, was everything. He took her face in both his hands and kissed her, and for the next while, there was only Mary.

When *Le Tigre* slid into view two hours later, Hugh was at the window again, looking down. He'd put on his better gray suit, combed and tied back his hair, and in deference to Mary wore no sword at all.

"You don't need to," she'd said. "You're all knives as it is. I've lost count of how many you carry."

He could have replied that he carried thirteen, plus the dirk at his waist and the pair of small pistols concealed in his inner coat pockets, but he took her point. Swords were of next to no practical use in a dining room, and any man who dared draw on him would, soon enough, learn he'd made a mistake.

Mary added, "Besides, I'd be grateful if you didn't kill anybody at dinner."

Had she made that comment not ten minutes earlier, he might have promised with confidence that he'd behave, since as far as he knew there were only two other guests in the whole inn. He'd heard them come upstairs not long ago, talking in hushed voices, laughing. A man and a woman. With only the four of them seated at dinner, Hugh thought it unlikely he'd face any threat.

But *Le Tigre*'s arrival had changed that.

That ship's captain had made Del Rio concerned enough to run for shelter, and that in turn made Hugh inclined to be vigilant. Just now the ship was still turning to nose its way into the harbor. It would be some time before anyone on it could lower a boat in this weather and row to shore. If he and Mary were fortunate, they would be finished with dinner and back in the room before anyone did.

She'd finished arranging her hair. "I am ready."

Downstairs, there were two public rooms—one for dining, and one for a parlor, the latter with comfortable chairs and a carpet and even a table for cards, but the dining room they were now entering was set more plainly, one long common table with benches and chairs on a tiled floor, brass sconces with candles hung round on the plastered walls above dark wainscoting. There was but one door, a hearth, and a window whose lower half had been protectively shuttered.

Hugh would have preferred one more door, but a door and a window were good enough. Choosing the chair that allowed him a clear view of both, he stood waiting for Mary to sit, but she'd paused and half turned at the sound of the other guests' voices approaching, preparing to give a polite welcome.

The couple that entered the room were about their own ages—a tall, dark-haired man in his mid-thirties, leaner than Hugh but with shoulders as wide. And a woman who looked to be several years younger than that, with a lively, bright face that lit up in a smile when she caught sight of Mary.

"Well, this is a pleasant surprise, Mistress Dundas." She held out her hands, coming forward, and Mary returned the warm greeting.

"MacPherson, now," Mary corrected her. "This is my husband. And Hugh, this is—"

Anyone who didn't know Mary well might have thought she had paused to hold back a small cough, but he knew better, just as he knew that she hadn't forgotten the woman's name. Mary had one of the best memories of any person he'd met in his life.

He was careful to keep his expression unchanged but he studied the woman more closely as she smoothly stepped in, not missing a beat, and said, "Anna O'Connor. And my husband, Edmund."

Her husband paid his honors in the same way Hugh did, with a nod and not a bow, and each man took the other's measure as they sat.

The Irishman was gifted with the sort of charm that women liked, a face of even features and an easy smile and eyes that held a challenge. Hugh returned it with a level gaze that for some reason made O'Connor look amused and glance away as he leaned back to make room for the maid to set their dinner platters on the table.

Hugh paid little attention to what they were served, but the moment the maid had retreated again he found Anna O'Connor assessing his own face with keenly intelligent eyes.

"You're a friend of the Earl Marischal." She was stating a fact, and not asking him. "I've heard you well described. Good. You can help us."

Her husband said, "Anna."

"Edmund, Mistress MacPherson and I are acquainted. Her husband's a man of impeccable honor. I know what I'm doing."

"Sure, I never said you didn't. But the wine jug's on that side of you. I'd be obliged if you would share it."

Passing him the wine jug with a sidelong look, she carried on, "You've only just arrived yourselves this morning, so I understand, but have you in your travels met a Scotsman by the name of Douglas? Fifty years of age or so, fair-haired, with a long nose?"

Hugh didn't answer, but the trust between the women clearly went both ways, for Mary told her, "No, we haven't."

"We have reason to believe he has been sent to kill the Duke of Ormonde, who right now is traveling from Avignon to Rome and may not realize that the English have him marked—" She broke off. Looked at Hugh's face closely. "But I'm telling you what you already know," she said. "You know there's an assassin."

Hugh said nothing, but she nodded as though he had told her yes.

"And you are on your way to meet the duke at…Genoa?" she guessed. "To be his escort as he makes his way to Rome."

The woman's mind was quick, and Hugh, despite his own misgivings, could not but admire it.

Still guardedly, he settled in his chair and took a drink of wine, and thought a moment.

"Tell me more," he said, "about this Douglas."

II

"She's rather remarkable, don't you agree?" Mary said.

They were back in their room upstairs, Hugh at the window as he'd been before, while Mary sat off to the side, having turned their small, round table into her writing desk so she could set down the day's happenings in her journal.

It was one of the things they had clashed about in the beginning—her keeping a journal. He'd thought it unsafe, and unwise. But she kept it in cipher, and as she'd reminded him, paper was easy to burn.

Besides, he'd come to like the way she wrote things down, giving the commonplace the air of an adventure. And from time to time, between the daily entries, she would drop one of the fairy tales she'd told to entertain Captain del Rio—who particularly liked them—or her maid. Or him.

Hugh liked her tales. He'd often watched her weave them out of strands of whimsy floating in the air, using the objects and the people who surrounded her the way his father once had tied off threads and set his loom in motion, letting fly the shuttle till it all became one cloth of substance.

And in the same way the woolen cloth his father wove had settled warm around Hugh's shoulders as a child, so sometimes now, big hardened man he was, and weary with the world, he'd sit with Mary at his side and she would tell a story that would settle over him and make him feel his troubles were far off, and all was right and well, and naught else mattered.

This was not a time for stories, though.

The storm had worsened and he could no longer see the harbor.

He was not at present in a mood for conversation, but Mary needed no reply from him to continue her praise of Anna O'Connor. She told him of how they'd first met, when Anna had been traveling under a different name and on a secret business in the interest of the king, which was why she'd been uncertain how to greet her in the dining room downstairs, lest Anna was on secret business now as well, and did not wish to be revealed. Mary described her as she might have done the heroine of some romantic tale—a bold adventuress, of diamond-rare abilities.

She finished with: "However much this storm is interfering with our plans, I am glad it has brought our paths together once again. What do they say about the ill wind? That it always blows some good?"

Hugh, watching the effects of that same wind, remarked, "Her husband lives by that, no doubt. He strikes me as the type to think there's no wind blows so ill but that a man might profit by it. Preferably him."

Mary seemed unsurprised that he'd formed an opinion of Edmund O'Connor—but then she'd known Hugh long enough now to read his reactions to people with maddening ease, even when he took care not to change his expression. She did seem surprised, though, that he'd taken time to express that opinion. He generally didn't.

Her rebuke, when it came, was more of a gentle reminder. "You cannot judge a person by the face they show the world. Someone judging you by yours would think you fierce and threatening, good for your sword and little else…you see? Yes, that's the very face I'm speaking of, that glare you have, right there. They see that, and they miss the man inside, the man who reads, and laughs, and was intelligent enough to figure out this cipher in… What was it now? Less than a week, as I recall?"

"Two days."

"Well, there you are, then." Having made her point, she inked her pen and went on writing in her journal. "Anyway, does Anna seem the sort of woman who would choose her husband so unwisely?"

Hugh considered that in silence for a moment. *No*, he thought. She'd seemed to him a careful woman.

Earlier, at dinner, when she'd told him what she knew about the man named Douglas, she'd shared only the essential information, saying nothing anyone could follow back to ferret out her sources.

She'd said only "I was told," not who had told her, nor if her informant had been friend or stranger. Only once had she let any detail slip, and it was inadvertent.

"Years ago," she'd said, "the English government sent Douglas into France to kill King James. Of course he failed, and so they must have thought his face forgotten, but when Douglas stepped ashore this time, he was soon recognized."

Obviously, then, whoever told Anna O'Connor that Douglas had "stepped ashore" lived on a coast somewhere—likely in France, even more likely at a port such as Boulogne or Calais, where the English were wont to land.

Hugh, giving no sign he'd sorted this out, had merely waited for her to go on.

She'd said, "We did not know his target, but we knew he was a danger, so we followed him. To Avignon. He made it very clear, there, who he'd come to find."

James Butler, Duke of Ormonde, made his home at Avignon. In his prime he'd been the dashing hero of the people, commanding all of Britain's armies in the final years of Queen Anne's reign. When she died, he stood with the Jacobites, backing the claim of her half brother, James, to the throne—and was charged with high treason. Outwitting his opponents, he'd avoided arrest and imprisonment and escaped to safety, but Ormonde was a fighting man. No death sentence could stop him taking part in the late uprising, and even though he had not won, the current English government yet feared his popularity.

To many throughout Britain, Ormonde was a hero still. A man like that could lift his sword and, with a word, stir loyalty in sleeping hearts, and raise an army at his back. A man like that, the English knew, was dangerous to them.

And to the Jacobites, invaluable.

"Thankfully," Anna had continued, "we discovered that the duke had left his house already, well disguised, and set off on the road. We stayed behind Douglas as far as Marseilles, where we lost both his trail and the duke's, though I'm told the duke sailed from there on the *Gallant Jack*, headed for Genoa."

Hugh had repeated, "The *Gallant Jack*?"

"Yes." She'd eyed him closely. "Do you know the ship?" Not waiting for his nod, she'd asked, "And do you know her captain? I had wondered if he was perhaps a kinsman of the duke's, for I believe his name is also Butler."

At her side, her husband with a lazy smile had commented, "An Irish name. Let's hope that means he's someone we can trust."

"He's Cornish." Hugh's tone had been clipped. "And aye, he can be trusted."

More than some, he thought.

He pushed the conversation from his mind.

It took him a moment to realize that Mary, at her table with her journal, was still talking to him. "...must admit this ill wind blew us something else of value."

"What is that?" he asked her, absently.

"We knew the English dispatched an assassin. But we didn't know his name, nor his description. Now, because this storm has blown us here with Anna and her husband, we know both these things."

The knowledge helped him less than he'd have liked, for Douglas was a common name, and he'd met many Scots of middle age with fair hair and long noses.

Hugh would have much preferred to know where Douglas *was*. That was what had him worried. If the *Gallant Jack* had managed to escape this storm, she might already have arrived at Genoa, and Douglas, too, might be there. And the Duke of Ormonde would be unprotected, unaware of the assassin stalking him.

Meanwhile, Hugh was trapped here, blinded by the weather, unable to see past his own reflection in the window. He always hated feeling helpless.

Although he knew the winds couldn't be blowing from all four directions at once, still it seemed that they were, hurling rain with such force at the glass of the window it overrode all other sounds for a moment, and Hugh nearly missed the quick knock at their door.

It was Anna O'Connor.

She entered the room when invited to do so and closed the door behind her, but kept one hand on the latch.

A careful woman.

She asked Hugh, "I don't suppose you also know the captain of the ship *Le Tigre*?"

"No."

"Because our landlord's just had word he's on his way to shore and needs two rooms prepared, and now our landlord's wife is praying. I had hoped you might know why."

"No."

She accepted this. "We'll learn the facts ourselves, I should expect, when he arrives. Edmund and I thought we'd go down and wait in the parlor, since anyone coming in has to go by there. You're welcome to join us. I'll save you the elbow chair," she said to Hugh, as though that meant something, though if there was a meaning it escaped him.

Till she smiled and explained, "It's in the corner, well away from any windows, with a clear view of the parlor's door, so you can sit and have your back well guarded while you keep your eye on everyone, the way you did at dinner."

She was gone again before he could respond to that, so quietly and swiftly that she might have been a shadow slipping through the door.

He heard the lightly exhaled breath from Mary, like a sigh, and when he glanced her way he saw the admiration in her eyes. "You see?" she said. "*Rather* remarkable."

The upheavals of Mary's life had left her with a family scattered wide and, from what he'd observed, no friends at all except himself and their devoted maid, who'd stayed behind this time at Rome with Mary's dog. Hugh, after living so much on his own, felt complete in his life now with Mary, and needed no other, but clearly she longed for a friend and believed she had found one in Anna O'Connor.

He hoped she'd not be disappointed.

Not waiting for him to reply, Mary said, "You should trust her more, though. You may not know the captain of *Le Tigre*, but you know his name as well as I do. There was no avoiding it aboard our ship. The crew had much to say about Captain Vautour."

Captain Lambert Vautour, a pirate descended from pirates, whose father had been one of the infamous buccaneers of Saint-Domingue. Hugh had heard tales of those buccaneers, and last night on the ship Del Rio's crew had added to them, having sailed much in those waters. The cabin boy Juan came from Cartagena, which had been attacked and plundered many times over the years, and he had shared the stories he'd heard from his mother, who had hidden as a young girl in a small and airless space within the rafters of her home throughout the terror and brutality of one such raid.

The stories were ugly. Mary, still asleep within their forward cabin, had been spared the worst of them, but the crew had still been talking when she'd wakened, and she'd clearly heard more than Hugh would have liked.

Now she said, "It's a very good name for a pirate: Vautour."

He hadn't considered that, but he supposed it was. In the French language, which Mary spoke best, it meant "vulture."

She asked, "Are there vultures in Scotland?"

Hugh privately thought that depended on whether you meant birds or humans, but he knew what Mary meant. "No. Take this."

Absently, she took the little pistol with the silver-inlaid handle that he gave to her, and laid it on the table near her journal. "And no mermaids, either, I'd imagine. Although of course it wouldn't be a real mermaid. La Sirène," she clarified, when he glanced at her. "We still don't know who *she* is, only that she's not a ship, which is not very helpful. Perhaps she's a beautiful woman."

Hugh knew women, too, could be a danger if a man let down his guard.

He carefully eased a thin Corsican dagger from the lining of his waistcoat, turned it lightly in his hand, and held it handle-first to Mary. "Take this, too. Keep it close. Don't let anyone in except me."

He was turning away from the window when he saw the look on her face as she registered the full significance of both the blade and the pistol, and what he'd just said, and he caught himself briefly.

He knew she'd grown accustomed, in her life, to being left behind. She hid the hurt of it with a convincing mask. But he had studied her so closely these past months they'd been together that he wasn't fooled.

A year ago, he'd not have wasted time explaining why she could not come with him. He would have thought it obvious. But now he found himself explaining patiently, "Del Rio did not fear the storm. He feared whoever was aboard *Le Tigre*. I would judge the threat afore I put ye in its path."

She nodded, and did not complain.

He promised her, "I'll not be long."

And in the end, it was a promise he could keep with ease. He'd only been downstairs for a few minutes when the inn's front door blew open, hard, upon a gust of wind and rain, admitting two cloaked guests.

The first flung off the folds of sodden cloth to show a face and form so perfectly aligned with the description that Del Rio's crew had given of Lambert Vautour there was no doubt in Hugh's mind who it was. Warily, he watched the slightly smaller figure standing just behind Vautour. Del Rio had shown less fear of the pirate than he had of La Sirène.

But when that second cloak was pushed back, it revealed a face he'd not expected.

The face of a man, not a woman.

A man who, in features and coloring, looked to be Scottish.

Fifty years of age or so, fair-haired, with a long nose.

III

"Mr. Douglas!" Anna called to him across the parlor in a tone so pleasant none would have suspected she was being anything but genuinely friendly.

Hugh was still reluctant to believe his luck. Fate had just neatly brought to him his enemy, which meant the duke—wherever he might be—was, for the moment, safe. And even better, Douglas was yet unaware that anyone suspected him of being an assassin.

Hugh, who'd had some hours now to observe the man, felt confident that Douglas had never seen nor heard of the O'Connors, and so did not recognize them now, for all they might have followed him from Paris to Marseilles.

He had, though, heard of Hugh.

When they'd been introduced, there had been no mistaking the slight alteration in the other Scotsman's features as he marked the name and placed its relevance. And while Douglas claimed that he was only traveling at leisure, from a wish to see the ancient wonders of the world, Hugh knew that Anna had been right.

This man, without a doubt, was their assassin, sent to kill the Duke of Ormonde.

For that purpose, he had been well chosen by the English, being one of those men who could blend with any company and neither call attention to himself nor be remembered the day afterward. He was of middle age, of middle height, of middle build. His clothes were tailored well enough—not of the latest style, and yet not out of fashion—of a middling blue that neither pleased the eye nor yet offended it. He was in all things, by design, supremely unremarkable.

Which made Hugh more inclined to notice everything about him.

During supper, while Vautour had sought to charm the women, Hugh had kept his eye on Douglas.

Not that Vautour didn't need to be watched. He was larger than Hugh, and beneath the fancy clothes and fancy wig and fine French manners lay a rough and ruthless core that made him dangerous.

But when a man like that came at you, it would be straightforward, and the fight, however fierce, would be predictable.

How Douglas would attack was yet a mystery.

He wore no weapons Hugh could see—no sword nor dirk nor pistols. If he had blades concealed in his clothes, then his tailor was fully as skilled as Hugh's own, for the seams showed no signs of it. All he had taken so far from his pockets had been a plain handkerchief and a small snuffbox of tortoiseshell inlaid with silver, neither seeming deadly.

But he definitely wasn't someone Hugh would turn his back to.

After supper, when the group moved into the parlor, Hugh had settled in the chair that Anna had predicted he would choose—the elbow chair set in the corner, well away from any windows, where his own back would be guarded while he watched the others.

There were few diversions in the parlor. No musical instruments, thankfully, save an old Spanish guitar which, when properly tuned, was a sound he could tolerate. Not that anyone seemed of a mind to play a song. Close by the window was a table set with chairs for gaming, although there again the choice of games was limited, at first glance, to a chessboard that was missing several men.

In Hugh's own corner there were books that had apparently been left behind by former guests, being in several languages and all conditions, stacked without care on a cabinet. Had he been truly at leisure he might have enjoyed searching through them to find one that suited his tastes. As it was, he'd reached out for the nearest one, which turned out to be the second volume of a novel titled *Zayde*. The first volume being nowhere in sight, his only option was to wade into the midst of the action and try to sort out what was happening—which, he reasoned, was not all that different from his daily life, come to that.

Mary, searching through the cabinet, smiled at his choice. "You know they have a copy of the *Stratagems* of Frontinus," she told him, "if you'd rather read that. Very stirring, war-like stuff, and not so sentimental."

He was fine with what he had, and turned a page to let her know it.

"As you like. It's set in Spain, that one," she told him, "though I doubt the author's knowledge of that country will be equal to your own. I don't believe she ever went there."

"He." Correcting her, he turned the book toward her so that she could see the author's name stamped in gilt letters: *Monsieur de Segrais*.

"You should not be so quick to trust your eyes," she said. "A woman can do many things and yet remain invisible."

She straightened from the cabinet, having found a pack of playing cards, together with a basket full of counters for quadrille. "You won't care if I play for a penny per corner?"

"No."

That hadn't been the whole truth, because while he was not the least bothered what stakes Mary played for, he did care very much that she'd be playing in a vulnerable position with a pirate—for Vautour had settled his large frame already at the gaming table—and a woman he had barely met, and...

"Mr. Douglas!" Anna called a second time across the parlor. "Come and play quadrille with us. We need a fourth."

Hugh very nearly sympathized with Douglas when the man half turned from studying a framed print hung on the wall, his features silently revealing he would rather face an army on the battlefield than women at quadrille.

Hugh had no patience for playing at cards. If a game employed logic or cunning, then he could endure it, but mostly he found games a waste of his time, and quadrille was especially torturous.

He knew Mary knew his views well, but even so he took a fiercer interest in the pages of his novel, so nobody would call on him to play.

Douglas parried with, "Surely your husband—"

But Edmund O'Connor dropped into the chair next to Hugh's and said, "I'm not allowed to play."

His tone was entirely matter-of-fact.

"With good reason," his wife said, indulgently. "Show them why."

Hugh didn't like parlor tricks, either, but by the time he raised his eyes O'Connor had a pack of cards within his hands and had begun to shuffle them. Although the Irishman's left hand had scarring straight across his knuckles in a thin, raised ridge that might have come from any type of fighting, it appeared to be no hindrance to the movements of his fingers, which were deft and sure. Spreading the cards in the shape of a fan, faces down, Edmund held them to Hugh and said, "Choose one."

As challenges went, it seemed harmless enough. Hugh chose a card.

"Now, look at it, but hold it to yourself, so I can't see it," Edmund said. "And put it back again." He closed the fan and shuffled it a second time, and then a third. "Cut that anywhere you like," he said, "and turn the top half over."

Hugh obliged. And frowned a moment at the card he'd just turned upward, for it was the same card he'd been holding: king of diamonds.

Edmund smiled. "Your card? Of course you'd pick something all pointy and sharp. Give it here. Let's see where he ends up."

He did it another three times—turned the card from the pack, the same card, and then shuffled and cut and produced it again, without Hugh seeing how it was done.

Douglas, who had moved closer to watch, remarked, "It's a simple enough thing to tailor a pack of cards, shaving the edges or giving them marks, so you know what they are. Any sharper who cheats men at gaming can do it."

Leaning back in his chair, Edmund offered the cards in a neat stack to Douglas. "You're free to inspect them, if you think them marked."

His wife, from her seat at the table by the window, said indulgently, "It is a special talent of my husband's, I'm afraid, that he can do the same with any cards. Here, try these."

Douglas crossed the few steps to exchange the cards he held for the pack from the inn's gaming table. It was a newer pack of cards, with brightly printed faces, ordered in the Spanish suits of cups and swords and coins and clubs. He handed them to Edmund. "I suppose you'll have to start again."

"Why's that?"

"There are no diamonds."

Edmund shrugged, shuffled, and held the pack out to Hugh. "Yours had a point on it, as I recall?"

Hugh, frowning, cut the pack, and turned it cautiously. And found the king of swords.

Edmund smoothly said, "Your card, I think."

Hugh had met other men like Edmund—men whose languid actions hid a quick and agile mind. They'd all been equally annoying.

"Aye," he said, returned the cards, and raised his book while Edmund looked to Douglas—who through all this had been standing close beside their chairs.

"You see now," Edmund said, "why I am not allowed to play."

"Indeed. An honest man would be at a decided disadvantage."

The Irishman smiled. "I confess I don't meet many honest men."

Some people might have missed the change in Douglas's attention as he focused with a keener interest on the lounging Edmund.

Hugh was instantly aware of it, and of its cause. When he was on a mission, he, too, kept an eye out for those men who might provide him information or be turned to serve his purpose—men whose moral boundaries had a certain flexibility. And Douglas plainly saw the same thing he did in the Irishman.

Vautour was losing patience.

"Come now, Douglas, a penny a corner won't make you a bankrupt. Come and join the game."

Douglas, smiling thinly back at Edmund, turned and told Vautour, "I will, but only if we play 'the king surrendered.'"

It was a reasonable request for a man to make when playing quadrille.

Bad enough the game's rules were complicated for the sake of it, and the bids and scoring unnecessarily convoluted, but it didn't even allow a man to choose his own partner. Instead, if he were unlucky enough to be holding the king of the suit called as trump, he was bound to become the secret partner of the player who had called it, and so might find himself forced into playing with any incompetent idiot. The variant known as "the king surrendered" meant exactly that—when the trump was called, whoever held the king could then exchange it for another card. There'd be no secret partnership. It made the game much faster and more serious.

But Hugh suspected Douglas had requested it for other reasons.

No doubt an assassin who had tried to kill King James and was now sent to kill the Duke of Ormonde would find it amusing to sit undiscovered—as he thought—amidst a group of ardent Jacobites. Perhaps he thought it would be a good story to tell later, to his friends, if he had any. "I played at cards," he'd tell them, "with the wife of Hugh MacPherson, and we played 'the king surrendered.'"

He had clearly underestimated Mary.

Hugh, from where he sat, had a fair view of Mary's cards. He knew she held the king of clubs before Vautour called it as the trump.

He'd wager any odds Anna O'Connor knew it, too. As the dealer, she appeared to be controlling the game's play with a skill equal to her husband's, and so likely knew exactly who held each card she had dealt.

Nor could it be coincidence that Anna faintly smiled when Mary tucked the king of clubs more firmly in her hand and carried on the play without revealing that she held him.

Much as Mary loved winning at cards, they would never persuade her to give up her king—and especially one with black hair like King James.

"But your hand was weak," said Douglas, all impatience, when the tricks were counted in the end. "Had you surrendered up your king, as you were meant to do, you might have gained a better card in the exchange, and thus improved your score."

"I shall do better next time," Mary promised, in the careless way that convinced so many people she was nothing but a pretty piece of fluff, when truthfully her mind was full as sharp as any blade Hugh carried.

He enjoyed watching her best Douglas at the game, though she was wise enough not to take obvious pleasure in doing so.

"Well," she said, when the last tour had been played and the winnings were tallied and paid, with the bulk of them hers, "this *has* been diverting. Shall we try a different game?"

"Or no game," was Vautour's suggestion. Easing his chair back enough to draw Hugh's wary notice, the pirate said, "Let me consult La Sirène."

IV

"It's a watch," said Mary, looking at the object in Vautour's hand with amazement, before covering her own surprise with half-truths. "Do forgive me, but our landlord's wife was quite beside herself, sir, when she saw your ship come into harbor here, and though I could make little sense of what she said, this name was mentioned several times with worry: La Sirène. So I confess I thought whatever bore that name must then be something fierce and dangerous." Half turning in her seat, she told Hugh, "Darling, come and see."

Hugh had started to stand when Vautour first moved his right hand toward what might have been a weapon concealed in his coat. Now he rose to his full height and, tucking the novel away in his own pocket, crossed to the table.

Douglas said dryly, "I cannot imagine your husband takes very much interest in timepieces, madam."

Mary did not answer. She would always guard his privacy. So Hugh himself revealed what few men knew about him.

"Ye'd be mistaken," he told Douglas. "Watchmaking was once my trade." A minor revelation that provided him a chance to view this object that had caused a hard man like Del Rio to know fear.

Vautour allowed it, holding it up closer for inspection.

In the pirate's roughened hand, it was a thing of unexpected elegance, well crafted of the finest gold, the dial bearing the name of a French maker of great quality, and the outer case chased and engraved with the scene of a ship tossed at sea in a tempest, surrounded by pierced scrollwork meant to be waves mixed with menacing sea creatures.

Anna O'Connor leaned in for a careful study of those decorations, and remarked, "I cannot see a mermaid. And yet there must be one, surely, if this watch is named for one."

Vautour's smile held approval and a trace of admiration. It was clear she'd caught his eye.

"Yes," he said, "La Sirène is safe within. Not many have seen her, but for you, madame, I will make an exception."

Opening the outer case, he lifted out what Hugh would call the watch's "box"—its inner case that held the dial itself and housed the workings and was also pierced with scrollwork. Carefully, Vautour turned this over, briefly revealing an inscription on the back of the inner case before he opened that as well to reveal the inner movement, gleaming brightly gold, with an exceptionally fine balance cock covering the top of it all, pierced and engraved with the form of a mermaid.

"She's beautiful," Anna said.

"She is," Vautour agreed. "But you and I, madame, might be the only ones who think so. Most people, like your landlord's wife, consider her a demoness—a bringer of misfortune."

"Why?"

"Because they think the gold this watch is made from has been cursed."

He said it undramatically, but at his back the storm rattled at the shuttered window and swept air so sharply up the chimney that the flames within the fireplace sputtered wildly, and created drama all their own.

Edmund, still lounging in his chair across the room, asked, "And pray what did the gold do, to deserve a curse?"

Rather than rise to the Irishman's mockery, Vautour faintly smiled and set the separate cases of the watch upon the table, with the inner case still upside down and open, so the mermaid on the balance cock appeared to be observing them. The warm light of the candles set around the room in sconces made the gold gleam richly. "This gold, monsieur, my father took from Cartagena on the second day of June, in 1697."

For all he said it cordially, the speaking of that place and date aloud had the effect of someone rapping at a door—it gathered everyone's attention.

Edmund turned his head. "Your father took part in the siege?"

"We both did, although I was young."

"Convenient for you," Edmund said, "since now you can excuse yourself by claiming you were too young to know what you were involved in." His voice had grown a darker edge.

Vautour's expression altered, too, as he assessed the challenge. "I knew, monsieur, what I was involved in. And I needed no excuse for it. Not then. Not now."

Anna aimed a glance at Edmund that, upon its surface, seemed no more than any wife might send a husband to remind him of his manners in a social situation, but Hugh knew it went beyond that, in this instance. Anna's purpose, all through dinner and the game of cards, had clearly been to keep Vautour relaxed and try to use that to draw Douglas also into conversation, for it was through conversation that a man revealed things—and when speaking to a woman, men were more inclined to leave their words unguarded.

She showed a smile now to Vautour, and said, "You'll think me very ignorant, I fear, but I confess that I know little of the siege apart from stories I've been told, and stories, as I'm sure you know, are often wrong."

Vautour's face cleared. "Exactly." When he looked at her this time, his eyes were openly admiring. "I would never think that you are ignorant, madame. You may be young, but already you know this truth: you cannot trust a book. It is an unforgiving weapon."

Hugh could tell that Mary, with her love of books, was keen to intervene in their defense, and he could see the effort that it cost her to keep still as Vautour continued on, not noticing, to Anna, "All these stories you have heard came from a book—you know this? A book written by the nobleman who led our raid, betrayed us, and then scurried home to France to publish his relation of events and twist the truth to his own purposes. The great Baron de Pointis." He all but spat the name, and Mary could not hold her silence.

She lightly said, "I think you are unfair to blame the book, sir, for a book cannot be faulted for the writing that it holds. It is the baron, surely, who deserves the blame."

He seemed unswayed by her opinion. "But the baron has been dead longer than you have been alive, madame, and yet his book lives on, and wounds my reputation still. How does a man fight that?"

Anna leaned forward, laid her hand upon his arm, and said, "By telling us your side of it."

Hugh, having heard the young lad Juan aboard Del Rio's ship relate his mother's tales about the devastation visited on Cartagena in that fateful raid, had no wish now to hear the explanations of a man who'd done the raiding. Shifting half a step back, he took up a quietly comfortable standing position behind Mary's chair and resumed his close study of Douglas, whose own focus seemed to be wholly diverted by La Sirène.

In Hugh's experience, men came into this type of life by different paths. Some, like himself, were driven by the demons of their past to kill from duty, and for honor. Others became zealots for a cause. And some killed purely for the money.

None could doubt which path was Douglas's—not seeing how he gazed at that gold watch, eyes bright with greed.

For Hugh, it made things easier. A man who killed for honor, for a cause, even if that cause was in opposition to his own—he could view such a man with some respect. But no respect was owed a man who sold his sword for profit.

Not that he used a sword. Even from this angle, Hugh saw no weapon on Douglas.

"How very annoying," said Anna, replying to something Vautour was now saying.

"Indeed, it was incompetence," Vautour agreed. "But then, that was the way of our French navy in those days. They'd suffered such humiliations they relied upon us flibustiers to help them win their victories."

Douglas, without looking up from La Sirène, said, "I am not familiar with that word. What is a flibustier?"

Vautour shrugged. "It is what I am, and what my father was before me."

"Well, yes, but—"

Mary, half-French herself and with a love of all languages, answered, "It comes from the English word 'freebooter,' and means the same thing."

"A pirate," said Edmund, across the room.

Mary said, "I would translate it as 'buccaneer.'"

Vautour accepted this. "Our late king, God rest his soul, knew well the value of his flibustiers. As did our governor of Saint-Domingue."

Hugh had a rough knowledge of the isles of the West Indies. Saint-Domingue, he knew, was on the isle of Hispaniola, which in settlement had been divided between France and Spain—uneasy bedfellows.

"Our Governor Du Casse thought we would have the best effect by making our attack upon the Spanish at their town of San Domingo on our island. Had we struck them then, we might have pushed them out forever. But De Pointis—when he finally arrived, so late, from France—he was for making an attack on Cartagena, and his voice was the more powerful."

With one finger Vautour turned the outer watchcase on the table so the golden ship carved on it chased a circle through the endless, storm-tossed waves.

"And so we sailed. Together with the ships and men De Pointis brought, we had six thousand in our fleet, in more than twenty vessels, and twelve hundred of those men were from our island, Saint-Domingue. And half of those at least were flibustiers. De Pointis promised us we'd have an equal share of any treasure, man for man, to his own men. But it was clear he thought our lives were more expendable.

"He gathered us and set us down by stealth in boats the first night that we came to anchor, sending us ashore to seize a church and hill that would give us command of all roads to and from the city, in case the people tried to take their treasure and run inland, to escape.

"This taking of the hill, it held great danger, which was why he did not choose to risk his own men in the mission, but we did it for him," Vautour said. "We helped him take the fort as well, and marched beside him in the street to keep the peace while he read out the terms of the capitulation. Not that terms on paper had much meaning for De Pointis. Oh, he went to the cathedral like a pious man and stood for the 'Te Deum,' but with his next breath he said to the religious leaders of that place that, while the terms might promise that their houses would not be molested, that did not include their money, and so they had to render half of all they owned to him, like every other person who chose to remain now in the city."

Douglas dryly pointed out that one could hardly say a man held in a city under siege "chose to remain." He asked, "Did anybody choose to leave?"

"On paper it was possible, if they gave to De Pointis all they owned. But I saw no one do that," Vautour said. "At least, not willingly. And I saw many things."

Hugh did not doubt he had. And though Hugh seldom spoke up much in social gatherings, he stood prepared to do it now to stop Vautour from reminiscing, should the pirate feel inclined to offer any gruesome details of the things he'd seen, in front of Mary.

But Vautour, upon reflection, only said, "De Pointis, in his famous book, he paints us all with one black brush, the flibustiers, but I tell you his men were equal to our own in violence. And some of us did try to help the common people. Some of us, we hired ourselves out to be guards. They won't tell you that in the books, but we did."

"Yes," Edmund said, "and very noble of you, to be sure, considering it put you even closer to the common people's money."

Vautour paused. Then raised a hand toward his collar, which put Hugh on guard because he also kept a blade hid there. But all the pirate did was draw the collar down enough that, when he slightly turned his head, it showed a narrow scar that marked his neck.

Hugh had one very like it, and in much the same place, so he could well guess what weapon might have been its cause.

Vautour confirmed it when he coldly said, "I got this from the blade of a gallant French officer, one of De Pointis's men, when I stood between him and two boys younger than myself at Cartagena. I saved their lives, but not their family's savings, nor their sister's honor—the French officer took those. So do not speak to me of what is noble."

Anna, again playing peacemaker, told him, "I'm sure you did all that you could. It cannot have been easy."

"It was not." He set his collar straight. "Men will be men, but his men were as bad as any pirate, and De Pointis sat as though he were collecting taxes in the grand house he had taken, counting all the money that was brought to him and plotting ways to keep it for himself. And then he calls us all together, all the flibustiers, and says there is an enemy approaching by the land, and we must go out and stop them. But there was no enemy. We could find no one, and when we returned to the city, we found the gates were barred to us and guarded by his men." The memory drew his brows together darkly. "Fifteen days they held us there, and by the time the gates were opened to us once again, De Pointis and his men had finished their collection and loaded the money on their ships. Governor Du Casse, who had first brought us into this business, said, 'Wait and be patient, he is making up the accounts now, and before he sails we'll have our share.'"

Vautour set the outer watchcase slowly spinning for a second time, and smiled faintly at the serpents rising from the sea.

"De Pointis, in his book, claims the treasure taken in that siege at Cartagena was eight million livres, maybe nine. He's a liar. Even Governor Du Casse thought it was more than twenty million, and my father and his friends counted it closer still to forty. Man for man, an equal share, that's what we had been promised. And in the end, do you know what he paid to us? For all of us—the governor, the colonists, and all us flibustiers to have between us? Forty thousand crowns." He damned De Pointis with a phrase that Hugh suspected might have been more choice if there had not been ladies present.

"Governor Du Casse was too ashamed to tell us what we had been given until we had started home. And then…" His gesture left no doubt what the reaction of the buccaneers had been to the discovery they'd been cheated. "And so yes, we went back. Yes, we took what rightfully was ours to take. De Pointis could have stopped us, could have paid us what he'd promised, but he didn't. When he heard we were returning, he turned tail and ran for France."

It had been an unlucky day for Cartagena. Plundered once already, the inhabitants had found themselves attacked and newly terrorized and held for ransom once again.

"But," said Mary, "you'd just taken all their money, days before."

"Not all. There was still wealth to find. My father with his own hands took this gold from the cathedral." Vautour touched the watchcase lightly. "He took emeralds, also. Beautiful. And silver. We had asked five million livres, and in four days we had nearly that. And we had rules, at least. Two of our men, they killed two local women, and we held a trial and condemned those men to death, and saw them executed. *That*, you will not read of in your books, but it is true. We were not animals."

Douglas had heard only part of that. He asked, "What happened to the emeralds?"

"We took them back with us, to Saint-Domingue. We took it all. My father's ship was one of those that did not perish in the storm that followed, or fall victim to the English fleet that had been sent against us, and we made it home in safety. But we carried yellow fever, and of all our crew only my father and myself and two more men survived the sickness, and so this is where the rumors of the curse of La Sirène have their beginning."

It was a trick of light, Hugh knew, but still it seemed the room grew darker as he focused on the fine gold inner watchcase with its even finer balance cock engraved with that small mermaid.

Vautour was looking at her, too. "It is the gold, and not the watch itself, mind you, that's meant to bear the curse."

Mary, predictably, was taken by the intrigue of the tale. "Because the gold was stolen from a church, you mean, and people think that angered God?"

Vautour shrugged. "There are older gods in Cartagena, and the gold the Spaniards used to build their churches was already stolen, madame, from the Indians who had that place before them. You may choose which god you think would seek its vengeance on my father. For myself, I don't believe in curses. But my father…he had much bad luck, my father. He lost ships, and half his fortune, in bad ventures. People whispered that it was the curse of this gold he'd brought back from Cartagena. So he took that gold, my father, and in France he had a watchmaker craft La Sirène—the mermaid for our ship's name, and this," he added, turning the inner case over to show the inscription that Hugh had glimpsed earlier, "to show he was a Vautour, and not God's plaything." Holding it close to Mary, Vautour said, "You translate well, madame. Read that, if you will, for your friends who have no French."

Mary obliged. "It says: 'Je suis le seul maître de mon temps.' In English that would simply be 'I am the only master of my time.'"

Vautour liked that. "The only master of my time. Yes, this is how my father thought. But then there came a sudden illness, like a mystery, and in one day it had taken all my sisters, and my brother, and my mother. And the whispers of the curse grew louder. So my father, in his grief, he went to see my uncle's wife, who was herself an Indian from Darien. And she said yes, this curse is very real, and he must break it, and to do that the gold must be embraced by all four elements in turn—by water first, then by the earth, and by the air, and finally fire—and then the curse would break, and all would be forgiven."

Hugh knew the fantastical elements of Vautour's story would hold Mary's rapt attention, and would most probably find their way into one of her own tales in the future, but he would still have preferred her to not lean so close to the pirate.

She asked Vautour, "What did your father do?"

"Well, he could not do much, for the same illness that had killed my mother and sisters and brother struck him at this time. But my uncle's wife had reassured him the gold had already been over the water when he'd brought it from Cartagena, so that was one element already dealt with, so my father called me and said, you must take La Sirène now and bury her in the ground, so that the earth can embrace her."

He looked for a long moment at the words proclaiming him the only master of his time.

Then Mary asked, "And did you?"

"Of course not." Vautour turned the inner case over again in his hand, so the mermaid showed, smiling serenely. "She was too beautiful to bury. And as I said, I don't believe in curses." With the ease of long practice he fitted the inner case into the outer one and snapped them firmly together. "Anyway," he said, "I'm still alive."

Pushing back his chair, he sent an indulgent sideways look to Anna. "And you, madame, have heard my story. But a hundred years from now, when we are dead, men will not know the truth of how things happened. They'll know only what De Pointis wrote, and so to them we flibustiers will be the villains, and the good things that we did will be forgotten."

"Perhaps," she said, "you ought to write your story down."

"To what end? His is famous, and has sold so many copies, and been translated to English. When he lived, he was a nobleman, with friends at court. Even if I could find a publisher who dared to print my side of things, there would be few who'd read it. Men with power write the histories that survive. Men like your husband read them, and believe." He aimed a narrow glance across the room, although it was difficult to tell whether he was aiming it at Edmund or the jumbled stack of books atop the cabinet just beyond his chair.

"This is the unkindness of history, madame. The exploits of the greatest general will not be remembered if none choose to write them down for him, yet all men's lives lie vulnerable to any who would hang them out and twist them on the page with all the cruelty of a common executioner. No, I would rather face the Scottish blade that your unsmiling friend here carries at his belt"—he gestured to the dirk that Hugh wore openly—"than battle with a book, for as I say, it is an unforgiving weapon."

Consulting his watch for the hour, he returned La Sirène to his pocket and, standing, bade them a good night and excused himself gallantly, kissing the ladies' hands with a French flourish.

When Vautour had left the room, Edmund unfolded himself from his chair and crossed over to join them. He stayed standing. With the kind of measured lightness that Hugh knew could mask deep irritation, he remarked, "I didn't learn about it from a book." And then, when Anna looked at him, a question in her eyes, he said, "The raid on Cartagena. When I lived in Spain I met a priest who'd had the great misfortune to have been there. Lost an eye and his left hand and somehow kept his faith. He told me stories also of the flibustiers, the buccaneers, that were less... complimentary."

Douglas turned his head. "You lived in Spain?"

"I did indeed. I lived at Valencia for several months with my kinsman, Sir Toby Bourke."

Lord Bourke's privileged standing at King James's court in Rome, as well as his long service to the king in Spain and elsewhere, meant his name would catch the notice of a man like Douglas. Edmund, unless he were a great fool, would surely know that. And whatever else Hugh thought of Edmund, he did not suspect he was a fool.

Douglas said, "He sounds a man of worth, your kinsman."

"He is that. I am traveling now on his business, as it happens."

Anna murmured, "Edmund."

"What? We are some leagues from Rome, and Mr. Douglas is no spy."

She said, "Nonetheless."

"You worry overmuch," he told her. "Anyhow, I'm off to find our landlord, for I need a drink, my darling, before settling for the night."

Observing this small interchange between the couple, Douglas made an effort to disguise his interest with an idle tone. "Perhaps I'll join you in that drink. I had some thought, when I have done my tour of Italy, of voyaging to Spain myself. I'd be most grateful to have your advice, sir, on the places I should visit, for I've learned the finest information comes firsthand."

Hugh would not have left Mary unattended at any rate—not with Vautour upstairs, and only Anna to guard her—so joining the other two men for a drink in the dining room was something he'd have declined, even if Edmund had not subtly signaled by means of a look and a half nod of warning that Hugh should remain with the women.

But that didn't make it any easier to stand there, while Anna and Mary took up the cards once again and played a game of piquet, and the storm battered loudly enough at the windows that Hugh could not catch any words of the talk from the dining room.

Frustrated, he crossed to the fireplace and, taking out his pipe, began the ritual of cleaning it and filling it with new tobacco. Rituals were steadying.

He selected a spill from the few in the holder and used it to transfer the flame from the fire to his pipe, and then neatly extinguished the spill and replaced it. There. Better already.

As he exhaled smoke, he became aware Anna was standing not far from his shoulder, and watching him.

Mary was now by the cabinet, apparently choosing a book. They had finished their game of cards.

Anna's voice was conversational. "Have you ever *not* been in control?" she asked. Then, at whatever expression had shown in his eyes at that, added, "I mean as an adult, of course. No? It's only that—forgive me, but you seem so ill at ease when you cannot direct the game. Is that why you don't like to play at cards?"

He studied her a moment. "Ask yourself."

"I beg your pardon?"

"Your husband's card trick earlier was only so that ye could switch the packs with him, because ye had need of the one he carried." They were somehow marked, he reasoned, so she could more easily control the play.

He had surprised her, he could see that, but she owned it without shame.

"My husband can do what he does with any pack of cards," she told him. "My skills are more limited. But I am learning."

"Ye knew Mary held the king of trumps."

"I did. I dealt him to her."

"Why?"

She said, "Because I knew she'd not surrender him."

Coldly, Hugh remarked, "I'll thank ye not to use my wife in games."

Anna's gaze was very level, very calm. "In my life, knowing whom to trust has never been a game, Mr. MacPherson."

The sound of Edmund's laughter carried briefly from the dining room. Hugh raised an eyebrow, pointedly.

"My husband can be trusted," she assured him. "Shall I tell you what they are discussing? Would that ease your mind?"

He waited.

"My husband, while pretending he's had far too much to drink, will be revealing he's been sent to fetch the Duke of Ormonde, who has been instructed to meet us at Monaco. No part of that is true, of course, but Douglas does not know that, and it might succeed in drawing him off long enough for you to get to Genoa to find the duke and see him safely out of danger."

She'd surprised *him*, now, and well she knew it.

"I confess," she said, "it's not the best plan, but with little time to think, and when this storm could clear at any moment, we felt it was better to do something than do nothing."

He said, grudgingly, "It's not a bad plan."

"Thank you."

His was better, though, he thought, as he watched Anna cross to be of aid to Mary in her choice of book.

His plan would see them all safe, and would let him meet the duke, and best of all, was simple: he had no intention of allowing Douglas to depart this inn alive.

SECOND DAY

"I am not what I am."
—Shakespeare, *Twelfth Night*: act 3, scene 1

I

February 12, 1733

THERE WERE NEW SAILS in the harbor when Hugh wakened the next morning.

Mary stirred and turned in bed and frowned to see him standing once more at the window, looking out. She asked, "Is something wrong?"

This problem was so new he was still working it within his mind in silence.

Mary sighed. "I once told you the story of a lady who was changed into a falcon, but I fear you have forgotten it."

He felt his eyebrows lift a fraction as he turned to meet her gaze. She could not truly think he ever would forget that particular story. She'd told it to him on the night she said that she would marry him. He'd take that memory to the grave.

"Examine me on any point," he challenged, "and ye'll find I've not."

"Why was the lady changed into a falcon, then?"

He knew why, but he also knew that Mary would continue without needing his reply, and so she did.

"I'll tell you why," she said. "It was so she could travel with the man she loved and be his true companion, so that they might share all things together—good *and* bad."

He would have little choice, he knew. This wasn't news he could withhold. He said, "The *Gallant Jack* is in the harbor."

Mary sat up in the blankets. "The ship the Duke of Ormonde boarded at Marseilles?"

"According to your friend, aye."

The wind of the storm was still rising and falling and masking their voices but he spoke with care, so that Douglas in his room next door to theirs would not hear.

Hugh didn't know if Douglas knew the duke was on that ship, but if Anna O'Connor had managed to learn the ship's name at Marseilles, then he had to assume Douglas might have done likewise.

Mary moved swiftly and softly across from the bed to stand close by Hugh's side. "Which one is it?"

"There. Next to *Le Tigre*."

Their view through the window was easier now that the rain fell less violently and was, from time to time, blown aside by the strong wind to allow them a shifting and watery glimpse of the harbor as Mary pressed close to the glass. "Are you sure it's the *Gallant Jack*?"

"Aye."

"Then they ought to be warned."

Hugh swore quietly. "Too late." He should have been watching the beach, not the ship. They had already sent in their longboat to shore, and the passengers it had deposited were coming straight for the inn. Two people—two men, it looked like. One walking ahead with authority.

Hugh swore a second time. Shrugging into his coat, he passed Mary one of the silver-handled pistols that he carried, like before, but when he would have given her the dagger from his waistcoat lining, too, she stopped him, and instead placed her hand on his upturned cuff, and drew the Flemish small knife from its tailored scabbard in the seam that kept it well concealed.

"This one is easier to hold," she said. "Now, go. You're losing time."

Hugh wished he were a man of words, but he was not. He kissed her briefly. Hard. He told her, "Bolt the door." And then was gone.

He had not been the only one to notice the arrival of the *Gallant Jack* and her approaching passengers.

He'd barely made it to the entry hall when he became aware that Douglas, too, had left his chamber and was coming down the stairs.

And then the inn's door opened in a burst of wind and weather, and the new arrivals, unsuspecting, stepped inside.

The man at the front, shaking rainwater from his cloak, noticed Hugh first.

But before he could do more than smile and say "MacPherson!" Hugh had quickly crossed the space between them, moved in close, and knowing the assassin—although not yet fully down the stairs behind them—would be keenly watching, told both men beneath his breath, "Don't argue," before bending low to pay his honors with a gallant bow.

"Your Grace," he said, to Captain Butler.

II

"I thought it inspired," Daniel Butler commended him, with a broad smile.

They could speak freely now, having moved from the inn to a church not far distant, at Anna's suggestion. How she'd known the church was there, Hugh wasn't certain, but he was grudgingly starting to share Mary's view of her.

Anna had swept down the stairs after Douglas, had taken one look at them there in the entry hall, and fallen in with the play without missing a step. Greeting Butler with her finest curtsy, she'd said, "We must give thanks, Your Grace, that you have been delivered to us from this terrible storm." And, declaring there wasn't a moment to lose, she had gathered her husband and Mary and, turning to Douglas, had asked, "Mr. Douglas, you'll join us for prayers?"

She'd have known he'd decline. He'd revealed very little to them last night, but when Anna had made mention of the pope at supper, Douglas's reply had made it clear he was no Catholic, and not likely to feel comfortable in any of the churches here. Besides, he'd see no point in it. He didn't know they suspected him—he thought he had the advantage of time on his side. He'd await their return.

And so now here they all were. Well, nearly all. Daniel Butler's friend and first mate, Fergal, who'd come with him to the inn, had taken leave of them at the church door, once he had heard the first rough explanations.

"I'll go back and guard the duke, then," he'd said. "And MacPherson? If you let that bastard harm a hair on Danny's head, I'll make you wish we'd never met. You hear?"

Hugh did not doubt it. There were few men he'd rate tougher than himself. Fergal was one of them. The Duke of Ormonde would be safe enough aboard the *Gallant Jack*, in Fergal's care.

Which freed Hugh's thoughts to turn now to the situation near at hand.

The church was empty, thankfully, but for themselves. They sat together in a single line with Hugh at one end, Edmund at the other, wives beside them, Daniel Butler in the middle, shouldered close to one another as though praying. It allowed them to speak privately.

Beside Hugh, Mary leaned out slightly to ask Edmund, "Are you certain Mr. Douglas has not ever seen the Duke of Ormonde?"

"He has not. He told me so last night, while we were drinking. Ask your husband, if you don't believe me. I've no doubt he overheard Douglas himself, else he'd never have been bold enough to make the play he did back at the inn."

Hugh did not alter his expression. His play had been a gamble. Last night's storm had meant he couldn't overhear the talk between

Edmund and Douglas. Still, there was no harm in having Edmund think that Hugh might be forever just around the corner, out of sight, and hearing everything.

"Inspired," Butler said again. "Though I am younger than the duke, and am not much like him to look at."

Anna countered, "But if Douglas has not met him, then he will have nothing more than a description to be working from. At most a portrait done in miniature. And being kin to him, you have at least your height and build in common, Captain Butler, though you are much better looking."

Butler smiled warmly at her. "Call me Daniel."

"Anyway," said Edmund, "Douglas knows *I've* seen the duke, and that MacPherson has, so if we say that's who you are, he'll have no reason to suspect you're not."

The logic, stated in that way, seemed sound enough, but Butler asked, "You're sure of that?"

Edmund shrugged. "People will see what they wish to see."

The lightness of his tone seemed pitched a little too deliberately, and could not fully cover a faint underthread of bitterness, which made Hugh take note of the words.

Butler accepted them at their face value. "And then what?"

Everyone turned to him, questioning.

"Well, having me impersonate the duke and getting Douglas to accept me in that role is half a plan, but to what end? I'm sure MacPherson here would simply rather kill him and be done with it, but that's not always practical in such close quarters."

"No," said Mary. "It is not." She laid her hand on Hugh's.

Butler smiled. "So then our plan must have a second half."

Anna said, "Originally, Edmund and I were going to lead Mr. Douglas away and off course, pretending we'd arranged a rendezvous with the duke. Except now that *you're* here…"

"Yes." The problem was obvious. Butler considered this. "I could still lead him away. He would follow me." As though he sensed that the others were doubtful, he added, "It worked for the king, when he had to leave Rome to meet Ormonde in Spain in the spring of '19. Hugh was there. He'll remember."

Hugh did remember. He could have recounted the plain facts in a single sentence to the others, who'd been either too young or too distant from the danger at that time to be aware, but he let Butler tell the tale instead. The Cornishman had an easier way with words.

"Our hope in those days," Butler told them, "was to raise the Highlanders in Scotland, and all the Spanish ships were set to sail for us, and Ormonde sent for the king to come join him. Only the king was encircled by spies and could barely move. And then, bravely, with Lords Mar and Perth as companions, the king came out into the open and headed northward, made a show of it. Except it wasn't him. It was some other member of the court, whose name escapes me—"

"Paterson," said Hugh.

"Yes, that's it. Paterson. And while those three went north, drawing attention to themselves and being dogged at every step by English spies, our real king quietly slipped out of Rome and headed south, to meet the ship that waited ready there to carry him to Spain. It was a brilliant ruse."

Mary, who enjoyed all tales of such adventures, asked, "What became of Paterson and the others?"

Butler admitted they had not made it as far as Genoa. "As soon as they entered the territory of the Emperor, they were arrested and imprisoned in the castle at Milan, but not for long, and they were fairly treated, and released when it became clear Paterson was an impostor. Meanwhile, they had done what they'd set out to do, and if I did the same, and led your Mr. Douglas off somewhere while you escorted Ormonde down to Rome—"

"Douglas would kill ye." Hugh believed in speaking plainly.

"I'd have Fergal."

Risking Daniel Butler's life was not an option, in Hugh's view. Hugh stared him down, and Anna broke the impasse.

"Thank you, Captain Butler." She was calm. "I hope we will not need to put you in such danger. After all, we are still held here by this storm, which gives us time to think. Some better plan might yet occur to us." She looked toward the altar of the church as though for inspiration. "Until then, the duke will, at least, be kept safe in the harbor."

Mary turned to Butler, too. "And you'll be safe with us."

Butler told her, "That I can be sure of, with your husband at my back." But he had not lived so long from being reckless. As the others filed toward the church door, he kept pace with Hugh and asked, in a low voice, "How will he come at me?"

"With me between ye."

"Yes, but how? What weapon does he favor?"

Hugh was forced to answer that he did not know. "Not yet."

"I see. Then I am indeed glad that I have you between us. I may also need your protection," he said, with a faint smile, "when Ormonde learns I've taken his bed at the inn, while he's left on the *Jack* with a humorless Irishman." On that last word, his eyes shifted to Edmund, who walked with the women ahead of them. "I'm not one for gossip, you know this. But I've heard some talk, in Spain, of an O'Connor who went into Russia a few years back. Young man, like that one. A kinsman of Sir Toby Bourke. Carried letters for our loyal friends, and betrayed them the first chance he got. Might be nothing but rumor," he said, meeting Hugh's angled glance, "but, my friend, while you are watching my back, you would do well to watch your own."

III

Butler played his part as well as any actor, and with such complete conviction that the innkeeper evicted Douglas from his room and moved him to the smaller, plainer chamber in the farther corner, next to the O'Connors, so the "duke" could then be housed in greater comfort.

This pleased Butler, since it meant his room was next to Hugh's. As Hugh hauled in the trunk of clothing that had been sent over from the *Gallant Jack* and slid it into place alongside Butler's bed, the older man said, "At least I'll be guarded if I sleep tonight, for I know you do not. Unless married life has changed you."

Hugh made no reply to that, nor did he, later on at dinner, step into the friendly snares that Butler set for him in conversation in an effort to discover more of his relationship with Mary.

Butler was, at heart, a man of science and of inquiry. It was his nature to desire to learn what had made Hugh—who'd more than once, throughout the years, said he would never take a wife—discard his earlier beliefs, but Hugh believed in setting boundaries with his privacy.

Mary guarded those same boundaries like a gentle watchman at the gate, and though she smiled and seemed to answer Butler's questions, she let nothing pass.

"Of course, I need not bore you with the details" was the end of her reply to one of Butler's questions, "since I'm sure you'll have heard all of it already from the Earl Marischal."

Butler's smile was amused. "Indeed."

And with the meal eaten and plates cleared, when Anna and Mary excused themselves to play at cards in the parlor while the men stayed for a drink in the dining room, Butler leaned back in his chair and regarded Hugh, seeming well satisfied. "I like your wife."

Douglas had also been noticing Mary. "She has an unusual accent," he said. "Half-French, is she? Or, perhaps, raised in France? What is her family name?"

Hugh did not answer, and into the brief silence Edmund lied smoothly and with what appeared full authority: "Jamieson, same as my own wife. They're cousins." He looked at Hugh, feigning defensiveness. "What? As I said, we're among friends. 'Tis no place for secrets." To Douglas, he added, "You'll have to forgive him, he's worked for so long guarding people from danger he doesn't remember the way to trust anyone."

As always, with Edmund, Hugh wasn't entirely sure of the game, or the partnership. Having him offer the false name for Mary had been the clear move of an ally, but this move was murkier.

Still, it had been obvious enough to Hugh himself that Douglas, when they'd first been introduced, had known exactly who Hugh was. *He'd* used no alias, and any good assassin having made a study of King James's court at Rome would know that a MacPherson matching his description lived there.

So, though Douglas pretended surprise and asked, "Is that what you do? Guard people from danger?" Hugh knew there could be no harm in saying truthfully, "Aye."

"Well, then." Douglas looked to Butler, seemingly impressed. "I'm very glad, Your Grace, to see you well defended."

Butler thanked him. "I am fortunate to have such friends around me."

Edmund raised his glass. "To friends."

They drank the toast, which left but little wine remaining in the jug, and when they called the landlord to bring more he brought, in place of the more common local stuff, a bottle of fine burgundy he had been saving for a special moment. He also brought a single silver drinking cup—engraved and showing signs of recent polishing. "For you, Your Grace," he said, and offered both to Butler solemnly, with ceremony, "because you bring us honor, being here."

Butler, clearly moved by the gesture, made a great show of gratitude, passing the cup around so they all could admire it. This pleased the landlord, who bowed low and left them.

Douglas, who had taken out his snuffbox in the interim—a foppish habit, in Hugh's view—appeared now to think better of the impulse, closed the box, and put it once more in his pocket as he took the silver cup in his turn. "Very finely made." He felt the thinness of the rim with evident appreciation, though his tone as he remarked, "Our landlord treats his noble clients nicely," held a trace of churlishness that made it clear he had not been best pleased at being forced to change his room in Butler's favor.

Butler heard the tone as well. "Come now, I'm a man, like any other. I should hope I've never asked for special treatment." As the cup passed next from Douglas to Vautour, he added, "Neither do I need a special cup to drink from. Captain, you may hold that for your own use, and enjoy it. Pewter does as well for me."

Vautour, delighted, filled his cup and raised it with a flourish. "Let us drink to your King James. May he reclaim his father's crown from those who stole it."

"Well spoken, Captain." Butler held his plainer cup aloft and said, "King James!"

They all five drank the toast. Hugh knew that Douglas, from experience, would drink as though he meant it, so he did not bother watching him. Instead, he watched Edmund.

Was that hesitation? Possibly.

Edmund met his eyes and, saying nothing, drank. He filled his cup and passed the bottle round and made a new toast to the queen, then Butler made one to the two young princes, and so it progressed until the bottle had been emptied and Vautour suggested moving from the dining room to join the ladies in the parlor.

"I have a mind to play your wife at cards," he said, to Edmund.

For a man of size, he did not hold his wine well. He was showing its effects when he bowed gallantly to Anna and suggested that they once more play quadrille, but she'd proven herself capable of keeping him in hand, and now that Butler, too, was seated at the card table between Vautour and Mary, with Douglas sitting off to one side by the window, watching but not playing, Hugh felt comfortable taking the same chair he had the night before, close by the cabinet that held the books.

Until Edmund came to sit next to him.

"We're long past due for a change in the wind. Can you ever remember a storm like this?"

"No."

The Irishman's mouth faintly curved at the corners. "We're

meant to be friends. Douglas has that belief, and it's useful to us if he goes on believing it, so it might help if you did more than glower."

Hugh looked at him.

"That would be glowering," Edmund said. "If we speak low, we won't be overheard. You can curse me however you like, but you might at least smile while you're doing it."

Hugh made an effort to hold his face neutral, but knew that if this conversation was truly intended to make Douglas think he and Edmund were friends, its results would be questionable.

"That's a smile?" Edmund's eyebrows rose. "Your wife's a saint, so she is."

"Leave her out of it."

"That would be unkind to her when she so clearly longs to be right in the thick of things. Surely you see it? Your wife's an intelligent woman. She notices everything. You should be letting her help you by putting those talents to use, and not—"

"Leave Mary out of it."

Edmund shrugged, looking across to the card table, where the two women were laughing at something that Butler had said. "My wife told me that when she met your wife last year outside Paris, there was in that house a caged bird of some sort, that refused to sing. The lady of the house, she could not understand it, why this bird that was so coddled and well cared for would not sing, and your wife said... Have you already heard this? Has she told you?"

"No."

"Your wife said she believed it was because the cage was close beside the window so the bird could see the sky, yet never fly in it, and so it was too sad to offer any song at all."

Hugh looked at Mary closely, saying nothing.

Edmund carried on, "You're thinking, she's not sad, for she would tell you if she were, but I can promise you, a woman of her character will never be content to only see the sky. She'll wish to be a part of all you do."

Hugh did not answer that, and Edmund smiled.

"You are not married yet a year, while I've been married nearly seven. If you truly think you'll keep your Mary sheltered all her life and clear of any danger, I will only say I wish you luck with that."

Hugh wasn't sure why he replied, for he owed Edmund no explanations, but still he said, "I'll keep her safe."

"You can do that as easily with her beside you as with her behind. Look, I know how you feel—"

"I doubt that."

Edmund paused, as though his temper, too, needed calming. As though he were finding words. "She's the most perfect and wonderful thing ever happened to you in your whole life," he said, "and you know you've done nothing at all to deserve her, and you'd do whatever it takes to defend her. You'd die if it meant she'd breathe one hour more."

Hugh turned his head sharply, surprised that a stranger would so know his feelings. Except when he saw the direction of Edmund's gaze it became clear he was speaking of Anna, not Mary.

Still, Hugh found it vaguely unnerving, this glimpse into the workings of a man he'd only halfway figured out, and was prepared to think the worst of.

Edmund turned that same gaze on him, but all its mockery and wit was gone. In its place there was only impatience. "My life, if she died, would be over, you follow? But hers would be over if I kept her caged."

And with that, he stood, crossing over to stand near the others, and leaving Hugh sitting to think on those words for a while in silence.

IV

Their life together had been forged in small and private spaces—hours and days spent in the close confinement of a carriage or the cabin of a ship at sea, or in some water-coach or corner of a wayside inn, like this one. Hugh never used to think such places comfortable, but Mary made them so. She made them home.

There was a peace he felt in being here, within their room. The wind might shake the window glass, but it could not intrude. The candle she had set upon the small round table while she wrote the day's events into her journal cast a warming golden glow against the wall and gave Hugh light enough to read by as he settled wearily into the chair across from hers, the half-read novel in his hand.

She wrote the final few words of her entry, set her pen down, closed the journal, and took up another book to read.

Hugh asked, "What did you finally choose?"

"The *Stratagems* of Frontinus." She held the cover up, as proof. "My uncle had a copy in his study, and I read it years ago, though I was too young to appreciate it properly. There is much to be learned from such a book."

"Aye? And what have ye learned?"

"That it's useful to have elephants and camels in a battle, for they do confuse your enemies. And it's unwise to trust a Carthaginian." She nodded at the novel in his hand. "And what of you? How are you liking *Zayde*?"

"'Tis passable."

"High praise indeed."

"The scenes of war are not too badly done."

She smiled. "From you, that *is* high praise. Perhaps Madame de La Fayette consulted Frontinus for research."

"You are certain this was written by a woman?"

"Very certain. Monsieur de Segrais put his name to the book in order to protect her, because in those days, for a woman, it was dangerous to publish. But with that seeming kindness, he has robbed her of a key part of her legacy, for few will now believe she wrote the novel, even though he did confess it." Mary paused, as though to think on this injustice, then remarked, "Sometimes, when trying to protect someone, you do them harm that you did not intend."

It was not an idle comment.

He might not yet be familiar with all his wife's ways and moods, but he had learned when she was saying something from her heart and hoping he would hear.

Lowering his novel, he looked steadily across at her so she would know he'd heard. He was searching for the words to ask if she believed he'd done her harm, when they were interrupted by a heavy and persistent knocking.

Hugh impatiently pushed back his chair and stood.

Vautour was at the door.

"I give you my apologies," the big man said, "but you did say you were once a watchmaker, yes? Because La Sirène, she has stopped."

"So wind her."

"I have tried. This is more serious." Indeed, Vautour seemed troubled. He looked pale. "Please, I will pay you very handsomely."

Hugh had no wish to fix the Frenchman's watch, nor to allow cursed gold into this room, but Mary was already at his side, and taking pity on Vautour.

"Of course he'll fix it for you," she said. "And you needn't pay him. He enjoys the challenge, don't you, darling?"

Hugh glanced down at her, but did not argue. From his pocket, he withdrew a handkerchief and lined his open hand with it and held it out resignedly.

"Most kind," Vautour said, as he placed the gold watch with its small key on the handkerchief. "It is not good when La Sirène decides to stop."

"I'm sure he'll have her working by the morning," Mary said.

And with that reassurance, Vautour thanked them and retreated down the corridor toward his room.

Hugh closed the door.

His looks had long since ceased to have a withering effect upon her, but he made the effort, nonetheless. When she pretended not to notice and began her little rituals of readying for bed, he said, "I ought to throw it in the fire."

"The fire," said Mary, lightly, "is the last thing La Sirène must pass through, if the curse is ever to be broken. Weren't you listening? Water, earth, then air, *then* fire. It must be done in proper order."

"There are no such things as curses."

"I'm aware of that. But I am not the one who will not touch it with my naked hand." She looked with meaning at the handkerchief he held.

He said, stubbornly, "'Tis gold. I would not see it damaged."

"What is it about the Highland air that makes you all so superstitious?"

"Cautious."

Mary tried to hide her smile. "At least the watch will help to keep you occupied while you are sitting up tonight," she told him, "for I know you will not sleep."

She knew him well. There was no question of him sleeping—not with Douglas thinking Butler was the duke, and liable to attempt to strike by stealth at any moment.

He waited until Butler gave the predetermined signal, by two raps against the wall, that he was ready to retire for the night. Then Hugh saw Mary safely into bed and took a chair and went into the corridor and sat against the wall between their door and Butler's, from where he would see if anybody dared to stir.

He brought the watch with him, upon the shallow tray that normally sat underneath their washing basin, and that seemed well suited to his purpose, being wide enough to sit across his knees to make a surface he could work on. Overhead, there was a candle sconce set on the wall that gave good light to see by, though it cast annoying shadows when it flickered in the drafts.

He did not have his proper tools with him, but with his most delicate, small blade and one of the pins Mary used for her hair, he was able to make a fair survey of the watch and all its parts. It seemed, to him, to be in perfect working order. He could find no reason why it should have stopped.

With patient care, he reassembled it into its separate cases, and tried winding it again. The watch stayed silent.

From the cover of the balance cock, the mermaid eyed him mockingly.

I am the only master of my time, the watch reminded him.

A sudden, colder draft swept down the corridor. The candle guttered, and went out.

"To hell with ye," Hugh told the darkness. But he took care not to touch the cases of the watch as he placed one inside the other and rewrapped it in the handkerchief and thrust it once more deep into his pocket.

THIRD DAY

"Time shall unfold what plighted cunning hides."
—Shakespeare, *King Lear*: act 1, scene 1

I

February 13, 1733

MORNING BROUGHT A CHANGE Hugh could not place at first until he realized that the storm had died. The rain had ceased. The wind had shifted; pushed the clouds aside in places so a watery, uncertain daylight angled briefly through the window glass.

He finished shaving. Cleaned his razor.

Mary, who was nearly dressed, passed him a new shirt. "You've worn the other now for days," she said, as if that somehow mattered, as she took up his coat and began to brush it. Though he would not have admitted it openly, he liked the fact she cared for him.

"Clever man," she told him fondly. And then, to his questioning expression, she held out his coat for him. "Did I not say you would have the watch fixed by the morning?"

He frowned. But now he heard it, too—just as she must have done—from the depths of his coat pocket. Ticking.

Unease tapped cold on the back of his neck. He didn't correct her, but he knew he hadn't repaired it, and if it was running now, some hand more powerful than his had wound the key. All the more reason to have naught to do with the thing. "I'll return it."

"We'll be seeing him at breakfast shortly."

"I'll do it now." Shrugging into his coat, he went quietly out of their room. At Vautour's door, he knocked. It was early enough that the others had not gone downstairs yet to breakfast, but late enough that they should all be awake.

Vautour did not reply.

Hugh knocked, sharply, a second time. And then a third.

The door to the O'Connors' room opened, and Anna and Edmund stepped into the corridor. Anna frowned. "Is he in there?"

"Aye."

Edmund asked, "Are you certain? I mean, he couldn't have gone out when you weren't looking?"

Hugh allowed that Edmund did not know him well, and was thinking he should simply let the insult pass, when Anna said, "I'm sure Mr. MacPherson's always looking, Edmund, even when he isn't looking, if you understand me. If he says Captain Vautour's in this room, he is. But I do fear—" She broke off, and then said, "He looked unwell, last night."

She was not wrong.

Hugh thought back to the pallor of Vautour's face when he'd told him La Sirène had stopped. When he had said to Hugh, *This is more serious.*

He tried the door and found, as he'd expected, it was bolted from the inside.

Anna asked him, "Shall I fetch the landlord?"

Edmund flexed the fingers of the hand that was not scarred. "No need for that."

He had a skill for forcing locks, and did it quietly and swiftly. Hugh was not convinced that he himself could have done better.

"How did ye learn that?"

"In Ireland we're taught this in our cradles, so we are." There was that edge again, in Edmund's voice, of bitterness and hard disdain, hid carefully beneath the lighter carelessness. "It makes us better criminals."

His wife said, "Edmund."

"What? He has no right to judge me. There," said Edmund, as he swung the door wide. "And you're welcome." But that was the end of his defiance.

For they saw, then, what was in the room.

Although she had already seen, Edmund stepped forward, shielding Anna's view from instinct. "Now would be the time," he told her, low, "to fetch the landlord."

II

Vautour had been surprised by death. He had, from all appearances, been sitting at his bed's edge and preparing to undress, with one boot off, when death had come to him and caught him unawares.

He'd toppled back onto the mattress in what seemingly had been a sudden fit that had convulsed his frame and left a blood-hued froth around the corners of his mouth, and now the stiffness that came after dying had drawn back his features into an expression of astonishment.

"Poor man." The local doctor, who'd been called in by the landlord, had exhausted all the tests for life and come to the conclusion none remained—which Hugh could have informed them all for nothing when he'd first laid eyes upon the corpse two hours earlier. "May God have pity on his soul."

The landlord would not be consoled. "But this has never happened, that a guest has died here. Never!" Sadly he regarded his remaining male guests, standing now at Vautour's bedside. "This will bring much harm," he told them, "to my reputation."

"Nonsense." Butler tried to calm him. "It was not your fault."

To which the doctor added, "No, no, it was by his own hand that he died, my friend, and I assure you that was accidental. See there, on the table by the bed, that little vial labeled 'mandragora'? That is an old-fashioned form of sleeping draft."

Anna had discovered it and shown it to the doctor when he'd

first arrived, before he'd promptly sent her from the room so he could make a full examination of the body with no women present. She had gone downstairs, Hugh thought. And Mary had, on Hugh's instructions, stayed within the safety of their own room.

Which left only the men, gathered where he could keep an eye on them. The landlord was the exception, having been in and out several times attending to various matters like the fetching of the doctor. Evidently he'd not been there when the doctor had explained before about the mandragora, since he listened now as if it were a new discovery.

"Yes," the landlord said. "I understand. So he has taken this to help him sleep, but drank too large a dose."

The doctor nodded. "No one could think you were to blame."

"I hope his ship's crew will agree. This may be one of them," the landlord added, as the voice of somebody arriving drifted up from downstairs, and although he blanched a little at the sound of booted footsteps, he turned bravely to address the newcomer, and offer his condolences. "I am so very desolate."

Captain del Rio stood framed in the doorway. "I thank you," he said, with a glance at Vautour, "but in truth, we were never great friends." His gaze fell on Butler.

Hugh thought he saw a gleam of recognition in Del Rio's eyes, and interjected, "Captain, ye'll have met the Duke of Ormonde, have ye not?"

"Yes, of course. We have a long acquaintance." Without missing a step, he bowed gallantly as he attempted, no doubt, to sort out what the devil was going on.

"I am confused," said the landlord. "You're not of the *Tigre*?"

Del Rio at least knew the answer to *that*. "No." He smiled. "But you sent to *Le Tigre* a messenger earlier, saying their captain was dead, yes? And letting them know they could come to collect his remains?"

"Yes."

"And they sent to my ship a messenger after that, and asked me would I deliver to you their reply. Why not? So, here I am, to deliver it." He drew a velvet purse of coins from deep within his coat pocket and passed it to the landlord with a flourish. "They regret they cannot take their captain's body, but they give you this, as payment for his funeral."

The landlord, with the purse held in his hands, looked down, uncomprehending. "Cannot take his body?"

"No, because they are already leaving, as you see."

Douglas, who had been standing furthest from the window, crossed to look out on the harbor. "The rest of my belongings are onboard that ship!" He swore, and turning to Del Rio asked, "I don't suppose they asked you to deliver those, as well?"

"They did not, no. Just at this moment I think they wish only to put as much distance as possible between themselves and La Sirène." Del Rio crossed himself when he pronounced the name, and crossed himself again when Hugh produced the watch from his own pocket.

Held within the handkerchief, the gold watch ticked as brightly as if it had never stopped.

Hugh said, "If he is to be buried, let this thing be buried with him."

Edmund frowned. "How do you come to have it?"

"Vautour needed it repaired." It was no lie.

He moved toward the bed, and Douglas protested.

"You cannot mean to let a gold watch languish in the ground. It's far too beautiful to bury."

"Aye," said Hugh, and nodded at Vautour's contorted face. "He thought so, too."

And with that terse reminder, he tucked La Sirène into the pocket of the dead man's coat, where she belonged.

III

Mary was a fair way through the *Stratagems* of Frontinus. She glanced up as Hugh set the vial of mandragora on the little table. He said, "Find a place for this, to keep it safe."

"Where did you get that?"

He explained, as economically as possible.

"And no one saw you?"

"No."

There'd been much confusion of movement in Vautour's room with everyone leaving, and he had been quick. If, later, anyone noticed the vial was gone, they'd most likely assume that the doctor had taken it.

"I disagree with the doctor," said Mary. "If Captain Vautour died, as you say he seems to, of some kind of fit, it was not mandragora. That's not how it kills you. You just go to sleep and you never awaken."

Hugh looked at her, waiting.

She said, "My aunt used it for some time. She'd injured her shoulder, and had trouble sleeping. She tried belladonna but it gave her nightmares, and so an old apothecary made her some of this." Before Hugh could guess what she intended, she'd picked up the vial and uncorked it and sniffed it. "Yes, that's it, I remember the scent."

"Are ye mad?"

"I am careful." She recorked the vial and set it down, appearing unaware she'd nearly stopped his heart. "It's perfectly safe if you know what amount to take, and I'm sure Captain Vautour knew the proper amount for his needs. Its effects are well known. It's been used for some centuries." She took up her book again, leafing back as though in search of a reference she wished to reread. "Did I hear Captain del Rio?"

She notices everything, Edmund had said.

"Aye. He's waiting for us to decide when to sail."

"Is that him in the next room now, with Captain Butler?"

He confirmed this. "Del Rio's acquaintance with Butler is nearly as old as my own." That fact, learned just this morning, had been a surprise to him.

Mary looked up. "You have known Captain Butler a long time."

"Aye. Since I was fifteen years old."

At the end of the doomed uprising of 1715, it had been Butler and his wife and crew who'd sheltered Hugh and carried him to Spain. Hugh owed him much. His life. His freedom. Debts he knew could never be repaid.

He did not doubt that Butler was still making some plan to draw Douglas off in one direction, so that he and Mary could escort the real duke safely on his way to Rome, but Hugh could not allow that.

He would have laid odds that Douglas had just somehow killed Vautour. He knew the way a killer looked. He knew the signs of false emotion, and the coldness that lay underneath the words of seeming sympathy. Vautour's death had not been natural, of that much Hugh felt certain, and yet how the man had died remained a mystery.

If Douglas could do that beneath Hugh's nose, there was no chance Butler—even with his trusted Fergal—could hope to survive the assassin.

Which meant Hugh would have to kill Douglas.

"That's a very heavy exhaled breath," said Mary. "What has vexed you?"

Hugh searched for an answer that wasn't a lie. "My head aches."

"It's this room," she said. "Having the door shut so long makes the air stifling."

"Open a window."

"I have. It does little to help."

She was making a statement of fact, not complaining, and yet he remembered what Edmund had told him about the caged bird in the house outside Paris, that, seeing the sky but unable to fly in it, chose not to sing.

Once again, he felt moved to explain, where a year ago he would not have seen the point. "The closed door is to keep ye from harm."

There was more that he ought to have said, and he knew it:

that she was his reason for breathing. That if she were harmed, he would never forgive himself, and if she died, he would never survive it. But all of that, even unsaid, must have shown in his eyes, and she saw it, and he saw hers soften in answer.

"I know," she replied. Then her smile tilted faintly with mischief. "But you'll have to let me out for dinner."

"Why is that?"

"Because Captain del Rio will doubtless be staying. And he'll want a story."

She had a point.

"But till then, ye stay here, with the door bolted. And keep that close," he said, nudging the pistol nearer to her on the table.

"I'll be fine." She raised the *Stratagems* as proof. "Captain Vautour believed a book could be a deadly weapon," she reminded him, "so, as you see, I am well armed."

And as he left her, she went back to reading.

IV

Hugh was watching Douglas over dinner, so although he was aware that Mary murmured to the landlord twice, he did not pay much heed to it until, after the plates were cleared, the landlord brought the necessary serving things for tea.

As the silver pieces were arranged with ceremony on the table, Mary smiled across at Douglas. "I thought it might cheer you. I remember you said to us yesterday, while we were playing at cards, that you had missed the taste of tea while on your travels. And you have had a trying day."

"How very thoughtful." Covetous, as usual, of things of beauty, his eyes had gone straight to the small cups of Chinese porcelain, and the canisters and pots of silver.

Mary said, "Your Grace, I know that you do not enjoy tea, but perhaps, Mistress and Mr. O'Connor, you'll join us?"

Del Rio declined, as did Hugh. He found tea bitter and unsatisfying. And Butler, as Mary had predicted, was content to keep to wine, which the innkeeper found disappointing.

"It is the best tea, Your Grace. Brought by my wife's brother on his last voyage from China."

"But your wine is also excellent," said Butler. "Especially in these." He held up his stemmed glass, one of the set they'd all been given for their wine today in place of the more ordinary pewter and the silver cup of yesterday. The landlord did like showing off his treasures.

Immediately he began to tell them all the history of the glassware, in excruciating detail, until Mary—having taken on the task of pouring out the tea—discreetly interrupted with "Do you take sugar, Mr. Douglas?"

She had his cup poured and ready, but it took some minutes for her to dispense tea to the others, by which time Del Rio was impatient for his story.

"It is time," the Spanish captain told her, "for entertainment. When you were last on my ship, you left your pirate-hunter hero in great peril."

Edmund looked from Mary to Del Rio, quizzically. "What's this?"

"She tells the greatest tales. One day they will be published, and she will be very famous," said Del Rio, "and the world will read them also."

Mary blushed. "You are too kind."

"No, I am right," he told her. "I am always right about such things. But now, about your pirate-hunter's next adventure..."

Mary thought a moment. "It might be too difficult for those who have not heard the parts that came before."

Del Rio shrugged. "They will be fine."

If Hugh had been the sort of man who smiled, he might have done it then, because Del Rio's pridefulness amused him. It had been Del Rio who had first decided, upon hearing Mary tell her tales, that she should choose a pirate-hunter as her hero, and that his name should be the same as Del Rio's own—and in the time they'd spent aboard his ship it had become their daily custom to sit longer after dinner listening to Mary's stories, with Del Rio prodding her at times with his suggestions to ensure his namesake got a happy ending.

Once again, as she prepared herself, Hugh was reminded of his father's weaving—threads that he could barely see in the half-light of their small cottage turned to cloth of a whole pattern.

Magic was what it had seemed to him then as a child, and magic it seemed to him now, watching Mary.

"In a time before this, in a faraway land, lived a fisherman," she began.

Del Rio frowned. "Not a pirate-hunter?"

"A fisherman," she told him, firmly. "When he had been but a youth, a violent storm had swept across his island and had taken those he loved, and he had vowed that he would never feel the pain again of such a loss, and so he kept his heart well guarded; but a mermaid, being also lonely in her way, began to follow him each day while he was walking near the shore, and keeping near the shore began to sing to him and tell him stories, and at length his heart began to soften, and they fell in love."

Del Rio considered this variant, and said, "A mermaid can be a most fortunate match for a fisherman, because her songs can do many things. Even calm storms."

Edmund added, "Or raise them. Like La Sirène."

Del Rio nodded. "But we interrupt the tale. The fisherman, he fell in love," he prompted Mary.

"This made him very happy, but his happiness was bounded by great worry that his love would come to harm. 'For what defense has she,' he asked, 'against the dangers lurking deep within the sea?'"

Even Douglas appeared to be taking an interest, relaxed in his chair, sitting quietly.

"For many weeks he worried, till the kindly west wind, Zephyr, could no longer bear to see him suffering. Up rose the wind and said, 'I know a cave where lives a wise enchanter who can answer any wish if he believes it worthy.' With the fisherman and mermaid holding fast to one another, Zephyr blew the boat across the sea, along the path of moonlight, to the cave of the enchanter.

"When he saw the couple so in love with one another, the enchanter felt his own heart moved to help them. 'I perceive,' he told the fisherman, 'you wish she could have human legs, that she might be your true companion.' Whereupon the fisherman, in awe at first, recovered his resolve and answered, 'Truly, all I wish is that you cast your strongest spell to keep her safe.'

"The mermaid would have much preferred the legs and argued thus, but for the fisherman the memory of his losses was too sharp for him to chance her safety if it could be guarded. 'For what use are legs,' he asked, 'if you should meet with misadventure?' So he held to his convictions, and received his wish. ''Twill be a powerful enchantment,' he was promised, 'and not easily undone.'

"No sooner were those words pronounced than an impenetrable mist rose from the cave's floor and swirled over and around them all, and when it had receded, the poor fisherman discovered he was holding, not the hand of his true love, but an exquisite watch of precious gold, wherein she had been sealed.

"'But now,' he cried, 'I can no longer hear her voice.'

"'The price,' said the enchanter, 'for her safety.'"

Mary paused to drink, and Hugh allowed her one brief sideways glance to let her know he knew what she was doing—that she meant the tale to be a private message to him, showing him her heart, cloaked in a story.

She did not return his look, but Edmund, on the far side of the table from him, next to Douglas, caught his eye as he looked back with a degree of knowing Hugh found irritating.

Mary lowered her cup. "The fisherman in sadness put the watch into his pocket"—she resumed the tale—"and climbed again into his boat, and Zephyr filled his sails with wind so he could cross the sea and take his mermaid home. But when his neighbors saw the golden watch, they eyed it with such envy that he feared it might be stolen, so in stealth one night he dug a hole and buried it for safety in the sand along the shore. When morning came, his neighbors, seeing he no longer wore the watch, searched for its hiding place, and in their frenzy took apart the rustic shack he lived in, and his fishing boat, and so at once he lost both home and livelihood.

"In all despair he sought the shore again, only to find a storm approaching, and without the mermaid's voice to calm the sea, the waves had risen high and washed the sand away so that the watch lay now exposed and glinting brightly. And as quickly as he bent down to retrieve it, still more quickly came the shadow of a raven that, attracted by the golden gleam, swooped down and snatched the watch into its beak and flew away with it, the mermaid trapped inside.

"The fisherman followed the raven, across a wide valley and over a mountain, until he arrived at the edge of a forest so thick that the trees hid the sky. Not even his old friend, the west wind, could see through the tangle of branches to locate the raven's nest.

"And in that dark forest, the fisherman met with a fox at the side of a stream where the fish were so plentiful, each time the fox dipped its paws in the water it caught one, but could not keep hold of it. Seeing the problem, the fisherman said, 'Friend, you are seeking to grip them too tightly. The harder you hold them, the more they will slip from your grasp.'

"Taking heed, the fox reached with more care, and with gentle paws captured a fish. 'You are wise,' said the fox, 'though you'd do well to take your own counsel.'

"And standing, the fox shed his animal form and revealed himself as the enchanter, the fish turned by magic now into a tinderbox. 'If you had not tried to hold to your mermaid too tightly, you might not have lost her.'

"The fisherman sadly agreed. 'But I cannot undo what's been done, as you warned me yourself.'

"The old enchanter smiled. 'I warned you it would not be easy, but in truth there is no spell, or curse, that cannot be undone. When each of the four elements—first water, and then earth, then air, and finally fire—have held your mermaid in their turn, the spell will break. And three of those are already accomplished, are they not? The first when you sailed home with her, the second when you buried her for safety by the shore, and the third when she was flown here to this forest by the raven. There remains but one.' And he held out the tinderbox. The fisherman was hesitant."

"I do not blame him," Edmund said. "If your fisherman sets the whole forest alight, he'll be setting his true love on fire as well, surely?"

His wife replied, "I should imagine that's why he was hesitant." With a warm smile, Anna added, to Mary, "You truly are good at this. Captain del Rio is right."

"I am always right."

Thanking her, Mary went on, "Now, the whole time the men had been talking, the mermaid within her watch had been directly above them, concealed in the nest of the raven. She'd heard every word, and with all of her strength rolled the watch so the glint of its gold caught the raven's attention, and as the bird pecked at the watchcase the outer case opened, allowing the mermaid to press herself close to the keyhole and sing. Only faintly, but such was her power that even that breath of a song raised a storm, and a spear of bright lightning struck straight to the tree where the raven's nest lay, and engulfed it in fire."

"That's unfortunate, surely," said Edmund.

"Only wait," said Del Rio. "She always finds a way to end things well."

Mary smiled slightly. "Then came thunder and rain, and the flames of the tree were extinguished, and to the great joy of the fisherman, there was his mermaid."

"You see?" said Del Rio. "That is a good ending."

"I certainly hope," Anna said, "after all her adventures, she finally had legs, as she wished at the first."

"She had legs," Mary promised. "The fisherman built a new boat, and—as you so wisely observed, Captain—he found his wife a great help in his work, and they traveled together in happiness for all the rest of their days."

"A *very* good ending," Del Rio observed. "Only—"

Whatever he was about to say never got said, because at that exact moment, Douglas collapsed forward onto the table, his slack fingers loosing their hold on the fine, empty teacup. It fell to the floor, where it shattered.

V

The innkeeper, who during Mary's story had retreated to the kitchen, now came running back and gave a cry of anguish, although Hugh would not have cared to wager whether that distress was from the sight of Douglas lying senseless or the broken teacup.

Mary, generous as she was, assumed the former. "Do not worry, he's not dead," she reassured the landlord. "See? He's breathing. He has merely fainted."

It occurred to Hugh that she alone, of all of them, appeared completely unsurprised.

He looked at her more closely.

Mary said, "Poor man. It must be difficult enough for him to lose his friend Vautour, but then to have his transport and belongings lost as well, it would force any one of us beyond the limits of endurance. I am glad, Captain del Rio, he was able to arrange his passage to Genoa with you."

Del Rio's mind was quick. Perhaps not quite as quick as Mary's, but he did not drop the ball she tossed in his direction. "Yes, of course," he told her, catching on. "It is most fortunate indeed that we were able to arrive at this arrangement." Though his face and tone were serious, his eyes held dark amusement. "He was most insistent we should sail upon the evening tide."

Mary thought that excellent, and said so. "For the sooner he can leave the scene of his misfortune, it will be the better for him." Turning to their landlord, Mary asked him, "Would you be so kind as to collect whatever few belongings Mr. Douglas might have in his room upstairs, and bring them down? I fear he is in no condition to do so himself."

The landlord cast a wistful eye over the splinters of the teacup, but he nodded and went slowly up the stairs.

When he had gone, the others turned to look at Mary.

Very calm, she took the little vial of mandragora from her sleeve and passed it to Del Rio. "You may need this later. He should sleep for several hours, if I am right about the dose." She told him what amount to give, if he had need to do so.

"You are wasted on a man such as MacPherson." Lifting Mary's hand in his, he lightly kissed it, and then turned to Hugh and said, "Come, help me carry Mr. Douglas to my ship. My men will take charge of him there, and see he causes no disturbance."

Only Del Rio, Hugh thought dryly, could insult a man and ask his help in the same breath. And yet he knew he'd help. Del Rio couldn't manage an unconscious Douglas on his own, and anyway, it would give Hugh time to explain who Douglas was, and why he was so dangerous, and why it would be useful to have him removed completely from their path.

Del Rio asked, "What weapons is he hiding? I saw none."

Hugh would have said he did not know, but Mary spoke up, unexpectedly.

"He only carries one, that I've observed. You'll find a snuff-box," she said, "in the right-hand pocket of his waistcoat. Tortoiseshell, with silver. When he's on your ship, I would advise you not to open it, but throw it overboard, and burn whatever you have used to touch it. I believe its contents are the poison that was meant to kill the duke."

The Calm

"I shall the effect of this good lesson keep,
As watchman to my heart."
—Shakespeare, *Hamlet*: act 1, scene 3

I

February 14, 1733

The Duke of Ormonde, holding court at midnight in the captain's cabin on the *Gallant Jack*, seemed happy to be finally once more under sail.

"It's been a restless time for me," he told them.

Fergal slanted him a look. "It's been two days."

In all the time that Hugh had known Fergal, the dark Irishman had never held a high opinion of the duke, and did not always try to hide the fact. Still, Fergal was loyal to Butler, and Butler was loyal to Ormonde, and Ormonde liked Butler, so Ormonde and Fergal had danced around each other this way for years.

"Has it? Only two days?" The duke shook his head. "It seemed much longer. In spite of your efforts, my dear," he said, smiling at Butler's wife.

Hugh had been surprised, at first, to find her standing on the deck to welcome them an hour ago. And yet in truth he knew that he should not have been surprised, because where Butler went, she seemed to go, the two of them forever bound.

Like Butler, she was aging well, and was attractive in her features and her figure and her character, the warm embrace she gave Hugh when they greeted one another just the same as that she'd given him the first day they had met, when he was but a lad and close to death and needing mothering.

Indeed, one might have thought she was his mother from the pure delight she'd shown when Butler, crossing close behind her while they boarded, had remarked, "He has a *wife*."

And in that hour since, she had done little else than question Mary.

But then, everybody was questioning Mary.

"So you and Captain del Rio," asked Anna, "did not have this prearranged? No? Then he could have a second career on the stage, for that was a convincing performance." She thought for a moment. "Where will he take Douglas?"

No one was entirely certain, but "Since we are headed to Rome," Butler said, "I suspect Del Rio will head in the opposite direction, and deposit Douglas someplace where he'll be no danger to our cause."

Edmund winced. "Rome." And to Anna, said, "Not that I'm truly complaining, but promise we'll not stay there long. I can't bear hot weather, you know that. 'Tis why I left Spain."

Hugh hadn't made his mind up about Edmund. He said, "I heard ye left Spain for different reasons."

Edmund met his gaze with a light challenge. "Did you, now? Someday I'll tell you the truth of that, when we have time."

Anna said, "You will have time in Rome."

"Maybe, and maybe not. Anyhow, it's as I told you," he said to Hugh. "People will see what they wish to see. What do *you* see?"

Anna answered for Hugh: "Trouble."

Edmund smiled. "True enough."

He looked a rogue, yet it was obvious the couple was devoted to each other, and considering that Anna was no fool, Hugh thought it might be worth his time to seek out Edmund while in Rome and hear his side of things.

But this was not the time nor place for that discussion. Not within the gaiety of this cabin, with the candles in brass holders on the walls reflecting light against the row of windows in the broad squared stern, old books, good wine, and Butler looking fully like himself again, less fettered, as he always did when on one of his ships.

"It was a stroke of genius," Butler said, "to spot the snuffbox. I would never have suspected it was anything but what it seemed to be."

Beneath his admiration, Mary blushed anew. "It is not so original to think of poison in a snuffbox. Why, in France the dauphiness was poisoned by a gift of Spanish snuff when I was two years old, so I was raised to look upon all snuff as dangerous. Indeed, in one of the novels I loved as a girl, that was how the king's mistress endeavored to poison him. Mr. Douglas carried snuff but never used it. That seemed strange. It made me wonder."

It was a good thing she had, thought Hugh.

When he had helped Del Rio carry Douglas down to meet the longboat for Del Rio's ship, the Spanish captain, unable to curb his curiosity, had put on Douglas's own gloves and eased the snuffbox out of the assassin's waistcoat pocket. Inside, where the powdered snuff should have been, they had found a substance much like beeswax.

"Most intriguing," had been Del Rio's pronouncement, as he'd closed it, stripping off the gloves and rolling them around the snuffbox before tucking it securely into his own coat.

Hugh had said nothing, only looked at him with meaning.

"What?" Del Rio had remarked. "I know a man who makes a study of such things. He will be very interested."

And doubtless would pay handsomely. Del Rio might hunt pirates now, but what made him effective was that he had once been one of them, and knew the way to plunder.

Hugh had let it pass, because he also knew Del Rio had a sense of honor underneath his tangled set of morals, and would take care where the poison went; and also because, in the end, what mattered was that Douglas went, as well.

Mary was saying, "I wondered, though, why Mr. Douglas

would poison poor Captain Vautour, when his mission was killing the duke."

Edmund said, "But he did try to kill the duke." Then, as she looked at him, "The cup was meant for the duke, not Vautour." She still looked blank. "The little silver cup, don't you remember?"

Anna admitted she had no idea, either, what he was talking about, and suggested that it might have happened during the time she and Mary had been in the parlor after dinner on that fatal day, playing at cards. "We were not there."

"Ah. You're right, I've forgotten. The innkeeper brought out a silver cup specially for the duke's use, and we all passed it round and admired it, and Douglas had opened his snuffbox before that, and then he felt round the cup's rim with his fingers—to measure its quality, we were to think, but that's obviously when he laid on the poison."

The Duke of Ormonde said, "It's very odd, I must say, to be talked about as though I were present for all of this when in fact I was not."

Edmund laughed. "You were with us in spirit, Your Grace."

"And I'm grateful I did not become one. But if indeed this poisoned silver cup was meant for me—for Butler, rather—why did it not reach him?"

"Because he is too good a man to sit on airs and graces, and instead of accepting the cup, he said—"

Butler mused, "I said that pewter would do well enough for me."

"Aye, that's exactly what you said, and Vautour took the cup instead," said Edmund, finishing his summary, and in the little silence that fell afterward, Hugh reasoned they were all reflecting on how closely Butler had avoided death.

Then the duke drank deeply from his glass and sought to set their conversation on a new path. "Do you know, MacPherson, I'll admit I might be biased as a military man, but there's a fine poetic beauty in the fact your wife used mandragora. One of Hannibal's generals used much the same trick, as I recall, in ancient times, when his armies were fighting in Africa, though I've forgotten the general's name..."

Mary said, "Maharbal."

Ormonde blinked. "I do believe that's right. However would a young woman like you know that?"

Fergal muttered something underneath his breath and Butler's wife nudged him to silence, but unflustered, Mary simply said, "I read it in the *Stratagems* of Frontinus, Your Grace. He mixed the mandragora into wine which he deliberately left lying in his camp, then he retreated, so his enemy would overrun the camp, find the drugged wine, and drink their fill of it. That night, Maharbal and his men returned, to capture them or kill them where they lay unconscious. It was in the section about ambushes. A most ingenious plan. When my husband brought the mandragora to me to take care of, I remembered I had read that passage, and it gave me an idea how to deal with Mr. Douglas, so he might be taken off by ship without a fuss."

The duke, with eyebrows raised, remarked to Hugh, "A woman who reads Frontinus! You'll want to guard her well."

"He does," said Mary fondly.

Hugh looked down at her, and did a thing he only rarely did when other eyes were watching them—he put his arm around her. Drew her close against his side. "We guard each other."

Her eyes, briefly bright with emotion, met his before she cloaked it in the quick smile that she showed to the rest of the world and, addressing the others, made light of the moment. "Though, granted, I'm much less effective," she told them, "as books are my weapon of choice."

II

Thc sky was full of stars.

Hugh knew them intimately, having spent a lifetime sleeping

under them and finding his way home by them and, when that home had vanished, using them to find his way within a newer, stranger, less forgiving world.

On any other night, he might have searched among them for the constellations that would show him where he was, and which way he was heading. But tonight, he only glanced at them and leaned against the ship's rail, next to Mary.

She was watching, not the stars, but the calm swelling of the sea, and the broad path of moonlight that stretched out to the horizon.

He asked what she was thinking.

"I am trying to commit to memory something Captain Butler's wife remarked to me, because I wish to write it in my journal later. Something that her husband told her when they were both young. It was poetic."

One thing Hugh would never be. "Oh, aye?"

"He said that life will always be uncertain, and we cannot let the fear of what might happen stop us living as we choose." She turned her face to his. "Is that not beautiful?"

"Poetic," he agreed.

"He also said, whatever time two people have together, when they love each other, that is time enough."

He was in less agreement with that sentiment. "It never will be, though."

"I know." She turned away again, to watch the play of moonlight on the waves. "But it is ours, while yet we have it."

They were silent for a moment, with the water moving under them and past them, and their hands upon the railing.

Hugh, as always, could not help but think upon the difference in their hands—hers small and fine and meant to hold a pen and to create, while his were hard and rough from years of taking life. He'd very nearly taken one more in their time at Portofino.

As though her thoughts were fed by his, she said, "I could not let you kill him, when I had the means to find another way."

"He's not worth saving."

"It was not him I sought to save. You've killed before, and will again, but Douglas was not worth your blade. And I would have you standing at my side," she told him, "when we face Saint Peter at the gates of heaven."

Hugh angled a look down at her in silence. And then he said, quietly, "I'll stand beside ye always, be it in this life or after, for without ye I've no life at all."

She met his eyes, and once again he saw the brightness of emotion in them. He turned his hand, open, toward her and she placed her smaller one trustingly into his hold as his fingers closed over hers gently, with care.

Mary whispered, "Now *that* was poetic."

"If ye write that into your journal, I'm burning the page."

She assured him his fierce reputation was safe. "Though it would make a very good line for a hero in one of my stories. Those are safe in my journals, including the story of the lady who was changed into a falcon so that she could ride to battle on her true love's hand—for as Captain del Rio says, one day my tales might be published. One can never tell." She paused in the way he'd learned meant she was gathering thoughts. "I read somewhere the English King Henry the Eighth had a hawk he'd release in the air at the start of a battle, so that it would fly ahead, seek out the enemy's army, and circle there, letting him know where the danger was."

Hugh waited, knowing with Mary such speeches were made for a purpose.

She said, "A hawk is very like a falcon, is it not?"

"Aye."

"They are both small, and strong, and can be very useful."

Life will always be uncertain…

Hugh heard Butler's words drift past him like a spoken voice upon the wind, and knew it to be truth.

But Mary's hand was warm in his, and Mary's eyes were all the light he wanted.

"Aye," he said, "they're very useful, falcons are. But only if the fool who holds their jesses has the faith to let them fly."

She caught her breath at that. Her eyes filled, and began to shine. And as she turned and reached for him, he bent his head to hers, the stars forgotten.

III

The innkeeper had always liked the quiet of the night. His wife—good woman that she was—filled all his daylight hours with chores and obligations and left little time for him to spend communing with the things that gave him pleasure.

"There's no harm in it," her brother had defended him. "Be glad it is not younger women who do catch his eye."

"As if they'd have him," she'd replied. But she indulged her husband's love of beauty.

She had not objected when he'd built this cabinet to display the things he loved, although it was for his own sight and no one else's.

Carefully, he set the silver drinking cup back in its place. There'd been a stain around its inner rim, but he had polished it with diligence until it shone like new.

The Duke of Ormonde drank from that, he told himself with pleasure, *and from this.* He slid the stemmed glass at its side along the shelf until it caught the light—just so.

It was a shame about the Chinese tea set having lost a cup, but through the years he'd learned such seeming tragedies left space for him to gather and display new treasures.

All the guests were gone.

There was no one to hear him as he climbed the staircase to the upper floor.

The Duke of Ormonde slept in that room, he thought, passing the doorway. He could tell his future visitors, and charge them an enhanced rate for the privilege of resting where so great a man had lain his head.

The body in the next room would be taken in the morning for its burial.

Already it appeared more peaceful, but out of respect he crossed himself and said a thoughtful word of prayer before he felt the dead man's pocket.

There it was—where the big Jacobite had placed it.

He was saving it, he told himself. No thing of such great value, such great beauty, should be buried in the ground and lost. It would be his. He'd care for it, and keep it safe forever.

With a barely contained thrill that left him short of breath, the innkeeper drew out the watch.

And stared in disappointment.

It was not of gold, but some ignoble metal.

It was plain.

It had a porcelain face.

It was not La Sirène.

IV

His dreams had been troubled.

He'd dreamed darkness, movement, rough hands and rough voices, and clear, blinding light. He awoke to a brilliant blue sky stretching over him, and the sharp salt scent of seawater.

Rolling, he hastily rolled back when he found the world moving under him. Rocking. Unsteady and dangerous.

Douglas forced open his eyes to their fullest and looked around, wildly.

He lay on his back in a small boat. Beside him lay oars and two earthenware jugs beaded with perspiration—presumably containing water. And close by his feet lay two loaves of hard bread that the ocean birds, silently wheeling above him, had already spotted.

He pushed himself upright and sat with great care.

He was floating adrift in the middle of what might have been any sea.

In the distance to one side he could make out the purple line of what might have been land. And in the other direction, the sails of a ship were receding along the horizon.

He swore.

Then because there was no one to hear him, he swore still more violently.

Feeling his pockets, he swore for a third time, with all of the feeling his hatred could muster.

They'd taken his traveling papers. His money. His snuffbox. *His snuffbox*!

His...

Still coming out of his fog, but remembering slowly, in pieces, he plunged his hand into his final coat pocket and pulled out his traveling watchcase.

He'd bought it in London, to keep his own watch in. A useful thing, fashioned of wood lined with velvet to keep the watch safe and to muffle its infernal ticking.

Except, of course, it was not his watch inside the case. He had exchanged it for what he desired.

It was still there—the gold gleaming brightly.

He smiled in relief.

They had left him this much, at least. And with a note, in an elegant hand, reading: *This you can keep.*

Fools, he thought, to believe in a curse.

A shadow flitted underneath his boat, as of a school of fish. *A mermaid, keeping pace with him*, he thought in his delirium.

"I am the only master of my time!" he called across the waves.

And turned his boat toward the distant shore.

A Note of Thanks

No work of fiction is ever the product of solitude.

To those who gave me help whose names I didn't think to ask, and those who helped but whom I have forgotten to acknowledge here, please know I'm in your debt.

I'm very grateful to my three fellow anthologists—Anna Lee Huber, Christine Trent, and C. S. Harris—for including me in this adventure, and supporting me at every step along the way. It's been a wonderful experience.

I'm also grateful to Diana Gabaldon for pointing out that the scene I'd been seeing in my mind with Mary and Hugh wasn't simply a leftover bit from my previous novel, *A Desperate Fortune*, but the beginning of an entirely new story—and for reassuring me I could write a novella, even though I'd never written one. Her friendship, generosity, and mentorship mean more to me than she will ever know.

My thanks to Suzette Hafner for creating the perfect French motto for La Sirène.

And to my fellow writer and Spanish translator Sarah Callejo, who kindly corrects all of Del Rio's speech, my thanks, as always, for her expert eye.

To my editor, Deb Werksman; my copy editors, Heather Hall and Diane Dannenfeldt; and to everyone at Sourcebooks: thanks for giving me the time and space to finish this. I love you all.

Thanks to my agents, Shawna McCarthy and Felicity Blunt, for everything.

To the bloggers, readers, booksellers, librarians, and others who continually lift me up when I am in my writing room, I thank you for your patience and encouragement, and hope you'll find this story worth the wait.

And to my mother, who is always my first reader and first editor, and always will be who the books are written for, my thanks for all you do.

About the Author

New York Times and *USA Today* bestselling author Susanna Kearsley is a former museum curator who loves restoring the lost voices of real people to the page, writing stories that typically interweave modern adventure with romance, historical intrigue, and sometimes an edge of the unexplained. Her books, available in translation in more than twenty countries, have won the Catherine Cookson Fiction Prize, RT Reviewers' Choice Awards, a RITA Award, and National Readers' Choice Awards, and have finaled for the UK's Romantic Novel of the Year Award and the Crime Writers of Canada's Arthur Ellis Award for Best Novel. She lives in Canada, by the shores of Lake Ontario.

In a Fevered Hour

A Lady Darby Novella

Anna Lee Huber

CHAPTER 1

"We Spaniards know a sickness of the
heart that only gold can cure."
—attributed to Hernán Cortés, Spanish conquistador

Edinburgh, Scotland: May 1831

"MY LADY?"

I glanced up in surprise at the timid sound of our butler's voice. Usually stalwart and distinguished, Jeffers seemed hesitant.

"Yes?"

His jaw clenched. "There is a…Mr. Kincaid asking to speak with you." His lips pressed together before adding, "He insists it's urgent."

My eyes widened as I turned to meet my new husband's equally startled gaze. I knew of only one Mr. Kincaid who would both seek me out and elicit such disapproval from our butler, but it seemed impossible that he should be calling on me at our town house in opulent New Town. Nearly complete, this northern section of Edinburgh, with its graceful Georgian facades and neat squares, contrasted starkly with the dark stone and cluttered squalor of Old Town—Mr. Kincaid's usual haunt. In the past when we needed to confer, he would summon me in his brusque manner to some meeting place or suddenly appear at my elbow while I strolled the streets of the city.

Without waiting for my husband to recover, I stammered a response. "Show him up."

Jeffers nodded and backed out of the drawing room, his posture even more rigid than typical.

Sebastian Gage's brow furrowed, falling into lines of displeasure. "Is that wise, Kiera?"

Well aware of my husband's not-undeserved animosity toward the Mr. Kincaid I expected, I was not shocked by his irritation. After all, upon our first meeting, the man had kidnapped me and then accosted Gage, and their mutual antagonism had not stopped there.

I fussed with the stylishly puffed sleeve of my Pomona-green gown where it tightened just above my right elbow, still uncomfortable with this new style. "We can hardly turn him away without finding out what he wants. You know he'll just seek me out in a more inconvenient manner."

Gage's eyes hardened at the reminder. "I thought we'd finished with the man. After all, we repaid the favor we owed him."

At no small risk to ourselves, he didn't need to add, for it glimmered in the pale-blue chips of his eyes. I too had believed we'd seen the last of the maddening man, but apparently he wasn't content to leave us to our matrimonial bliss.

Not for the first time, I wished we could have made our escape to the Lake District of Cumberland for our honeymoon following our nuptials a fortnight ago, but Gage's testimony had been needed in the trial of a poisoner we'd recently apprehended. As a gentleman inquiry agent, he was accustomed to such proceedings, and I would grow to be so in time. We would embark on our wedding trip as soon as the trial was over, so the delay was to be of short duration. But just then, it was quite vexing.

Before I could speculate on the reason for his visit, the man in question barged through the doorway ahead of a scowling Jeffers, displaying the same devil-may-care attitude I was accustomed to. His clothes were fashioned of the highest quality and finest fabric, but as always, he seemed to have misplaced his cravat and his shoulder-length tawny hair was in disarray.

"A Mister Bonnie Brock Kincaid," the butler intoned belatedly.

Bonnie Brock turned to glare at him, but far from being

intimidated, Jeffers ignored his glower. This was no small feat, for I had witnessed how the notorious criminal's stare could make even the burliest of men quake in their boots. Of course, he could also turn that ruthlessness into devastating charm. They didn't call him "Bonnie" for no reason.

I hid a smile at Jeffers's refusal to be cowed. "Thank you, Jeffers. That will be all."

He nodded and I thought I detected a satisfied narrowing of his eyes, obviously not having missed my failure to request tea for our visitor. Gage and I might be reluctant allies with the charismatic and cold-blooded head of Edinburgh's largest gang of criminals, but that didn't mean I welcomed the association or wished to prolong his visit.

Bonnie Brock crossed the room in three long strides. His eyes strayed distractedly around the cozy drawing room, taking in the wallpaper patterned with delicate yellow twining roses or the sage-green damask drapes and Axminster carpet. He did not spend much time within the sumptuous parlors of New Town. Not unless he did so uninvited while the occupants were either absent or asleep, but I suspected he left the details of actual housebreakings to his underlings.

Had I not known him better, I would have thought he was nervous, for there was a restlessness to his movements, an almost frantic energy. Even his eyes were wild with some suppressed emotion. I had never seen him so agitated.

"To what do we owe the pleasure?" Gage drawled, eyeing the man with displeasure. In contrast to our guest, my husband clearly suited the stuccoed elegance of our surroundings, from the artful style of his golden curls to his sapphire waistcoat with a rolled shawl collar and the cut of his coffee-brown frock coat.

Normally, Bonnie Brock would have responded with equal hostility, skewering my husband with some quip, but this time he seemed preoccupied. "I need yer help," he replied in his deep Scottish brogue. His eyes darted toward the giltwood armchair adjacent to the daffodil-silk-upholstered walnut sofa on which I perched next to Gage, and I gestured for him to be seated. "I need ye to find a watch," he demanded, sitting uneasily on the edge of the dainty chair. "I need ye to find it before it's too late. Before all o' Edinburgh's doomed."

"Just a moment," I interjected, unsettled by the brightness of his eyes and the sharpness of his words. "Let's take a step back. What watch?"

"It was cursed by a Jacobite. I dinna ken his name, and it doesna matter. And when it fell into the hands o' Lord Avonley and then my mother, it cursed all o' us, too."

I exchanged a look with Gage, trying to tell if he was following Bonnie Brock's words any better than I was, but his eyes were wide with the same unnerved expression I knew must cloud mine.

"I know you think you're explaining yourself," I told the hardened criminal. "But you're not. In truth, you sound a bit... delirious." I studied his face, noting the clammy pallor, the dampness of his tawny hair at his temples. "Brock, are you well?"

He inhaled impatiently, clenching his jaw as he forced himself to exhale slowly and begin again. "My sister's father was Lord Avonley, the current viscount's uncle. He was my mother's protector for some years. Longer 'an most o' the swells she entertained."

Kincaid's eyes locked with mine, as if to be certain I understood what he was relaying. As a gentlewoman, I wasn't supposed to know about the seedier side of gentlemen's lives—mistresses, courtesans, and such. We were supposed to look the other way and pretend they didn't exist. But I wasn't any normal gentlewoman.

"Go on," I told him.

"Lord Avonley inherited a pocket watch from his uncle." He grimaced. "One wi' a notorious reputation."

"The curse?" I guessed.

"Yes. None o' us believed it at first, though he told me the story o' the watch's journey through the hands o' several unlucky men, includin' his uncle, who'd researched it after sufferin' his ain turn o' fate wi' the Walcheren Campaign."

I didn't know much about the doomed naval expedition to the Netherlands during the Napoleonic Wars except that it had ended in disaster and disease. Thousands of soldiers had fallen ill with Walcheren fever. Surely he didn't intend to blame that on some curse.

As if reading my thoughts, Bonnie Brock nodded. "Just a coincidence, right? 'Cept no' long after Avonley inherited, he began to lose money at the tables. Then his livestock died, and the south tower o' his castle collapsed."

"That sounds more like poor judgment and mismanagement to me," Gage said.

Bonnie Brock's eyes narrowed. "Ye might think, but I can assure you him bein' trampled to death by horses wasna a matter o' poor judgment."

I flinched at the rawness of his words.

"The watch was passed on to my mother when he died, an' no more 'an two months later she was dead, too. Killed by the same sickness that almost killed me and my sister."

"How old were you?" I couldn't help asking, somehow knowing this incident had played an integral part in his mysterious past that had made him the criminal he was today.

He furrowed his brow in aggravation, and I thought he would refuse to answer, but he bit out a retort. "Thirteen. Maggie was three." Then he turned back to Gage with a mutinous glint in his eyes, communicating he would answer no more questions about that. "I rid us o' the pocket watch, though it didna go lightly, an' no' wi'oot exactin' another pound o' flesh. But somehow it's surfaced again."

"What do you mean?" Gage asked. "Have you seen it?"

He shook his head. "Nay. But several o' my men have seen a pocket watch wi' a siren engraved upon it that sounds remarkably like the Jacobite's watch that cursed my family. And those men have all fallen ill. As have hundreds more across Old Town." He leaned forward, his voice sharp with urgency. "'Tis the watch, I tell ye. Must be."

I turned to meet Gage's eye, reading the skepticism there.

It was true. I'd heard mumblings about a baffling illness sweeping through Grassmarket and some of the more squalid sections of Old Town, but I had a difficult time believing the cause was anything more than the damp and filth of too many bodies living packed together in poor conditions. If the knowledge I'd accrued from my first husband—the famous anatomist, Sir Anthony Darby—had taught me anything, it was that there was almost always a rational explanation for such occurrences. However, being half-Scottish and witness to any number of strange occurrences over the last year, I had a difficult time dismissing the existence of curses altogether.

"So you think this illness is the fault of the watch?" I asked, trying to keep my incredulity from coloring my voice. "Because it was cursed? By a Jacobite?"

"No' just a Jacobite," Bonnie Brock insisted. "'Twas first cursed by God when French buccaneers stole the gold from the holy altars as they sacked the city of Cartagena."

I arched my eyebrows, not having imagined this tale could grow any more fantastical. "Then why is it called the Jacobite's watch?"

He huffed, scraping a hand back through his hair before dropping it in his lap again. I couldn't help but note how it shook.

"Because the man who first brought it to Scotland was a loyalist assassin workin' for the English Crown. And *he* got it by way o' a Jacobite watchmaker, who passed its foul luck on to him. Even set him adrift in the middle o' the sea wi' naught but the watch and the clothes on his back." He glared at me in challenge. "It killed him at Culloden."

I frowned. Many men had lost their lives at the Battle of Culloden, and far more Jacobites than loyalists, so I didn't understand how this added to his claim that the watch was cursed. In fact, very little of what Bonnie Brock was saying made sense. And, frankly, the manner in which he spoke of the watch, almost as if it had a mind of its own, sounded a bit mad.

"You must realize all of this sounds…incredible," I told him gently, knowing that if I didn't speak first, Gage would use terms that were far less diplomatic. "A cursed watch spreading disease and death. I'm not sure such a thing is possible."

Bonnie Brock jumped to his feet, pacing before our settee in agitation. "But it is, I tell ye." He threw his arms in the air, his breathing growing ragged. "Do ye think I woulda come here if I werena certain?"

He did have a point. I couldn't imagine him asking for our help if the situation wasn't dire. But that still didn't mean it had anything to do with the watch, only that he believed it did.

I inched forward on the settee, hoping to calm him. "There may be some other explanation."

He ceased his pacing, pressing a hand to the back of one of the Chippendale chairs and lowering his head.

"Some unknown malady or contagion. Some…"

Before I could say more, Bonnie Brock collapsed to the floor. I gasped, leaping to my feet to hurry over to him. However, when I reached out to attend to him, Gage stopped me.

"Stay back," he ordered. "We don't know what the man is suffering from."

I snatched my hand back, startled by the snap of his voice. "But we can't leave him lying here. I need to know if he's still breathing."

"Then let me check," Gage insisted, dropping to his knees on the other side of the man. He lifted his hand, feeling Bonnie Brock's wrist for a pulse. Gage's face was grim. "His heartbeat is steady, though not strong."

I hurried across the room to pull the cord to summon Jeffers, who must have been hovering nearby, for he responded in seconds. "Send John to fetch Dr. Graham," I instructed, trusting our footman to be fleet of foot. "And tell him it's urgent. Then Mr. Gage will need your assistance in moving Mr. Kincaid to the guest chamber."

Jeffers hastened to comply, while I turned back toward Gage, who rose to his feet to stand beside me where I stared down at the large man. He looked infinitely less frightening and intimidating when sprawled in such an awkward position. An uncomfortable sensation crawled up the back of my neck seeing him like this, for I knew Bonnie Brock despised weakness. For him to display such feebleness in front of me, and especially Gage, he must be very ill indeed. He was completely at our mercy.

"I suppose it's out of the question to propose he be moved to his own lodgings and examined by the doctor there," Gage suggested.

I glared at him. "Not unless you want the fault for his death laid at our door."

He sighed heavily, but nodded in acceptance.

"I suspect two or more of his lackeys are hovering outside on the street or in the mews," I murmured, knowing full well that Bonnie Brock rarely traversed the city alone. "I suppose they should be informed, or else we might have a pair of blackguards breaking down our door."

Gage's brow furrowed. "We'll send one of them to fetch his sister, for I'm not going to allow you to care for him. Not when we don't know what pestilence he's brought into this house."

I didn't argue, knowing such a thing was futile. He was only trying to protect me. Besides, I could hardly conduct an investigation while tied to Bonnie Brock's bedside. His sister should be capable of tending to him. In fact, it might do her some good.

Maggie had run away with one of her brother's former minions six months prior. A disastrous decision, for when Gage and I had rescued her, she'd been in dire straits, indeed. And the subsequent loss of the babe conceived by that encounter had made matters worse.

Perhaps if Maggie were allowed to be of actual use to someone, to focus her thoughts on something other than her own foolishness and loss, maybe she would recover some of her old spirit. Of course, if her brother died while under her care, she might also never mend.

I shook the dismal thought away.

"What do you think of his claim?" I asked. "Do you think the watch could have anything do with this?" I gestured toward the criminal's collapsed form.

Gage's handsome face creased into a scowl. "I don't see how it could." But then his lips pursed. "I suppose we shall have to wait to hear what the physician says."

I nodded, recognizing this was as open-minded as my husband was able to be about the matter. As an Englishman and an inquiry agent of some repute, he would insist there was a logical explanation. The more analytical bent of my brain agreed with him, even if the Scotswoman and the portrait artist in me could never close off the possibility of the mystical.

I pressed a hand to my chest, wishing there was more I could do for Bonnie Brock. Unfortunately, my medical knowledge extended to anatomy and the signs of disease and decay in corpses, not the methods of diagnosing and treating the living. I prayed Dr. Graham arrived quickly, or our only hope of finding answers for the rogue might be during a postmortem examination.

CHAPTER 2

I ROSE FROM MY PERCH on the edge of the chintz window seat where I'd been watching Bonnie Brock's henchmen tramp up and down Albyn Place, never allowing their eyes to stray far from our town house, as Gage and Dr. Robert Graham returned to the drawing room. The physician mopped his broad brow with his handkerchief and gratefully accepted Gage's offer to be seated. The table before him was laden with a tray filled with tea and assorted cakes, and I hurried forward to test the heat of the pot, wondering if it had sat cooling too long and would need to be replenished. Finding it warm, I poured the doctor and Gage a cup before settling again on the settee where I had been seated when Bonnie Brock entered.

"How is he?" I asked after Dr. Graham had taken his first fortifying sip.

"Resting now." He frowned. "But time will tell." His eyes examined my features in thoughtful speculation. "You have some interesting friends, Lady Darby."

This wasn't the first time this had been pointed out to me, nor did I suspect it would be the last. I respected Dr. Graham, and perhaps more importantly, I liked him. He was one of those rare medical men who could look beyond the strange circumstances in which I'd received my anatomical training to the mind beyond. He was forthright. He did not suffer fools gladly. But he was also tolerant and open-minded. As Regius Keeper of the Royal

Botanic Garden Edinburgh, chair of botany at the University of Edinburgh, and a physician to the Royal Infirmary of Edinburgh, I suspected those traits came in handy.

I would have liked to give him a straight answer, but we hadn't the time for a lengthy explanation. So I deflected his curiosity with a question of my own. "Do you think he has sickened from the same illness sweeping through Old Town?"

Dr. Graham frowned into his cup. "I can't be certain. In many respects, his symptoms do seem to mimic those of the patients we're treating at the Royal Infirmary. The headache, the high fever, the muscle pains, chills, and falling blood pressure"—he glanced up—"which caused him to collapse." His eyes strayed toward Gage. "I understand he was speaking almost deliriously."

I turned to look at my husband, whose steady glare dared me to disagree. "Yes. He did seem overexcited. Which is not like him." Even when Bonnie Brock lost his temper, his words and actions were carefully controlled. It added to his aura of menace.

Dr. Graham nodded. "If a mottled, rubeloid rash should develop, then I think it very likely is the same culprit. *However…*" He shifted forward in his seat, his expression growing dissatisfied. "I can't help but feel there is something strange, something suspicious about it." His dark eyes lifted to meet mine. "Normally, I would hesitate to speak without further evidence, but given our history, I know you will understand."

My muscles tightened, knowing he was speaking of his involvement in one of our previous inquiries.

"Mr. Kincaid is not presenting *exactly* like the majority of other patients," he began to explain. "For one, he has confessed to having had a stomach upset. For another, he is not displaying sensitivity to light or sound. It's early days yet for the rash to have appeared, but somehow I don't expect it will."

"What are you saying? What do you think it is?"

He pressed his lips together, as if still questioning the wisdom of making such a prognosis without more information, before answering reluctantly. "I believe Mr. Kincaid *may* have been poisoned."

My eyes widened. "Poisoned?"

"It's only a supposition," he hastened to add. "But yes."

I shared a glance with Gage, whose brow was heavy with unspoken thoughts. "Do you know by what?"

The doctor shook his head. "There are any number of plants and chemicals that could be the culprit, but without further examination and data, I can't tell you which is most likely." He set his cup and saucer on the table to his right. "The patient isn't precisely forthcoming or compliant."

I sighed, having worried Bonnie Brock would prove difficult if he awakened to find himself being examined by a physician.

"Could the poison be some type of metal?" I asked, thinking of the components of the pocket watch Bonnie Brock had been so intent on finding. "Like that which you'd find in a piece of jewelry?" I felt Gage's gaze on my face, but ignored him.

Dr. Graham tilted his head, considering the matter. "Unlikely. Most metal poisonings happen gradually over a period of time. As I'm certain you're aware, handling the pigments and other components that contain such metals, as you do when you mix your paints."

I nodded, well aware of the caution necessary when creating the portraits that were my passion.

"But this poisoning is more acute. And it seems to have occurred in a short time. Possibly from one exposure. That suggests to me either a well-known poison such as arsenic, or some botanic substance."

Drumming my fingers against the cushions of the settee, I turned to study the brick hearth, reviewing everything the doctor had told us. "You said his symptoms weren't presenting like *most* of the other patients." I glanced back at the physician. "Have some of them displayed similar abnormalities?"

He nodded. "Yes. That's one of the reasons my colleagues

and I have had such a difficult time agreeing on the source of the outbreak. Until we can pinpoint the cause and why it's spreading so rapidly, it will be difficult to stop." He tapped his fingers together, his eyes losing focus as he ruminated. "But if we're dealing with more than one culprit, if there is both a disease and a poison to be blamed for the illnesses, that might prove the answer." He rose to his feet. "I must repair to the Royal Infirmary at once to examine this hypothesis."

"Might we join you?" I asked, as he stooped to pick up his black medical bag.

He turned to look at me, almost as if he'd forgotten I was there. "If you wish." His steps carried him toward the door. "I'll leave word at the admittance desk that you should be allowed access. One of the younger lads should be able to point you in my direction." Then he was gone.

Gage shifted in his seat beside me, recalling my attention to his presence. "You wish to visit an infirmary overrun with patients suffering from some unknown disease?"

I stared up into his reproachful gaze. "How else are we going to find answers to Bonnie Brock's wild accusations about the watch?"

As I began to stand, he caught hold of my wrist, gently restraining me. "Kiera, the man was delirious. I shouldn't take him seriously."

"Yes, but if he isn't suffering from this illness, if he's been poisoned, that means someone else is almost certainly to blame. And if others have fallen victim to the same poison, doesn't that mean we have a potential mass poisoner on our hands?"

Gage's brow crinkled, troubled by such a realization.

"We can't ignore the matter until we can either confirm or refute the fact that poison might have been involved, whether it has anything to do with this Jacobite's watch or not."

He nodded, acceding my point. "You're correct." His eyes brightened hopefully. "But you could always allow me to visit the infirmary alone to ask questions for us."

I arched a single eyebrow, telling him what I thought of such a suggestion.

One corner of his mouth quirked upward. "Right. Well, I suppose I knew what I was letting myself in for when I married you."

"And if you didn't, then you were being remarkably thick," I quipped. Gathering my green skirts, I prepared to rise to my feet, but not before leaning toward my husband with a mischievous grin. "And I've never thought you were that, darling. A bit impenetrable at times, but never thick."

I began to stand again, but he pulled me back once more, this time with an arm around my waist. "Yes, well, even the most impervious of substances have a weakness. You just happened to be mine." He pressed a swift, but delightfully thorough kiss to my lips before pulling me to my feet.

I clung to him a moment longer than was strictly dignified, trying to regain my equilibrium.

Meanwhile, his eyes had hardened. "Let's find out who uncovered Kincaid's weakness."

The large brick-and-stone building of the Royal Infirmary of Edinburgh dominated the aptly named Infirmary Street on which it stood, just a block south of the squalid, tightly packed buildings of Cowgate. Set back from the road at some distance, two massive wings thrust forward on either side, forming a stark and gloomy forecourt through which one passed to reach the main entrance. It didn't help that the sunny spring skies of the morning had turned leaden, heralding the approach of rain. Regardless, I couldn't help but speculate that some flowers and a bit of thoughtful landscaping would have made the space more inviting, and less like a place where the old and young came to die.

Clasping my forest-green pelisse closed at my neck, I allowed Gage to hustle me along the path to the heavy wooden door, eager to finish this task and depart this place, preferably this side of the grave.

True to his assurances, Dr. Graham had left word at the admittance desk, facilitating our entry to the building. The young man stationed near the entrance guided us along the corridors to where Dr. Graham stood conferring with a pair of physicians.

"Ah, Lady Darby, Mr. Gage." He bowed his head in greeting. "I was just explaining my theory to my colleagues."

He performed the introductions, properly addressing me as Lady Darby despite my marriage to Gage a fortnight ago. I continued to retain the title by courtesy rather than by right since my first husband outranked my second, even though I was none too happy to keep Sir Anthony's name. There had been nothing happy about my first marriage, and I would have been pleased to discard such a reminder of it. But thus far most of my requests that acquaintances call me Mrs. Gage had been met with awkwardness and confusion. Given the fact that my association with Dr. Graham was so limited, and that we were in the presence of his colleagues, I decided to forego the appeal—and the explanation that would by necessity follow—for the sake of expedience.

"It is an interesting proposal," the youngest of the three physicians, a Dr. Nickels, replied, rubbing his smooth chin with a sharp cleft in it.

"Aye," the white-haired Dr. Maxwell agreed, crossing his arms over his chest. "I've been thinkin' many o' the patients are presentin' like the typhus of old, but no' all. Could we be contendin' wi' more than one ailment?"

"But typhus does not react like this new fever. In the past, bloodletting has always helped to bring it down," Dr. Nickels argued.

"Ah, but you're no' thinkin' o' the spotted fevers o' the seventeenth and eighteenth centuries. It's been some time since we've seen such a strain, but they, too, caused faintin' when only a few ounces were drawn. Those fevers require fortification, no' a release o' the humors."

As fascinating as all this was, it was not helpful to me and Gage in finding the answers we sought, at least not in regards to the poison or Bonnie Brock's insistent claims. "Excuse me," I interrupted. "But can you recall whether any of the patients have mentioned something about a gold pocket watch? Even in passing."

It was immediately apparent from their bemused expressions and the way they glanced at each other in astonishment that this was not the first time the subject had been raised. My hand tightened around Gage's arm, anxious to hear what they had to say.

"Aye," Dr. Maxwell replied. "Several o' the patients have been noted to babble—and in one case bicker—o'er some sort o' watch. At first we thought to attribute it to their delirium, but 'twas such an odd coincidence so many mentioned it, we've all been wonderin' what it's to do wi' any o' this."

Gage and I shared a look mingled with surprise and misgiving.

"Are those patients who babble about the watch all presenting the same symptoms?" I asked excitedly as a theory formed in my mind.

The physicians shook their heads.

"No," Dr. Nickels replied testily. "That's why I haven't worried overmuch about the watch, for those patients who mention it fall into both categories. There doesn't seem to be any rhyme or reason as to who speaks of it and who doesn't."

Ignoring the younger man's affront, Gage spoke to Dr. Graham. "Might we speak with those patients?"

"Follow me." He led us down the corridor and then through a series of doors before pausing in front of the final wooden door that would lead us into one of the wards. "I warn you, what you're about to see will not be pleasant. Our infectious wards are overrun with these cases, and we've been forced to crowd in more patients than we prefer." He sighed, allowing us a glimpse of the weary frustration and worry he'd until now been hiding rather well. "Many more and we'll have to start lining the corridors."

I hoped Gage wouldn't use this information as an excuse

to keep me from entering. One look over my shoulder at his furrowed brow told me he was considering that very thing, but he simply closed his fingers around my upper arm, keeping me close to his side.

The smells were the first thing to assault me as Dr. Graham opened the door, and instinctively I recoiled. The sour reek of sweat and human waste could not be blotted out even by the harsh odors of vinegar and alcohol. I'd experienced worse standing beside my late husband in his tiny medical theater in the cellar of our London town house while I sketched the bodies he dissected for the anatomy textbook he was writing. I had never learned to ignore the stomach-churning smells, though in time my ability to withstand them had improved. Exhaling through my nose to rid it of the stench, I summoned that same resolve and breathed shallowly through my mouth.

The number of cots crammed into the room, each of them filled with one, if not two patients, was staggering. The infirmary staff moved down narrow aisles barely wide enough for them to pass between the tightly packed rows of bodies. Some of the beds had small tables beside them, but the supply was limited, and those cots without a nightstand boasted only enough space between them for the staff to stand sideways to minister to the patient.

My eyes slid over the mass of ill people, coughing and moaning, and fixed on Dr. Graham's back. My heart softened toward all these suffering people, wanting to help them, but my back remained stiff as an icy drop of fear slid down my spine. Typhus, in whatever form, was no laughing matter. Nor were any of the other numerous diseases that could easily sweep one away to one's deathbed.

Dr. Graham paused beside the cot of a man with a head full of thick, red, sweat-slicked hair, much of which was standing on end. Patches of a blotchy rash dappled his face. He shivered almost uncontrollably, huddled beneath his blankets, and blinked his eyes open blearily at the physician.

"Mr. Aikin, these people have a few questions for you, namely about that pocket watch you've been telling us about."

The man's eyes flared wide. "I d-dinna ken anything aboot n-no watch," he denied, though it was clear he did.

Dr. Graham frowned. "Come now. You and Mr. Dornan nearly came to fisticuffs over the matter. Mr. Gage and Lady Darby are here to help. I don't want you wasting their time."

At the mention of my name, a change came over Mr. Aikin's face as he stared raptly up at me. "Y-yer Lady Darby?"

Whether or not it was good he recognized me, I didn't know. There were many in Edinburgh who viewed me as a figure to be reviled and feared because of the things that had been written about me in the penny press after my anatomist husband's death. Vile rumors that made me out to be even worse than Burke and Hare, the pair of body snatchers turned murderers who less than three years prior had prowled the streets and taverns of Grassmarket in Old Town for their next victims. But if he was one of Bonnie Brock's men, then perhaps he knew enough about my association with his leader to grasp he could confide in me.

In any case, I could hardly deny who I was now. "I am."

His gaze flicked toward Gage, narrowing in suspicion, but he subsided. "What do ye want to k-ken?"

"This pocket watch," I began, stepping as close to the end of the bed as Gage would allow. "What did it look like? Did it have a siren on it?"

He shrugged. "Gold. Expensive-like. I didna get any better look at it than that. No' in the tussle."

"There was a tussle over it?"

"Aye. Some flat brought it into the White Hart. Asked if any o' us had lost a watch. So course Dornan tells 'im he had, though we all ken our lad was pitchin' the gammon. He dinna have a feather to fly wi', let alone enough lard for such a flashy bit o' bob."

At this last comment, a man lying in the next aisle several cots away spoke up in a rattling voice. "'Tis no' my fault the rest o' ye turned Mary, sittin' wi' yer gobs hangin' open." He pounded his chest, though it made him cough. "I woulda split the brass wi' ye."

Aikin scoffed. "Aye, an' if that's no' a clanker, I'm Saint Paul."

"What happened then?" I prodded, trying to direct his attention away from Mr. Dornan's trustworthiness, or lack thereof, and back to the watch. "You fought over it?"

"Well, we werena gonna let Dornan keep it."

"How many men were involved? How many of you actually touched the watch?"

"Started wi' half a dozen o' us or so, but by the end the whole inn was part o' the mill." He stifled a cough. "I dinna ken who touched the watch."

Gage and I shared a look. We'd visited the White Hart Inn located in dark, filth-ridden Grassmarket on one notable and frightening occasion. Fifty or more men could crowd into its barroom on an evening. If the watch had anything to do with this matter, as it seemed to, who knew how many people it had affected?

"What of the other men involved in this scuffle? Did any of them also fall ill?" Gage asked.

Aikin scowled at this question. "Aye."

"Are they here at the infirmary?"

"Maybe."

Confused by his sudden reticence, I glanced at Dr. Graham.

"Two of them died yesterday," he confirmed.

I'm not certain why this unsettled me. Perhaps it was the realization that Bonnie Brock might be laid low by the very same thing. For if these men were part of his gang, as I suspected, then they could have spread it to him. My feelings on the notorious criminal were conflicted to say the least. He was annoying and infuriating, but also oddly endearing, and I certainly didn't want to see him die in this way.

Whatever the case, the matter had just gotten deathly serious. Not just for Bonnie Brock, but for all of Edinburgh.

"You said you didn't get a good look at the watch, but did you or Mr. Dornan"—I swiveled to include the other man in my question—"notice anything particular about it? Perhaps the way it smelled or felt in your hand?"

Aikin shook his head, but Dornan seemed to be giving the matter some consideration.

"'Less ye mean how 'twas dirty, then nay," he finally replied.

I shifted to peer more closely at the grizzle-headed man. "What do you mean 'dirty'?"

"'Twas covered in dirt or dust. Like someone had dug it up." His breathing grew labored, as if this conversation was taxing him. "Figured he'd found it kicked in a rubbish heap or close to the mound."

I wasn't certain such a detail meant anything, for he was undoubtedly right. Muck and grime coated the broken cobblestones of Grassmarket, as well as everything else in that dank, overpopulated area of Old Town where it huddled beneath the great rock on which Edinburgh Castle perched. Nevertheless, I filed the fact away to be contemplated later.

"Where is the watch now?" Gage asked, scrutinizing the older and clearly sicker man. "You don't still have it, do you, Mr. Dornan?"

"Nay. Lost in the scuffle. Someone prolly pocketed it and slinked away 'fore the rest o' us realized."

Which meant that at this point it could be anywhere in the city. Tracking it down was not going to prove easy.

Gage's eyes narrowed in consideration. "This man who said he found the watch. What did he look like?"

"A bit o' a chawbacon, if ye ask me," Aiken mocked, drawing our attention back to him.

Whether this was because he truly appeared to have come from the country or the fact that he had so willingly given over such a valuable article made him seem so, I didn't know. And I doubted Aiken had a discerning enough eye to tell either.

Dornan agreed. "But no' a bruiser. Looked more like a bag o' bones."

Gage and I thanked the men, and then nodded for Dr. Graham to take us to speak with two more patients who had mentioned the watch. One of these men had also been involved in the brawl at the White Hart Inn; however, the other had encountered the watch in a different manner. He claimed a man had traded it to him for services rendered. What possible services he could have performed to earn such a costly item, he wouldn't say, but I suspected that in actuality he was a pickpocket. Regardless, the truth didn't matter, for the man had promptly lost the watch in a hand of cards.

Curious whether we could connect those other people with disparate symptoms to the watch in some way, I also asked to speak with a few of the patients whose illness mimicked Bonnie Brock's. I understood what Dr. Graham and his colleagues had meant when they said there didn't seem any direct connection between one set of symptoms and the watch, for two of the men had exhibited the measly complexion associated with spotted typhus while the others did not. However, there might be some association we were missing. Four subjects were not enough to substantiate anything, so I wanted to widen the sample.

The next two men we spoke to insisted they hadn't encountered a gold pocket watch nor had they taken part in any public brawls. One of them seemed insulted by the suggestion. But the woman Dr. Graham introduced us to next proved more interesting.

She lay in a cot in the far corner of the women's ward. The skin around her eyes was dark and sunken and her brown hair matted and snarled, as if she'd been tossing her head restlessly on her pillow. But when we moved close enough to stand over her, she blinked open her eyes to reveal them bright green and glistening with lucidity.

"Mrs. Brown, do you feel well enough to talk?" Dr. Graham asked.

"Aye," she replied, studying us curiously.

Her eyes lingered on Gage, something I couldn't fault her for. His golden good looks were difficult to ignore. My husband had also noticed her interest, for he stepped forward to question her.

"Mrs. Brown, we do hate to trouble you, but we believe you might be able to help us." He bestowed on her one of his warm smiles certain to make any female within twenty feet flush with pleasure.

Mrs. Brown was no exception. Her cheeks crested with color, and even the tips of her ears blushed pink. "W-what can I do?"

"Have you by chance seen or heard of a gold pocket watch, even in passing?"

From the look in her eyes, it was evident she had, but she seemed hesitant to speak.

"We aren't looking to cause trouble for whoever currently possesses the watch. But it's very important we find it," he implored her. "It could be a matter of life and death."

She flinched at his words, almost recoiling from them. But they also seemed to convince her to talk, for she swallowed and clasped her hands over her torso. "Aye, I've seen one. Wi' a wheel and a sword on the coverin' and some sort o' selkie or mermaid on the inside." Her gaze flicked up at us. "Be that the one?"

We'd yet to receive a detailed description of the watch, but Bonnie Brock had mentioned a siren. And honestly, how many gold pocket watches could there be flitting about Old Town?

"Yes," Gage replied. "Where did you see it?"

"I found it." She swallowed again. "In my husband's coat pocket."

My hand tightened around Gage's arm.

"Does he happen to frequent the White Hart Inn?" he asked.

She stiffened in insult. "He does no'. He's a kirk elder."

Which didn't necessarily preclude him from visiting such an establishment, but it was clear she believed so, and I wasn't about to argue the point, and neither was Gage.

He dipped his head in comprehension. "My apologies. Do you know how he came to hold the watch then?"

"I dinna. He..." Her skin stretched taut over her features as she struggled with her words. "He was killed by a bit o' fallen masonry."

My eyes flared wide in shock. To be killed by a brick or stone from a building was certainly a freak incident, and a piece of rotten luck. But for it to occur while he possessed the watch was both troubling and suggestive. Had it been the cause, or simply an inexplicable coincidence?

I glanced up at Gage's profile, curious what he thought of the matter, but he seemed determined not to meet my eye.

"I'm sorry for your loss," he told the woman gently.

She nodded, turning her head to stare at the wall. "In truth, I didna ken what to make o' the watch when I found it. So I gave it to my brother. He promised to take care o' it."

Dr. Graham's gaze met mine, sharp with alarm.

When none of us responded—for what was there to say, and in front of Mrs. Brown—she turned to look at us, her eyes clouding with worry. "Should I no' have?"

"I'm sure you did the best thing you could at the moment," Gage assured her in a stilted voice.

There was no point in telling the woman she might have unknowingly exposed her brother to some sort of illness or poison, or even possibly a curse. Not when there was nothing that could have been done to stop it, and we didn't yet know what the result had been.

After ascertaining her brother's name and direction, we left her to rest and followed Dr. Graham back out into the corridor, for it was evident he had something more to tell us.

"I need to check our records, but I believe we've already seen her brother."

"What? Here at the infirmary?" I clarified.

He nodded grimly, striding down the hall. I practically had

to run to keep up. "If he's the man I'm thinking of, then her husband isn't the only loss she's suffered in the last fortnight."

My chest tightened. Poor woman.

But a glimmer of hope also sparked inside me. For if her brother had been brought to the infirmary, there was a chance the watch had also. Perhaps it was even then sitting in a box, waiting to be claimed again.

CHAPTER 3

THE POCKET WATCH WAS not at the infirmary. However, Mrs. Brown's brother had been, though he'd since gone on to join his brother-in-law in Greyfriars Kirkyard. What had become of the watch between the time Mrs. Brown had given it to him and he'd arrived at the infirmary was a mystery. There was always the possibility an enterprising member of the staff had filched it, but it seemed more likely it had passed out of his possession before he was admitted.

We traveled on to the boardinghouse Mrs. Brown directed us to—a shabby, but respectable establishment north of Canongate. Unfortunately, upon learning of her boarder's demise, the proprietress—a pinch-faced woman prone to voicing her disdain in the form of sharp sniffs—had carted his belongings off to the local poorhouse. She declared she'd waited three days for his next of kin to collect his things, which was two days beyond the rent he'd paid. It wasn't her fault his family had dawdled. She couldn't be expected to keep his room and his effects forever. She had bills to be paid. When asked whether she'd seen a pocket watch, she flatly denied searching through his things, even though someone had packed up the man's possessions.

Realizing it was futile to expect a straight answer from the woman, we abandoned the boardinghouse and returned to our carriage to set off for our town house on Albyn Place.

"If that pocket watch is cursed, that's one person I hope did finger it," Gage muttered under his breath as the carriage rattled forward over the cobblestones.

Harboring my own indignation at the woman's actions and demeanor, I had to agree with him. "*Do* you think it's cursed?" I asked, scrutinizing his bronzed features.

I expected him to answer immediately in the negative, so when instead he frowned back at me thoughtfully, I knew he was trying to keep an open mind.

"Frankly…I do not." He tapped his fingers against his thigh. "But I will admit there does seem to be some sort of mischief surrounding that timepiece. What exactly it is—poison, malady, madness…" He shook his head. "I cannot say. But I'm loath to believe it's the result of some curse."

I nodded in agreement. There were too many other factors to consider first. "If nothing else, I believe the watch might be some sort of…facilitator for the trouble surrounding it. Passing from person to person to person, spreading whatever ill luck is attached to it."

Gage grimaced, reaching for my hand. "We need to find it."

I squeezed his fingers back. "And quickly. Before more people are stricken by whatever illness is following in its wake. Before it spreads too far to be stopped."

Given my and Gage's eventful courtship and our roles as inquiry agents, I had predicted our married life would be somewhat unconventional. However, I could honestly say I'd never anticipated I would spend an evening huddled in our butler's tiny sitting room with two hardened criminals. From the long-suffering look on Gage's face, I suspected he hadn't either.

We'd returned from the infirmary to find that Bonnie Brock's condition had deteriorated, even with his sister there to tend to him. His henchmen had continued to pace the pavement outside, fairly champing at the bit to enact some sort of punishment or revenge for his debilitated state. At this discovery, we'd decided we needed to direct them to some task, or risk having them turn on our neighbors or an innocent passerby. But one simply didn't invite thieves and ruffians into one's drawing room for tea. Not even with their leader lying ill in the guest chamber above. So we had commandeered Jeffers's sitting room for the task, bringing them through the mews and inside via the servants' door.

I flicked a glance at our punctilious butler, expecting him to give notice after such a breach in protocol. But despite his hardened scowl, I detected a faint twinkle in his eye that made me question whether he might actually enjoy being forced to consort with cutthroats. Perhaps our oh-so-proper butler craved excitement more than I, and perhaps even he, realized.

Stumps and Locke shifted their feet uncomfortably in the confined space, and I could not blame them, for they were both large men, suited to their roles as bodyguards and lieutenants to Bonnie Brock. Stumps was a great ox of a man with dark, curling hair springing from every surface and orifice, even straining through the buttons of his shirt. Meanwhile, Locke was packed with lean, wiry muscle all through his six-and-a-half-foot frame. A man would have to stand far back to be out of reach of a jab or a stab from his long limbs.

This was not the first time Gage and I had encountered the men, for they were often at Bonnie Brock's side, and Gage had even had occasion to indulge in a scuffle with one of them several months past. Nevertheless, this was the first time we'd spoken with them, and I found them more intelligent than I'd assumed. Given what I knew about Bonnie Brock, and the fact his gang had its hand in everything from body snatching to theft, I chastised myself for having such poor insight. Of course, Bonnie Brock would never tolerate imbeciles as his right-hand men, no matter their fighting prowess.

"I suspect you're aware of the pocket watch Bonnie Brock believes is responsible for his illness," Gage began, eyeing both men critically. Whether intentionally or not, he'd positioned himself between me and them while still turning to include me in the conversation.

"Aye," grunted Stumps. "The Jacobite's watch. He ordered ye to find it."

Gage narrowed his eyes at this choice of verb, but he didn't correct him. "And we are endeavoring to do so. But we need your help. You know the streets and citizens of Old Town far better than we do."

"We've already searched for it," Locke scoffed. "Do ye think Bonnie Brock would o' come to ye afore we had?"

"But I imagine you did so quietly. That he ordered you to keep the matter as secretive as possible."

The two ruffians glanced at each other, giving us our answer.

"Well, we want you to do the opposite. Spread the word far and wide that we're looking for information on the whereabouts of a gold pocket watch with a wheel and sword on the case, and a siren somewhere inside." He lifted aside his frock coat and pressed his hands to his hips. "There will be a monetary reward to anyone who supplies *legitimately useful* information." He nodded to our butler. "Jeffers, here, will be scrutinizing them and whatever tales they have to tell. So those who think to defraud us should be warned not to waste our time."

"Bonnie Brock agreed to this?" Locke asked doubtfully.

Gage glowered at him. "Mr. Kincaid is in no state to agree or disagree about anything, and your best chance to assist him is to *find that watch*."

Locke's jaw hardened as if he wished to argue that point, but before he could do so, Stumps spoke over him.

"Maybe so." He shook his head in puzzlement. "But that's no' the right watch."

Gage and I shared a look of mutual confusion.

"What do you mean?" I queried.

"Bonnie Brock said the pocket watch had a siren on the back

o' the cock cover inside the watch, but he didna mention any wheels or swords. Said the case be decorated in some motif wi' a ship bein' tossed aboot in a storm."

I tilted my head in contemplation. Could there be more than one lost gold pocket watch flitting about the city? More than one that boasted a mermaid? More than one that left mayhem in its wake? It seemed improbable.

"Perhaps Bonnie Brock was describing the inner case?" I suggested, knowing that pocket watches often came in three pieces—the watch mechanism itself, including its watch face and back cock cover; an inner case with a lid of glass; and an outer case, which could be spectacularly ornamental.

Stumps shook his head again adamantly, making his shaggy hair shake over his forehead. "Nay. That part was engraved wi' something in French. Something about being the master o' time."

I didn't know how to reconcile this new information with what we already knew. Unless the pocket watch Mrs. Brown described to us was, in fact, a different timepiece altogether. Or perhaps she'd become muddled after lying ill in the infirmary for so long. Maybe she'd confused the watch she found in her husband's coat pocket with another watch.

Except, she hadn't seemed confused.

Gage gestured impatiently. "Whatever it looks like, we want information about all gold pocket watches seen in Old Town in the last fortnight, particularly those with a siren engraved somewhere inside it." He glanced between the two criminals. "Can you have it done tonight?"

Locke and Stumps conferred with each other with their eyes, and then Locke nodded. "Aye. Our runners will have spread the word all over the city afore midnight."

"Good," Gage replied with satisfaction.

Once the two men had filed out, shown to the door by our footman, Gage turned to face Jeffers with a grim smile. "I'm afraid we've just burdened you with a terrible task. Despite our warning,

I suspect we shall be inundated within the hour by people claiming to possess useful information about the location of the watch."

"Yes, well, don't bother about me. I shall sort them out quickly enough and send them on their way." His eyebrows lifted as if he relished the prospect. "But might I recommend we position Mr. Anderley at the front door and John at the servants' entrance," he said, speaking of Gage's exceptionally capable valet and our sole footman. "Lest we have meddlesome riffraff trying to sneak past to speak with you."

"Excellent suggestion."

"I'll also ask the coachman and stable lads to keep a sharp eye on the exterior. One can never be too careful."

"Very good."

"Perhaps Miss McEvoy could lend some extra assistance with our anticipated visitors," I interjected, suspecting my maid, Bree, would not mind being volunteered for the duty. She often aided in our investigations and would doubtless take the unusual assignment with her usual good humor. I turned toward the door. "I'll also ask Mrs. Grady to prepare tea and set aside some extra sustenance. We may all need it before the night is through."

A few minutes later, after speaking to our cook, I climbed the stairs and rounded the banister toward the warm wooden entry hall to find Gage shrugging into his dark greatcoat. "Where are you off to?"

"I want to apprise Sergeant Maclean of our current inquiry before we're descended upon by the masses."

Sergeant Maclean was a former pugilist turned officer for the Edinburgh City Police. We'd worked with him upon occasion to solve a number of troubling investigations.

"He might have some insight into the matter." Gage offered me a wry grin. "And I'm hoping he might be able to send a few extra patrols our way this evening."

The police house off Old Stamp Office Close where Sergeant Maclean could most often be found between his rounds was not a place for a lady, so I didn't expect Gage to invite me to join him. Nor, in this case, did I wish to. "Give him my regards then." I arched up on my toes to press a parting kiss to Gage's cheek.

But before I could turn away, he caught me about the waist. "I'll offer him that bit of esteem, but how about a proper farewell for me?"

Given the fact there were no servants about, I was more than happy to oblige.

Intimacy with my first husband had been far from enjoyable, so relations with Gage had been something of a revelation. He had the pleasant, if bemusing ability to make me completely forget myself.

So when the sound of footsteps finally penetrated through the haze of my enjoyment, I pulled back with a blush.

Gage shook his head at whoever was standing beyond me in the corridor. "Abominable timing, as always," he remarked drolly, leaving me no doubt as to who it was.

I turned in my husband's arms to see his valet, Anderley, begin to move toward us from the servants' staircase at the opposite end of the hall. The two men had a long history and a far more friendly and complicated past than most employers did with their valets. But I supposed that could only be expected given the nature of Gage's work and the fact that his valet often assisted him in his efforts, diving headlong into whatever danger awaited.

Anderley smirked. "My apologies. Jeffers told me to report to the entry hall *immediately* for sentry duty. I thought I should take him at his word."

Gage shook his head at his valet's impudence, but didn't say more. Instead, he pressed his hat to his head and squeezed my fingers. "I'll return as swiftly as I may."

Anderley opened the door for him, shut it behind him, and then turned to me and tipped his head toward the stairs. "Miss Kincaid was asking for you a short while ago."

My embarrassment fading, I searched his bland expression. I'd seen the way Maggie's eyes brightened at the sight of Anderley earlier. A fondness had developed between them during the days following her rescue several months earlier, something akin to what I felt for my cousins, and it appeared time hadn't diminished it. "How is she?"

His shoulders began to lift in a shrug, dodging the query, but then he stopped, as if realizing it might be best to give me an honest answer. "Sad. Drawn."

I moved a step closer, lest she or someone else hear us talking about her. "Did she talk to you?"

Anderley was a handsome man—a dark foil to Gage's golden good looks. He usually caused quite a stir among the female staff of whatever establishment he and Gage lodged in, and most young girls were easily persuaded to talk to him.

But not Maggie, it seemed, for he shook his head. "But…" He hesitated. "I did discover she likes shortbread, and she could use a bit of bolstering. Told Mrs. Grady that you and Mr. Gage had requested some special. So if she should ask…"

I smiled softly at this unexpected display of kindness, even as he tugged at his waistcoat, trying to hide his awkwardness. "I will not give you away." Though I doubted our amiable cook would begrudge the girl such a treat.

He nodded.

I found the door ajar to the guest bedchamber where Bonnie Brock had been installed. After rapping, I pushed it open further to find Maggie seated in one of the walnut fireside chairs positioned near the hearth. Earl Grey, my gray mouser lay curled in her lap, purring contentedly. Maggie looked up at me anxiously, but I was distracted by the sight of her brother sleeping under a mound of blankets on the bed.

His face was ashen, his lips cracked, and his tawny hair had fallen back on the pillow to reveal the puckered scar running from his hairline down across his temple to his left ear that his overgrown tresses normally hid. He would have hated for me to see him like this. And that made the unexpected pulse of affection I felt for the exasperating scoundrel all the more poignant.

I turned away resolutely and gestured for Maggie to follow me. She glanced down at the cat who lay in her lap, refusing to be dislodged, and I smiled.

"Bring him with you," I murmured before leading her out into the corridor. "We can talk out here so we don't disturb your brother. With the door cracked, we should be able to hear him should he need assistance."

I crossed the forest-green carpet running along the wide corridor to the cream cushioned bench positioned in front of the window at the back of the house. At this hour, the space was shadowed, the light from the nearest wall sconce failing to illuminate this far, but it made for a cozy tête-à-tête.

"How is he?" I asked as she settled onto the bench beside me, resting Earl Grey on the lap of her floral-printed chintz dress.

Her fingers combed through the cat's silky hair as she shrugged. "I...I dinna ken," she began hesitantly. Her eyes darted up to meet mine, the green irises bright with distress. "He...he hasna cast up his accounts since just before I arrived. Though he's no' eatin' anything. He mostly sleeps. And moans sometimes. I dinna ken what to do for him. Whether I should let him rest or wake him."

"Is his breathing even? Not too fast or too slow?"

"Aye."

"Then I would let him sleep. He needs it." I smiled tightly. "Has he said anything?"

Her fair skin flushed. "No' worth repeatin'."

What that meant, I could only guess, especially since this was Bonnie Brock. I strongly suspected he'd toned down his coarse language in my presence, so I could only imagine how crude it was when he wasn't minding his tongue.

Maggie resumed her attentions to Earl Grey, who closed his eyes in bliss. They made a somewhat incongruent picture; the round tomcat perched on the waiflike girl's lap. Earl Grey had grown fat on the tidbits my nieces and nephews snuck him when I still lived with my sister before the wedding, while Maggie had withered away. When I'd first met her in the wilds of Northumberland in January, she'd already been slim, but now she was skin and bones. It was no wonder Anderley had coaxed Mrs. Grady to make shortbread, hoping to tempt the girl.

I watched as her shoulders began to relax, the repetitive movement of her strokes down the cat's back and the sound of the feline's purring working their own sort of magic. She lifted her eyes to stare at me from beneath her lashes before dropping them back to the cat. "I ken he wouldna wish me to tell ye this, but…he mentioned our mother."

I didn't speak, worried any interruption might break the spell and stop her from sharing.

"He doesna talk aboot her often." A pleat formed between her eyebrows. "But…I ken he thinks of her." Her voice dropped. "I can see it in his eyes when he looks at me."

"Do you look like her?" I ventured to ask when she fell silent.

Her lips creased into a smile. "Nay. Least, no' how I remember her." She shrugged. "I was just three when she died. But I suspect Brock looks quite like her." She scoffed. "For he doesna look anything like his father."

As if realizing what she'd just admitted, she turned to me abruptly, biting her lip. I didn't know who Bonnie Brock's father was, though I'd long suspected it was someone from the upper classes. Someone prominent. Possibly even someone I knew. But the chances of me discovering it were slim. Particularly if there wasn't some obvious resemblance.

"In any case," she rushed on to say, "he's been thinkin' o' her a lot lately." Her face tightened into lines of remembered pain. "And now my father's old pocket watch has resurfaced."

"He spoke to you about it?" This surprised me, for it seemed just the sort of thing Bonnie Brock would try to shield his sister from learning.

"Nay. But I heard him discussin' it with some o' his men. He sounded…frightened." Her eyes lifted to meet mine almost in shock. I could understand why such a revelation would unsettle her. Bonnie Brock was not the type of man to be frightened easily, if at all. But then to *show* that fear…

I pressed a hand to my stomach. Such a discovery unsettled me, too.

I reached out a hand to scratch underneath Earl Grey's chin. "I know you were young, but do you remember the watch?"

She narrowed her eyes as if seeing into the past. "I remember Brock gettin' angry at me for playin' wi' it, and my father tellin' him I was allowed to look at it, too."

I couldn't help but smile at this evidence that he had been a typical older brother.

She shifted her legs slightly, making Earl Grey turn his head to glare at her. "I remember enough. And what I might've forgot came back to me after lookin' through my mother's journal." She reached into the pocket sewn into her dress and extracted the slim volume bound in merlot leather.

I didn't know if Bonnie Brock had shared with her my part in retrieving the diary, so I feigned ignorance as she flipped through the pages, finding the one she wanted before passing it to me.

I leaned forward to better catch the light of the sconce some distance away, recognizing the image at once, for it had caught my eye the first time I'd seen it. From what I'd been able to gauge from the sketches in her journal, their mother had been a talented artist. As a gifted portrait artist myself, I could distinguish the difference. But some of the drawings were more skillfully wrought than others, including this one. It captured Bonnie Brock at the age of about thirteen, standing with his head held high and his shoulders squared as he clutched a pocket watch in his hand like a compass.

Maggie inhaled a deep breath. "That's why I'm certain I'm right when I say I've seen it again."

CHAPTER 4

I SAT UPRIGHT. "YOU'VE SEEN it? Recently?"

Maggie's expression was contorted with apprehension as she nodded.

"When?"

"In January," she whispered.

My eyes widened in astonishment.

"John gave it to me. But 'twas just the case, fashioned into a necklace."

She must have meant Sore John, the man she'd run away with, believing he meant to marry her.

"That must have been a rather…large necklace." To say the least. And ungainly.

"Aye," she admitted.

"Do you know where he got it?" I had a difficult time believing the body snatcher had obtained such a piece of jewelry by honest means. It was far more likely he'd stolen it, either from the living or the dead.

She shook her head. "It wasna 'til later that I kenned enough to wonder. By then he was at ebb water, and he took the necklace from me so he could sell or gamble it away. I dinna ken which, but I never saw it again."

I puzzled over this new piece of information, wondering what, if anything, it meant to our current search for the watch and all the mysterious occurrences surrounding it. It seemed impossible to believe it was a coincidence the case had fallen into Maggie's hands. "And you're sure it was the same watchcase?" I questioned.

"Absolutely. 'Twas engraved wi' a ship surrounded by roilin' waves and writhin' sea creatures, as if they meant to devour it. They scared me as a child. And I didna find them any more comfortin' a few months ago neither," she mumbled. "There was also a tiny nick near the hinge. No' deep enough that ye can see it, but if ye run yer finger o'er the smooth metal, ye could feel the scratch."

That was definitely specific, and something her three-year-old self might have noticed and locked away in her memory. Stumps had mentioned the ship motif, if not the scratch. I trusted she was right, and that she was innocent of any of the implications surrounding its reappearance after all these years. But it still raised questions about where exactly Sore John had gotten the case.

Could he have stolen it from Bonnie Brock? Brock had said he'd gotten rid of the watch, and I'd presumed he meant the entire piece—cases and all. But perhaps I'd been hasty in my assumption. Perhaps he'd kept the outer case, not believing the curse was associated with that part of the timepiece.

I frowned at the door to the bedchamber where he lay inside, battling illness or the effects of poison. The question needed to be asked, but somehow I suspected that scenario was not quite right either. Not that Bonnie Brock would hesitate to mislead me or even lie outright, if necessary, though he did have his own strict code of honor. That was why such a large portion of Edinburgh was content to live under his sway, seeing him as a sort of Robin Hood figure. But there was undeniably more to the mystery of this pocket watch than I'd first assumed.

Leaving Bonnie Brock to his rest, I turned to study his sister, wondering if she might have some of the answers I sought. "Could your brother have kept the outer case? Could Sore John have stolen it from him?"

Maggie nibbled her lip in thought. "I dinna think so. No' unless Brock found it in recent years and dinna tell me."

"What do you mean?"

Her eyes blinked up at me, plainly pondering whether she was about to say too much again. "He was thrown in jail no' long after our mother died. So even if he had kept it, it would've been long gone by the time he was let oot."

It didn't surprise me to learn that Bonnie Brock had spent time in jail, only that he'd been so young. Just thirteen. And what of three-year-old Maggie? To lose her father, her mother, and then her brother in such quick succession must have been devastating.

I closed her mother's journal before passing it back to her. "That must have been hard."

Her gaze dropped to the cat still in her lap. "Yes, he was never the same after that." Her brow furrowed. "But maybe I'm misremembering. I was quite small."

"I meant, it must have been hard for you."

"Oh! I… Yes," she stammered, evidently unused to such consideration.

The sound of a low groan came from inside the guest chamber, and then a louder one.

Maggie pushed to her feet, dislodging Earl Grey. "Excuse me."

I watched as she hastened back to her brother's side, slipping the diary back into her pocket. Though it was clear she was concerned for her brother, I suspected she was also relieved to be rescued from our conversation. The stark look in her eyes had told me I'd prodded close to something she didn't wish to discuss.

Regardless, she'd given me much to contemplate.

I opened my eyes blearily, gazing through the darkness at the blurry outline of the bed curtains. It took me a few seconds to recall where I was, still growing accustomed to living in this town house. Then the warmth of my husband's solid form at my back flooded me with remembrance.

Since our wedding night, we'd fallen into the habit of sharing a bedchamber. Though it wasn't common among the upper class, I knew that my sister and brother-in-law—the Earl and Countess of Cromarty—did so, and they led one of the happiest marriages I'd witnessed. I decided that was reason enough to follow their example. Gage seemed more persuaded by the fact it was delightfully convenient.

I closed my eyes, preparing to sink back into slumber, when I realized his body was no longer comfortingly compliant. Tension radiated through his frame. The muscles in his arm draped around my torso tautened as if ready to swing. Alarm coursed through me, making my heart race.

Sensing I'd awakened, his arm tightened slightly, stopping me from speaking. That was when I realized he was listening for something, and I also strained to hear it—whatever it was. We didn't have to wait for long.

A muffled thud reverberated from the corridor outside our door, and Gage sprang to action. He rolled from bed and pulled his trousers up over his legs before throwing his dressing gown over his bare shoulders. Tugging a hasty knot at the waist, he pulled his percussion pistol from the bedside drawer. Whether it was loaded or not, I didn't know, but it would make an effective threat. I sat up and pulled the covers to my chin as he moved stealthily toward the door. He listened a moment longer, hearing a strangled voice followed by another solid thud, before throwing open the door.

I couldn't see much beyond his tall frame, but I gathered there was some sort of scuffle in the hall. Gage observed the melee for a second, perhaps trying to deduce which shadow was who, before he strode forward, pulling the door shut behind him. Scrabbling for my night rail and dressing gown, I hastily donned them before joining him.

I watched from the doorway as Gage and Anderley stood over another man seated on the floor. The man tried to push to his feet, but the valet shoved him down again. Rolling his shoulder, the man grimaced in pain. Anderley's coat and cravat were askew, but he ignored them in favor of glaring at the man below him.

"I haves some'in' he should hear," the man protested, his voice slurring. His jaw was shadowed with several days' worth of beard and his grimy hair was plastered to his head, his hat having been knocked off.

"And you thought the best way of sharing that information was to barge into a gentleman's town house and dash past his servants?" Anderley snapped.

Instead of expressing remorse, the man scowled. "They said ye'd pay for information," he groused. "Said ye'd reward us."

"Only if the information proves truthful and useful," Gage replied, still managing to appear intimidating despite his rumpled curls, bare feet, and general state of undress.

The man arched his chin in challenge. "Ye callin' me a liar?"

Gage lowered the pistol he still held to his side, tapping it against his leg. "I wouldn't dream of doing so." His voice dipped. "But if I should discover you are here to cheat me, you will not like the consequences."

His threat seemed to sober the man somewhat, for his gaze darted back and forth between the two men towering over him and he nodded. "What I got to say be truthful."

"Then out with it."

He swallowed, moving as if he meant to push to his feet again, but then changed his mind after Anderley loomed forward. "There's a lad. Works in a shop off Blair Street. He's been tellin' stories aboot some cursed watch to any who'll listen."

Though his tone of voice remained indifferent, observing from behind, I could see how Gage's back straightened in interest. "And what has he been saying about it?"

"How some prince who owned it were killed wi' a cricket ball. And some officer on the *Queen Charlotte* had it when the ship blew up, and he lost his arm."

I was familiar with both instances he was referring to, as I'm sure

Gage was. However, I had never heard tell of any pocket watch connected to either the death of Frederick, Prince of Wales—King George II's son and heir to the throne—in the middle of the last century, or the fire and explosion of the HMS *Queen Charlotte* off the coast of Italy thirty years ago.

Gage's stance widened and he began to shake his head, communicating his skepticism. But before he could respond, the man added one last comment.

"Oh, aye, and he be sayin' some loyalist spy had it, and was killed at Culloden."

He continued speaking, but neither Gage nor I paid much attention as he glanced over his shoulder to meet my gaze.

"Some scavenger lad found it then, but got caught wi' it and charged wi' theft for his trouble, and accused o' bein' a Jacobite to boot. Sent him to prison and the Sassenach officer who nabbed him kept the watch." He chuckled. "Though the lad had his revenge when..."

"Which shop does the boy work in?" Gage interrupted.

The man crossed his arms over his chest, a canny look entering his eyes. "Noo why would I be tellin' ye that afore I get my reward?"

"Because I could find his exact location in all of five minutes on my own, and should the information you've shared actually prove useful, I'll be deducting that amount of effort from the amount I *would* have paid you."

The man scowled at his folly in mentioning the street where the boy worked. It took him a moment to reply, but he grudgingly gave a response. "Hamilton and Whyte's."

Gage nodded and then looked to Anderley. "Escort Mr...?"

"Smythe."

This was almost certainly a false name, but we didn't need his true one.

"Mr. Smythe out to the stables and offer him a bed for the night. See that one of the stable lads attends to him. We'll ascertain whether his information is, in fact, accurate in the morning and then return to pay him his reward."

Mr. Smythe was half-bosky, but he was attentive enough to realize the accommodations Gage was providing for him were not entirely for his benefit. He eyed Gage with naked mistrust, but followed Anderley down the stairs. Evidently, his concern that if he left Gage would later deny the conversation ever happened outweighed his fear that we would report his forced entry to the authorities.

Gage slid the pistol into the pocket of his dressing gown and swiveled to face me. His gaze rested for a moment on something further down the hall before meeting mine. I turned to find Maggie standing in the doorway of the guest bedchamber. She must have heard the tumult and opened the door to investigate.

"I'm going down to watch the front entry and have a word with Jeffers while Anderley escorts our guest to the mews." He nodded to Maggie. "I suggest you remain here with Miss Kincaid."

I agreed, holding back my questions about Mr. Smythe's revelation for the moment. In any case, Locke had been proven right. The speed of the young runners Bonnie Brock's gang employed was envious. It was no wonder the city police had so rarely been able to catch him in any wrongdoing. And when they did, the citizens muddied the evidence or positioned someone to take the blame for him. Anything to keep their Robin Hood out of jail.

"Who—who was that?" Maggie asked, her eyes wide and luminous.

"Someone far too impatient to share information about the pocket watch," I replied somewhat sardonically. "Did he wake you?"

She didn't look as if she believed me. "No. I..." She swallowed. "I was waitin' for one o' the staff to come. We need water."

I studied the dark circles under her eyes, the lines of worry etched on her young face. "And perhaps some tea?" I suggested gently.

"Yes. That'd be nice."

"I imagine the staff is a bit inundated at the moment. I suspect that's the reason for the delay." And if it wasn't, they would soon hear from me.

"I could fetch it, except..." Her eyes strayed over her shoulder toward where her brother lay, candlelight flickering over his features.

"I can stay with him if you're worried about leaving him alone," I offered. Gage wouldn't like it, but there was little risk to me if I hovered in the doorway.

"Could ye?"

"Of course."

"Thank you." She grabbed the ewer from the nearest table and hurried past me. "I'll be back in a trice."

I watched her go, crossing my arms in front of me and rubbing my upper arms against the chill of the corridor. When I glanced back to check on my charge, I was surprised to find his eyes open. It was difficult to tell much at such a distance, but I could see lucidity shimmering in their depths.

"Were you listening to us?" I asked even though I already knew the answer.

He all but ignored the question, instead asking one of his own in a gravelly voice. "Are they here for me?"

I took several steps closer to better hear him and studied his face. There was no trace of fear stamped there. Not that I'd expected any. Only fatigue and a touch of wariness. He was unaccustomed to being at such a disadvantage.

"No. Merely someone with information for us. Someone a trifle too eager to collect the reward we offered."

His eyes flickered with interest. "Is it good information?"

"I believe so. We'll know more tomorrow."

"Ye could find oot tonight."

I arched an eyebrow in challenge at his surly response. "We could. But we're not going to. In this instance, morning is soon enough."

His mouth pressed into a mutinous line, emphasizing the pale-gray cast to his skin and the sunken orbs of his eyes. His hair rested lankly against the pillow—no longer a riotous lion's mane. I waited for him to argue even though he was in no position to make demands, but his rebellion slipped away as he seemed to sink deeper into the mattress, closing his eyes.

I took another step forward in concern. Bonnie Brock had never been one to relent, to wait passively. If there was something to be done, he wanted it done immediately. The very fact that he was not attempting to exert his will told me more than anything just how weak he was.

"I wouldna come any closer," he murmured, peering through his lashes. "Yer husband wouldna like it." His gaze dipped to my form. "'Specially no' dressed like that."

A blush began to burn its way into my cheeks, and I frowned in irritation that the rogue had still managed to disconcert me.

His voice softened. "Though, ye do look bonnie wi' yer hair doon."

I fumbled for a response. Thanking him for such a compliment seemed inappropriate, but so did chastising him.

Then his eyes sharpened with wicked glee. "How'd it become tangled so?"

The light flush in my cheeks turned scalding, and he gave a low chuckle.

"Wouldn't you like to know," I snapped and then narrowed my eyes when this only seemed to add to his amusement. "I'll let Gage know you'd like him to explain the mechanics."

This was a lie, and we both knew it. For if I told Gage what Bonnie Brock had said, he would likely smother the scoundrel in his sleep, and Brock in his current state would be too weak to fight back. But he did stop teasing me.

I swiveled to return to my place near the door, putting more distance between us, but his next words halted me before I could take more than two steps.

"Look after her, will ye?"

I glanced back at him, not having to guess which "her" he meant.

"Should the worst happen, should I not recover. I dinna trust anyone else."

I stared at him, stunned into silence once again.

His brow furrowed. "At first I wasna happy to find ye'd brought her here. That ye'd exposed her to me. But noo..." He sighed wearily. "Noo, I'm glad. At least, I ken here she's protected. Gage's honor will see to it. And if no', then you will."

"Well, push that nonsense from your head," I replied sternly. "You'll recover and see to her yourself." My voice was harsher than I'd intended, but it had to be to counteract the suspicious burning at the back of my eyes.

"Aye, harpy," he replied almost affectionately, evidence that he wasn't the least bit intimidated by my reprimand. He settled deeper into his pillow and closed his eyes, content I would do as he asked.

I returned to the doorway, squashing the emotion his words had stirred inside me. Bonnie Brock Kincaid was *not* my friend. He was a blackguard and a criminal—the very antithesis of the good that Gage and I strove to bring to this world. When the time came, as it must—sooner rather than later, given his chosen form of employment—I would *not* mourn his sorry hide.

I inhaled a shaky breath. Unfortunately, my rattled composure proved that to be a lie.

CHAPTER 5

A few moments later, Maggie appeared before me empty-handed.

"Where's your water?" I asked, before my eyes drifted over her shoulder to see Gage trailing behind her. His features were sharp with displeasure.

"Miss McEvoy is bringing it," she replied quietly, her gaze remaining on the floor.

I scowled at my husband, for he'd evidently made her feel as if she'd done something wrong, even if he hadn't directly reprimanded her. Softening my gaze, I touched a hand to her arm. "Your brother is still resting. Let Miss McEvoy know if you require anything else."

She nodded, her eyes still lowered.

I wished her a good night before allowing Gage to escort me back down the corridor to our room. I trusted Bree would take care of the Kincaids. Given her own painful past, Bree was the perfect companion for the girl in her current state, and I knew my maid well enough to know she would ply her with sweetened tea and Mrs. Grady's shortbread, in addition to bringing her water.

Gage shut the door to our bedchamber with a decisive click and I rounded on him in the darkness before he could speak.

"There was no need to upset the girl. I volunteered to stay with her brother while she procured the water she'd been waiting on."

"I suspected as much," he retorted, matching my low tone.

"Even though you *knew* I wished you not to go near Kincaid until we know what sort of foul illness we're dealing with."

"Or poison. It may be poison."

He glowered down at me. "For now that's unclear. You agreed to stay away." His stance softened, and he reached out to clasp my upper arms as he lowered his forehead so that it almost touched mine. "Kiera, my request was not unreasonable. What kind of husband would I be if I didn't try to protect my wife, my *new wife* from contracting a deadly disease?"

In the face of this plea, my own anger dissolved. "I wasn't trying to defy you. I didn't touch him or move close to the bed. I took precautions."

"Did you speak with him?"

I hesitated, and Gage lifted his head, one corner of his mouth curling sardonically.

"From a distance," I protested. Distance being a relative term.

He sighed in aggravation. "And what did he have to say?"

I pulled from his grasp, crossing toward the bed, eager to return to its warmth. "He was concerned that the scuffle in the corridor had been with someone intent on harming him." I elected not to tell him about Bonnie Brock's inappropriate comments.

Gage followed me, watching as I removed my dressing gown and slid beneath the covers. "Well, I wish you had remained in the doorway," he groused. I'd never said I'd left it, but he knew me well. "I wish you'd stood in the corridor to the side of the door."

I paused, comprehension dawning. "So he couldn't see me?"

Gage tugged the tie of his dressing gown loose, tossing the garment onto the end of the bed. "There are some things a gentleman does not wish to share with others. And that includes the sight of his wife in her nightclothes with her hair down."

Perhaps it was incongruous, but my heart warmed at his display of affront and jealousy. As a rule, men did not pursue me. I was the scandalous outcast, my reputation nearly destroyed by my involvement with my first husband's anatomy work. What attractiveness I possessed was not compensation enough for the oddity I presented and the awkwardness I often exhibited in social situations. On the other hand, Gage was the golden boy of the ton, sought after for his charm and staggering good looks. I didn't miss the way women looked at him. He could have selected his wife from any of the eligible ladies. And yet, he'd chosen me.

I rolled toward him as he slid under the covers beside me. Snuggling into his side, I rested a hand against the warm skin over his heart. "I apologize," I murmured. "When I volunteered, I expected him to remain asleep, and I didn't consider my attire until it was too late."

He exhaled, clasping a hand over mine. "Perhaps it's absurd of me to be irritated by such a thing..."

I shook my head. "It's not. I wouldn't want another woman seeing you in your..." I gestured to his bare chest, fumbling for words, "...your nightclothes." Or lack thereof. I assumed he owned some, but thus far he'd slept without them. Though this certainly wasn't something I would mention aloud.

Even so, he knew what I was thinking. I felt more than saw the amusement flicker across his features as he lowered his face toward mine. "And they never shall," he assured me. His mouth covered mine, sealing the promise.

Sometime later, I reclined with my head cushioned on his shoulder, thinking of our nocturnal guest. From the sound of my husband's breathing, I could tell he wasn't yet asleep, so I ventured a question.

"Do you think Mr. Smythe was being truthful?"

Gage stirred, taking a moment to gather his thoughts before he replied in a voice gruff with fatigue. "I think it unlikely there are two timepieces associated with a curse and an enemy of the Jacobites dying at Culloden." He rolled onto his side toward me, forcing my head off his chest and onto the pillow. "I think we'll find out in the morning."

It was a not-so-subtle hint to stop talking and go to sleep. But with my mind still whirling, I couldn't resist one more question. "Have you ever visited Hamilton and Whyte's?"

He blinked his eyes open to glare at me. "Clearly my recent efforts were not enthusiastic enough," he drawled. "The answer is no, I've never visited. And before you ask, no, I don't know what type of shop it is. We'll find out in the morning." His strong arm pulled me closer to his side. "Now, go to sleep, wife."

I smiled at his grumpiness and nestled closer, shutting my eyes. In the past, I'd spent many a restless night in other pursuits, reading and sketching and such, as sleep eluded me. But with Gage now sleeping by my side, it was far more pleasant to remain wrapped in his warmth and his scent.

Despite the previous night's interruptions, both pleasant and unpleasant, I woke refreshed and eager to journey into Old Town. The same could not be said of Gage. He scowled out the carriage window at the bustling cobblestone streets, which teemed with people going about their usual business. In truth, I don't think he saw them through the veil of his fingers as he rubbed circles over his temples.

"I thought you took the headache remedy Anderley brought you," I said, craning forward to see out the opposite window, curious how much farther we had to travel.

"I did."

I glanced back at him, feeling a moment's qualm that his head pains hadn't yet subsided. How many illnesses started in just such a way? Perhaps even the ones currently rampaging through Edinburgh's lower denizens.

I shook my head, pushing my fear aside. There was no use borrowing trouble when there was no proof his headache was anything more than the natural result of a fitful night of slumber.

Gage and I had only been wed for a little over a fortnight,

but I already knew his temperament well enough to know any further comment on his beleaguered state would be met with terse remarks, so instead I focused on the task at hand. "Blair Street begins just beyond the Tron Kirk, does it not?" I asked, trying to recall the area.

"Yes. Off Hunter Square."

"A respectable address that might still serve the higher classes even though it's not located in New Town." After all, not everyone with property in Edinburgh's Old Town had relinquished it for a cleaner, brighter space to the north in New Town. For instance, the Earl of Moray still owned a large swathe of buildings and land several blocks east on Canongate.

"But also near enough to Grassmarket and Cowgate to draw the notice of a seedier element." He winced as the carriage jolted over a deep rut in the road.

Fortunately, the carriage made a sharp turn and then rolled to a stop, saving us from any further rough treatment. Gage sighed, shrugging off the pain that pinched his weary features and donning his usual affable demeanor. It said much about how our relationship had grown that he allowed his facade of careless charm to slip away when we were alone.

He descended to the street and then reached up to help me down, guiding me away from a foul-smelling puddle. I was glad I'd worn my brown kid-leather boots—a habit I'd long adopted for ventures into Old Town—even though they did not complement my amethyst redingote.

My husband threaded my arm through his and led me down the street. We passed a cobbler and a haberdashery before coming to a rather astonished stop in front of an ordinary-looking little shop with a single window. The sign above the door hung from an intricately worked support of wrought-iron and proclaimed *Hamilton and Whyte's* in block gold letters. However, it wasn't the words that arrested our attention, but the image of a clock, its face adorned with a golden thistle.

The back of my neck tingled in anticipation as Gage stepped forward to open the door.

Inside, the shop was narrow, its walls lined with shelves on which were positioned a number of finely crafted clocks nestled in beds of deep-blue velvet. Their gold and silver gleamed even in the dim lighting. At the far end of the space stood a counter that boasted a display case filled with pocket watches of infinite variety, most of them exhibiting the hallmarks of a true craftsman's skill.

My gaze ran lightly over the contents of the entire case, but there was no watch adorned with either a ship in a storm or a wheel with a sword. If the Jacobite's watch had been here at one time, it was no longer. At least, not in the display case.

We looked up as a boy of about eight strolled through the door from the back of the shop. His complexion was olive-toned and his hair a thick, black mop. But his eyebrows were his most distinguishing characteristic, for they were far bushier than most children boasted. Thicker even than most adults. He grinned at the sight of us and hurried over.

"Can I help you?" he asked in a very English voice.

The corners of Gage's lips curled upward at the puppy-dog eagerness of the boy. "We're here for information. Are you apprenticed here?"

"Not really. This is my uncle's shop. I got sent down from school for pulling too many pranks, and my parents sent me here as a sort of punishment."

This was said with such artless cheerfulness that I strongly suspected this "punishment" was not having the desired effect.

"I see. Well, we're looking for information about a cursed pocket watch."

The lad's eyes lit with excitement, making Gage's next question somewhat redundant.

"Have we come to the right place?"

"Yes, you have. I've seen it."

Gage offered the boy his hand. "Then I'm pleased to make

your acquaintance. My name is Sebastian Gage, and this…" He turned to introduce me but the boy cut him off, nearly springing across the counter.

"*The* Sebastian Gage? I've read *all* the stories about you in the papers. Did you really catch that thoroughbred thief by tackling him from a hot-air balloon?" he asked eagerly.

Gage seemed to find his enthusiasm amusing. "I didn't leap out of the contraption, but yes, I convinced a balloonist to help me chase the thief."

The boy beamed. "Zooks!"

He opened his mouth to ask another question, but Gage cut him off. "And your name is?"

The lad straightened. "Teddy Beecham. Well, Theodore Beecham. But you can call me Teddy."

"Pleased to meet you, Mr. Beecham. Now, the pocket watch. When did you see it?"

"Oh! Are you investigating it? Let me see." He scrunched up his face very seriously. "It must have been about four weeks ago. My uncle might know better. He worked on it for Mr. Douglas."

"And Mr. Douglas was the man who had it in his possession?"

He nodded. "Wanted my uncle to make some adjustments to it. Said he'd wait, even though my uncle told him it would take him the better part of an afternoon."

Plainly this Mr. Douglas had not trusted the watch to be far from his sight.

"And let me guess, it was your job to keep him entertained?" Gage queried, leaning toward the boy confidentially.

"More like he kept *me* entertained. Told me all about the curse on the watch—one put there by God himself because of some French buccaneer."

Gage flicked a knowing look over his shoulder at me. "Is your uncle available, by chance?"

But there was no need for Teddy to answer, for a man with honey-blond hair and ruddy features entered the front of the shop through the door behind the counter. His clothing was more fashionable than I'd expected and his eyes bright with curiosity, but the most interesting aspect about him was the bandage wrapped around his right hand. My gaze immediately riveted to it, and he lowered it behind the counter as he addressed my husband.

"May I help you?"

Gage performed the necessary introductions, all while Teddy bounced on his heels waiting for him to reach the most interesting part. We learned that Teddy's uncle was the Hamilton in Hamilton and Whyte's, and he had indeed made adjustments to a pocket watch for a Mr. Douglas.

"Do you mind telling us more about it?" Gage asked.

Mr. Hamilton hesitated for a moment, scrutinizing each of us in turn.

"He's that gentleman inquiry agent from London," Teddy declared in a loud whisper. "The one who solves thefts and murders."

His uncle touched him on the shoulder, staying him. "I'm aware." Then he turned back to us, apparently deciding to trust us. "It was an intricate timepiece. I would have thought it quite valuable based on the quality o' the gold alone, no' to mention the craftsmanship. I remember thinkin' that this Mr. Douglas, if that was his name, hardly seemed the type o' man to own such a piece. But after he spouted off aboot the watch's curse and the unfortunate events associated wi' it, well..." He shrugged. "I decided that might account for it. For who would want to own a watch wi' such a history?"

The manner in which Teddy's eyes gleamed answered that question.

"Can you describe it for us?" Gage asked.

"The watch itself had a mermaid engraved on the cock cover and some words inscribed on the back. 'Je suis le seul maître de mon temps,' it said."

I am the only master of my time. Interesting in its defiant tone.

"The outer case was adorned wi' the Wheel of Fortune wi' a sword stabbin' through its spokes. Except..."

His words died away as he pressed his lips together in some internal debate.

Gage perked up. "Yes?"

"Well...I feel quite certain that wasna its original outer case." He frowned. "The gold was o' a lesser quality. And the craftsmanship was no' done by the same man."

If the watches and clocks in this shop were any indication of the caliber of this man's work, I trusted his opinion. He knew his trade, and excelled at it.

"What alterations did he wish you to make to it?" I asked, speaking for the first time since we'd entered the shop.

Mr. Hamilton's sharp brown eyes swung toward me. "He complained that the watch kept stoppin' at odd times, but I couldna find anything wrong wi' it. All the parts were in good workin' order, so I simply cleaned away some dust and tarnish."

But the men at the hospital had described the watch as dirty, dusty. If Mr. Hamilton had cleaned it, then why had it been in such a state when it made its appearance at the White Hart Inn?

"That probably happened when he secreted it away in his family's attic for all those years," Teddy supplied, evidently referring to some part of the tale Mr. Douglas had told him.

His uncle ignored him. "*And* he wanted me to make some alterations to the new outer case so that the inner case fit more easily inside." His brow furrowed and he shook his head. "Such a strange piece," he murmured almost as an aside.

"Strange how?" Gage asked, sensing as I did that this detail might somehow be important.

He shifted his stance and exhaled, gathering his thoughts. "Well, the outer case had a tiny channel fashioned aroond the interior o' the hinged lid." He demonstrated with his hands. "For what purpose, I couldna tell you. I've never seen anything like it."

An idea that might explain it all began to percolate through my brain. The variance in symptoms between some of the patients at the infirmary and Bonnie Brock, the two outer cases—one of which Maggie had possessed for a short time as a bulky necklace—the strange feature in the new outer case, the dirty appearance of the watch. It wouldn't tell me where the watch was now located or who this Mr. Douglas really was. But I suspected Bonnie Brock might, perhaps unwittingly, be able to.

I swiveled toward Gage, who had asked Mr. Hamilton and Teddy for a description of Mr. Douglas. His eyes darted to meet mine when I touched his arm, their pupils dilating as he acknowledged my restrained urgency. But then he turned back to hear what they had to say.

"No' very tall. A little below average height. Wi' dark hair and a scar runnin' across his cheek here." Mr. Hamilton brushed his finger horizontally from his nose to his ear.

"And he was missing three of his fingers on his right hand," Teddy chimed in, his excitement undimmed.

His uncle glanced at him, startled.

"He took off his glove and showed me."

Mr. Hamilton glanced down at his own bandaged hand.

"How did you injure it?" I asked softly.

His face pinched. "A foutering group o' lads tripped me, and I fell into a broken gate wi' some jagged metal bits. Cut my hand."

I flinched.

I didn't have to ask him how long ago this happened, or whether his right hand was his dominant hand. It was written in the tense lines of his face, in the hollows beneath his eyes. A watchmaker depended on his ability to perform minute, detailed tasks with his hands. If his hand didn't heal adequately, he wouldn't be able to practice his trade. Perhaps that wasn't the fault of the watch, but he had handled it, and that knowledge sat heavy on his shoulders.

Chapter 6

No sooner had Gage and I descended from our carriage before our town house than we heard shouts coming from inside, foul curses that made my eyes widen in shock and my steps falter.

Gage released my arm and hastened up the stairs ahead of me, throwing open the door to find Bonnie Brock struggling against Anderley and our footman. The table in the entry had been knocked over, and the footman sported a sizable contusion on his cheek. Bonnie Brock was in no state to be out of the bed. In fact, he sagged against the men, dragging them downward. Once Gage joined the fray, it didn't take much to force the rogue's feet back toward the staircase and push him down onto the second step where he slumped.

"Why are you attacking my staff?" Gage demanded to know. "You can barely stand. You're as feeble as a kitten."

Bonnie Brock's shoulders stiffened, not taking kindly to this last statement. He lifted his head to glare at Gage in such a way that if he had not been ill, I would have expected to find a dirk buried in my husband's side. Even in such a weakened condition, he might still attempt it, at that.

I rushed forward to intercede. "You're too ill to be moving around. You should be in bed," I scolded him.

He flashed me a wolfish grin. "I'll go if you'll join me." His eyes darted toward Gage, baiting him.

I held a hand up to restrain Gage as his muscles tensed. "I've had quite enough from you," I snapped at Bonnie Brock. "Here, I've shown you every kindness and consideration when we could as easily have labeled you a raving lunatic and tossed your carcass out into the street. And how am I repaid for that courtesy? With insults. And in my own home. I'll not have it, I won't."

Bonnie Brock's features tightened, and his complexion paled in what I thought might actually be chagrin.

I inhaled a deep calming breath through my nose, reminding myself he was rebelling against his state of helplessness. For a man to whom power was not only a way of life, but a matter of survival, the loss of it had clearly rattled him. And perhaps brought back some rather unpleasant memories of the times before he had wielded such influence. "We've uncovered information, and we would like to confer with you."

He straightened with interest, and I narrowed my eyes.

"Do you think you can be civil, or do we need to send for Sergeant Maclean and ask him to transport you to the infirmary, where you *should* be?"

"I can be civil," he grumbled. Though his tone wasn't exactly contrite, I suspected it was the best I would get.

I nodded sharply, and then gestured for Anderley and the footman to help him to his feet. I half expected him to shake them off, but his foray had weakened him and he accepted their assistance, leaning heavily on their support as they mounted the stairs. Maggie, who had stood at the top of the stairs wringing her hands through this altercation, hurried on ahead.

I took a moment to remove my hat, gloves, and redingote while I settled my frayed temper. Then, after smoothing the hairs on top of my head, I swiveled to take Gage's proffered arm.

"I know I shouldn't," he murmured as we climbed the stairs. "But I thoroughly enjoyed that."

I looked up to see a satisfied smile stretching his handsome lips. "Well, don't let Bonnie Brock see how pleased you are. I'm in no mood to watch the two of you trade barbs."

"Duly noted."

I studied his profile, uncertain whether he was being sarcastic. However, by the time we reached Bonnie Brock's assigned chamber, he had donned a suitably indifferent expression.

Maggie smoothed the covers over her brother while Anderley and the footman departed. At the sight of us, she straightened and moved toward the door as if to give us privacy, but I halted her.

"You should hear this, too," I told her.

She hesitated, glancing at her brother, who voiced neither assent nor an objection, before she crossed to her chair positioned near the fireplace. Gage pulled me toward the settee on the opposite side of the room from the bed, and I didn't even think of objecting.

"You gave us very little detail about the appearance of this cursed pocket watch you charged us to find," I told Bonnie Brock. "But allow me to describe it, and you tell me if I'm correct."

He nodded as I rattled off the features and engravings we were aware of on the watch mechanism and inner cover, including the inscription "Je suis le seul maître de mon temps."

"Now, we come to the matter of the outer case, where there seems to be some discrepancy. The outer case you recall was adorned with a ship being tossed about in a storm by waves and attacked by sea creatures, yes?"

"Aye," he confirmed.

I glanced at Maggie, who gave a minute nod of her head.

"Though the case my men saw on the watch makin' everyone ill was different." Bonnie Brock scowled. "'Tis why I didna immediately recognize it. No' 'til they described the siren and the inscription."

"It was engraved with the Wheel of Fortune being stabbed by a sword," I replied, lacing my fingers around one of my knees.

"Aye." He lifted his head from the pillow expectantly.

I shared a look with Gage, voicing the matter we'd discussed in the carriage after leaving the watchmaker's shop. "Did you know that those are both symbols of the Greek goddess Nemesis, the goddess of revenge?"

Bonnie Brock's eyes flared wide for a second before narrowing. I took that to mean no.

I tilted my head. "Some of the men in the infirmary, men I suspect are known to you, also told us that the pocket watch they fought over in the White Hart Inn was dirty, as if it had been buried."

"Aye. I heard the same. They said the dust had worked itself into some o' its crevices."

"Did they mention the strange channel that had been fashioned around the interior of the hinged lid? Was that one of those crevices?"

Maggie pressed a hand to her lips, and I wondered if she had an inkling of what I was hinting at.

"I dinna ken." His brow lowered in impatience. "But I'm guessin' yer gonna tell me."

I glanced once again at Gage, wondering if my supposition was too bizarre. After all, I had no proof, only inferences and guesswork. My husband nodded in encouragement, and I turned back to face Bonnie Brock.

"I suspect," I began slowly, "that channel was created so that it could be packed with something. And I suspect that dirt the men mentioned wasn't dirt or dust at all, but poison, in powder form."

Bonnie Brock surged upright, and Maggie rushed across to him.

"The poison got all over them when they scuffled over the watch, and then they spread it throughout Grassmarket and Old Town. Including to you."

I didn't know what poison it had been, or if passing it in such a way was possible. I would have to confer with Dr. Graham to find out what he thought about my suppositions. But it was the best explanation we had, and one that, in an odd way, made the most sense. Why else had that man—who I now suspected was Mr.

Douglas—asked a tableful of Bonnie Brock's men at the White Hart Inn whether one of them had lost such an expensive-looking watch? He wanted them to touch it, to dislodge the poison and pass it along to Bonnie Brock. Perhaps he'd even hoped the watch would end up in his hands. Fortunately, it had not. Otherwise we might not be having this conversation.

"So you dinna believe it was the work o' the curse?" he challenged, breathing heavily.

I shook my head. "No. At least, not entirely," I hedged. Mr. Hamilton's injured hand, the death of Mrs. Brown's husband and her brother—they couldn't all be attributed to a vengeful man. I didn't know if their misfortunes could be attributed to a curse, but there was certainly something eerily unsettling about the fact they'd all come into contact with the watch.

"Who?" he growled. "Who did this?"

Gage's hand squeezed mine and I hesitated once again. Perhaps we knew the man's correct name, perhaps we didn't. But I had no doubt that mentioning it would rain trouble down on whoever he was, whether the man who visited Mr. Hamilton's shop deserved it or not. Bonnie Brock was not the forgiving type.

He narrowed his eyes. "I ken you ken. I ken where you've been. If you dinna tell me, I'll find oot in my own way."

I sighed, not missing the way Maggie cringed where she stood beside the bed. Evidently she'd told him what she'd overheard Mr. Smythe tell us the night before. "I don't know if this is his real name or not, but he seems to go by the name of Douglas."

This caused such a swift and immediate reaction in Bonnie Brock that I straightened in alarm. His face paled, and then a moment later flushed fiery red with anger. His hands clenched into fists at his side, shaking with repressed fury.

"You know him?"

"Aye," he bit out. "Has a scar across his cheek?"

"Yes," I admitted somewhat reluctantly, given the wrath we were facing. I knew it wasn't directed at me, but all the same, his expression sent a shiver down my spine. Even Maggie backed a step away from him before checking herself.

"I'll kill him! I'll kill him dead this time."

"That's well and good," Gage drawled as he draped his arm across the back of the settee behind me, astounding me with his insouciance. "But do you mind explaining who this fellow is you mean to kill so thoroughly, and why he's so determined to slay you first that he risked poisoning half of Edinburgh?"

I braced for Bonnie Brock's rejoinder, prepared for him to blister us with his tongue at the very least. His face turned almost purple with rage, making the scar across his nose stand out starkly against his features. But then suddenly all color fled as he dropped back against his pillows. His eyes closed, and his chest rose up and down as if he'd run all the way from Grassmarket. Such was his pained expression that I began to rise to my feet, anxious to assist him, but Gage held me back.

A tense moment passed as Maggie rubbed a hand over his arm, her worried gaze riveted to his face. His breathing gradually slowed, and his complexion regained a tinge of pink.

Bonnie Brock blinked open his bloodshot eyes to look first at his sister and then us. "Angus Douglas was the oldest son o' our neighbor, an innkeeper. No' like the taverns in Grassmarket, but a respectable establishment. At least, as respectable as they run in much o' Old Town."

He paused, glancing up at his sister again. Her face was pained, clearly knowing this story well.

"Go on," Gage prodded.

"One day I made the mistake o' showin' the Jacobite's watch Lord Avonley had given me to Angus. He tried to claim it'd been lost by his father's ancestor long ago." He scoffed. "Aye, his last name was the same as the Douglas Lord Avonley told me first brought the watch to Scotland. The man who later died at Culloden wi' the watch the Jacobite had cursed gripped in his hand. But he was no relation. That man was a Douglas o'

Drumlanrig. The idea that one o' his descendants would be a lowly innkeeper is daft. No' to mention, according to the history o' the watch's previous owners Lord Avonley's uncle dug up, all o' Douglas o' Drumlanrig's children died in infancy, even his by-blows. 'Twas part o' the curse."

Bonnie Brock shook his head, staring broodingly at his feet covered with blankets. "But Angus was determined to have it. And soon enough he seized his chance." His mouth twisted. "No' long after our mam died, I decided to take the watch and pawn it." His gaze flicked toward his sister. "We needed the money, and I wanted to be rid o' the cursed thing. It'd caused us enough trouble. Unbeknownst to me, Angus had discovered my plan and visited the shop where I later took the watch." His hand curled into a fist again. "He claimed I'd stolen it, so when I arrived to pawn it, I found myself accused o' theft and thrown in jail."

I must have gasped aloud, for his bright eyes lifted to meet mine.

"After all, what was the word o' a bastard against a respectable innkeeper's son?"

"I'm guessing Mr. Douglas then arrived to claim his 'stolen' property?" Gage said.

"Aye. Though I wasna aware o' his deception at the time."

"What happened to Maggie?"

She had fixed her gaze on the headboard and did not turn to look at me despite my query.

Bonnie Brock looked up into his sister's averted face. "Angus's family *kindly* took her in. Gave her a bed in their frigid attic and scraps from their table, so long as she emptied chamber pots and scrubbed the floors."

My heart squeezed at the thought of such a young girl living in such conditions. Unloved, unwanted when not so long before she'd been doted on by a loving father, mother, and brother. It was no wonder she'd run off with Sore John after he'd professed to love her. I'd seen the way Bonnie Brock treated her. It was evident to me that behind that surly gruffness, he cared for her dearly, but I could understand why that would not be obvious to her.

"When I was released, I reclaimed my sister and learned o' Angus and his family's trickery," Bonnie Brock continued. "Though they hadna escaped the intervenin' years unscathed. No' wi' the watch in their possession. Their inn's custom had declined, the building had flooded twice, Mrs. Douglas had lost an eye, and Angus noo sported his scar." He shook his head slowly. "But that wasna enough. No' for what they'd done to me and my sister."

His eyes shifted to meet Gage's. "I'd gained something o' a reputation while in jail, and a whole host o' new friends. So I put 'em to good use. And later, when I'd amassed enough wealth and loyalty from the citizens o' Edinburgh, I *ruined* the Douglases." His eyes flared with unholy vengeance. "I'll no' tell ye the details, but 'tis enough to say none o' 'em should ever have dared showed their face in the city again."

"What of the watch?" Gage asked.

"I made certain it went wi' them." He gestured with his chin. "Let the curse work its woe on 'em."

"And you haven't seen or heard of it since?" I looked to Maggie again, and this time her gaze turned to meet mine. "At least, not until your men came to you with tales of a gold pocket watch that some of them had fought over at the White Hart Inn."

"Aye."

I arched my eyebrows, telling her now was the time for her to share what she'd told me the evening before. She began to shake her head, but I did not soften my gaze. If she didn't speak up, I would.

She exhaled a shaky breath, staring down at her brother in trepidation. "I-I have."

His head snapped around.

"Th-the case, that is." She relayed to him everything she'd told me about the original outer case with its motif of the storm-tossed ship. How it had been fashioned into a necklace and given to her by Sore John before being snatched away again. How the drawings in her mother's journal had helped her recognize it.

Bonnie Brock stared up at her mutely, his face tight with anger and confusion.

When he didn't respond, Gage chimed in for him. "So it appears that Mr. Douglas has been attempting to enact his revenge for some time. Unless you believe in coincidences?"

Bonnie Brock's pointed glare answered that.

"If he's this determined to have his vengeance that he would risk the lives of so many bystanders, I'm afraid he may not stop until he gets it," I stated solemnly.

Gage's brow furrowed, as troubled as I was by the possibility. "How else might Douglas strike at you?"

Bonnie Brock clamped his lips together, scowling back at him.

"What is his real plan? Releasing poison into a crowded tavern, even if it is populated by your men, is hardly the most direct way to get to you. Surely there are better methods of targeting you instead of spreading poison and infection throughout Edinburgh."

When Bonnie Brock still did not respond, Gage pushed to his feet and strode closer to the bed. I stood as well, trying to figure out what the scoundrel wasn't telling us. What had made his eyes blaze with such ferocity?

"What could Douglas achieve by causing chaos, particularly in the parts of the city that surround Grassmarket?" Gage's voice made it clear he expected an answer. "What does he gain?"

"*You* asked us to investigate," I reminded him. "If you want us to help you, you can't withhold information from us now."

For a moment, I thought he would continue to do just that. But then Maggie pressed a hand to his shoulder and he huffed an aggravated breath. "Greyfriars Kirkyard," he growled. "I keep a great deal of money and other goods there, hidden in one o' the vaults."

"You store your money in a tomb?" Gage asked incredulously.

"Given the fact most are wary o' the place, and that I employ all o' the grave robbers in the city, 'tis the safest place to put it. No one but me and the most trusted o' my men ken where it is." His voice hardened. "Most people wouldna dare try to steal from me, for they ken what I'd do to them if they did." He scowled. "But perhaps in all the chaos the normal protections have broken down. Maybe the guards have fallen ill or been poisoned as well."

Gage planted his hands on his hips and turned his head to look at me. Indecision furrowed his brow. I understood why he was conflicted, for I was contemplating the same things. Neither of us cared a jot about protecting Bonnie Brock's ill-gotten gains, but Douglas needed to be apprehended and soon, lest he have more mayhem in store for the city. And the only place we had any inkling he would appear was Greyfriars Kirkyard.

Coming to some sort of decision, Gage glared down at Bonnie Brock. "Are Stumps and Locke two of your trusted men?"

Bonnie Brock seemed reluctant to answer, but then he must have realized he had no other recourse. "Aye."

"Then we'll take them with us this evening when we pay a visit to this vault of yours. Let's hope the deed isn't already done," Gage added before striding from the room.

I turned to follow him, but Bonnie Brock stopped me.

"Kiera."

I glanced over my shoulder, arching an eyebrow at his impertinence in calling me by my given name when I'd not given him permission to do so.

His clenched jaw was as hard as granite. "I owe ye," he finally bit out.

I frowned. Bonnie Brock and his ridiculous tally of favors. We'd been trading them back and forth since we met, one of us constantly in debt to the other. For all its benefits to previous investigations, it had also caused me considerable trouble, and I had no wish to continue the ripostes.

"No, you don't," I replied.

He began to argue, but I held up my hand. "Gage and I help

people." My lip curled wryly. "Even, from time to time, irritating criminals. We're both doing this to prevent further calamity for the people of Edinburgh." I spread my hands. "This is what we do. That doesn't place you in our debt."

Maggie glanced back and forth between us as her brother arched his chin stubbornly.

"Mayhap, but I've my own rules. And I never leave a balance unpaid."

Or forget to collect on one either.

But I would be departing Edinburgh soon. As soon as the trial in which Gage's testimony was needed came to an end, we planned to travel to the Lake District of Cumberland on a delayed wedding trip. In many ways, this was a good thing, for it would allow Bonnie Brock some time to reclaim his dignity after being so vulnerable before us. On the other hand, I did not imagine he would be best pleased to be in my debt for so long. Who knew when I would return to Edinburgh or have reason to collect on that favor?

"Then perhaps you would allow me to transfer this favor to someone else?" I asked.

He narrowed his eyes suspiciously. "Who?"

My gaze slid to Maggie. "Your sister."

They both startled, as if stunned by my request.

"Why should my sister need a favor?" he snapped. "I dinna deny her anything she asks for."

"Really?" I challenged. "Or is it more that she never actually asks you for anything?"

He opened his mouth to respond to this and then fell silent. I glanced at Maggie, who seemed to shrink into herself.

"I think what she needs is for you to listen to her. And now is as good a time to start as any."

I had no idea whether either of them would take my advice, but when I turned back to close the door, I was heartened by the sight of Bonnie Brock gazing up at his sister with such gentle curiosity.

CHAPTER 7

OUR FEET CRUNCHED IN the dirt and detritus strewn over the cobblestones as we departed the safety of the confines of our carriage and picked our way down Candlemaker Row. Shouts and laughter rang out in the distance, mostly coming from the direction of Grassmarket, but before us the shops and buildings lining this street were largely silent. I stuck close to Gage's side, ever conscious of the potential for violence that simmered within the breasts of the inhabitants of this lowly, beaten-down part of the city. My reputation only heightened the danger, being linked to the despised body snatchers turned murderers Burke and Hare, who'd prowled these wynds and closes less than three years prior.

The air was thick with damp and soot. Mist would form before the night was through. I hoped it held off long enough for us to catch the men we were after. Greyfriars Kirkyard had enough dark corners and concealing gravestones to obstruct our efforts without the added hindrance of fog.

"They're meeting us at the gate?" I whispered, ever conscious of listening ears. Just because I didn't see anyone didn't mean they weren't there, hiding in the shadows.

"Yes. Along with Sergeant Maclean and a few of his men from the Edinburgh City Police."

I glanced sideways at Gage around the folds of my cloak's hood, unable to mask my surprise. I could see the faint outline of his lips as they curled into a sardonic smile.

"You didn't think I was going to confront a revenge-mad

murderer, and whatever associates he might have, with only Kincaid's dubious henchmen in tow, did you? Especially not with you, dear wife, on my arm."

"How…?"

"I sent Maclean a note the moment I left Kincaid's room. I'm sure he's walking some distance behind us now."

I began to glance over my shoulder, but Gage tugged on my arm to stop me.

"I thought it best if we met Stumps and Locke at the gates before he approached. It's less likely they'll run off."

"Or pull a knife," I muttered.

"Yes. That, too."

We fell silent again as we approached the narrow passage that led between the buildings to the kirk's iron gates. The darkness fell thick around us, high walls blocking the light of the nearly full moon. I wrapped my fingers around my Hewson percussion pistol tucked inside the pocket of my cloak, just as Gage shifted his arm behind his back, drawing his own weapon.

The spear-topped gates loomed before us out of the gloom. We slowed our steps, our eyes straining to pierce the blackness at the corners where metal met stone and brick. Slowly, one shape materialized out of the shadows and then another, taking the forms of Stumps and Locke.

"We were aboot to go on wi'oot ye," Locke grumbled, jerking his head toward the entrance. "Saw 'em enter aboot a quarter of an hour ago."

"How many of them were there?"

"I counted five." He looked to Stumps for confirmation, and the other man grunted.

"Weel, then. I'm glad ye didna," Sergeant Maclean said out of the darkness. His bass rumble made both men wheel about.

Both men wheeled about at the sound of Sergeant Maclean's bass rumble. Gage thrust his arm across my chest, drawing me behind him as Stumps and Locke both pulled knives.

"There's no' need for that," Maclean protested, widening his stance as two other policemen drew up beside him. A club dangled from the former pugilist's side, though it wasn't truly necessary. His muscular bulk spoke for itself, even against Stumps's large frame. "This time, we're on the same side." He nodded toward the kirkyard. "After those blackguards. Though, I suspect ye had something else in mind other than arrestin' 'em," he added dryly.

"What is this?" Locke demanded of Gage.

"Reinforcements."

"Bonnie Brock'll no' like it," Stumps griped.

Gage's retort was curt. "That's not my concern. But catching Douglas is. Whatever he's doing in there, clearly our prediction he would visit here was correct." He glared at them through the gloom, making certain they'd grasped he hadn't mentioned anything about Bonnie Brock's fortune.

"Dinna worry," Maclean assured them, striding closer to peer through the gates. "You'll get yer pound o' flesh." He glanced over his shoulder at them. "Just dinna kill 'em. Then I'll have to arrest ye."

With that, he pushed the gate open, the metal swinging quietly inward. Our motley group followed him inside, keeping close to the wall as we circled to the right of the kirk, the glass of its Gothic-arched windows appearing an oily black in the moonlight. Monuments adorned the wall's surface, and listing gravestones crowded near, forcing us to watch our steps. Maclean and Gage looked to Bonnie Brock's men to lead the way, but the sound of raised voices soon negated that necessity.

Abandoning the stealth we'd been attempting to employ, we crossed the open space, weaving between grave markers and trees toward the opposite wall. In front of a vault decorated with pillars, a trio of men clustered around a tall figure as he shook a shorter fellow by the collar. At the base of a statue nearby lay a third man, his arms bound behind his back. I suspected he was Bonnie Brock's guard.

"This is yer bloody fault! *You* did this," the tall man howled, sprinkling his accusations liberally with curses. "My bairn is crippled because of you an' yer acurst watch." Then he drew back his arm and punched the shorter fellow in the eye, knocking him to the ground. "Take it!" He hurled an object down at him. "Take it and choke on it!"

The man on the ground, who I presumed was Douglas, flung it aside as if it were on fire. "I dinna want it."

"Because it *is* cursed, isna it, ye bloody…"

The tall chap never got to finish his accusation, for Douglas swung out with his leg, tripping him. With that, seething tempers exploded. Each criminal dove into the fight until it was a melee of swinging limbs.

Maclean and his cohorts, as well as Locke and Stumps, charged forward to subdue the thieves. And, at least in Bonnie Brock's men's case, to land a few blows of their own. Gage and I approached more cautiously, waiting until the brawl had subsided and the police stood over the perpetrators before we joined them.

"Are any o' these the man yer lookin' for?" Maclean asked Gage as he glared down at each of them in turn.

"That one," he replied, pointing toward the shorter fellow. The scar running across the man's face proved my suspicion correct.

Douglas scowled and then spat at Gage, though fortunately his aim was poor. His insolence earned him a thwack to the back of his head and a stern warning from Maclean.

"Did ye wish to question him?" the sergeant barked, obviously eager to haul these blackguards back to the police house and seek his own bed.

"Briefly."

But no matter what query Gage put to him, Douglas refused to answer, even after suffering several more slaps to his head. When it became clear he was not going to cooperate, I began to lose interest, allowing my gaze to travel down the line of other criminals.

My eyes rested on the tall man who had punched Douglas. His head was bowed in bitter defeat.

I released my grip on Gage's arm, unable to deny my curiosity and the sense of foreboding creeping along my skin. Crossing to stand in front of him, I waited until his head lifted so that I could look into his eyes. The anguish written there made my breath catch.

"Your child?" I murmured. "You said she was crippled. What happened to…her? Is the child a girl?"

He nodded, visibly swallowing. "She found a watch in the gutter at the edge o' the street where she was playin'. Thought 'twas a pretty bauble, so she ran home to show her mam. 'Cept a cart came 'roond the corner too quick."

My stomach dropped and I watched as he began to tremble, his face an ugly mask of rage and grief. "Struck her and dragged her 'neath its wheels."

I pressed a hand to my mouth.

"Crushed her legs."

In the ringing silence that descended, I noticed that Gage and Maclean had stopped talking, but I ignored them, unwilling to walk away after hearing such a pronouncement without offering him some hope. "Has a surgeon seen her?"

"Aye. There's naught they can do."

I bent closer, gentling my words. "Will you give me her name and direction? Will you let me try to help her? I'm acquainted with one of the best surgeons in all of Edinburgh, perhaps all of Scotland. If anyone can do something for her, he can."

I prayed he would assent. Let the connections and knowledge forced on me by my late husband count for something other than helping me solve murders. Let it do some good for the living.

I could tell he wanted to reject my offer, so I made one last plea. "Please. Do it for her."

His throat worked up and down as if choking down his pride. He gave one curt nod before relaying her information.

I promised him someone would examine her first thing in the morning.

Gage took my hand, pulling me away from the men as Maclean ordered them to their feet. My insides had turned as cold as ice, and I shivered in the cool night air. Grateful for his solid presence beside me, I allowed him to guide me across the kirkyard.

Then something flashed in the grass next to a gravestone. My footsteps faltered and I hesitated, wondering if my eyes deceived me.

"What is it?" Gage asked in concern.

I released his hand and stepped forward to kneel beside the marker. My heart thudded sharply against my ribs as my fingers brushed something smooth. Lifting it from the ground, I opened my hand to stare down at a gold pocket watch.

"Kiera…" my husband protested, but then his words choked off as he stared over my shoulder at the object in my palm. "Is it…?"

He didn't need to finish the sentence. I held the watch up to the bright moonlight to see a wheel pierced by a sword. Seeing those symbols made my skin crawl with dread.

As much as the logical side of me wanted to tell myself it was all nonsense, my fear of the timepiece and all the inexplicable tragedy that surrounded it was stronger. I began to draw my arm back to hurl it away, but then I stopped.

Flinging it across the kirkyard might distance it from me, but sooner or later someone else was going to find it. Someone who had no idea what sort of disaster and suffering followed in its wake. If this cycle of calamity was ever to end, then the watch had to disappear or be destroyed. I hadn't with me the means to destroy it, and I certainly wasn't going to keep it in my possession any longer than I absolutely had to.

My gaze drifted over the gravestones to my left.

But I might have the perfect means to make it disappear.

Gage followed as I glided between the markers, almost as if sensing my intentions. Here was a gravestone with a dancing skeleton I noted almost absently, and there a ghoulish angel of death stared back at us from the stone. Realizing what I was doing, I shook my head, ordering myself to stop observing such details. I didn't want to recall where I was walking. I didn't want to know the positioning of the newly dug grave before me, the scent of its freshly turned soil perfuming the night air.

I slowly peeled my caramel-brown leather gloves from my hands, wrapping the pocket watch inside. Then before I could give the matter a second thought, I dropped it into the yawning hole in the earth still awaiting its new inhabitant. Lifting my skirts, I kicked loose dirt over the side to cover it and continued on my way without looking back.

Gage caught up with me several steps later, linking my arm through his. He clasped my chilled hands in his own, lending me his warmth as well as his support. I thought he might scold me for my superstitious foolishness. I thought he might object. But he never said a word.

Acknowledgments

First and foremost, my heartfelt thanks goes to my fellow authors of this anthology, my partners in crime. You leapt at this idea with boundless enthusiasm and creativity, and stuck with this project through thick and through thin, each executing brilliant stories. It's been an absolute joy and pleasure to work with all of you.

Huge helpings of gratitude also go to my agent, Kevan Lyon, who supported this concept from day one and wrangled our pitches together; Deb Werksman, our editor extraordinaire, who shaped our vision into something even better; and to the entire Sourcebooks team for their exemplary work on all facets of the book.

Much thanks also goes to God, for the will and the insight; my husband and daughters, for their unending love; my family and friends, for their tireless support; and my readers, for their zeal and excitement.

My appreciation also goes to the city of Edinburgh—one of the greatest cities in the world, in my opinion—where I have set yet another tale. Thank you for allowing my characters to wander your streets, and allowing me the liberty of inserting a cursed pocket watch into the events surrounding your minor outbreak of spotted typhus in early 1831. I'd like to think it could have happened, and perhaps many of you would agree.

About the Author

Anna Lee Huber is the Daphne du Maurier Award–winning author of the national bestselling Lady Darby Mysteries, the Verity Kent Mysteries, and the Gothic Myths series. She is a summa cum laude graduate of Lipscomb University in Nashville, Tennessee, where she majored in music and minored in psychology. She currently resides in Indiana with her family and is hard at work on her next novel. Visit her online at annaleehuber.com.

A Pocketful of Death

Christine Trent

For Anna Lee Huber, Susanna Kearsley, and C. S. Harris.
It has been a joy to collaborate with you.

CHAPTER 1

Greyfriars Kirkyard, Edinburgh: March 1870

VIOLET HARPER STOOD OVER the open grave, lamenting the day she had agreed to help Lord Ashenhurst move his dead relatives to the new family plot at Abney Park Cemetery.

"Almost there, Mrs. Harper." Harry Blundell, her business partner, grunted as he plunged the spade downward again. "Mighty hard this ground is."

That was only one of the problems Violet had with this commission. It might be March, but the earth was still far too frozen to be penetrated without great difficulty. Harry was built like an ox, but he wasn't exactly a canal dredge.

Despite the frigid temperature, Harry was sweating profusely while Violet hugged herself and pulled her cloak more closely around her. The sun shone as brightly as it could in March, but it was no help against the pervasive damp cold that had a way of penetrating clothing, skin, and bones and curling up like an unwanted visitor in the soul.

Violet was displeased with this commission she had taken at the behest of the Ashenhurst family. Lord Victor Ashenhurst was Queen Victoria's newly minted viscount, a title given in appreciation for his lordship's work last year in achieving a treaty between the United States and Britain for the suppression of the Portuguese slave trade.

Although Violet was happy for Ashenhurst's good fortune, she regretted having become encumbered with his success.

His lordship had summoned Morgan Undertaking to have numerous relatives disinterred from various cemeteries in order to have a funereal reunion at the new Ashenhurst plot at Abney Park Cemetery in London.

Violet dropped her measuring tape into the hole Harry was digging. He had finally reached down two feet. "You should be at more pliable earth now, Harry," she said.

As if on cue, he brought the shovel down with brute force, and this time it sunk past the top of the blade instead of piercing through a couple of icy inches.

"Hah!" Harry barked in relief, finding renewed energy now that he was dealing with loose dirt.

Violet stood back once more, stamping her feet to get feeling back in them. This commission was irritating her in many ways, not least of which were the miserable conditions. Lord Ashenhurst was imperious about reuniting a family that had been separated for centuries and could not possibly wait until the April thaw.

More importantly, it seemed distinctly sacrilegious to unearth coffins for no other reason than consolidation. Despite the current fad for disinterment out of ancient, crumbling burial grounds into the new and popular garden cemeteries, Violet remained unconvinced of its propriety. To have the deceased jostled and bounced about when they had been lying in repose for decades upon decades...it was unseemly and intrusive.

The protests from the kirkyard's day watchman further emphasized her own discomfort.

Violet sighed and rubbed her gloved hands against her arms. There was nothing to do about it now; she had agreed to the work. At least the Ashenhurst plot, which covered an astounding quarter acre, had already been adorned with a stunning monument resembling the Parthenon. It wasn't quite life-size, but it was one of the largest and most impressive monuments Violet had ever installed for a customer.

Lord Ashenhurst was clearly determined to make the world aware of his growing fortune and fame.

A thud and scrape broke Violet out of her reverie, and she moved back to the edge of the grave to peer down once more. Harry laughed spontaneously at having reached the coffin, and he began applying the shovel more gingerly to the dirt as he worked to loosen it.

Soon though, Violet stopped him. "Look!" she exclaimed, pointing at the unearthed ground near one side of the coffin.

Harry looked around, puzzled. "I don't understand," he said.

"There," she said, pointing again. It appeared to be a bit of clothing.

Harry finally saw what Violet had noticed and bent down to brush dirt away from it, lifting it up into the sunlight for a closer look.

"Here you go, Mrs. Harper," he said, handing the dirt-encrusted, tattered piece up to Violet. She bent down to take it and realized that it was a pair of small leather gloves folded inside each other. They had probably been dropped by whomever had originally dug the grave, she imagined, except that—

Violet hefted the gloves. There was weight to them. She gently brushed away the black earth and slowly pulled the gloves apart. A round, shiny object fell out, and she managed to catch it before it hit the ground.

As Harry continued to unearth Mr. Ian Gilchrist, a distant cousin of Lord Ashenhurst, Violet examined the strange object.

It was a pocket watchcase. Made of pure gold, she thought, since age and burial had not caused any tarnishing. Despite the freezing cold, Violet removed a glove and ran a bare finger over the case. It was decorated with what appeared to be a wheel with multiple spokes extending from the center to the outer rim. Curiously, there was also a sword through the center of the wheel.

This was certainly not a watch that belonged to a humble grave digger. Perhaps it had been thrown in by a mourning family member. The gloves were small, so they probably belonged to a lady.

Violet's imagination vividly conjured up a sorrowful wife throwing herself against the coffin and pledging to join her husband in the grave. Maybe the watch had been a gift from Ian Gilchrist to his wife and she was leaving it as a beloved memento.

How very heartbreaking to think how it might have ended up in the grave.

Violet decided to open this outer case in order to more carefully scrutinize it. Watch inscriptions were frequently located on the inner cover, so maybe that would reveal the owner with more certainty.

She was stunned to find that the inner case was far more highly decorated than the outer case. If she wasn't mistaken, the gold was of higher quality here, as well. The inscription around the edge of the inner watchcase quickly caught her attention.

She squinted at the writing. "'Je suis le seul maître de mon temps,'" she read aloud, grasping for her rudimentary French. "'I am the only master of my time.'"

"What's that?" Harry said, stopping his work and using the opportunity to wipe his sweat-beaded brow with a handkerchief.

"Oh, nothing," Violet said, dismissing his query as she dropped the watch into her own reticule. Surely Lord Ashenhurst would be pleased to have both Mr. Gilchrist and this bit of memorabilia back in the family.

Violet and Harry accompanied Ian Gilchrist's coffin on the eight-hour train ride from Edinburgh back to London's Euston Station. There a hired wagon finished the journey to Abney Park. Once they passed through the Egyptian Revival front gates—a decorative affectation of most of London's Magnificent Seven cemeteries—she parted ways with her partner.

Leaving Harry to see to Mr. Gilchrist's reinterment, Violet made her way to the west side of Arlington Street in St. James's.

This area of stately, gleaming-white town houses, with drapery-laden windows and freshly scrubbed stoops, was also home to the Ashenhurst family. Lord Ashenhurst had moved his family here not six months ago and immediately embarked on his self-aggrandizement program.

The last time Violet had mounted the steps to Number 19, his lordship had been planning a design for his coat of arms.

She twisted the bell knob to the front door, in complete disregard of Lady Ashenhurst's request that Violet use the rear trade entrance. In Violet's opinion, an undertaker joined a family, even if for a brief period of time, and family was not relegated to using the back door.

To her surprise, Mrs. Chase, the Ashenhurst housekeeper, opened the door, rather than the maid, Maisie, who usually did so. The Ashenhursts appeared to be managing with a spartan staff, with no butler, footmen, or other male servants yet on hire for their new London home.

Mrs. Chase's smoothly welcoming countenance immediately twisted into evident annoyance at the sight of Violet. She greeted the undertaker, her look one of disapproval over the wire-rimmed glasses that seemed destined to perch precariously at the end of the woman's nose. She ushered Violet into the front parlor to wait among the heavy walnut pieces upholstered in scarlet velvet.

The walls of the parlor were fashionably done with nearly every square inch covered in framed oil landscapes, charcoal drawings of European landmarks, and sepia-toned tintypes. All this on top of swirled wallpaper in a green so dark it was nearly black. One section of the wall above the fireplace mantel contained carved shelves, each bearing an objet d'art. The mantel itself held an imposing framed portrait of Queen Victoria, flanked by dual-branched candelabra. A fitting touch, given that the queen was the source of Lord Ashenhurst's happy change of circumstances.

All in all, the room was typical of many upper-class ones that Violet had visited over the years.

And, as with almost every upper-class home visit, Violet was required to wait an interminable amount of time as punishment for her audacity in entering a hallowed home through the front door.

By the time Violet had examined every framed item on the wall, including several postmortem tintypes of young children, she finally heard the telltale tapping of heels on wood that announced Lady Ashenhurst's arrival.

"Mrs. Harper," the viscountess said from the doorway. She stood there uncertainly in her well-made crimson wool gown trimmed in fur. Violet was about to invite the woman into her own parlor when the viscountess finally edged her way in, looking all the world like someone who was afraid of her own home.

Curious.

Nevertheless, the new viscountess attempted some regality. "Have you completed Mr. Gilchrist's move?" she asked, drawing up her tiny frame. Lady Ashenhurst was like an oil painting that had been left hanging far too long on a wall that faced a window—once beautiful and arresting, but now rather pale and faded. Her blond hair, streaked with the red of youth, was fashionably arranged around her face, but it only served to emphasize blue eyes so drab that the woman seemed to have a blank stare.

"He is being reinterred into the Ashenhurst plot as we speak, madam, but I—" Violet started to withdraw the watch from her reticule, but Lady Ashenhurst stopped her.

"You aren't here to collect payment, I presume? My husband—"

"No, my lady," Violet replied. Heaven knew she would spend weeks, if not months, attempting to collect from his lordship. Society was notorious for not paying bills, and the family undertaker was usually at the bottom of that delayed list. "I came to give you this." Violet withdrew the pocket watch and held it out.

Lady Ashenhurst frowned. "What is it?"

"An old watch. It was wrapped inside a pair of lady's gloves and was in Mr. Gilchrist's grave. I suspect his wife or sweetheart threw it into the grave in her grief."

"A lady permitted to be at graveside?" the viscountess said, aghast.

Violet nodded. "Unusual, yes, my lady, but a woman in deep grief can be very determined. I have found that—"

She was once more interrupted by the arrival of Lord Victor Ashenhurst, the new viscount himself. He addressed his wife first. "Vernon said you were down here." Then he noticed Violet in the room. "Mrs. Harper," he said, inclining his dark, oiled hair and beard at her. He was as vibrant and energetic as his wife was bland and mousy. He radiated nervous vitality, and Violet wondered if he was still anxious about his coat of arms.

"My lord," she said. "I was just showing Lady Ashenhurst what I found in Mr. Gilchrist's grave." Violet proffered the watch again and explained how she had found it. "The gloves it was wrapped in were tattered, so I took the liberty of discarding them."

The viscount casually examined the watch and shrugged. "A pretty little trinket," he said, handing it off to his wife. "I don't recognize it as a family piece."

"I see," Violet said. "If I may be intrusive, my lord, did Mr. Gilchrist have a well-to-do background?"

Ashenhurst's focus instantly became razor-sharp upon Violet. "Why would you ask such an impertinent question?"

"The watch, sir. The inner case is made of exquisite-quality gold and has an intriguing inscription on it. It seems a valuable item for a grieving widow to have thrown into the grave."

"Hmm." He took the watch back from Lady Ashenhurst to scrutinize it more closely, removing the outer case as Violet had done. "'I am the only master of my time.' What does that mean?"

Now it was Violet's turn to shrug. "I am at a loss to answer that. Perhaps it was just a clever saying and has no meaning at all. But I think the watch might benefit from a cleaning and prove to be a fitting heirloom."

As expected, the man preened at her words. "Quite so," he agreed. "Our fervent thanks, Mrs. Harper, for returning it to us. I will see to restoring it to its proper glory."

A strange look passed between Lord and Lady Ashenhurst, but Violet gave it but a moment's thought. No doubt Victor Ashenhurst needed his wife's help in causing the watch to become part of *his* glory. Maybe he would work the inscription into his personal motto.

The thoughts and deeds of society members were beyond Violet's concern. Until they died, of course.

Back at Morgan Undertaking, Violet found her American-born husband, Sam, at work developing slides in his makeshift studio. He had found an interest in photography over the past few months, after seeing many of Matthew Brady's still pictures of the recent war in the United States, a conflict in which Samuel Harper had been wounded.

Having learned the rudimentaries of photography—using Violet, Harry, and random objects for experimentation—Sam had carved out a corner of the shop as his studio. Now he accompanied Violet and Harry to clients seeking postmortem photography of their loved ones, as well as assisting with other undertaking tasks.

Sam was a natural at the work, having a perfectionist's passion for it. His background as both a lawyer and a diplomat serving the Union's interests during his home country's conflict made him well suited to handling delicate negotiations with grieving—and sometimes angry—relatives.

"Tarnation!" Sam exploded at precisely the moment the door's bells jangled upon Violet's entry.

"Sam," Violet said quietly, removing her tall, black hat with its long crape tails and setting it on its oak stand. Her shop rule was to maintain an air of somber competence at all times.

Her husband stepped out from behind the screen that shielded the rest of the shop from his work. He was wiping his hands on a rag. His fingers remained perpetually stained from the silver nitrate he used to develop his albumen prints. These prints were a new improvement upon the popular tintypes that had been in use for over a decade, as the albumen prints were the first to develop photographs onto paper rather than metal. Sam's entrepreneurial mind loved learning about the newest processes in the field.

The sweet, cloying odor of ether wafted over Violet. Sam used collodion, a syrupy solution of ether and alcohol, to coat his negatives. The smell was, unfortunately, exceedingly repellent. They really needed to consider constructing walls to contain Sam's work, Violet thought. How he didn't fall into faints from the sharp and overpowering chemicals used to process his egg-dipped cotton prints, she would never know.

"My apologies, wife. I thought I was alone," he added in excuse. "My bottle of collodion had entirely too much alcohol in it. Ruined my negative. All of that exposure work for nothing." He shook his head in disgust.

Violet readily empathized with her husband over the difficulty in finding scrupulous suppliers. The funeral business was also rife with shifty purveyors of funerary goods. Just last week, she had sent a salesman packing when he had tried to pass off cheap imitation glass as genuine Whitby-factory jet.

"It's an unfortunate consequence of this business, I suppose," she said. "Harry hasn't returned yet from Abney Park?" she asked.

Sam shook his head. "Nary a soul all day. I do believe I'm hungry," he said, tossing the rag back behind the screen. "Do you think Mrs. Wren might produce something cheerful for supper tonight?"

Mrs. Wren was their day cook, whose lips rarely broke into a smile. However, she could bake, sauté, and roast with the best Parisian chefs, so Violet and Sam had learned long ago to ignore the woman's sour disposition.

An hour later, sated on pork chops with fried apples at the dining table in their lodgings over the shop, Violet told Sam about her strange find in the grave.

"The watch was genuine gold?" he asked, frowning. "Doesn't seem like something even a distraught widow would intentionally throw down to be sealed away forever in dirt. You'd think she would have put it in the coffin with her husband. In his hand."

Sam had a valid point.

By the next morning, though, Violet had forgotten about the watch, since news of a gruesome murder always occupies one's entire mind.

CHAPTER 2

After a good night of sleep, Violet was back in the shop and preparing to leave to meet with a monument maker when the *Times* was delivered. Ordinarily she would simply take it home with her at the end of the day, but the very large headline caught her attention.

Murder In Jermyn Street!

That was a few blocks from the Ashenhurst home. How unusual for a murder to be committed in such a genteel part of the city. Violet peeled off her gloves and picked up the paper to read the accompanying article.

> *At around ten o'clock last night, LORD MANSFIELD was brutally MURDERED in the street near his home by several blows to the head. He had been recognized by Her Majesty in 1859 for his architectural assistance to Messrs. Barry and Pugin in the neo-Gothic design of our new Houses of Parliament. Lord Mansfield was found, BLEEDING and barely conscious, by a passing night watchman and was taken across the river to St. Thomas's Hospital. He died of his wounds later without having revealed the name of his attacker; if, in fact, he had even seen the miscreant. If the DERELICT and DERANGED have intruded upon the neighborhood of St. James's, what hope is there for the rest of the city? Scotland Yard has taken up the investigation, with Detective Chief Inspector Magnus Pompey Hurst leading the inquiry.*

Violet knew Inspector Hurst, having worked with him on multiple cases—much to the man's great chagrin and discontent. Despite Hurst's general competence, his blustering manner caused him to overlook simple details and dismiss the helpful suggestions of others. Violet was an especial target for dismissal and disregard, despite having led the detective to more than one criminal culprit.

She folded the newspaper, hiding the disturbing headline from her own view. This murder had likely shaken the Ashenhurst family to its core. The deceased might not be a body in Violet's care, but the viscount and his household were until the last relative had been transferred to Abney Park.

Perhaps Violet had nothing to offer regarding the situation, but her instincts told her that a prompt visit to the Ashenhurst home might be in order.

Maisie opened the door to Violet, but the housekeeper was towering right behind the girl, almost as if she had sensed Violet's presence by the way Violet had twisted the knob.

Mrs. Chase's glance of reproof was emphasized with "A second day in a row, Mrs. Harper?" before she motioned for Maisie to permit the undertaker in through the front door. Violet heard a cross between a harrumph and a wheeze emitting from the aging housekeeper as she followed the woman back into the parlor. Maisie bobbed her head and scurried away.

The pocket watch had replaced a trinket on one of the wall shelves next to the fireplace. In a mere day's time, it had been thoroughly cleaned, repaired, and polished. It was quite remarkable how quickly tasks could be performed when requested by an address in St. James's rather than, say, Whitechapel. Violet leaned her ear up to the shelf, but could not hear any ticking.

"Mrs. Harper?" came a voice from behind her, causing Violet to whirl around in surprise, feeling a twinge of guilt at her disparaging thoughts.

"I am Miss Whitton. You are the undertaker for my sister and brother-in-law?" In the doorway this time stood a woman who wasn't Lady Ashenhurst, but a younger, more brightly tinted replica of the viscountess. Her features resembled that of her sister, but her blue eyes nearly watered with intensity, and her hair dropped in flaming ringlets around her head.

Violet nodded. "Of a sort. I am moving the family relations from various ceme—"

Miss Whitton shook her head violently. "All of this national conceit to move bodies about is evil and will result in tragedy! The evil has entered this household and must be purged." She raised a hand toward the ceiling, as though summoning the Almighty. "Since the day you started your ungodly practice of unburying the dead, I have seen horrifying specters who do terrible deeds."

Violet instinctively took a step backward, bumping her shoulder against the fireplace mantel. Ignoring the sharp twinge of pain, she held her hands palms up in supplication toward Lady Ashenhurst's sister. "I'm sorry, Miss Whitton, but I don't understand. What have you—"

"In the streets! There are spirits in the streets! They flit about, this way and that, in their unearthly light." Miss Whitton put her hands to either side of her head and rocked back and forth.

The poor woman was obviously not right in her mind.

"Josephine!" Lady Ashenhurst appeared in the doorway. "What sort of nonsense are you spewing? Come now." She took her sister's elbow while calling out for Mrs. Chase. But Josephine wasn't finished with Violet. Even as the housekeeper was attempting to pull her out of the room, she yanked out of Mrs. Chase's grasp for one last volley at Violet. "The spirits will never leave until you have ceased your gruesome activities. You are the one to blame!"

"There, there, miss," Mrs. Chase said, comforting the woman as she led her out of the parlor. "A nice teaspoon of your tonic and you'll be right as rain, now won't you?" The housekeeper continued her soothing assurances as she led the other woman up the stairs.

Lady Ashenhurst put a palm to her head as if to press away a headache. Dropping her hand, she waved to a chair. "Please, Mrs. Harper, have a seat. You must excuse my sister. She is prone to... rantings. Her husband left her after two years of marriage and we moved her in here, but I'm not sure Victor will tolerate too much more of her and then what will I do? Commit my own sister to Bedlam? To a workhouse?" The viscountess took a deep breath, as if suddenly remembering who she was and Violet's lower status before her. She sat down opposite Violet, her back straight and her chin up. "What may I do for you today, Mrs. Harper?"

"I must confess, my lady, that I had hoped to help you somehow, although now I feel a bit foolish. I read about the murder that took place..."

"Oh, that," Lady Ashenhurst said with a quick toss of her head. "My husband says that Sir Holland Mansfield had made many enemies and so it was undoubtedly some sort of revenge crime. Victor says we are in no danger, since it obviously wasn't the work of a random madman. Whoever it was will be apprehended in short order and will hang for his crime. Victor is certain."

"I see." Violet thought that Victor Ashenhurst's confidence might be misplaced. Murderers rarely acted rationally, and slaughtering a man in the street was as far from a rational act as Violet could imagine. "Forgive my intrusion, my lady. I just wanted to be certain all was well here after the traumatic events of last night, but clearly my visit was unnecessary."

Lady Ashenhurst rose and Violet followed suit. "Thank you for your concern, Mrs. Harper. I do not believe I need to impress upon you that the status of our family is quite important, and that my husband would be most...displeased...to learn that we were being gossiped about."

Violet nodded at the woman's veiled petition. "I understand you perfectly well, my lady. A good undertaker is as silent as a crypt, and remembers nothing about a family other than its tender grieving."

Lady Ashenhurst clasped her hands together. "Well then, we shall have no further troubles, shall we?"

Violet had left the Ashenhurst home and was halfway to the omnibus stop when she paused in the middle of the busy sidewalk. A nanny almost collided into her with a perambulator. "Pardon me," Violet said absentmindedly as the nanny and squalling infant made their way around her. Violet was too lost in thought to pay much attention to them.

What an odd thing Lady Ashenhurst had said after cautioning Violet about her sister: "We shall have no further troubles." How was Violet part of any trouble in the household? For that matter, what trouble was there to begin with?

Two days later, Violet and Harry moved a Liza Millis, some distant cousin of Lady Ashenhurst's, from St. Mary's churchyard to Abney Park, a brief journey of less than a mile. Even Harry, bless his soul, was starting to complain about the absurdity of the Ashenhurst commission. "Why are we using a hearse to move a body such a short distance when I could practically carry the coffin on my back?" he demanded, testy in a way that Violet had never witnessed.

She couldn't blame him. Here they were removing a coffin that had only been in the ground for five years inside the churchyard, which was less than two decades old itself. The parish priest, Reverend Le Guyt, stood over them as they worked, clucking over the removal of one of only a handful of bodies buried there.

"I do not approve of this, madam," he said sternly, frowning behind wire-rimmed glasses as he stroked his chin beard. He watched as Harry thrust his spade against the frozen ground over and over. "Those at rest here are not piled atop one another as they are in other churchyards. You are disturbing their eternal peace. It is ungodly what you are doing."

This was becoming a common refrain, and at this point Violet was no happier about it than either Harry or the priest were. How many more of these removals could she endure?

That afternoon, after locking up the shop and saying farewell to a grumpy Harry Blundell, Violet and Sam stepped outside of Morgan Undertaking. They had intentions of leisurely browsing at a nearby bookstore before returning to their lodgings above the shop for some of Mrs. Wren's mouthwatering rabbit pie.

A newspaper boy was in the street, eagerly brandishing the day's edition of the *Times*. "Another murder in St. James's! A man's brains bashed! Read it here, just a ha'penny!"

With an unspoken question of concern passing between them, Sam quickly purchased a copy from the boy. With his eagle-headed cane tucked beneath one arm and oblivious of the foot traffic rushing around them, Sam quickly scanned the headline. Violet practically wore holes of anxiety into her gloves as she rubbed them together.

"Sweetheart," Sam said, extending the article out to her. "Isn't this where your viscount lives?"

Violet took the proffered article. The article detailed a vicious beating in Arlington Street that had resulted in death, this time of a Mr. Ralph Fitzworth, known for his great number of charitable works since making a fortune in building and selling cotton machinery. Although he had not been granted a title, the queen had invited him to Buckingham Palace to thank him personally for his contributions to the poor.

A small knot of alarm formed in Violet's stomach, eliminating her desire for Mrs. Wren's gravy-laden rabbit dish. She wondered what Lord and Lady Ashenhurst thought now about the terrible exploits occurring in their stately neighborhood. "Sam, I think we should—"

"Yes," he said, taking her arm in one of his and hailing a cab with his cane. "It's time for you to visit the family again."

The scene that greeted them was vastly different than Violet had experienced just two days ago. The entire neighborhood seemed to have taken up residence outside in the street, blocking carriage traffic so that Violet and Sam had to exit their cab a couple of blocks away from the Ashenhurst home.

The mood in the crowds was fearful, with mothers huddled together, clutching their children to their skirts against the cold. Further beyond that group were normally placid society gentlemen, bellowing at two men in dark-brown overcoats.

"Isn't that...?" Sam's voice trailed off as he pointed at one of the two, a great bear of a man who looked as though he might take a swipe at the portly gentleman who was red-faced from shouting.

"Yes, it is." Violet had never felt so sorry for Detective Chief Inspector Hurst before this moment.

Sam nodded in grim determination. "Believe I will give him a hand."

Sam and the detective had a cordial relationship. Violet now saw that Second Class Inspector Langley Pratt, Hurst's junior colleague, was also there, furiously scribbling notes in his worn leather journal.

Violet considered joining Sam, but she was distracted by a man who was staring openly at the windows of the Ashenhurst home. He was well dressed in a spotless suit and kid gloves. His closely trimmed beard, tinged with gray, was equally well groomed. The only indication that he was not placid beneath his exterior was his quick expulsion of breaths, making tiny puffs of vapor in the freezing air, as though he were a steam engine chugging along in place. After watching him gaze at the viscount's home for several moments, she approached.

"Pardon me, sir, I am Violet Harper, an undertaker doing some work for the Ashenhurst family, and I couldn't help noticing your great interest in their home."

The man slowly turned his attention to her. "I'm sorry, did you say you are an undertaker?"

Violet braced herself for the disbelief and incredulity to come, but the man was actually disinterested in the fact that she was a woman performing funereal work. "Has someone else died, in addition to Lord Mansfield? Someone in the Ashenhurst household?" he asked. Violet noted a hopeful tone in his voice.

"No, no, nothing of the sort. I am merely helping the family with some previous burial matters, Mr...?"

"*Lord* Claybrook, madam," he said, pulling himself up to full aristocratic height.

"Of course, my apologies," Violet murmured, hoping she struck the correct note between deference and acknowledgment. So much of society was sensitive about others knowing they were important community members just by a glance at the cut of their clothes, but the world seemed to be changing quickly. Many men were making fortunes in railroads, banking, and other ventures, and they frequently dressed just as well as their aristocratic betters.

"So you say no one has died there?" he repeated, and now the wistfulness was unmistakable.

"I'm afraid not. Have you an interest in the family, my lord?" Violet asked.

Claybrook huffed. "Hardly. I just wish this blight could be removed from the street."

Violet glanced back at the Ashenhurst home. It gleamed just as white as the homes to either side of it, and in fact as far down either side of the road as the eye could see. It was as if the coal smuts that choked the air throughout most of London and mercilessly blackened roofs, windows, and walkways, did not dare make an appearance in this exclusive neighborhood.

"I don't understand," she said. "Does the viscount's home offend you somehow?"

"Hardly. I admit it has never looked better with its fresh coat of black paint on the fence and the new marble inlay on the stoop. No, it is the viscount himself that I find objectionable."

Had the baron been victim to Ashenhurst's obsessive quest for prestige? Such a thing would be most repugnant to members of society. And yet, the baron's distaste seemed to go further than that.

Violet tried one more time, her curiosity overwhelming her. "Has his lordship…committed a crime of some sort against you, sir?"

"Now you are much closer to the truth of it, madam. The man is an upstart with no real money to speak of. And a viscountcy because of some minor diplomatic work? Unthinkable. He must be blackmailing the queen, or maybe he kidnapped one of her infernal yapping dogs." He shook his head in bewilderment. "How is it that in six months he has accomplished more than my family has in…" Claybrook's expression took on a faraway look as he turned his attention once more to the Ashenhurst home windows.

Violet waited, wondering if he would say more. Her patience was rewarded a few moments later when he turned back to her. "Do you know, Mrs. Harper, that my family obtained its baronetcy under the Conqueror?"

"Most impressive, my lord. Your family has enjoyed centuries of recognition, then." Now she thought she had an inkling of the baron's immense irritation.

"And yet a man like Ashenhurst leaps along like a rabbit to his burrow, collecting accolades along the way to bury in his underground chambers. While my family is like Aesop's tortoise, shuffling along at an interminable pace."

As far as Violet knew, a man achieved rank for service to country or to sovereign. If Lord Claybrook had risen no higher than baron, there was only one logical conclusion for why his family had been denied advancement. "I understand that he helped with a diplomatic end to slavery in Portugal—" Violet began, but Claybrook rudely waved her off.

"And of what possible benefit was that to Her Majesty, madam? Are we conquering that insignificant little country now? Yes, I see you are at a loss for words, as I have been for the past year. It is unconscionable, I tell you, and I'm quite certain that Ashenhurst's rapid rise is due to other circumstances than his *diplomatic service*." Claybrook practically spat the veiled insinuation at her.

How contemptible that in the middle of a pair of murders in St. James's, the baron was still more concerned with another man besting him in the corridors of Buckingham Palace.

Sam waved Violet over to where he stood with Inspectors Hurst and Pratt, so Violet took her leave of the baron and joined her husband. The assembled crowd seemed to have exhausted its anger on the detectives and was breaking up in groups of twos and threes to gossip and worry over the great malevolence that hung over the streets like a thundercloud, ready to deluge them with rain and lightning at any moment.

"Mrs. Harper," the massive, barrel-chested Hurst said, tipping his hat to her. Pratt followed suit, his graphite-covered fingers leaving a smudge on his hat brim.

"A pleasure to see you here, I'm sure," Hurst said, his tone only slightly less sarcastic than Claybrook's had been. Violet had been an unwanted assistant to the inspector on several occasions, although he had softened some toward her, especially now that he had developed an interest in Violet's recently widowed friend Mary Cooke.

"I have read, sir, that you are investigating the murder that occurred two nights ago, so I imagine your hands are full now," Violet said.

"Yes," Pratt said as though the question were directed at him. "A very peculiar case, one that—"

"Nothing I cannot handle, Mrs. Harper," Hurst declared, sending Pratt a withering look. "Certainly nothing that I haven't handled before," he added for emphasis, effectively subduing the other detective.

But Violet knew that he would soon remember that she was Mary's closest friend, and that fact would override his resistance to what he deemed Violet's intrusion on his cases.

"The inspector has discovered something interesting, sweetheart," Sam said.

Hurst reluctantly responded to Sam's urging. "Yes, well, the two dead men both belonged to Arthur's."

"Arthur's," Violet repeated flatly, unfamiliar with what this was.

"Yes, a *gentlemen's* club, if you don't mind me saying, madam, so you won't be able to follow me there when I go to do interviews."

"Why, Inspector," Violet said, feigning indignation, "I wouldn't dream of interfering in your work."

"Hmm," was all the detective said.

Sam shifted his cane—earned from injuries during the recent American war—to his other hand, a sign of impatience. "I told Hurst that you were performing some undertaking work for the Ashenhurst household," he said, clearly wishing to elicit more from Hurst. "You will be surprised to hear that he has encountered the Ashenhurst family before."

Violet's ears immediately perked up at this. "Is that so, Inspector?"

Hurst muttered something unintelligibly beneath his breath before responding. "Yes. All of these society types have eccentric little eggs hatching all over the place, don't they? Some neighbors complained about one of the occupants—the cousin or sister of Lady Ashenhurst—who stands on the stoop and accuses people on the street of wild crimes. Like stealing all of her unmentionables from her bedchamber. Or poaching her dinner out from under nose while she's in the midst of eating. I interviewed the woman myself, and she's clearly—" Hurst tapped a finger to the side of his head in a knowing manner.

Violet was disappointed, since this certainly wasn't news to her. "I believe you are referring to Josephine Whitton, Lady Ashenhurst's sister."

"Then you've met her, too. Poor woman is terribly young

to be so dotty. But it seems to be common in these families. I'm surprised they don't keep her hidden in the attic."

"Surely you aren't suggesting that Miss Whitton has done anything criminal, are you?" Violet asked. Josephine Whitton was clearly troubled, but just as clearly did not deserve to be locked away.

"No, not her. But I do think it's possible that some other batty relative living in St. James's could be behind these two murders. I imagine I'll know more when I go to the club and have some chats. Doesn't seem to be anything linking the two men other than the club, so my assumption for now is that one of these relations got worked up about an imaginary crime and decided to do something about it. No doubt more than one of them sees evil in everything and feels personally responsible for stopping it. Like the temperance people." Hurst nodded, confident in his working theory.

Violet thought back to Josephine Whitton's wild accusations. Was it possible that Hurst was right? Miss Whitton herself seemed harmless enough, but perhaps there was someone else in the neighborhood who was deranged, and there was no other purpose behind the two murders than randomness on the part of the murderer and the worst of luck on the part of the victims.

Hurst was implying—as he always did—that this was none of Violet's business, and she knew that it really wasn't, but obtaining justice for the dead had undeniably become a passion of hers over the past year. Particularly when the dead were so maltreated. Coshing a man in the street and abandoning him certainly qualified as cruel treatment to Violet.

"Well, if you have no other probing questions, Mrs. Harper, Mr. Pratt and I will be leaving now." Hurst turned to leave, then turned back with a sly smile.

"Ever been to a gentlemen's club, Harper?" he asked of Sam. "You should come along."

Sam mouthed something to Violet that she couldn't under stand, but his wink told her he intended to humor Hurst. The two detectives and Sam started to move off, but then Mr. Pratt lagged behind hesitantly.

"Will you not be attending Mr. Hurst during the questioning, sir?" Violet asked of the shy, lanky detective.

"No, madam. I mean, yes, I will, but I wanted to say...to tell you..." Pratt reddened, clearly embarrassed by whatever it was.

"Pray tell, Mr. Pratt, what is troubling you?" The young man was always quiet and retiring, but she had never seen him quite so reserved.

He glanced at where Hurst and Sam were moving up the street. Seemingly satisfied that they were out of earshot, he said, "It's your friend Mrs. Cooke."

"What about her?" Violet had not seen Mary in a few weeks.

"Yes, well, ahem. The inspector has been putting himself in her path lately. At the butcher's, running into her 'accidentally' in front of the draper's shop, that sort of thing. I am always with him, so we are on official Scotland Yard business when it happens, you understand."

"Of course." Violet had a very good idea where Pratt was leading her, and she supposed she shouldn't be surprised. Violet had been trying to guard Mary in her official year of mourning since the death of her husband, George, despite his being a no-good louse. Her protections had included keeping the attentions of Mr. Hurst at bay.

In time, though, she had begun to realize that Mary, twenty years Violet's senior, was very flattered by the detective's attentions and, in fact, welcomed them. Violet was baffled by what Hurst's attractions could possibly be to her friend, but knew it was wrong to play the part of wicketkeeper to Hurst's batsman in a futile attempt to ruin his play on Mary. Especially when the two of them so obviously enjoyed each other's company.

The other benefit of their burgeoning relationship was that it had caused Hurst to be a little gentler with Violet. Today, though, his steps at reconciliation with the undertaker had disappeared.

Yes, Violet had a very good notion what Pratt was about to say.

"The inspector believed his affections were well received, so he planned to, er, to—" Pratt's ears had turned bright red.

"And so he decided to test her affections in some grand manner?" Violet suggested.

"Yes, madam. He invited her to go ice-skating last month, and proposed marriage to her when they went for tea afterward." Pratt said this dolefully, as if announcing a death. "Mrs. Cooke refused him, said you had impressed upon her the importance of waiting at least a full year of mourning before any other, er, considerations could be made."

So Mary hadn't rejected Hurst outright, just asked him to wait a while longer. What was the problem?

"I don't understand. Mary simply wanted him to keep his peace another"—Violet made a mental calculation—"three months before she would consider remarriage. Perfectly reasonable."

Pratt cleared his throat. "You would think so. The inspector has had his share of rejection to marriage proposals—"

No surprise there.

"—but this one he blames on you, for controlling Mrs. Cooke like a…a…" Pratt's words drifted off.

"Like a what?" Violet prodded.

"'Like a spinsterish old governess clinging to her charge for fear of being tossed out of the family and ending up in the workhouse.'" Pratt rattled off his words in an embarrassed rush. "His words, madam, not mine."

At that, Violet forgot all about the Ashenhursts and their bizarre reburial commission, the two murdered men, and even about the strange Baron Claybrook and the even odder Josephine Whitton. She burst into uncontrolled giggles, loud enough to attract the interest of several neighborhood onlookers who were still gathered in the street. Violet knew she was being wildly indecorous, an undertaker laughing hysterically at the scene of a man's death, but oh, the idea that she had Mary metaphorically chained inside a musty old classroom with no escape route was too amusing for words.

"Therefore I am at the top of Scotland Yard's list of most dangerous criminal suspects?" Violet swiped at a moist eye with her gloved finger.

"Quite nearly. You are taking this news better than I had expected." Pratt's ears were flesh-colored once more, and his expression was that of relief.

"This problem hardly rises to the level of murder," Violet said, still controlling her laughter. "But it is 'certainly nothing that I haven't handled before,' in the words of the illustrious Magnus Pompey Hurst. Do not worry, Mr. Pratt. I shall make all well again with the inspector."

Pratt shook his head. "He's quite angry, like I've never seen. It will take more than a soft word to soothe that savage breast."

"Pardon me," came a male voice from behind Violet. "Did you say you've found the brute who committed these crimes?"

Violet turned to include the stranger in the conversation. He wore expensive clothes, but they hung on his haggard frame. He was either ill or carried the worries of the world on his shoulders. Based upon the pouches under his eyes, Violet surmised that the man had deep troubles. What she couldn't guess, though, was how old he was. Thirty? Forty? Even older? It was remarkable how distress and torment could age a man.

His wan appearance was further emphasized by the multiple scarves he wore, swaddling his neck.

"Actually, sir," Pratt said. "I was speaking in metaphors. I don't believe I have interviewed you yet. Do you live in this street?"

The man put out a hand to both Violet and Pratt, introducing himself as Edgar Dye. "Yes, I live there." He pointed to the town house directly to the right of the Ashenhursts'.

Pratt withdrew his journal from his coat and flipped to a page with no writing on it. "If I may ask you a few questions, sir..."

Dye nodded. "Of course. The sooner you find this miscreant, the sooner we can rest in our beds."

This was a man who likely spent much time resting in his bed.

With his dull pencil tip poised over the little book in his hand, Pratt asked, "Tell me about yourself, Mr. Dye. Your family, how long you have lived here, your general activities."

Violet had to admire Pratt's initial angle of questioning, which encouraged Mr. Dye to elaborate about himself. It was hard to admit, but Pratt was growing as a detective, under Hurst's harsh tutelage.

"Why, I own Dye Matchworks. I not only have a group of girls making matches, but I'm expanding into candles, wicks, that sort of thing. I'm the third-largest matchmaker in London already, and I plan to have an even greater business soon." Despite his dismal pallor, there was no mistaking the great pride in his voice.

"And your family?" Pratt said politely, flipping to a new page.

"My family," Dye repeated with a sad smile. "God has seen fit to take away almost everyone I love. My parents died long ago of cholera, and my sister and her husband were killed as missionaries in Africa. Murdered by a native in cold blood, they were. Then my beloved Adele was carried away two years ago while giving birth to my son, who lived but two weeks."

Violet's heart surged with sympathy for the man. "Have you no other relations, sir?"

"A younger brother, John. He manages Charfield's cotton mill up in Manchester. He's blessed with seven children, not a stillbirth in the lot. Yet he's jealous of my success, if you can believe it. He doesn't like me having an address in St. James's, nor seeing our name on the side of my factory, so he doesn't come to London often."

The poor man. Violet didn't see her own parents often as they lived down in Brighton and seldom ventured from their cozy seaside cottage. She had no siblings, and her adopted daughter, Susanna, lived in far-off Colorado, but the separation was one of circumstances, not bad feelings. But Violet had Sam, as well as Mary, for company. What did Mr. Dye do for companionship and friendship?

An idea occurred to her.

"Do you belong to a gentlemen's club called Arthur's?" she asked.

He frowned. "Never heard of it, madam. I don't have much time for social events, as my business takes up much of my time."

May that fact save him from being the next victim, Violet thought in silent benediction.

Before she or Pratt could ask the affluent businessman any further questions, a man came up the stairwell from the servants' entrance of Dye's home. Carrying a bundle of charcoal gray wool in his hands, he scurried to where Violet and the other two men stood, saying breathlessly, "There you are, sir. You'll catch your death out here if you don't mind me saying. Here's your cloak." He swung it over Mr. Dye's shoulders. "And who might you be?" he asked sharply of Violet and Pratt.

"Second Class Inspector Langley Pratt. The better question might be who you are, sir?" Pratt said officiously, in his best imitation of Hurst.

Edgar Dye held up a hand as if to ward off Pratt's inquisition. "This is my valet, Hutton. He is quite above suspicion."

The valet looked to be no more than thirty years old, and Violet would call him handsome were it not for the pained expression that seemed to be permanently etched around his eyes.

Hutton did not notice Violet's scrutiny, for his focus was on his master. "You should come inside, sir. We don't want your condition to worsen. You cannot stand out here talking to others and risk yourself."

Dye smiled as he said apologetically to Pratt and Violet, "Hutton has cared for me since…since everything has happened. I don't know what I would do without him."

The valet cleared his throat. "Just doing my duty, sir. As for the rest," he said, turning to look at them also. "My master must have a lie-down and cannot answer any further inquiries. I'm sure if you have a list of questions delivered, I can see that they are answered and delivered back to you."

To Violet's great surprise, Dye meekly allowed Hutton to take him by the arm and guide him back to the house. This time, the valet climbed the steps to the front entrance, strolling inside with his master as if he were a good friend and not a servant.

Who was this man, Hutton? Was he truly a servant? If so, he behaved with outrageous insolence. Violet felt he was not so much *protecting* his master as he was *controlling* the owner of Dye Matchworks. The reason for that would be an interesting discovery.

Pratt's expression suggested he was as baffled by it as Violet was, but he made no move to follow the two men to demand that the interview be finished. Instead, he took his leave of Violet to join Hurst and Sam at the gentlemen's club.

As for the undertaker, despite her great curiosity over it, she didn't think Edgar Dye was in any imminent danger of death, so his valet's behavior was ultimately no business of hers.

Violet returned to the lodgings she and Sam shared above Morgan Undertaking. She loved this cozy place of just four rooms overlooking Queen's Road in Paddington. Mrs. Wren served them chicken fricassee in her typical grumpy fashion, complaining about having to keep it warm while Violet gallivanted about the city. She seemed most peeved that Violet hadn't even bothered sending a messenger to let anyone know where she was.

"I must apologize for my wife's rudeness, Mrs. Wren," Sam said, barely hiding a grin. "I'll emphasize to her that dead bodies are no excuse for tardiness."

"Harrumph," their day cook said before leaving them to their meal, her long, talon-like fingers grasping the door of their dining room and shutting it behind her.

The food might not have been as hot as it was when freshly prepared, but it was delectable, with its tender meat sautéed in a rich, smooth sauce. Violet and Sam barely spoke as they ate, so intent were they on devouring what lay before them. When they were finally finished, Sam leaned back. "Good God, that woman is worth every barb-covered insult she throws," he proclaimed heartily. "I tell you, wife, she could murder someone in our bedchamber, and I still wouldn't want to dismiss her."

Violet laughed before taking a final swallow of cider. "She could stir, toss, and knead her victim right back to life, I imagine. But speaking of murder, what did you find out at the gentlemen's club?" she asked, dabbing at her mouth with a napkin and contemplating the blessed removal of her corset after a long day within its tight confines.

"It's not much. Sir Holland Mansfield and Mr. Fitzworth were known to play an occasional game of cribbage and share a bottle of brandy together, but that's apparently nothing unusual in these places. The only interesting thing is that Fitzworth was a great benefactor of the Establishment for Gentlewomen during Temporary Illness in Cavendish Square, and Sir Holland's wife was there for a spell back around '61 or '62. Again, I doubt that's a particularly extraordinary coincidence."

Violet knew the Establishment, which had been run by Miss Florence Nightingale until she left for the Crimean War in 1854. It was renowned for excellent standards of care. If Fitzworth had been a benefactor, his money had been well spent.

"Do you know why Lady Mansfield was there?" she asked.

"Apparently some sort of nervous ailment," Sam said, rising from his chair and offering Violet his hand, helping her up, too. "'Hysteria,' I think they called it."

Violet followed her husband back to their bedchamber to prepare for the night's sleep, but knew she would spend most of the night pacing the floors in thought.

Was it coincidence that Lord Mansfield's wife as well as

Josephine Whitton had an excitable disposition? Did Fitzworth's charitable efforts toward the Establishment begin before or after Lady Mansfield's stay?

Regardless, the answers didn't seem to have much bearing on two dead men from St. James's.

As she changed into her nightclothes, Violet shared with Sam the details of her encounters with both Lord Claybrook and Mr. Dye.

"Strange men," was Sam's succinct commentary.

"Yes. I worry for Mr. Dye. His valet is a little too influential over his master's movements, I think, and Mr. Dye seems quite ill. I hope nothing untoward happens to him."

"One other thing," Sam mused as he sat against the pillows, stretching out his long legs and interlacing his fingers on his chest.

Violet turned from where she was brushing her hair repeatedly, in accordance with *Godey's Lady's Book*'s instructions for shiny tresses. The American magazine was full of advice that Violet only half-heartedly followed. "What is that?"

"Hurst proposed to Mary. She turned him down as if he were a deuce in a hand full of aces."

Violet sighed. "Mr. Pratt told me. I am apparently at fault for it, in Mr. Hurst's mind."

Sam's laugh was a low rumble in his throat, a sign that he would soon be drifting off. "Yes. And I suspect he will not welcome your assistance on his investigations for quite some time," he added with a grin.

"In other words, then, nothing will be different," Violet replied tartly, but her sarcasm was lost on Sam, who was already softly snoring.

As she spent the night wearing a path on the parlor carpet, Violet came to the conclusion that everything that had happened thus far was merely coincidence and that she was weaving cobwebs in her mind to think otherwise.

Thus reassured, she finally tumbled into bed in the wee hours of the morning, seeking the reassuring warmth of her husband's form.

The next day, there were no formal appointments for Morgan Undertaking, and Harry went to meet with the monument company that Violet had foregone several days earlier. While Sam developed photographic plates for a family who had just lost its matriarch, Violet spent an hour cleaning the shop. Then she spent several hours relaxing by herself in the rear of the shop, tallying up figures in their business ledger.

Around noon the door's bells jangled, so Violet put down her pen and heavy book. She entered the front of the shop with her best undertaker's expression, a learned one of deep concern and open friendliness intended to set people immediately at ease.

"Good afternoon. How may I be of service in your time of sorrow?" she offered while assessing her patron. Oddly enough, it was a young woman in her twenties, well dressed even if not fashionably so, accompanied by a far more well-dressed boy of about five years of age. The child, whose blond hair was carefully groomed away from his cherubic face, gazed about openmouthed at the contents of the shop. The woman clutched his hand tightly in hers, as if she were afraid to lose him. They seemed perfectly respectable, but what struck Violet as most peculiar was that she was in the shop at all. Women were not typically sent to fetch the undertaker unless it couldn't at all be helped.

As if uncannily reading Violet's thoughts, the woman said, "I am not here for a funeral. I am here to see you, Mrs. Harper." Her brow furrowed as though she was bundling up the courage to say something of great import.

At that moment, the boy chose to wrench himself away from the woman, throwing himself against Violet's display case of empty mourning brooches and jet jewelry. He pressed his nose and fingers against the glass as he peered intently inside. Violet cringed at the thought that she would already have to wipe her case down again. She tore her attention away from the boy, who now trailed his fingers along the glass as he walked back and forth along the long walnut-trimmed case.

"Let me take your cloak," Violet said, offering out a hand. "Have we met before?"

Without the boy's hand in hers, the woman unhooked the braided frog closure at her throat. "No, but I have seen you. I am Miss Johanna Froste, governess to the Ashenhurst household. This is Master Lucius Ashenhurst, the family heir." She nodded at the boy, who had just discovered Violet's hat stand, which held her black top hat with its long, flowing crape tails. The inquisitive child was in the process of setting it down on his own head.

Johanna offered an apologetic smile but did nothing to stop Lucius. "I apologize for disrupting you in the middle of your work. I don't know how you can bear to be in the midst of death every day."

Violet took the pale-blue cloak from the governess and hung it on a coatrack near the door. "Miss Froste, the *Book of Common Prayer* says that even 'in the midst of life, we are in death.' I just try to help those on the side of death, since the living can usually manage themselves. I hope that one day someone will help me. But I don't think that is why you are here. Is there something troubling you?"

Miss Froste bit her lip in hesitation, then forged ahead. "I am worried about my master's family. His mood has been unusually...erratic...since he has started having family members reburied. His demeanor is affecting Lady Ashenhurst's sister, too. You may not know it, but Miss Whitton is rather... She tends to..." Miss Froste's voice trailed off as she searched for an apt description.

"I think you mean to say that Miss Whitton is a bit excitable," Violet offered gently.

"Yes, that's it. And she has become much more excitable since you gave his lordship that old pocket watch. Lucius, please, you mustn't paw through Mrs. Harper's laces." Violet followed Miss Froste's line of sight. Lucius had discovered Violet's stand of black ribbons and lace, used to decorate fans and accentuate mourning jewelry. He had a length of lavender ribbon lined with silk flowers in one hand, and was twirling it around the fingers of his other hand.

If Violet didn't do something immediately, the boy would have Morgan Undertaking ransacked faster than a Visigoth in a Roman marketplace. "Sam," she sang out brightly. "I would like you to meet our visitors, Miss Froste and Master Lucius Ashenhurst."

Sam emerged from behind his screens again, wiping his fingers on a rag. "Good afternoon," he said genially, and immediately spotted Lucius, who was tugging on the ribbon stand and threatening to topple the whole thing over.

"Master Lucius!" Sam barked, instantly stilling the boy's grasping and clawing. The boy turned, wide-eyed and startled into immediate compliance.

"Sir?" he said, timid for the first time since entering the shop.

Sam smiled. "You look like an intelligent boy. Come, I will show you how to make a person's likeness appear by magic on paper."

All undertaking supplies were instantly forgotten, and Lucius willingly followed Sam, who gave Violet a wink of complete understanding.

Without Lucius distracting her, Miss Froste seemed much more focused. "As I was saying, my lady Ashenhurst's sister is much more agitated than normal, and I fear she may do something harmful to her person. Or to someone else."

This was the second time someone was emphasizing Josephine Whitton's mental instability to Violet. Was the woman that troubled? Moreover, was her erratic behavior of such concern that the Ashenhurst governess would secretly visit Violet to talk about it?

"Miss Froste, why are you telling me this? I'm not sure what I can be expected to do."

Miss Froste frowned, apparently frustrated that Violet did not understand her concerns. She dropped her voice, and it was ominous in Violet's ear. "I think that pocket watch you gave to Lord Ashenhurst is…is…is *cursed*, madam."

CHAPTER 3

VIOLET SCHOOLED HER EXPRESSION to remain neutral, despite wanting to shake her head in disbelief. "My dear, it is simply not possible that a timepiece can control people's actions. If your master and Miss Whitton are behaving peculiarly, there must be another reason." Personally, Violet thought that the viscount's obsession with his prestige was enough to drive a marble statue batty. "Perhaps there is trouble in the household of a private nature, to which you are not privy."

Her brows still knit together, Miss Froste shook her head emphatically. "No, that isn't it. Please, madam, you must remove that thing from the house. I don't know of anyone else who can get possession of it legitimately, other than the person who brought it in to start with."

Violet was sympathetic to Miss Froste's distress, but saw no reason to return to her customer's home to ask him to voluntarily turn over one of his possessions to her. Especially one that was nearly sacred in Violet's mind, having been found inside a grave. No, the idea was ludicrous.

"I'm sorry, but I am merely an undertaker. I have no standing in the family to do such a thing. Perhaps there are other relatives who can—"

"No, that will never do," Miss Froste said flatly. "His lordship would never give over a possession unless he believed it in his best interest to do so. That's why I thought you, what with your..."

your…access to the afterlife and all, could convince him." Miss Froste turned to take her cloak from the rack and called out for Lucius. The young lad reluctantly exited from Sam's makeshift darkroom and took his governess's hand once more.

"I must leave," the young woman said. "I am supposed to be on a walk through St. James's Park with Lucius, and I've been gone for far too long. I beg you, madam, not to tell my employer that I was here."

That, at least, was a promise Violet could keep.

Miss Froste had not been gone two hours from the shop before a servant from the Ashenhurst household burst into the shop, breathless and wide-eyed.

"My master says you must come immediately, Mrs. Harper. He must talk to you." The servant looked as though he had seen not just one, but several shadowy specters calling out his name and urging him on to the other side.

"What has happened?" Violet asked, already reaching for her gloves and undertaker's hat. She didn't recognize this servant. He must have been new to the household.

The servant shook his head. "I cannot say, madam. Not my place, no 'tisn't."

Dreading what it was that Lord Ashenhurst wanted to see her about, Violet wrote out a note for Sam, who had gone out to help Harry pick up some coffin samples, then she followed the servant to the awaiting conveyance. Had Miss Froste's visit been discovered? Did the viscount expect Violet to betray her confidence? Worse, had he located more family members who required reinterment? The servant may have been rattled, but he was also tight-lipped, so Violet gave up asking him for more information during their ride together to Arlington Street.

At the Ashenhurst home, the servant led Violet quickly down through the servants' entrance and into the spacious kitchen, where she was shocked to find the entire family and a gaggle of servants—including Miss Froste—milling about and chattering anxiously in the chilly room. Clearly the Ashenhursts had been busy hiring staff.

The kneading of bread loaves and mixing of pie crusts had been abandoned on a marble side table, and a pan filled with a dark syrup burbled away unattended on the stove. Candlesticks, tureens, and other silver pieces lay haphazardly on a sideboard next to stained white gloves and a jar of polishing cream, as though that were yet another activity cast aside.

Not only had household tasks been abandoned, but...Lord and Lady Ashenhurst had deigned to enter this sacrosanct servants' realm? That was the most peculiar sight of all. With only a few lamps burning, even in the middle of the day it was dark in the basement, because the windows were few and high up in the walls, offering little opportunity for daylight to penetrate the space.

When Victor Ashenhurst acknowledged Violet with a curt "Finally you have come," she realized that everyone was actually huddled around a body lying upon the large worktable that dominated the room.

With that, Violet's undertaking instincts took over and she inquired commandingly, "What has happened here?" as she approached the body. "Heavens!" she gasped. "This is Mr. Dye."

Lady Ashenhurst nodded. "He was attacked in the street. The madman must have gone after him right in front of our home, Mrs. Harper. My sister found him."

With that acknowledgment, Josephine Whitton began wailing. "I warned you all. I told you that there were evil spirits in the streets. You would not listen to me." She slowly raised a hand and pointed an accusing finger at Violet. "I especially warned *you*," Josephine hissed, and all of a sudden Violet felt as though she had been transported into the pages of a Charles Dickens novel.

Miss Froste shot her an anguished look, emphasizing that she, too, had warned Violet.

Shaking her head to ward off an imagined chill, Violet put her hand to Mr. Dye's chest as if she could gather strength from his lifeless form. "Why did you call me instead of the police?" She cursed herself for leaving so quickly that she hadn't thought to grab her undertaking bag. Not that she had any reason to imagine that a visit to Lord Ashenhurst would require it.

The viscount stepped forward. "My dear lady, have we not had enough madness and panic here already? Can you imagine how the newspapers would descend upon me to know that a third body in a few days had been found near my home, with this one found directly in front of it? I would be a laughingstock. No, the man is dead and I am hiring you as an undertaker to, well, to take care of him."

Violet's skin crawled at the thought that his lordship viewed her role as one to ensure he wouldn't be publicly embarrassed. This was utterly disrespectful to Mr. Dye, who was already tossed onto the table like an ungainly sack of potatoes. She drew a deep breath to try to squelch her rising irritation. Multiple sets of eyes stared at her as she bent down to focus on the Ashenhursts' neighbor.

"What do you see?" Victor Ashenhurst demanded at once, before Violet had a chance to begin even a cursory examination. "How did he die? Was it the same as with the others?"

Violet rose to face everyone surrounding the table. "If you will not leave the kitchen altogether, I beg you all to give me space. And peace," she added, more waspishly than she had intended.

Everyone hurriedly stepped back.

It was hardly the proper surroundings in which to conduct her work, but it would have to do, as one could order around a peer of the realm only so far. Violet returned to Mr. Dye's body. He had his scarves around his neck, and naturally his face was devoid of color. She took one of his hands in hers. No apparent injury to it. Rigor mortis had not yet set in. She put his cool hand down gently and patted it, then put fingers to his scalp. The hair in one area was crusted. Probably blood, but it was impossible to say for sure in this dim light. Violet put a palm to the side of his face. He didn't have… Wait, what was this?

Violet's heart stopped for a moment, then began pumping wildly. "Excuse me, who found this man again?"

"I did," Josephine said. "I was in my bedchamber, counting my earrings, when I thought I heard cats fighting outside. Awful things, full of evil and spite. I had a ewer of water filled to toss on them, and when I went out, I found *him*. The spirits plan to murder all of us in our beds," she claimed, her voice rising hysterically. Her finger shook as she pointed to Mr. Dye. "He is the proof of the spirits' mockery. It won't stop until we are all dead. Dead, dead, *dead*!"

"Dear God," Lord Ashenhurst said. "Judith, do something about your sister."

But Lady Ashenhurst seemed frozen in place, staring openmouthed and mesmerized by her sister's unladylike rantings. Instead, Mrs. Chase once again stepped forward to manage Josephine Whitton, taking her firmly by the elbow. "Now, then, I'm sure you're right, madam. You know there's a new tin of biscuits in the dining room. The kind you like, Miss Whitton, with the honey in them, remember?" The housekeeper's coaxing voice trailed off as she moved Josephine upstairs.

For several moments, no one downstairs moved, the only sound in the room being the continued burbling of whatever was cooking on the stove. The smell of burning sauce began wafting over them. Lady Ashenhurst finally had the presence of mind to snap her gaping mouth shut. "Could she be right?" the lady of the house asked timidly. "Is there an unsettled spirit coming back to murder everyone in the neighborhood?"

"Not in this case," Violet said firmly. "Because Mr. Dye is still alive."

"What?" Lord Ashenhurst exclaimed. "How could he still be… What do you mean, he is alive?"

"He is breathing," Violet told him. "If someone will fetch me a mirror…"

Moments later she had a piece of silvered glass in her hands and held it up to Mr. Dye's mouth, showing that he was, indeed, faintly breathing. "This man needs help. We must call—"

Violet was unable to finish her sentence, for Hutton came barging in through the servants' entrance, immediately bowing and apologizing upon seeing the Ashenhursts standing in the room. "Forgive me, my lord, but I understand that my master is here. I—" Hutton caught sight of Edgar Dye sprawled on the table, and he reacted bizarrely.

"Who touched him?" he asked, his voice a low growl.

"Nearly everyone, I imagine," Violet said. "He was found by a member of the household, carried in here by men in Lord Ashenhurst's employ, and I began an examination of him. However, you will be pleased to know that—"

But the valet wasn't pleased about anything. "I will take him next door immediately. He cannot be touched any further. His body cannot remain here." The valet moved toward Dye and started to tuck his hands beneath his master's armpits, as though he expected to drag the man off the table himself.

"Stop!" Violet commanded, which startled Hutton enough that he dropped his hands. "What I am trying to say to you is that your master is not dead. He breathes, but I believe he requires a physician's help."

Hutton appeared visibly relieved at the news that Dye was not deceased, then shook his head. "No, if I can just get him back to his own bed, I will make him well."

"But that is not possible," Violet said. "He is likely to get worse and—"

"No, I agree with him," Lord Ashenhurst said, nodding toward Hutton. "I'll have some men help you carry him back over. If he's alive, the sooner he is gone from here, the better." The viscount began issuing orders to some of the male staff, who surrounded the body while the other servants rushed off to resume their usual duties. If Mr. Dye wasn't actually dead, there was less to be twittering about.

As she watched the men clumsily grabbing parts of the ailing man, Violet once more interceded. "Leave him!" she said, raising her voice as much as she could without shouting. "You will not carry him out of here as if he were a carpet to be beaten. We need some bed coverings, or at least a tablecloth, to shield him from any prying eyes."

"It's only a few feet," one of the Ashenhurst servants said. "And we can go out the rear entrance where no one will see from the street."

"Nevertheless, I insist," Violet said, placing a hand back on Edgar Dye's chest as if to protect him herself.

"Do as she wishes," the viscount ordered. "It will be faster than arguing with her."

Within minutes, Dye was covered with an incongruously cheerful mauve tablecloth with a white lace overlay in a rose pattern, then moved over to his own home and placed on a long settee inside his parlor. Violet hardly bothered to take note of the decor, except to have the impression that it was stark as compared to the Ashenhursts' elegant home, as if the home itself had felt Edgar Dye's keening loss of family.

The Ashenhurst servants slithered away as soon as their cargo was unloaded, leaving Violet alone with the sick man and his valet. None of Dye's other servants made an appearance, which Violet found odd.

She knelt next to his prone figure and slowly removed the tablecloth. Dye coughed weakly, and his eyes opened and closed several times before he focused on Violet's face. His expression was confused.

She took his hand in hers once more. He may as well have been a corpse, as cold as he had become in the few minutes it had taken to reach his own home.

"Mr. Dye, can you hear me?" she asked softly.

He nodded, his expression still bewildered. Dye's valet positioned himself next to Violet, thus inserting himself within eyesight of his employer. Dye's eyes widened for a moment upon seeing Hutton.

"You are safe in your home now," Violet assured him before urging him gently for answers. "Can you tell me what happened?"

"You needn't speak to her, sir," Hutton said, pushing himself forward and nearly knocking Violet to the floor. "She's just a nosy undertaker."

"Just a nosy undertaker," Dye mumbled in a low monotone.

Violet glared at Hutton. "Sir, is there reasoning behind your hectoring and browbeating?"

Her irritation had no effect on him. "Only that Mr. Dye is sick and needs my help, not your foolish questions, madam. The sooner you are gone, the sooner I can restore him to health." He turned his attention back to the man on the settee. "Sir, I will just go and get your tonic, and you'll be better in two shakes."

Hadn't Mrs. Chase assured Josephine Whitton the same way the other day? Surely that was a coincidence though. Undoubtedly half the homes in London had laudanum stashes.

Dye weakly waved a hand. "It's all right, Hutton. Mrs. Harper, I remember you. Yes, I stepped outside to head to the cab stand at the top of the street, when all of a sudden I felt something hard across the back of my head, and then…I woke up here."

"You didn't see who attacked you?"

"Who attacked me?" Dye echoed others' words once more. Violet suspected he had received more damage than anyone could have guessed. The man needed a physician's care. And as if he were that physician, Hutton left the room, presumably in search of the miraculous tonic.

"Mr. Dye, do you know of anyone who hates you enough to attack you?" Violet asked.

"Hates me?" He attempted to laugh, but it sounded more like a gurgle. "Most men don't think enough of me for it to rise to the level of hate, I don't believe, Mrs. Harper. If I could trouble you to assist me…" He indicated that he wished to sit up.

Violet helped the man into an upright position. He was still swathed in winter clothing, but didn't seem to notice, so she assumed he was still chilled enough to need them. She folded the tablecloth and draped it over her arm. At that moment, Hutton returned with a brown bottle and a spoon, as well as some linen bandages. While the valet gave his master a dose, Violet stepped away, taking in what little decor there was.

As with most London town houses, the Dye home was built on the same rough floor plan as the Ashenhursts'. Unlike the viscount's expression of prestige through artwork, Mr. Dye had little to show, other than a few scattered vases, marble fern stands, and mirrors. Most poignant was a table with several framed photographs on it, one a wedding picture of a healthy Edgar Dye with a golden-haired beauty on his arm. Next to it were a postmortem picture of the same woman and another daguerreotype of a dead infant.

How terribly sad for the man. It was fortunate that he had not joined his wife and son today in death, although he might do so from natural causes soon enough. Violet turned toward the two men once more. Edgar was leaning back with his neck resting on the back of the settee, his eyes closed and his breathing becoming even and peaceful. Hutton had just resealed the bottle and was unwrapping a length of the bandage.

As she watched the scene before her, it occurred to Violet that perhaps her insistence that the factory owner see a physician was not the best course of action for him. *Leave him in peace,* she thought. *Blow away cobwebs elsewhere.*

Excusing herself to the valet, she retraced her steps back to the Ashenhurst kitchen to return the tablecloth. The staff—excepting the governess—was seated around the freshly scrubbed table. They were having tea, chattering about inconsequentials as if there had not just been a seemingly dead man on the table less than an hour ago.

Violet proffered the tablecloth, which a young maid spirited away, and Mrs. Chase invited Violet to sit down to tea. She gratefully accepted the housekeeper's generous pour into an old, stained cup, and was especially appreciative of the cake plate that was passed to her.

The servants continued their gossiping as if Violet were one of them. She figured it to be a result of her willingness to perform a messy task with a dead body, much as they had to be covered in soot and grime in their own daily duties.

"Miss Whitton was not to be consoled," Mrs. Chase said, shaking her head dolefully and sipping at her teacup. A repaired crack ran along the rim of the cup near her lips. "Says the household is cursed. Alice, we must be very quiet around her for a few days and serve her meals in her room."

A mousy girl in a perfectly starched uniform quickly swallowed her mouthful of lemon cake. "Yes, Mrs. Chase."

Violet, too, finished off her first slice and surreptitiously took another from the serving plate. "Do you not think that Miss Whitton requires a physician?" she asked.

Mrs. Chase looked at her in shock. "No, madam. Lady Ashenhurst would never allow her sister to be subjected to a bread-and-water diet or to being chained to a bed. We will take care of her here for the rest of her life."

Violet nodded and changed the subject, as there was no reason to continue examining Josephine Whitton's fragile mental condition, much as there was no reason to dissect poor Mr. Dye before he was dead. "How long have you worked here, Mrs. Chase?"

The housekeeper considered this. "Why, I've been with Lord Ashenhurst's family since he was a boy, and he brought me along when he got married. I work in a household that is rising high in this world. My friends are quite envious of my position here." Mrs. Chase gave a self-satisfied smack and put her cup down. "I'll never leave this home, not for any reason."

Several heads bobbed up and down around the table in avid agreement.

"Lord and Lady Ashenhurst must treat you very well," Violet said.

"There's nothing I wouldn't do for them. There's nothing that any of us wouldn't do to protect them."

That avowal was enough to silence Violet. The cook turned their conversation to the more mundane topics of which serving pieces would be needed for the evening's meal of veal cutlets, baked tomatoes, and potato soup. The Ashenhursts could now certainly afford a paragon of culinary excellence, but Violet doubted that Mrs. Chase could outdo Mrs. Wren's wizardry with veal or any other meat.

Violet said her farewells shortly thereafter and took a crowded omnibus home, preferring to endure the elements in the open-air conveyance and save money. Clutching her reticule to her as she sat on the wooden bench, she closed her eyes and blocked out the sounds of the streets as she contemplated everything that had happened that day. By the time the omnibus pulled up to its stop two blocks from her shop, she had at least come to one conclusion: Miss Whitton's obsession with the supernatural was ridiculous. Spirits in the street and cursed pocket watches, indeed. It beggared belief.

And yet, something inexplicable was happening in Arlington Street. Was it Violet's responsibility to find out what it was, or was there danger lurking in the answer?

The following morning, Violet had hardly gotten the shop open when a delivery boy arrived. He handed her an envelope made of thick, creamy paper, and she rewarded him with a penny. As Violet slid open the flap, she had a reasonably good idea whose desk the high-quality stationery had come from. She unfolded the page and quickly scanned the one broadly scrawled line.

Please come immediately.
—Ashenhurst

Now what was this about?

Fitting her crape-swathed hat on her head and tying it under her chin, Violet told Sam where she was going. He looked up in distraction from creating an emulsion of egg white and salt for sealing his photographic paper and quickly kissed her as she leaned down to him. "Don't be too late," he admonished as he resumed his quick stirring of the mixture. "I can only save you so many times from Mrs. Wren's wrath."

"I'll take my chances," she replied drily. "Besides, I suppose it wouldn't hurt me to miss a meal or two." If Violet had hoped for Sam to make an encouraging remark about her figure, she was disappointed, for he was already back to his emulsion as if he hadn't even heard her.

She shook her head. *Surely God will not hear vanity, neither will the Almighty regard it*, she recalled from the book of Job. Poor Job, a blameless man leading an upright life who loses everything.

Just like the lamentable Mr. Dye.

Perhaps she should make another visit to him after seeing the Ashenhursts, she thought as she climbed the stairs to the viscount's front door.

A new footman answered, and once more Violet stood in the Ashenhurst parlor, wondering who would come to greet her this time. It was, in fact, both Lord and Lady Ashenhurst who came in almost immediately, with Lady Ashenhurst visibly trembling and clinging to her husband's arm for support. The footman rolled the pocket doors shut and left Violet alone with her customers.

It was then that Violet realized that Lord Ashenhurst was visibly shaken. He stroked at his face with his free hand, but it seemed to be an affectation to cover up a nervous tic in his hand. What had happened here in the past forty-eight hours?

"Mrs. Harper, you received my note. Good, good. I must confess I have never been one for my sister-in-law's twaddle, but I believe I have now heard and experienced just enough to make me a believer. Here..." Ashenhurst disengaged from his wife, who sat in a chair and clung to both overstuffed arms for dear life. He walked over to one of the wall shelves and pulled down the old pocket watch that Violet had unearthed. "Come here."

As Violet neared, he handed the case to her, and she held the hard gold piece in her hand. She was glad the heirloom piece had its own display shelf. Except that...

"It appears to have stopped working," she said, looking up at Lord Ashenhurst.

"Precisely," he agreed, nodding.

That was it? An old watch that had been buried in the ground for nearly forty years had stopped working, and he needed to inform her of it? "I don't understand, my lord. It is a very old—"

"Look at the time," he commanded, moving to stand behind his wife's chair and putting both hands on her shoulders, as if he didn't want to be anywhere near the watch when Violet examined it in further detail.

"Half past one," she said. "Is the time significant?"

"Of course it is," Lady Ashenhurst cried shrilly, leaning forward. "It's an hour before Edgar Dye was nearly murdered yesterday afternoon. Don't you understand?"

She said this as if the answer should be obvious even to a Bedlamite, but Violet had no idea what the woman's point was. The Ashenhursts were clearly distraught, though.

"My lord, my lady, are you suggesting that this watch stopped in anticipation of yesterday's attack?"

"No, Mrs. Harper." Lord Ashenhurst, pulled himself up to be every inch an imperious viscount. "We *suggest* nothing. What you do not know is that the timepiece in your hand has consistently stopped prior to each of the three deaths in this neighborhood, including yesterday afternoon when Mr. Dye next door was nearly killed."

Violet glanced at the gold case still resting in her palm. "But surely it is a coinci—"

"That is what we believed, at first," Lady Ashenhurst said,

finally regaining her composure and rising from the chair to stand next to her husband once more. "But we realized that it was not that the watch was ceasing to function at intermittent, random moments, as you might expect from an antique piece—"

"One that had been buried for nearly four decades, for God's sake," Lord Ashenhurst added.

His wife nodded in agreement. "Instead, it was stopping almost precisely an hour prior to the time the murders were reported in the newspapers. The first murder was at half past four in the morning and the watch stopped at half past three. Mr. Fitzworth was killed around two o'clock; the next morning we found the watch stopped at just after one. You can see that it has a connection to the deaths."

Violet wasn't sure what to say. It was clearly impossible that a simple little watch could wreak havoc in someone's life, but the viscount and his wife were clearly disturbed by the coincidences they had experienced.

She proceeded cautiously. "I can understand that you would be upset..." she began, deliberating on what to say next.

Immediately Lord Ashenhurst seized upon her words. "We knew you would. Thus why I summoned you here today. I want you to take possession of the watch. Remove the curse from our home."

So his lordship was suggesting that Violet carry the curse into her own home? To bring death to Paddington? She should—

Violet took a deep breath. She was letting these neurotic aristocrats affect her own rational thinking. "If the watch has such... potency...why not destroy it?" she asked sensibly, hanging it back on the hook of its display case.

Lady Ashenhurst gasped at Violet's action, rushing over and snatching the watch from the shelf again. She thrust it back into Violet's hands and folded Violet's fingers around it, as if removing the offending object from her sight would also remove its curse.

"No!" the woman whispered harshly. "I'm afraid the curse is all around the case. To destroy it would make whatever is surrounding it…furious."

"My lady…" Violet replied helplessly. She had never before been faced with customers displaying such vitriol against an inanimate object. Unreasonable anger like this was usually directed toward fellow humans.

She was saved from having to say more by the appearance of Lucius Ashenhurst, who came bounding in like a colt in an open field. "Mama, have you seen Robespierre?" he asked, pulling up short when he saw Violet.

Lucius frowned as he tried to place Violet. Remembering the governess's fear of discovery by her employers, Violet tried to ward off any recognition.

"Why, you must be Master Ashenhurst," she said politely. "I remember seeing you on a previous visit."

That seemed to resolve the perplexing question of who Violet was, and his face cleared of confusion. By this point, he had also caught a glimpse of gold in her closed hand, too.

"What do you have?" he asked, approaching her.

Unthinking, Violet unfolded her hand to show the boy. He snatched it away, like an avaricious crow, immediately running and plopping down in the chair his mother had recently vacated. In an instant, he had popped open the cover and was seemingly trying to take it apart.

"Lucius!" his mother exclaimed sharply. "You are a rude boy. Stop that this moment."

He looked up at Lady Ashenhurst in utter surprise. "Mine," he said simply.

"Son," his father said. "That is not yours. It belongs to—" The viscount stopped, apparently not willing to say it belonged to him.

"I like this. That lady was going to steal it. I saved it." Lucius spoke with the resolute confidence of a five-year-old boy for whom there is only one viewpoint of the world: his own.

Violet was forming a thought, though. "My lord, is it not

possible that Lucius has been playing with the watch, and that its delicate workings are being damaged each time he plays with it?"

Victor Ashenhurst sniffed at her. "Mrs. Harper, we have instructed the governess to keep a very tight rein on our boy. She would never permit him to touch an objet d'art like some sort of alley waif. Besides, how could he have reached it up on its shelf?"

Ashenhurst went to Lucius and removed the watch from his son's fingers, resulting in a petulant cry from a child who was likely overindulged. However, Lucius did not argue with his father, and instead sat red-faced as though suppressing tears.

Violet could think of a hundred ways the child could have gotten to the shelf. He could have dragged any number of chairs, occasional tables, or an ottoman to the wall as a makeshift ladder, then clambered up to grab the shiny watch.

A more disturbing thought was whether Miss Froste might have handed it to him for play, an action that any servant worth a tuppence would know was cause for instant dismissal.

Miss Froste did not strike Violet as that foolish. However, it certainly put her visit to Morgan Undertaking in a new light.

She had been so lost in thought that she hadn't realized that Lord Ashenhurst had placed the watch back in her hand and three sets of eyes were looking at her expectantly.

In that moment, she had an idea. A way both to comfort them and assure everyone concerned that there was no link between the watch and the murders.

"I have a proposal," she announced.

Lord Ashenhurst nodded, silently granting her an audience to air her proposition.

"Although I cannot countenance that the watch has any sort of supernatural capability, I do want to assist you in any way I can to set your minds at ease. What if I were to stay here overnight to keep a vigil over the watch to see whether any…spirits…tamper with it during the night?"

She had no idea how she could prevent another murder if the

watch did stop mysteriously, but presumably Inspector Hurst had his own investigation well in hand and an arrest would soon be made.

Lady Ashenhurst brightened considerably at the suggestion. "Yes, perhaps you can frighten the evil spirit away, Mrs. Harper."

Violet suspected she would only be chasing away a young sprite and maybe his governess, but she nodded in agreement.

The bargain was struck that Violet would return that evening around eight o'clock and be fed supper, then would sit in the parlor to wait for whatever might happen. Lord Ashenhurst made her promise to return every night until something did happen, a provision which Violet was loath to agree upon, but she found herself nodding submissively.

Sam was appalled at the idea. "You wish to sit all night in a lord's house, waiting for a watch to stop ticking?"

"I don't actually *wish* to do it, Sam, but—"

"Don't these aristocrats have servants to do such things?" Sam was stoppering a bottle of fluid with such force she thought the cork might fall into it.

"I don't think it is a matter of staff, despite their lack of a full complement of servants, but their notion—however misguided it might be—that because I am the undertaker, I will have a special connection to whatever supernatural events are occurring. And, of course, they trust me to be discreet."

Her husband was still unconvinced. "Do they believe you to be a medium? A conjurer?" He set the bottle down none too gently onto a shelf behind him, the contents sloshing around but thoroughly stoppered and unable to splash out.

Sam was making a distressing situation even more troublesome. Violet found it difficult to justify it all to her husband, when she could hardly understand what she was doing herself. "I think it will bring them some comfort to have me there, and I believe it to be my role to bring families comfort."

"Comfort!" Sam exploded. "There is no grieving going on here, just preposterous doltishness. I don't like it, I will tell you. My wife alone like that amid some dotty members of London's elite. No sir, I don't like it at all."

Sam didn't like it, but he did escort Violet to the Ashenhurst residence that evening, silently holding her for several long moments before watching her go up the wide steps to the front door.

He was still there a half hour later, his lanky silhouette outlined by the hissing streetlamp. Alone with her supper tray, Violet parted the curtains wide so he could see her in the room's lamplight. He held up a hand and slowly moved away, shaking his head.

CHAPTER 4

A BUNDLE OF BLACK FUR jumped into her lap, purring loudly as it made itself comfortable by pawing and kneading Violet's dress fabric.

"You must be the errant Robespierre," Violet said, scratching the cat behind its ears. He responded by reaching his head up for more ministrations, eventually falling asleep against Violet's chest.

"Well, aren't you sweet?" she murmured. "Nothing like your fanatical namesake."

Thus did she end up falling asleep before midnight, lulled into a dreamless state by Robespierre's throaty rumbles.

When she was startled awake sometime in the middle of the night, the cat was gone. With her heart racing, she had to orient herself, and it was a few moments before she fully remembered her purpose in sitting up in an overupholstered armchair in an unfamiliar parlor. As she glanced around the room, which was still lit by the oil lamp, Violet's next thought was to wonder what had wakened her so suddenly. Her heart was still galloping as if it were in the final stretch of the Royal Ascot. Had it been a noise, a movement? Had she simply been a victim of Robespierre's decision to jump to the floor?

She checked the watch pinned to her bodice. It was nearly half past two.

This reminded Violet of her duty to the Ashenhurst timepiece.

May as well check it now. She rose and stretched, grimacing at the stiffness in her neck.

She went to the shelf where the watch was displayed and gently removed it from its perch. She took it to the lamp to examine it in the brightest light possible. The watch was off by only a minute or so as compared to her own. She held it to her ear. It was still ticking.

It must have been the silly cat jumping off her lap that had awakened her.

Violet replaced the watch on its shelf and settled back onto the chair to try to get more rest. By morning, the watch still functioned and the newspaper did not report any overnight murders.

Perhaps the curse had been lifted.

The Ashenhursts seemed almost disappointed that the watch had not "performed" properly. After ensuring Violet had a meal of coffee, eggs, haddock, ham, and toast, they extracted her solemn promise that she would return again that evening.

In the bright, late-morning sun of a chilly, windy March day, Violet decided that rather than rush back to her shop, it might be wise to pay a visit to Inspector Hurst.

At Scotland Yard, she learned that Hurst was at a nearby cordwainer's shop. Instead of waiting on a hard bench for him to return, she sought the detective out at the shop, where he was seated, trying on a pair of black leather boots. Violet hadn't realized before that his feet were as big as bear paws, which probably made sense, given his large frame.

"Mrs. Harper," he said flatly. "Are you here to approve my purchase? Or did Commissioner Henderson perhaps give you money for my boots? I've been arguing with him about providing a boot allowance for his detectives, but so far have made no progress." He stood, rocking back and forth to test the heels, then nodded in approval.

"No, Inspector, I have come to discuss your investigation into the murders in St. James's."

He sighed. "Of course you have. Not here though." He paid the clerk for his new footwear, then inclined his head for Violet to follow him. He held the door for her as they stepped into the busy street full of private carriages, taxis, omnibuses, dogs, street vendors, and foot traffic all competing for space. "St. James's Park," he spoke, his only words as he jammed his hat down onto his head. He led her several blocks to the old royal park, which was surrounded by Parliament, Buckingham Palace, and, of course, St. James's Palace. Violet had to avoid the inspector's overcoat as she scurried to keep up with his long strides. It flapped wildly behind him as he forced a path through the crowds.

Inside the park, Hurst stopped and whirled around to face Violet so suddenly that she nearly ran into him. "What do you want to know?" he asked impatiently, folding his arms belligerently across his chest.

"Good morning, Mr. Hurst. I trust you are well today," Violet said, still breathless from running after him. The detective grunted in return.

She sighed. "Very well then, sir. Let us first discuss your ill temper. I am aware of your great displeasure at what you believe to be my interference in your courtship of my dear friend, Mary Cooke."

Hurst frowned, clearly annoyed that Violet had pierced through his choler. "I didn't tell you that," he said.

"No, but I know that Mary rejected your marriage proposal. You should know that she—"

"Forget it. It was of no consequence. I hardly remember it." He kept his arms crossed, though, communicating his ill-concealed irritation.

"Nevertheless," Violet continued, determined to resolve this with the detective, "you should know that Mary is quite pleased with your attentions. She has told me this on many occasions."

"She has?" Hurst asked, and a tiny crack opened up in his frosty reserve.

"Of course. And while I confess I had my own concerns about your, er, familiarity with one another, I swear to you that I had stepped aside and have not spoken against you in months."

"Then why did she reject me?" he demanded.

Violet wanted to slap him. Here he was, an experienced, toughened member of the Metropolitan Police who dealt with all manner of people and situations, yet he didn't understand the simplest social etiquette. "Because, sir, she's not through with her full year of mourning yet."

The detective shook his head, uncomprehending. "But George Cooke was a dim-witted muttonhead. Any idiot could see that. And Mary isn't some society miss to have to worry that she's serving out a prescribed number of days in bereavement. Why, she probably didn't grieve him more than a fortnight." Now it was as though Hurst was pleading his case with Violet.

"That is quite true, Inspector. But Mary does *serve* society women, and her livelihood is dependent upon them. She is a mourning dressmaker, after all. It would do her no good to have women gossiping about how quickly she remarried."

"I earn enough that she wouldn't have to continue serving society ladies, though. She could be Mrs. Hurst and stop working her poor fingers to calloused nubs. Perhaps I didn't make that clear enough to her when I—"

"Mr. Hurst, you must cease all thought in that direction," Violet said. "Mary loves her work of making beautiful confections for grieving women. You could no more take that away from her than Sam could wrest a coffin handle from my hand. Please, I beg you, wait until her one-year mourning period is over, and I assure you that her response to your proposal will result in mutual satisfaction and happiness." Was Violet actually saying these words? She could hardly imagine this grumpy bear of a man becoming her best friend's husband. However, Mary had suffered enough in her life, and if Hurst made her happy, well then…

Hurst changed subjects abruptly. "You wanted to know about the St. James's investigation," he said, apparently deciding he was no longer angry at Violet. He now ambled slowly, listening as Violet disclosed everything that had happened—the attack on Edgar Dye, the governess's visit to her shop, and the Ashenhursts' concern that the watch was foretelling deaths. To her surprise, Hurst merely shrugged as he led her onto a path next to the park's long lake. It was still icy in spots and had the stillness of death that always covers a lake before spring bursts forth with flowers, foliage, and birds.

"A cursed pocket watch is as good as any answer I might have," he admitted, surprisingly accepting of such a ridiculous conjecture. "I confess that I have few theories myself. Here's what I know: we have two dead men, Sir Holland Mansfield and Mr. Ralph Fitzworth; then a third who should have been dead, your Mr. Dye. Sir Holland and Mr. Fitzworth were known to socialize at Arthur's. Fitzworth was a benefactor of Miss Nightingale's hospital, where Sir Holland's wife stayed for a spell almost a decade ago. Something in common, I suppose, but what of it? It was so long ago. Dye doesn't belong to a club. Fitzworth and Dye are widowers; Sir Holland has a wife. Fitzworth and Dye have their fortunes through business; Sir Holland has made his through royal recognition. The only real commonality is that all are residents in St. James's. Should I suggest to the commissioner that someone is tearing through a wealthy neighborhood murdering rich men? Our killer has an extensive task before him in order to complete the job."

Hurst paused at a bench along the path and sat down, gazing out over the lifeless water as he continued. "You say Dye's valet is overprotective of him, but that's hardly suspicious. I've encountered many a servant willing to risk death for an employer. I'd say the Ashenhurst governess is also acting in a protective manner, even if her motives are less clear. Maybe the boy is tinkering with the watch, but maybe he isn't. Again, you aren't providing me with anything concrete to investigate."

He reached his arm along the back of the bench and looked directly at Violet, who paced back and forth, her habit when she was deep in thought. "And so, Mrs. Harper, what would you have me do?"

For once, his tone was agreeable, as if he truly wanted to know what more could be done. The problem was, Violet had no answer either.

Sam once again protested Violet's planned overnight stay at the Ashenhurst home. This time he threatened to destroy the watch himself to satisfy the viscount that there was no curse upon it, but Violet eventually soothed him enough to escort her there once more. Other than Josephine Whitton making a brief appearance in a billowing, stained nightdress to ask Violet if she had brought any charms or amulets to protect herself, it was an eerie replay of the previous night. She settled down to a supper tray personally delivered by Mrs. Porter, then relaxed in her chair with a copy of Mr. Collins's *The Woman in White*. She soon regretted having brought along such an eerie title, but Robespierre made an appearance, demanding affection and plopping down on the open pages of her book.

"Yes, Your Highness," she said to the cat, putting the book aside on the table next to her and giving full attention to the fur-shedding feline in her lap. As had happened the previous night, Violet soon found herself nodding off with the cat in her lap. And, once more, she was startled awake in the wee hours by *something*.

"What was that?" she called out to an empty room. She put a hand to her chest, as if that would calm her racing heart. The cat was gone and the table lamp was still burning. She glanced up at the shelf.

It couldn't be.

Violet jumped up to verify that the pocket watch had toppled over. She picked it up gingerly and opened the case. The face wasn't cracked. She held the watch up to her ear. It made no sound.

And it had stopped just after two o'clock. A quick check of her own watch showed that it was, again, around half past two.

What had wakened her? It couldn't have been the watch ceasing to function, which would have been noiseless.

In the middle of the night without even the cat for company, it was easy to imagine there were fiendish spirits in the room with her, shrieking with unholy laughter at having frightened her. Or were they guiding spirits, warning her that another murder was about to occur?

Stop it this instant, Violet Harper, she admonished herself.

What was she to do now? Wake the family? It didn't seem as if there would be any use in that. No, she would settle back down and wait until morning, praying that there wouldn't be any horrific headlines in the newspaper.

This time, though, she put the watch in her lap, spending the predawn hours in exhausted sleeplessness as she stared down at the gold case, willing it to start working again.

The hands remained stuck at seven minutes past two.

Violet delivered the bad news after breakfasting by herself in the sitting room, then being summoned into the viscount's library, where the viscount, his wife, and Miss Whitton offered her triumphant looks. It was a sad but unsurprising reaction.

"I believe the point is proved, Mrs. Harper," Lord Ashenhurst said. "You must remove the watch from here."

"But we do not know yet if—" Violet began, but was interrupted by Mrs. Chase, who entered with a folded newspaper in her hands.

"As you requested, my lord," she said, holding it out to Victor Ashenhurst like a religious offering.

There was utter silence except for the rustling of paper as Ashenhurst opened the newspaper. Even Violet held her breath as she waited to hear the headlines spoken.

The viscount slowly read out loud. "'Baron Newberry found murdered in Bury Street. Scotland Yard baffled.'"

He raised his eyebrow patronizingly at Violet, while the egg she had swallowed a few minutes past curdled unpleasantly in her stomach. Without bothering to read the article itself, he folded it back up and handed it back to the housekeeper, who nodded. She reached to the center of the viscount's desk, lifted the watch, and removed both items from the room as if they were three-day-old fish. Violet returned to sitting wordlessly with her hands in her lap, while Miss Whitton chose this moment to start ranting.

"No one listens to me when I warn of the danger," she cried, her voice rising on the word *danger*. "I don't know why my sister thought *you* could prevent anything by being here. You are part of the problem. The danger increases with every minute that you are in the house. You must go." Once more, Lady Ashenhurst's sister, like a ghost from some unknown Christmas era, was raising her finger and pointing accusingly at Violet.

The most mangled of corpses couldn't shake Violet's composure, but this raving woman set her scalp to tingling. Perhaps it was time to consider proffering her final bill and performing a Pontius Pilate on this case.

"My sister means no offense, Mrs. Harper," Lady Ashenhurst said. "Her constitution is delicate and we are all a bit on edge."

"The only edge any of us will witness is that on a knife," Miss Whitton said, her eyes welling with fanatical tears. "He is bound to come for someone in this household. How could he not, when the damage has already been wreaked so close by?"

"Enough, Josephine," Lord Ashenhurst commanded in the tone that he normally reserved for Lucius. He must have discreetly pulled a bell cord while Miss Whitton was babbling, for Mrs. Chase returned once more, and he instructed the housekeeper to ensure his sister-in-law received some sort of sedative and that she be taken into the rear garden to sit in the sun for a while.

Before obeying her master, Mrs. Chase held up a tiny package wrapped tightly in plain paper with string crisscrossing it myriad times as though it were restraining a violent prisoner. She handed it to Violet. With a quick glance at the viscount, Violet realized that the viscount was not going to permit her to leave his home without the offending watch in her possession.

Very well then. She would quit the Ashenhurst family and all of its silliness, and leave Mr. Hurst to solve the murders. Anyway, it was high time Violet returned to her normal undertaking duties in the community.

Standing on the walkway at the bottom of the stairs was a woman, who stared intently as Violet descended the stairs. She was tall, regal, and well dressed. She had clearly been a great beauty in her youth, but at the moment appeared ravaged by whatever tragedies the years had foisted upon her. Her auburn hair was heavily streaked with silver, and although her demeanor bore the hallmarks of aristocracy, she couldn't quite disguise an air of heavy melancholy.

As Violet reached the street, the woman pulled her expensive cloak tightly around her, as if protecting herself not so much from the weather but from whatever she was about to do. "You are the undertaker?" the woman asked without preamble.

"I am Violet Harper, yes," Violet said. "May I help you?"

"Come with me," the woman said, turning on her heel with the aristocratic expectation that Violet would naturally follow. Violet stayed rooted to her spot for only a moment, as curiosity quickly overcame any fear she might have. She had encountered a female killer before, but this lady didn't strike her as particularly threatening.

They didn't have far to go. The woman threaded her way across the street to a town house across from the Ashenhursts'. A footman opened the door, and the woman shrugged off her cloak into the man's arms while instructing him to bring refreshments to the parlor straightaway. After Violet also surrendered her own cloak, the woman led her into a parlor of the same design as the Ashenhursts' and Mr. Dye's, except that this one felt as though she were stepping back into a previous century. Unlike in the homes of her neighbors, whose windows were swathed with heavy draperies to keep out the smuts and fog that perpetually blanketed London, this home's curtains were pulled back, resulting in bright sunlight flooding the room. So used to dimly lit parlors was Violet that she found herself squinting against the glare.

Decorated in robin's-egg blue and peach and cream, the parlor was full of delicately carved French furniture. Marie Antoinette would have felt quite at home holding a card party here. Perhaps the home had been in the woman's family for a long time without there ever being a decor change. Of course, that wasn't possible, since the homes in this fashionable area were quite new. Maybe she collected antiques. Or perhaps she simply preferred French style, or was—

"Sit, please," the woman commanded. Violet complied, settling herself on a pale-blue damask-covered chair.

"I am Lady Pintwood." This, too, was almost a command, as if there were some expected reaction Violet should have.

"Yes, my lady," she replied, unsure what else to do.

The woman shook her head in irritation. "I am Sir Oliver Pintwood's widow."

Her ladyship clearly expected Violet to understand her importance, but even an undertaker who dealt with all classes of society could not be expected to know the names and relationships of every aristocrat who wintered in London.

Thankfully, the maid appeared with a tray of tea and cakes. It was entirely too early in the day for this afternoon repast, and

Violet was still full from her breakfast repast at the Ashenhursts'. However, as her gaze raked across the tempting array of glazed and buttered confections, she decided that perhaps she still had a bit more room left. After all, it wouldn't do to insult her hostess.

Violet steadied the saucer and cup of tea in her lap. A tiny rounded table at her elbow bore the weight of her pastry-laden plate.

Once the maid was gone, Violet offered the only reaction she could. "I am terribly sorry for your loss, my lady."

The baroness sniffed. "My husband, until he died just over a year ago, was an assistant to Sir George Biddell Airy. Since you are obviously not aware of who Sir George is if you don't know my late husband's position, I will tell you that Sir George is the Astronomer Royal. He is very important to the queen's government, and through him I was able to secure a widow's pension from Her Majesty. I do not intend to jeopardize that pension."

Violet took a nibble of cake while waiting to hear what this had to do with her, a mere undertaker. Heavens, but the orange peel sent a burst of tangy sweetness into her mouth. Wonderful. Even more wonderful was that Lady Pintwood was thankfully ready to put Violet out of her confused state.

"You must understand, I have a reputation to protect, both as the widow of a baronet and as someone who is, shall we say, *reliant* on the generosity of others. If it were to get out that I was even remotely embroiled in something as salacious as these terrible murders, I might be branded as, shall we say, troublesome. I cannot risk losing that goodwill. Yet, I lie awake at night, worried that I will be murdered in my bed. I have been at a loss as to what to do until now."

Violet stopped in midchew. Did this woman have important knowledge about the murders in the neighborhood? Surely it didn't have anything to do with members of the queen's government? She quickly swallowed, took a sip of tea to wash it all down, and said, "Is there a way in which I can help you, my lady?"

The baroness's lips finally relaxed into what passed for a smile on her face. "That is precisely why I have asked you here, Mrs. Harper. I believe you are trustworthy, as you carry the secrets of the dead about you all of the time, do you not?"

Violet set her teacup down in its saucer. "My lady, it can hardly be said that the dead have conversations with me."

Lady Pintwood laughed without mirth. "True enough. Nevertheless, I have looked into your dealings, and your reputation appears to be spotless, much like mine. Therefore, I am going to entrust you with some knowledge and rely on you to use the information appropriately to ensure the culprit is caught."

Violet held her breath. Did Lady Pintwood know who the killer was? If so, Violet intended to march straight to Scotland Yard to tell Mr. Hurst.

The baroness dropped her voice, even though they were alone behind closed doors. "I have been watching, you understand. I frequently cannot sleep at night, and so I sit at my bedchamber window, which overlooks the street."

If her bedchamber was anything like this parlor, it had largely exposed windows. That could only mean it wouldn't be terribly difficult for the baroness to notice outside activities, which would be illuminated by the gaslight of the streetlamps.

Violet set her teacup next to her plate, which was now devoid of anything except crumbs. "And you have witnessed something important," Violet prompted.

"Yes. More than once, I have seen someone exiting the Ashenhurst home in the middle of the night, headed to parts unknown and not returning for hours, sometimes until almost dawn. It is always on the nights in which a new murder is reported."

Violet blinked, unable to register what she was hearing. "But you do not know who it was?"

"It's so difficult to know someone in the winter, isn't it, what with coats and cloaks and boots covering up everyone's forms? No, I cannot be sure who it was."

So Lady Pintwood was implying that someone in the Ashenhurst household was responsible for the murders? It was impossible. The Ashenhursts seemed frightfully upset by what was happening, going so far as to blame a watch for the deaths.

Unless Violet was being misled. But why mislead an undertaker about it? Perhaps they had discovered she was acquainted with Mr. Hurst and hoped that she would clear their name. How, though, did Miss Whitton's wild rantings figure into everything? Was she, too, a dupe, or was she making a pretense to madness with the help of the family and its servants?

You carry the secrets of the dead about you all of the time, don't you?

Was Violet unknowingly carrying the secrets of the living as well?

Lady Pintwood concluded mildly with, "And so now I simply want you to take care that this messy business goes away so I can get about my own life in peace. Would you like another cake?" The baroness picked up the serving utensil and held it over the tiered plate.

It was remarkable how the aristocracy could cover their feelings through adherence to societal niceties. How could the woman contemplate eating more sweets after having delivered such ghastly news? However, Violet kept her calm. "Yes, my lady. A slice of the glazed orange cake, if you please."

The baroness's hand skipped over the two remaining pieces of the orange cake, and instead she slid the server under a slice of sugar-dusted sponge cake and put it on Violet's plate. Had Lady Pintwood deliberately snubbed Violet's choice? Why would she do something so petty after having asked her to carry out a mission for her that would save the woman's pension?

Violet Harper would never be able to understand society. She chose to say nothing, and instead bit into the sponge, which was as delicious as the orange cake. Lady Pintwood spoke of inconsequential pleasantries until Violet had finished the treat, at which point the baroness stood, clearly indicating that their meeting was at an end.

Violet waited in the entry hallway for the maid to retrieve her cloak. As she stood there, she noticed that the morning mail delivery had already been made. A lone letter rested on a silver salver atop an oblong table running along the wall. Violet glanced surreptitiously at it and noted that it was addressed to Lady Pintwood from "The Right Honorable William Gladstone." Mr. Gladstone was not only the prime minister, but First Lord of the Treasury, which gave credence to Lady Pintwood's claim that she was receiving the benevolence of some sort of government pension.

Did that really matter, though, in determining the truthfulness of Lady Pintwood's accusation of the Ashenhurst family? She might be receiving a pension at the queen's behest, but the viscount was also a favorite of Her Majesty. Did the murders have something to do with both the Ashenhursts and the queen?

Her cloak was duly delivered, and Violet went down the stairs into the street to find the nearest taxi stand.

It sickened her to think that the situation could have anything to do with Queen Victoria, for whom Violet had personally done some work. The queen was temperamental, dramatic, and grief-obsessed, but surely she had no tendencies toward evil.

Could the same be said of all the men who worked in Her Majesty's government? Violet shook her head as a driver helped her into his hack. The carriage rumbled off, springs creaking, as she contemplated the idea. No, it was foolish. The men who had been murdered had little in common, and nearly nothing to do with parliamentary affairs.

So far as she knew. Perhaps she needed to visit Mr. Hurst again.

"What you are suggesting is madness," Hurst proclaimed, although Violet didn't sense any true antipathy for her in his voice.

"I know," she agreed, her hands folded around her reticule in her lap as she sat at a round oak table with Mr. Hurst and Mr. Pratt. Outside the closed door was the bustle of Scotland Yard and its fledgling detective force, but in here it had been reasonably quiet as Violet laid out for the detectives what had happened both with the stopped watch and her talk with Lady Pintwood.

"Do you have an opinion on which of the household members it could possibly be?" Hurst asked. "I can't round them up en famille and toss them all into Newgate. A bit of detail from Lady Pintwood would be helpful. 'Someone from the house' isn't exactly a lead."

Before Violet could say anything further, there was a sharp rap at the door. Whoever was there didn't wait for a reply but opened the door immediately. It was Commissioner Henderson, who had been working diligently to develop a serious detective force at Scotland Yard for the better part of a year now. "Inspector, may I see you for a moment?"

Hurst lumbered out of his chair and followed his superior, leaving Violet and Pratt alone for a few minutes.

"Mr. Hurst's humor has improved greatly the past couple of days," Pratt said, giving her a wink. "Your talk with him was just the thing to chip away at his stony heart."

"Well, I suppose one day soon you may find yourself standing next to him on the altar," Violet said, smiling.

"No doubt you and I will both be standing at the altar with them. How do you imagine it will be to have Mr. Hurst as practically a brother-in—"

Hurst returned at that moment, silencing any further conversation. He fell back into his chair with a grunt. "Bad news. Another body has been found in St. James's. And this time it's someone quite important so we are due for some serious scandal. The Earl of Wyville is well known here at the Yard for sending us complaints for everything from barking dogs to noisy children. A bit of a rotter, but many of these lords are. We will need to go interview his household."

Violet instinctively clutched her bag as though it meant to fly off on its own. "But that means…" She stopped.

"Means what, Mrs. Harper?" Hurst asked.

"The watch. It stopped, and I took it away with me, so it wasn't able to stop again for this murder."

"Mrs. Harper, do you hear yourself?" Hurst said, not unkindly.

She shook her head. "You are absolutely right. This watch is nothing but a mechanical bauble and has nothing to do with the evil men do." Violet cleared her throat as she gathered her thoughts again. "So I guess that what the victims all have in common was the way they were attacked, with a coshing to the head."

Hurst shrugged. "That's simply a commonality in the killer's methods. What is different is that Wyville has been killed mere hours after Baron Newberry. Our killer seems to be accelerating his activities."

The three were silent for a time, then Violet asked, "I recall that Mr. Fitzworth made his money in business. Remind me again how he came by his fortune, exactly?"

Pratt flipped through the worn pages of his journal. "Let me see. Yes, here it is. Mr. Fitzworth had investments in speculative construction in addition to cotton machinery."

Violet nodded as the germ of an idea took root. "And Sir Holland had entered the aristocratic ranks with largess from the royal purse. Other than with the hospital, do you know how Mr. Fitzworth's money was invested?"

Pratt gave her a bewildered look but perused his notes again. "His daughter told us he had a variety of philanthropic projects: the hospital, the Society for the Relief of the Homeless Poor, the Asylum for Fatherless Children, the Governesses' Home for the Unemployed, and even the Temporary Home for Lost and Starving Dogs."

"Very respectable, don't you think?" Violet said.

Hurst looked even more puzzled than his compatriot. "What of it, Mrs. Harper? Do you think someone murdered Sir Holland because he behaved honorably?"

"No, I'm saying he died because he considered *himself* to be honorable."

"Woman, what in heaven's name are you talking about?"

Hurst said, a touch of impatience now shading his voice as he leaned forward across the table. "I have another murder to investigate. If you know something, tell me."

Violet rose, still clutching her reticule containing the wrapped watch. "Forgive me, sir, I don't wish to say any more, in case I have missed the mark. I must check one more thing, then I believe I will be delivering the name of a murderer to you."

Hurst and Pratt stared openmouthed as Violet hurriedly left, but she paid no attention. Her sole focus was on returning to the Ashenhurst home.

CHAPTER 5

First, though, she went to the Anthony Jarrett clockmaker's shop. It was an old place located inside the City, the part of London where the old Worshipful Company of Clockmakers used to hold far more sway as a trade association than it did now in modern times.

The stooped, bespectacled owner grumbled at Violet's insistence that the repair of the pocket watch be immediate. Nonetheless, he opened the case and went directly to work on it.

"Hmm. Seems to have been demagnetized," he muttered to himself as if he had already forgotten Violet was still there. "How did that happen? Highly unusual. Yes, highly unusual."

To Violet, though, it made perfect sense and gave her one more piece to fit into the puzzle that was breathtakingly simple now that she knew exactly the picture to be formed.

She practically wore a hole through the floor, pacing back and forth in front of the man's elevated workbench while he ignored her. He continued his painstaking repair work, peering down at the watch and its parts through a large magnifying glass held in a wooden stand.

Finally, he was done. Refusing his offer to polish up the case, Violet hurriedly passed coins to him and slid the watch back into her reticule.

The taxi ride back to St. James's didn't take long but felt interminable, and Violet's taut nerves threatened to undo her.

Especially when she realized that Sam did not yet know that she wasn't coming home at all today. She would have to find a boy to take a message to him.

In contradiction to her usual policy, Violet entered via the servants' entrance, much to the surprise of Mrs. Porter, who stood over a large circle of flattened dough. Flour dusted the woman's nose and chin as she pushed a rolling pin back and forth over the beginnings of a delectable pie crust in the middle of the kitchen table.

"Mrs. Harper," she said, setting the rolling pin aside and wiping her hands on her apron. "If you're here to speak with his lordship or her ladyship, it's best if you enter by—"

"I will, but I thought perhaps I might ask you a few questions first."

"Me?" The cook's voice cracked in outright surprise.

Violet nodded. "You could be very helpful in assisting me to figure out the strange goings-on in the neighborhood. May I?" She indicated a chair on the other side of the worktable from where Mrs. Porter stood.

The cook whisked away her apron and hung it on a wall hook. "Of course, where are my manners?"

She and Violet sat down across from each other overlooking the unfinished pie crust. The cook maintained an even expression, but her trembling hands gave away her nerves.

"Mrs. Porter, when you feed the family, do you frequently serve Miss Whitton in her chamber, or does she typically take her meals with the family?"

The cook seemed puzzled by Violet's question. "Miss Whitton? Well, I suppose it depends upon whether she is…doing poorly, if you understand my meaning. In those spells, she is in her bedchamber quite a bit. But I make sure she gets the exact same nutritious food as the rest of the family. I would never—"

Violet held up a hand. "I'm sure you are most conscientious. And when Miss Whitton feels poorly, as you say, does she spend her time alone, or does someone sit with her? Her sister, perhaps? The housekeeper? Someone else?"

The cook's frown deepened in confusion. "Why, I suppose Mrs. Chase is with her the most. Miss Whitton responds to the sound of the housekeeper's voice, you know. It calms her. But—how can that have anything to do with these awful murders, madam?"

Unfortunately, this was not the right moment to share what Miss Whitton's role was in the events unfolding in St. James's.

"I'm afraid that only time can tell us, Mrs. Porter."

With that, Violet departed back out the servants' entrance and went to the front door. Maisie ushered her to Mrs. Chase, who addressed Violet with a brisk "Mrs. Harper, I thought your work was finished here."

"Not quite," she replied. "I should like to speak with Lord or Lady Ashenhurst, if they are at home."

Fifteen minutes later, Violet faced the Ashenhursts once more in the parlor. She explained that she had had the pocket watch repaired and wanted to test it on the shelf one more time before making an accusation.

"Whom do you suspect?" Lord Ashenhurst demanded.

Violet shook her head. "I'd rather not say, my lord, in the unlikely event that I am wrong."

A look passed between the couple, then Ashenhurst nodded. "Very well, as you wish."

"Thank you. First, though, may I impose upon someone in your household to take a message to my husband, explaining that I will not be home again this evening?"

Apparently obsessed with curiosity, Lord and Lady Ashenhurst chose to remain with Violet this time as she settled in for her night's vigil over the watch. However, after two hours of uncomfortable silence in which the three of them sat studiously avoiding each other's gazes, the Ashenhursts left Violet alone in the room, much to her great relief.

The only problem was that with the Ashenhursts in the room, she did not feel sleepy. Now with them gone, it was difficult to focus on the words as she flipped idly through her novel. Soon, though, she had difficulty keeping her head from lolling forward.

The next thing she knew, she was bolting straight up in her chair because of a loud noise. Once more, her heart threatened to explode from her chest in shock and fear.

What was that?

Violet looked around wildly. Her book had fallen from her lap to the floor. Had that been the noise that awakened her? Regardless, she knew what she needed to do next. Rising quickly from her chair, she went to the shelf upon which the watch sat and removed it.

It had stopped. And Violet knew with certainty that it hadn't been the falling book that woke her out of her sleep. Dashing to the staircase, she shouted up to the next floor with what she knew were unintelligible instructions, but it was enough that she heard stirring within the household. Picking up her skirts, she ran hastily down the stairs to the front door. She cursed in frustration at the complicated set of locks, but managed to break herself out without the housekeeper's help.

As she fled out to the stoop and down the steps, she heard Mrs. Chase calling out behind her, but ignored the housekeeper's admonishments. At the bottom of the steps, Violet saw exactly the person whom she expected to see, outlined in the glow of the hissing gas streetlamp.

Hutton, Edgar Dye's servant.

The man was bundled up, his shoulders hunched and his hands buried in the pockets of his wool overcoat. He was striding away from his master's home east on Arlington Street, his frozen breath making visible puffs in the air.

Hoping that Lord Ashenhurst would soon be behind her,

Violet pursued the valet. "Mr. Hutton!" she called out. "Sir, please stop!"

She caught up to him, breathless, and grabbed his arm. She yanked on it, and as his hand came out of its pocket, something in a mangled shape dropped from his palm to the ground with a thud. Before Hutton could react, Violet bent down, scooped up the item, and took several steps backward away from the man.

Lord and Lady Ashenhurst had by now exited their home, looking disheveled and decidedly unaristocratic in their dressing gowns covered with cloaks. "What the devil are you doing with this man, Mrs. Harper?" Victor Ashenhurst demanded as he and his wife came to a halt.

"I have found a murderer for you," she replied calmly, holding up the item she had picked up.

"What are you talking about?" Hutton said, clearing his throat. "I am just taking a late-night walk. I do this often."

The commotion was enough to alert the neighborhood residents, as Lady Pintwood was now scurrying out into the street, as were the Baron Claybrook, Josephine Whitton, and most of the Ashenhurst staff, including Miss Froste. Edgar Dye even appeared, swathed in scarves, one hand clutching the handrail as he cautiously made his way down the steps.

Hutton was huffing loudly. "What is the meaning of this, Mrs. Harper? Why is a woman out in the streets in the middle of the night? You have unnecessarily disturbed my master. Sir, you cannot be out here. You'll catch your death." The servant began fussing with Dye's scarves as Dye joined the group, openly confused and disoriented.

Violet ignored him. "I am most glad to have found you, Mr. Hutton, since now justice can be served."

"Justice? For what?" The servant now held Dye's elbow in one hand as if to guide his ailing employer back to the house.

"My apologies, but you cannot return inside," Violet said, holding up a hand.

"Good Lord," Victor Ashenhurst exclaimed. "It's like sitting on an ice block out here. I think we all need to go inside. Mrs. Porter, perhaps some tea is in order?" He also signaled to his own valet, Vernon, who ran off to do his bidding.

The cook, as hastily dressed as everyone else, scurried back down to the servants' entrance of the Ashenhurst home. "Well, shall we all repair to the parlor to hear what the eminent Mrs. Harper has to say?" Lord Ashenhurst said, his tone a command, not a question.

Hutton made another feeble attempt to take his master back to his own home, but Lord Ashenhurst clapped a hand on Dye's shoulder, nearly knocking the man over. "Women and their notions, eh?" he said, guiding the man out of his servant's grasp.

With most of the Ashenhurst staff surrounding him, Hutton reluctantly followed.

Eventually everyone was ensconced in the parlor with cups of tea. While servants aligned themselves in front of the double doors, the women—Josephine Whitton, Lady Ashenhurst, and Lady Pintwood—sat huddled together on a settee as if drawing strength from one another. The men stood in various places about the room, except for Edgar Dye, who sat hunched in a chair with Hutton standing behind him. *Did Mr. Hutton think the chair offered protection?*

Even young Lucius Ashenhurst was present, calm for once as he leaned against Miss Froste and rubbed sleep out of his eyes.

Victor Ashenhurst was the only one without tea, instead nursing a crystal goblet full of a ruby-red drink. "Perhaps you can now explain that little lump in your hand, Mrs. Harper," he suggested, waving the glass in her direction with his usual imperiousness and narrowly avoiding splashing some of it out.

Violet looked down, having forgotten that she was still clutching it. From her position in the center of the room, she now held it up for everyone to see. It resembled a black sponge, full of holes and crusted with what looked like dirt, but what Violet knew to be blood.

"Why, it's a silly little rock," Lady Pintwood said. "Are we here to study stones?"

Violet carried the item over to where Lady Pintwood sat with the other women and showed it to her. Lady Pintwood gasped in recognition. "Wait a moment. That looks like one of the meteorites my husband collected. He was the Royal Astronomer's assistant, you know," she stated for the assembly's benefit.

"Indeed," Violet said. "No doubt if you were to check your late husband's collection cabinet, you would find one to be missing."

Lady Pintwood put a hand to her throat, as if aghast at the idea that a stranger had been in her home unbidden.

"Or perhaps, my lady," Violet continued as she returned to the center of the room. "You would not notice that it was missing, am I right?"

Lady Pintwood frowned. "I do not know what you are implying, Mrs. Harper, but I am sure it is improper. My husband was—"

"Assistant to the Royal Astronomer. Yes, my lady, I know. I must say, I found it odd that you would approach me in the street and invite me over so that you could inform me of having witnessed someone from the Ashenhurst home leaving in the middle of the night. Why were you telling me instead of going to the police? You claimed you were trying to preserve your pension, but I think perhaps you were afraid of exposing someone in the viscount's family and having his lordship know it was you who did so."

At that, Victor Ashenhurst gulped the remainder of his drink and slammed the glass down on the fireplace mantel, causing his wife to jump nervously in her seat. "You are attempting to accuse someone in my household?" he demanded of Lady Pintwood. Then he immediately turned to his wife, whose expression was now ashen. "I knew we should have never let that lunatic sister of yours live here. If she has ruined my good name—"

"Please, my lord," Violet interrupted quietly. "If I may continue?"

Ashenhurst grunted at her but remained silent otherwise.

"What I realized later is that although Lady Pintwood had seen *something*, she was mistaken in what it was. It was her serving of cake that made me realize it, but only much later. She offered me a second helping and I requested the orange, but she served me sponge instead. At first I thought it was a deliberate slight, but now I know it is that Lady Pintwood has difficulty with her vision, is that not so?" Violet looked questioningly at the lady.

"Well, I-I am sure I never… Oh, what of it, Mrs. Harper?" Lady Pintwood's tone was an attempt to be belligerent, but Violet heard great fear in it.

"Do not worry, my lady, I believe your pension to be safe," she said. "You made me realize something important. Because of your troublesome eyesight, you did not recognize that what you witnessed at night was not someone exiting the Ashenhurst household, but someone exiting Mr. Dye's home."

"Hah!" Miss Whitton interjected, lifting a finger and pointing in her spectral way at Lady Pintwood. "Your name is Pintwood. I hear your friends call you 'Pinty,' but we should all call you Squinty." She dissolved into cackles, but no one else laughed and the tension remained high in the room.

Violet held up a hand to stop her. "As for you, Miss Whitton, you were also mistaken in your visions of spirits and demons and such. You believed yourself to be seeing one thing, but you were actually witnessing something else."

Miss Whitton took umbrage. "I am very sensitive to the spirits and have seen them on many occasions."

Violet shook her head gently at the poor woman. "I am afraid not, Miss Whitton. Here is what you have actually seen." She moved to stand next to Hutton. "If someone could extinguish the lamps, please?"

There was shuffling as a couple of servants went to the two lamps in the room and lowered the wicks. The darkened room resulted in gasps as there appeared to be a small, glowing spirit hovering next to Violet.

"Bring the lights back up," she said.

As the lamplight slowly increased, illuminating the room, there were yet more exclamations and wheezes. For Violet stood next to Hutton, with Edgar Dye's scarves in one hand and the meteorite in the other. It was upon Dye though, that everyone's attention was transfixed. What lay beneath his ever-present scarves was probably more horrifying than anyone in the room had ever seen.

The left side of Dye's jaw was partially eaten away, revealing teeth, gum, and tongue, all in deplorable condition. Pus drained from an opening inside his rotting flesh, and there was an ethereal glow emanating from the gaping hole.

"This is what Miss Whitton saw from her window, understandably believing she was seeing a ghostly spirit. For Mr. Dye, owner of a matchworks factory, is the unfortunate victim of phossy jaw, the result of working so closely with white phosphorous. I'm sure many of his workers suffer from it, as well."

No one else in the room even blinked, much less moved, as Violet continued unraveling the tale.

"Mr. Dye has had great success in his life, but also great tragedy. Another lamentable side effect of phossy jaw is mental deterioration, and I believe that Mr. Dye began to blame others for his tragedies. Not everyone accepted his rise in economic stature as worthy of entry into this neighborhood of pedigrees and royal appointments."

Lord and Lady Ashenhurst, along with Lady Pintwood and Baron Claybrook, turned their gazes away uneasily.

"Other than thinking the killings to be conducted by some random madman, I could come up with nothing to link them together, until I remembered the baron commenting to me that Lord Ashenhurst himself was a bit of an upstart," Violet said. Lord Ashenhurst whipped a dark, pointed look around at Claybrook, who held his chin up defiantly.

"Regrettably, Mr. Dye decided to do something about those who looked down upon him." Violet handed the scarves back to Hutton, who immediately began wrapping them around his employer once more. For his part, Dye no longer appeared to be confused, as though he had drifted momentarily back into reality.

"And so, sir," she said, turning to face the seated factory owner, "you have been murdering your neighbors in some sort of grotesque revenge scheme for their incivilities toward you. No doubt there are people in this room who would have soon felt the cold, hard animus of your weapon." She hefted the meteorite in her hand again. Violet knew that meteorites were mostly found in deserts, but no doubt rock collectors were able to obtain just about anything from anywhere via the Royal Mail system.

"But surely that feeble creature could not have beaten anyone to death with such a small rock," Lady Ashenhurst protested.

"Never underestimate the power of a deranged person," Violet said. "He could and he did. He was also most skilled at deflecting suspicion from himself, practically without knowing he was doing it. For example, I should have caught him once before, when we found him outside, bleeding. I believe he was befuddled about what had happened to him, because he had simply fallen in the street and hit his head while on his way out to commit mayhem. But it appeared as though he, too, had been attacked, thus throwing any suspicion away from him."

"Mrs. Harper, you impugn my employer..." Hutton began defensively, and was met with derision by everyone else present. To his credit, he continued to stand resolutely behind Dye's chair, while his master stared ahead, his lips tightly compressed.

"But...what about the watch?" Mrs. Chase asked timidly. "Wasn't it the cause of everything?"

Miss Whitton bobbed her head up and down in avid agreement. "It caused the spirits to make their appearance." Apparently Violet's revelation of Mr. Dye's condition had no impact on her opinion.

"Yes," Violet said. "Although I was skeptical about my lord and my lady in their certainty that the watch was bringing about the murders, it turned out that the timepiece was an integral part of the events that transpired. At first, I thought perhaps Lucius was to blame. He was fascinated with the watch, and it seemed likely that he was climbing up on furniture and taking it down to play with it and thus breaking it.

"I even thought that Miss Froste had some sort of grudge against the Ashenhursts that I didn't understand, and was orchestrating Lucius's activities. But I realized that poor Miss Froste is like every other put-upon governess, simply trying to manage her young charge with little gratitude from her employers and no respect from the servants."

Miss Froste blushed furiously at Violet's words.

Hutton broke his silence. "Miss Froste, you deserve the utmost respect and kindness. How could someone not recognize your innate gentleness and sweet disposition?"

Miss Froste blushed even more, the pink reaching from her neck up to her temples.

Once more, Violet held up the rock in her hand. "No, in a strange way, this meteorite really *was* the harbinger of the murders. You see, when Mr. Dye would exit his home to seek out his next victim, his murder weapon was demagnetizing the pocket watch as he stumbled and stomped down his stairs, which is directly on the other side of this room where the watch resided on the wall. When it demagnetized, it stopped. Of course, Mr. Dye's victim was within an hour of death by that point, hence why the watch seemed to be predicting the deaths."

"Good Lord, man," Victor Ashenhurst said forcefully to Edgar Dye. "Have you no idea what you've put my family through? My peerage is precariously new. You might have destroyed it."

"Yes," Violet said. "There is also the matter of Mr. Dye having murdered four people."

"Er, yes," Ashenhurst said, taking his glass off the mantel and refilling it from a crystal decanter on a side table. "There is also that."

Violet turned her attention back to Dye. "Everything I have said is true, is it not, sir?"

Dye slowly turned his head toward Violet and smiled gently at her. "Of course, dear lady. The sewer rats who live here in this neighborhood have done nothing but mock me for not entering society in the proper way, and it was unreasonable to expect that I could tolerate it any longer. Anyone in my position would have done the same thing. If we are quite done now, it's late, and I must be on my way. I still have much to accomplish before dawn."

Violet hardly knew what to say. She was saved from responding by Dye's valet, who sighed as he addressed the room. "You must understand, my master has been unwell for some years now, both in body and mind. It was the death of his wife and child, you see…" Hutton spread his hands in supplication.

"I had my suspicions that Mr. Dye might be behind the murders, what with his secret late-night departures and all, but wasn't entirely sure. When I discovered the meteorite in his study yesterday, stained with what I was certain was blood, well, I quite lost my head over what to do. Foolishly, I decided to head out in the middle of the night myself, hoping that if I disposed of the meteorite in St. James's Park lake, he might forget about it and thus forget about his evil intentions. He has done wrong, I know, but he has been a kind employer to me. I hated the thought of seeing him at the end of a hangman's rope and thought that if I could just *stop* him, all would be well. But now he will meet a terrible fate, and I am to blame. Not only for trying to cover his crimes, but for not recognizing them from the start."

"Now, now, Hutton," Dye said, seemingly oblivious to the severity of his own situation. "You mustn't take this too hard. When I finish explaining my circumstances to the judge, he will understand and we will be back to normal by supper."

"Mr. Dye," Violet said, "I'm not sure you truly recognize—"

She didn't finish her sentence, for Vernon had now arrived with Hurst and Pratt in tow.

"We got word from Lord Ashenhurst's valet that we were needed," Hurst stated directly to Violet.

She quickly apprised the detectives of what had transpired. Hutton made a last-minute attempt to have them arrest him in his master's stead, to save the ailing man from the cruelty of what his trial and execution would entail. He even argued that his employer was not long for the world anyway, so why waste time with a trial?

Seeming to sense the servant's deep loyalty, Hurst surprised Violet with his gentle approach. "Your wish is admirable, sir, but Mr. Dye will be needing your care from outside of Newgate until after his trial, won't he? If you are arrested, who will watch over him?"

Violet was once more left in wonder when Hutton nodded, satisfied with Hurst's logic.

Dye, though, was confused when Pratt produced a set of handcuffs and requested the man's wrists.

"Wait," Hutton said. "My master is not well, as you know." He shot Hurst a pleading look. "You will allow me to give him a dose of his tonic, to prepare him for the hours ahead?"

Hurst nodded his approval, and Hutton pulled a brown bottle and a spoon from his pocket. Doubtless the man carried all sorts of remedies on him for attending to his master. "Here you are, sir," Hutton said, unstoppering the bottle, pouring a reddish-brown liquid into the spoon, and offering it to Dye. Violet assumed the medicine was laudanum, given its color and widespread use for various ailments.

Edgar Dye eyed the spoon uneasily, then pursed his lips, and Violet wasn't sure if he was refusing the medicine or contemplating his dire immediate future. Astonishingly, though, Dye pushed away the spoon, sending the laudanum splashing onto the Turkish carpet. Dye then yanked the brown bottle away from his servant and put it to his lips, tilting his head back and swallowing the entire contents before anyone in the room could react to what he had done.

"Mr. Dye!" Violet exclaimed. If the medicine was indeed laudanum, an adult could overdose with just a few tablespoons of the opium-alcohol compound. The man had surely just sealed his own demise.

Sure enough, within moments, the ailing Mr. Dye's pupils began to constrict, and he put up a fist, weakly beating against his own chest as the laudanum bottle joined the spoon on the carpet. "Cannot. Breathe." Dye gasped and wheezed as though he were already in the throes of a death rattle. It confirmed Violet's opinion that he had consumed an enormous quantity of laudanum.

Everyone in the room seemed gripped by paralysis at the gruesome scene playing out before them. Violet sprang into action. Edgar Dye might be a foolish, unthinking killer, but his mind and body were diseased, and he would soon be in need of her help.

"Help me," she commanded Hurst and Pratt. "Carry him to the settee and lay him on it." The women sitting on it scattered as Violet issued her instructions and the detectives lifted Dye from his chair.

"See here, I strongly object to this," Victor Ashenhurst said. "It is one thing to learn one has a murderer in one's home; it is quite another to have him dy—"

"Silence!" Violet snapped. "If this troubles you, your lordship, please repair to your library until all is resolved."

Ashenhurst's mouth hung slackly open for several moments, then closed abruptly. He apparently decided that despite how distasteful the spectacle before him was, it was certainly not to be missed. Even Miss Whitton was enraptured, her knuckles white as she gripped the back of a chair while watching Dye gulp futilely for breath.

Violet went to work, loosening the man's scarf, jacket, waistcoat, tie, and shirt to give him as much air as possible. It was of no use, though, as within moments Dye had taken his last rattling wheeze, and now stared at her blankly.

She glanced at Hutton, who wore an expression of relief. She wondered if he had produced the laudanum in hopes that his employer would overdose on it, thus saving Dye from a trial and imprisonment. If true, should she admire Hutton's valiant efforts, or despise him for taking justice into his own hands?

Well, it mattered little now. Edgar Dye had paid for his crimes.

CHAPTER 6

VIOLET WAS HAPPY TO relax in her own armchair several weeks later, as she watched Sam place the antique pocket watch—cleaned and repaired one final time by Mr. Jarrett—in a display case on their fireplace mantel. She had attempted one more time to return the timepiece to Lord and Lady Ashenhurst, but they had refused to have the "accursed pile of gears" in their home, so Violet had decided to keep it as a peculiar memento of the events in St. James's.

Despite the darkness surrounding Edgar Dye's murderous rampage, there had been flickers of joy. Hurst had let Hutton go with a stern lecture, and the valet had soon learned that he was the sole heir of everything his employer owned: his match-works factory, his house, and his entire fortune. With all of that in hand, Hutton had marched next door and asked for Miss Froste's hand in marriage. According to rumor, the former governess had accepted without so much as looking backward at the Ashenhurst family and was now mistress of her own home.

Dye Matchworks was being sold to an industrialist in the north, and presumably Hutton would seek out less dangerous ways to invest his newfound wealth. The residents of St. James's would surely be aghast at the presence of a valet and governess as neighbors, even more so than at a murderous factory owner.

"Well, I don't like it as much as the Margaret Fleming piece I gave you," Sam said. "But it is a nice bit of decor. Now, how about some ice cream?"

Ice cream was Sam's favorite indulgence. Visiting ice cream shops had been a favorite pastime when they were courting, and even now they reminded Violet of those earlier days of Sam's wooing. She agreed to his idea, despite the fact that it was still entirely too cold outside to truly enjoy having the freezing treat melt in their mouths.

They returned two hours later, and Violet was relieved to see that the pocket watch was still ticking. Sam gently chided her for her superstition, and she laughed at herself with him.

Early the next morning, she awoke feeling thirsty. She slid quietly out of bed so as not to waken Sam, whose right arm was slung over his forehead in deep slumber. She padded out to the small parlor in their quarters. Mrs. Wren always left a covered pitcher of water and two glasses on a table next to the sofa, so Violet raised the wick on the lamp to increase the room's light. After pouring herself a glassful, she sat down on the sofa once more to enjoy the quiet.

She was soothed by the rhythmic ticking of the pocket watch, barely discernible from inside its glass dome. Despite the terrible way she had come in possession of it, it was such a beautiful thing. *I am the only master of my time*, the inner case had been inscribed. How devilishly appropriate. It was almost as if—

Wait. What was that?

Nothing. She heard nothing.

Not even the tick of the watch.

Violet hurriedly gulped the rest of her water and put the cup down on the table. She twisted the knob for the wick to go up farther, thus illuminating the room even more, then jumped up and went to the fireplace mantel.

Removing the display dome, she grabbed the watch with both hands and examined it. Violet exhaled the heaviest sigh of her life.

The watch had stopped. Violet's breathing momentarily did, too.

Strange how selective the timepiece seemed to be when it

came to its victims. She remained rooted to her spot for several moments, then lectured herself about all of the many reasons for the watch to stop; most likely because it was very old and had spent thirty years buried underground and was probably a lost cause to fix properly.

An hour later, nearby church bells tolled a death knell.

Violet stood in front of the shop in Bond Street, reading the sign.

The Raven's Nest
Fine Antique Furniture, Clocks, Weapons
Charles Corbett, Proprietor

This seemed as good a place as any. Violet Harper was not one for superstitious nonsense, except for those traditions that brought comfort to mourners. However, this watch spooked even her.

Violet had hardly been able to wait for London's busy shops to open. After Sam had awakened and she had explained what had happened, she had dashed out with the watch in her reticule to take care of the pocket watch once and for all.

"Perhaps someone else will have better luck with you," Violet muttered at her reticule, hoping no one nearby had heard her, since she surely sounded like a madwoman.

She went into the shop, which contained only one other customer, a middle-aged man intently examining a set of peacock-blue shrub glasses, labeled "Georgian, ca. 1807—Glasgow." The tinkling of the bells tied to the inner knob brought an elderly man out from a back room. He looked worn and musty enough to compete with his merchandise for age, but he offered Violet a welcoming smile and introduced himself as Charles Corbett.

Violet produced the pocket watch, which the shopkeeper pounced upon, admiring its excellent condition and fancy engraving, then removing the outer case and even reading the inscription aloud. Violet explained that the watch had a tendency to stop at unfortunate moments, but Mr. Corbett waved away her explanations. He proceeded to remove the cock cover as well and drew in a sharp breath before showing it to Violet.

On the actual inner timepiece was a finely engraved mermaid. Despite how anxious she was to be rid of the watch, Violet couldn't help but admire the artisan who had done the work.

A bargain was struck between her and the antiques dealer, and Corbett disappeared between a pair of pale-green and gold brocade curtains into the rear of his shop to retrieve money for Violet while she waited at the counter.

As she waited, the other store patron approached her and introduced himself as Theodore Beecham. He was tall and swarthy, with the thickest eyebrows Violet had ever seen. Those eyebrows sat atop heavily lidded eyes, which seemed to look at her with avarice. She soon realized, though, that his greed was not for her.

"I heard you speaking with Mr. Corbett," he said. "May I perchance have a look at your timepiece?" He reached out for the components, and Violet could see that the top of his hand was also covered in a mat of dense, black hair.

She nodded to him, and Beecham scrutinized the pocket watch with the same intensity as he had the glasses from Scotland. "Yes, yes, very interesting," he muttered, his ebony brows furrowing together. "I can hardly believe it. It is indeed a miracle. La Sirène makes her appearance again."

What was it about the timepiece that fascinated him so much? What did he understand that Violet didn't?

He finally looked up again and put the watch parts down on the counter. "I should like to make you an offer for the watch."

Violet was taken aback. "Sir, surely you heard me agree to sell it to the shopkeeper."

"I don't care. I'll give you double whatever he offered. I must have it."

Violet shook her head. "Mr. Beecham, first, I have already

accepted Mr. Corbett's offer. Second, if you knew how it seems to—"

Like Corbett, Beecham also waved away Violet's concerns. "I am well aware of how unusual the piece is. I am a regular patron here, and the proprietor won't mind if I—"

Charles Corbett emerged from the rear and immediately frowned as he took in what was happening at the counter. "Beecham, I have already purchased the watch. I plan to add it to my personal collection. Go back to your hot-air ballooning, sir, and leave the serious collecting to me."

"Yes, but it is imperative that I have it. I've offered her twice what you are willing to pay. It cannot simply sit in a velvet-lined box inside a drawer somewhere. It must be in proper use." Beecham's expression was taking on a fervor that was unnerving.

Corbett was not intimidated, though. "Its proper use is in my collection, sir. I have other watches much older and more delicate than this one, and I assure you that I will wind and clean it *properly*."

The proprietor leaned in Violet's direction and added, "Too much time in the air has addled his brain. He's always claiming he knows the dark history of pieces passing through my shop. His way of getting a bargain, but I pay him no mind."

Beecham slammed a fist down on the counter, causing Violet to jump. "You do not understand!" he shouted. "That watch has dark powers that you cannot comprehend, powers of life and death."

Violet stilled, hardly daring to breathe. What was this stranger saying? How could he possibly know anything about an old watch that Violet had plucked out of a grave just over two weeks ago?

But Corbett was unmoved, and Violet could not in good conscience break her bargain with him. Corbett handed her the money, and she turned to leave the shop.

Beecham followed her out, though, whispering to her, "The watch still has one more evil pursuit before its curse can be broken. I will have it in my possession. Corbett just needs to be *convinced*."

Violet shivered and turned to face him, a hundred questions on her tongue, but the man had disappeared into the crowd.

She was only grateful now that the watch had disappeared from her life as well.

Acknowledgments

Putting this anthology together was like fitting together intricate watch parts (forgive the pun). I am particularly grateful to Deb Werksman at Sourcebooks for her enthusiasm for this project, as well as literary agent Kevan Lyon who spearheaded the sale of the project. My own beloved agent, Helen Breitwieser, was instrumental in problem-solving issues and helping to assemble our writing team. My thanks to all of these wonderful players.

About the Author

Christine Trent is the author of the Lady of Ashes historical mystery series about a Victorian-era undertaker, as well as the Florence Nightingale Mysteries series. She has also published three other historical novels. Christine's novels have been translated into Turkish, Polish, and Czech. She writes from her two-story home library, where she lives with her wonderful bookshelf-building husband, five adorable and demanding cats, a large doll collection, entirely too many fountain pens, and more than four thousand catalogued books. Learn more about Christine at christinetrent.com.

Siren's Call

C. S. Harris

CHAPTER 1

New Godwick, Kent, England: June 1944

BLEAK AND ENDLESSLY BATTERED by the wind, Knowles Farm Cottage stood alone on a barren point overlooking a choppy sea. When the young woman left the hedgerow-lined lane to cut across the paddock, she could see the creeper-clad walls of the house and the shed where the major's Morris had stood up on blocks ever since the introduction of petrol rationing. Beyond that stretched nothing but a yawning white void of dense fog.

The field was still muddy from the early morning rain, so that Rachel's Wellingtons made squishing noises and sent up a pungent odor of old sheep droppings with each step. As she drew nearer the cliffs, a gust of cold, brine-laden wind hit her, and she turned up the collar of her mackintosh, her eyes narrowing as she studied the cottage's twin clusters of chimneys.

There was no smoke.

The house had been built centuries before of golden sandstone with a steep tiled roof and hipped dormer windows. Everyone still called it Knowles Farm Cottage even though the family of gentlemen farmers who'd lived there for generations was gone and most of the land that had once sustained its prosperity had crumbled over the years into the sea.

The last male Knowles had been blown into undeniable bits in 1916 in the trenches of the Somme. After that the cottage passed to his sister and her husband, Major Henry Crosby, a Northumbrian native in need of a place to retire after fighting the Empire's wars from Bengal to the Natal province of South Africa and the blood-soaked shores of Gallipoli. At one time he'd even roamed the Mediterranean in the service of military intelligence, posing as an antiquarian while secreting carefully rendered plans of enemy military instillations amongst his growing collection of rare clocks and watches. Rachel was one of the few residents of New Godwick who knew about that. Major Crosby might have lived at Knowles Cottage for twenty years and buried his native-born wife here, but he was still considered an outsider and always would be. New Godwick was that kind of village.

The major never seemed to mind it, though, and took his neighbors' provincial xenophobia in good humor. He liked to joke that once he was dead and planted beside his Margaret in the churchyard of St. Stephen's, they'd have to accept him as a part of Kent whether they wanted to or not. When war came again in 1939, he'd volunteered to organize the local Home Guard and serve as an enemy aircraft spotter for the Royal Observation Corps. He might be in his seventies, but he still kept his well-worn Webley revolver within easy reach, ready for any German spies or black-clad saboteurs who might try to sneak ashore and menace his adopted corner of England.

Of course the days when fears of an imminent German invasion had them all sleepless and jumpy were now, thankfully, in the past. These days, terror came in the form of V-1 flying bombs—the so-called doodlebugs that often fell short on their way to rain down death on London.

It was because of the doodlebugs that Rachel was here. As she approached the house, she kept running through various possible arguments in her head and trying out different openings. Maybe: *With so much of the past being destroyed every day by this dreadful war, Major, don't you think you owe it to future generations to—*

No, she decided; that sounded so accusatory and critical that she'd surely put up his back. Perhaps she should try something chirpy. Something like, *I've still got loads of crates and straw left over from packing up the museum; how about if I come up in the evenings and help you—*

No. That wouldn't work either. The major was being stubborn and selfish, not lazy. Flattery? *Your collection is world class and irreplaceable. You need to stop acting like a bloody idiot and let me store it someplace safe before a doodlebug falls out of the sky to blow you and every one of your priceless old watches and clocks to smithereens.*

Right, she thought in despair; that ought to do it.

At the base of the cottage's back steps, she drew up and took a deep breath, surprised to find the kitchen door ajar. Wisps of mist drifted across the flagstone floor to curl around the stocky legs of the farm table in the center of the room and the massive, crockery-laden Welsh dresser that stood beyond it. "Major?" she called, conscious of a faint whisper of apprehension that shivered up her spine. She could hear nothing except the buffeting of the wind, the crashing of the waves against the rocks at the base of the cliff, and the plaintive cries of gulls lost somewhere in the fog.

Her heart pounding, she climbed the steps to the kitchen. "Major," she called again. "Are you all r—" She broke off, then whispered, "Oh, no."

He lay sprawled on the far side of the kitchen near the door from the passage, an aged, white-haired man clad in an old-fashioned striped nightshirt such as her grandfather had once worn. His eyes were wide and staring and already beginning to flatten. In the first years of the war, Rachel had worked as an ambulance driver in Dover. She'd helped dig more shattered, bloody bodies from beneath the rubble of bombed-out houses and shops than she could count. She knew death when she saw it.

Her first thought was that he must have suffered a stroke or heart attack during the night and staggered down the steep, narrow back stairs from his bedroom to collapse here. But as she edged closer, she saw the big, old Webley service revolver that lay beside his outflung hand, saw the dark stain of dried blood around the narrow, telltale slit in the chest of his nightshirt.

"Dear God," she whispered.

Then she turned and ran.

Chapter 2

The memorial to New Godwick's war dead stood on the village green, not far from the weathered medieval market cross that had been relocated here in the early nineteenth century when the entire town of Godwick was moved a half mile inland from the crumbling sandstone cliffs overlooking the sea.

Jude Lowe, erstwhile Spitfire pilot now assigned to the section of military intelligence known as MI5, rested his left foot on the monument's base and read through the column of dead men. He'd only been in the village a few days, but he still recognized many of the surnames: Archer and Bancroft, Finney and Knowles, on and on. Jude counted twenty-three men. It was a long list for such a small village, and he suspected New Godwick had never really recovered from what had once been called the Great War but was now increasingly being styled the First World War. Jude found himself wondering how many more of the bloody things they were expecting if they had decided to start numbering them.

He straightened slowly, for the damp and cold always made him careful about how he moved. Instead of a uniform, he wore a gray Homburg hat with a black Petersham ribbon that matched the binding on its curled brim. His lightweight overcoat was of fine black wool and well tailored, although no longer as new as it had once been. Because he was a tall young man, broad shouldered and healthy looking, people in shops often glanced askance at him, wondering why he wasn't off doing his part to win the war. Then they'd notice the awkward way he held his left arm and the faint but unmistakable hesitation in his stride, and they'd understand.

Or at least, they'd think they understood.

The roar of planes overhead drew his gaze to the sky. The morning fog was only just beginning to lift, but even without seeing them, there was no mistaking the constant drone of these Allied bombers and their fighter escorts for the distinctive *woo-woo-woo* throb that characterized the German Luftwaffe. He felt a bitter wave of envy, anger, and shame slam into him. He wanted to be up there. And if he couldn't be up there, he wanted to be doing *something*—something other than poking around this quiet, out-of-the way village chasing a phantom German spy or saboteur that was more likely than not the figment of a War Office clerk's overheated imagination. If—

"There you are, mate," called a familiar, nasal voice with the inescapable inflections of London's East End. "Been looking for you."

Jude turned to find a short, heavyset man in his fifties cutting across the green toward him. Like Jude, Remus Stokes wore civilian clothes—in Stokes's case a badly fitting tweed suit of wool blended with some ghastly new synthetic. Unlike Jude, Stokes had been a detective inspector with Scotland Yard before the war. He still told people he was with Scotland Yard. They both did, although Stokes looked and sounded the part better than Jude.

"Right," said Jude, who had in fact been waiting for his partner. "I'm an easy bloke to miss, no doubt about it."

Stokes's eyes crinkled with a hint of amusement that faded as he tugged at one earlobe. "Something's come up."

"Thank God. We're being called back to London?"

"Not exactly."

Talk about the bleak midwinter, Jude thought when he first caught sight of Knowles Farm Cottage standing forlorn and isolated in a swirl of white. And it wasn't even winter; it was the bloody end of June. But "bleak" it definitely was, with the fog still hanging thick over the water and a cold wind moaning through the long grass. Maybe it looked more cheery in the sunshine.

When there wasn't a dead body inside.

The village police sergeant, a stocky, ruddy-cheeked local named Ned Gillingham, was waiting for them at the base of the worn steps that led up to what looked like the oldest part of the ancient, rambling house. He had his arms crossed at his barrel chest and his head thrown back at an angle popularized by millennia of balking donkeys, making it more than obvious he didn't take kindly to the need to defer to a couple of blokes from London. But the murder of a Home Guard commander who'd also been a spotter for the Royal Observation Corps was not something for a police sergeant to deal with alone—not when he knew precisely why the War Office had sent these men down to New Godwick. He was one of only two people in the village who'd been given that information.

The other was Major Crosby.

"You haven't moved him, I hope," said Jude as he and Stokes cut through the major's sopping wet victory garden. The mossy brick path was slippery, and he was careful to mind his step.

Sergeant Gillingham tightened his rather thick jaw and said, "No, sir. He's still on the kitchen floor where he was found."

Stokes nodded approvingly. "Did you touch anything at all?" The tone told Jude his partner was shifting into Scotland Yard mode. This was what he'd been trained to do, after all: peer at the mangled bodies of the dead and chase down their killers.

It had always struck Jude as a damned unpleasant way to spend your life.

"No, sir," said Gillingham again. "Soon as I realized he'd been murdered, I sent my lad to fetch you chaps right away. From the looks of things, I'd say he's been dead six or eight hours."

"Any idea how the killer got in?" asked Stokes, his head craning around as he squinted up at the old farmhouse's diamond-paned mullioned windows and dripping eaves.

"Walked in the door, I expect," said Gillingham, as if it were a daft question. "Front or back; no way to tell, really. This ain't London. Nobody around here locks up at night."

Perhaps they should consider it, Jude thought, but didn't say it.

"I had a good look around while I was waiting for you lot," said Gillingham in a way that subtly insinuated they'd taken their own sweet time moseying out to the point. "Didn't see nothing out the ordinary. No footprints. Nothing."

Not surprising, thought Jude. After a string of pleasant, dry days, it had rained hard enough shortly before dawn to wash away any traces a herd of elephants might have left. "Who found him?"

"One of the women from the village."

Jude was envisioning a charwoman with cleaning rags, a hand-knit jumper, and a sausage roll for her tea shoved into a bulging calico bag when the sergeant added, "She used to be the curator of the abbey museum before the war. Read history up at Oxford, she did." It was said with a combination of awe and puzzlement tinged faintly with derision, as if he found it impressive and yet faintly ridiculous that a female would want to do such a thing, and inexplicable that a self-respecting father had allowed it. "She's been trying for years to talk the major into storing his collection someplace safe till the war's over, and after that doodlebug come down on Joe Marsh's shed just across the lane yesterday, she says she decided to have another go at him."

"Must've been quite a shock for her," said Stokes.

"Aye. Although she's a plucky one, no doubt about that. Insisted on coming back out here with me. She's waiting in the front parlor, in case you need to ask her anything."

Jude nodded, although he couldn't see much use in talking to some village busybody who'd no doubt taken one look at the dead man and run screaming into the fog.

The bleak, bleak fog.

He gave an unexpected shiver and said, "Let's have a look at him, shall we?"

The kitchen had a low ceiling and didn't appear to have been updated for a hundred years or more, with the original dark, heavy beams still visible overhead and a wide stone hearth into which some forward-looking but doubtless long-dead Victorian had inserted a wood-burning stove. Between the old Welsh dresser, deep fireclay apron sink, and well-worn scrubbed table, it looked like something straight out of a Dickens novel. *Bleak House*, thought Jude, in keeping with his theme.

Major Crosby's stiffening corpse lay on the far side of the room, half in and half out of a doorway that led to a passage with the steep, narrow kind of stairs that had been intended for the "help." There would be a larger, grander, more impressive staircase somewhere else, near the front door, for the use of family and guests.

"No housekeeper?" said Jude, following the thought to its obvious conclusion.

Sergeant Gillingham shook his head. "He has—had—Mrs. Finney come in and do for him three times a week. Only not today."

He'd been of average height, the major, shrunken by age but still leanly muscled and determinedly straight-backed. The skin of his face was darkened and weathered by the decades he'd spent in hotter climes, so that it formed a stark contrast to the white of his thinning hair and the bushy mustache he still wore in the style that had been fashionable in the days of King Edward VII. The gun lying near his hand might have suggested suicide if the blood-soaked chest of his nightshirt had shown more than a neat slice.

"That's not a bullet wound," Jude said to Remus Stokes, who went to squat down beside the dead man.

"No, it's not," Stokes agreed with what sounded to Jude an awful lot like grim satisfaction. "He's been stabbed, all right—and by someone who knew what he was doing from the looks of it.

Got him right in the heart. He was probably dead almost before he hit the floor." Reaching awkwardly, for he was not as spry as he'd once been, Stokes slid the end of his pencil through the revolver's trigger guard and lifted it carefully to avoid smudging any fingerprints. "Given that it's an old Webley Mk IV, my guess is this belonged to the Major himself."

"Oh, no doubt about that," said the police sergeant. "Right proud of that revolver, Major Crosby was. Carried it through the Boer War and the Great War, he did. Took care of it as if it was one of those old watches and clocks he was so fond of collecting."

Stokes raised the revolver to his nose and sniffed. "It's been fired recently. I'd say our major heard someone moving around down here in the middle of the night, grabbed his gun, and came to confront him."

Our major. It was a peculiarity of detective inspectors, Jude had noticed, this tendency to refer to victims and criminals alike by the possessive *our*. A proprietary conceit, he supposed. Or was it motivated more by a sense of responsibility than ownership?

Jude glanced around the room. "If he fired the revolver, where did the bullet go?"

"Just there, behind you," said the police sergeant, his lips curling into a faint smile of condescension as he nodded toward the frame of the kitchen door. "I noticed it while I was waiting for you lot to get here."

Another subtle dig. *New theme*, thought Jude as he turned to look at the door: *Waiting for the Barbarians*.

A Webley Mk IV used a big .455 cartridge, and the bullet had torn a fist-sized chunk out of the old doorframe just below the center hinge in a way that suggested the door must have been standing wide open when the major fired off the last shot of his career.

Hunkering down, Jude studied the pieces of splintered wood that had sprayed across the lintel. The largest fragment was dark with what looked like blood. Eyes narrowing, he stared at the flagstone stoop just outside the door. A small overhang had kept off most of the rain, and he spotted what looked like several drops of blood near the edge. If there'd been more, they were now buried beneath the muck left by their own muddy boots. Barbarians, indeed.

He said, "There are traces of blood here. Looks like the killer got hit by some of the flying splinters from the doorframe."

Stokes shook his head. "That doesn't make sense."

Jude glanced over at him. "Why not?"

"Picture it. If our killer was already heading out the door when the major came barging down the stairs and took a shot at him, he'd just keep going and disappear into the night. Why stop and turn around? Why give the Major time to squeeze off another round by running back across the room to stab him? And yet the Webley was only fired once. So why didn't the major shoot again if he had the chance?"

Jude pushed to his feet, then had to steady himself with a quickly outflung hand as a burning pain shot up his left leg and he almost lost his balance. He squeezed his eyes shut for an instant before opening them to walk very carefully across the kitchen and stare thoughtfully down at the dead man.

"Must've been two of them," the police sergeant was saying. "The major shot at the one going out the door just as the second fellow stabbed him in the chest."

"Maybe," said Jude. "Or maybe our killer knows how to throw a knife." *Our.* He was doing it now.

The police sergeant laughed out loud, but Stokes looked thoughtful. "You think that German spy we're chasing did this?"

"You don't?"

Stokes shook his head. "I thought you'd decided that was all a hum."

"I had. Except a man with murderous enemies generally locks his doors." Jude glanced over at the police sergeant. "Do you know if Major Crosby had any enemies?"

Gillingham thought about it a moment, then shook his head. "Nah. Don't think so. He was a pretty easygoing, likable fellow. Not from New Godwick, you know. Only came here twenty years ago or so."

Ah, villages, thought Jude. Always so welcoming to outsiders. His father had come from such a place up in Shropshire, where anyone whose great-grandparents were born elsewhere was considered a newcomer and those who'd lived there for endless generations knew everyone else's business—and all their secrets.

But then, Jude's family had more secrets than most. Some very ugly secrets.

He pushed the thought aside. "You say the woman who found him is still here?"

Sergeant Gillingham nodded. "In the front parlor. She's the daughter of General Sir Garth Townsend-Smythe—him as owns the Grange and is with Montgomery himself in Normandy." He paused, then added helpfully, "That's Smythe with a Y. And an E."

Jude had seen the Grange. Along with a place called Bancroft Court, it was one of the two "big houses" in the village. Before the war it had probably employed a good third of the local population. "Of course it's Smythe with a Y. And an E," he said, and turned toward the parlor at the front of the house.

Chapter 3

Rachel Townsend-Smythe stood beside one of the parlor windows, her arms wrapped around her waist as she stared out at the fog. She'd laid a fire on the hearth, taken off her muddy Wellies and draped her damp mackintosh over a chair. But her socks were thin and had holes in the toes, and her baggy old sweater was woefully inadequate for the still-frigid room. She told herself that was why she kept shivering.

She'd been just five years old the first time she met the major, on a glorious, blue-sky day. She'd come to Knowles Point with her brother, Ben, to look for fossils in the sandstone cliffs. The cliffs were so crumbly all the village children were forbidden to venture close to the edge, but of course they did. They figured there was no one to tell on them, for the old cottage had stood silent and empty ever since the Widow Knowles died back in the spring of 1917. *Died of a broken heart*, said everyone in the village, on account of her only son, James, getting blown up on the Somme.

Rachel's grandpa had died of a "bad heart," but all that meant was that it quietly gave out on him one night as he slept—it hadn't *broken*. Her younger self had found it horrifying to think that something as vital as a person's heart could break as easily as an arm or a finger. Ben had assured her it was just something folks said, that you couldn't actually die of a broken heart. Rachel had believed him the same way she believed everything Ben told her, because he was her big brother and he knew all sorts of things.

But he'd been wrong about the broken heart. Because when Ben's ship went down in 1942 off Singapore and took Ben with it, Rachel had felt her heart break. And if she'd been as old as the Widow Knowles, she suspected she would surely have died of it.

It hurt to remember Ben the way he'd been on that long-ago day, sun-browned, golden-haired, and laughing. They'd both jumped when the major hallooed at them from the door of the cottage. They knew vaguely who he was, for he'd been to New Godwick once before on a visit with his village-born wife, Margaret. But they hadn't known he'd decided to move into Knowles Farm Cottage and live there.

He invited them to come back when he and Margaret were settled and have a look at what he called his "collections." He had the most amazing things: grotesque stone gargoyles from long-vanished abbeys, fancifully painted vases from ancient Greek shipwrecks, primitive masks from the darkest reaches of Africa. But more than anything, the major collected old timepieces—all sorts of watches and clocks, even an ancient marble sundial face he said had come from a Roman city half buried in the sands of Libya. Ben never had much interest in such things, but they fascinated the younger Rachel, and she'd come to visit the major many times throughout her growing-up years. She sometimes wondered if she would have gone to Oxford and become a museum curator, if she'd never met the major.

She asked him once how he'd come to be so interested in timepieces, and he'd taken a shadow box lined with faded blue velvet down from the wall and showed her the intricately carved outer watchcase he said had come to him from a great-uncle when he was a lad.

"Is it gold?" she asked in awe, studying the intricately pierced scrollwork of waves, the storm-tossed ship surrounded by menacing sea creatures. "Solid gold?"

"Oh, yes. Made from treasures stolen from the altar of a Spanish cathedral." The major looked a tad wistful. "It captured my imagination in a way nothing else ever has. I've always wanted to find the watch it once contained, but I never have."

The shadow box protected only one other item: a carved rosewood rosary neatly coiled around the watchcase. "Why do you keep a rosary in there with it?" she asked.

He chuckled. "That's because the bishop of the cathedral is said to have called upon God to curse it. The rosary is to ward off the evil."

"Ben says there's no such thing as curses," Rachel's younger self had announced, as if that settled it.

Of course, Ben had also said there was no such thing as a broken heart…

She'd left the parlor door open, so she knew when Sergeant Gillingham came back into the kitchen with the men he'd sent for, the ones he said were from Scotland Yard. She listened now to their voices, one older and with the harsh, nasal tones of the East End; the other younger, his voice deeper and more carefully modulated. Her hearing was keen enough that she was able to follow clearly what they were saying even though they kept their voices low. And so she heard the older man say, "You think that German spy we're chasing did this?"

Not *some German spy*, Rachel noted, but *that German spy we're chasing*. She was still trying to digest this when she heard the younger man's brisk, slightly uneven step sound in the hall. He drew up on the threshold, a tall, lean man with gypsy-dark hair and strangely faceted, piercing gray eyes. They stared at each other a long moment. Before she could stop herself, Rachel said, "You don't look like anyone from Scotland Yard I've ever met."

"So is that an insult or a compliment?"

"Perhaps it's simply an observation."

She thought she saw a faint gleam of amusement lighten his strange, crystal-like eyes. "The name's Lowe," he said. "You're Rachel Townsend-Smythe?"

"Yes. I'd say, 'Pleased to meet you, Mr. Lowe,' but under the circumstances it doesn't seem quite appropriate."

He turned away, his gaze drifting around the room as he took in the rows of priceless long-case clocks, and display cabinets crowded with fanciful pocket watches and ancient brass carriage clocks nestled amongst things like a beautifully carved series of wooden Renaissance santos Rachel knew had come from Italy.

"'Strange was the sight and smacking of the time,'" he said, or she thought she heard him say. "No wonder you wanted him to store this stuff someplace safe."

"What makes you think he was killed by a German spy?" she asked bluntly. He brought his gaze back to her face. And before he could deny it, she said, "I heard you."

The ambulance had arrived to carry the major's body off to the surgery of the village's aged doctor, and they could hear Sergeant Gillingham arguing with the driver. The other Scotland Yard man must have been taking photographs of the body because she could also hear the *snap, snap* of a camera shutter.

This Scotland Yard man said, "How well did you know the major?"

Snap, snap.

She hesitated just long enough to let him know she'd noticed his failure to answer her question. "He's been my friend almost as long as I can remember."

"Do you know anyone who'd want to kill him?"

"No. He had no enemies."

"Perhaps someone broke in to steal some of...this." His glance took in the room crowded with priceless treasures. "Would you know if anything's missing?"

"Nothing's missing." Major Crosby might not lock his doors, but he did keep his display cases locked. She'd asked him why once, and he'd said that while he didn't think any of his neighbors would deliberately sneak into his house to take something, he saw no reason to tempt visitors into casual theft.

The Scotland Yard man prowled the room, peering into cases, pausing to inspect a particularly lovely Regency mantel clock of veined green marble crowned with a gilt bronze eagle. He said, "The killer could have been interrupted before he had a chance to steal anything."

If Rachel were the type of woman to be easily bulldozed, she never would have made it into Oxford. She said, "I know what I heard. Is that why you're here, in New Godwick? Because you think there's a German spy hidden amongst us? It's ridiculous, you know. This is a small village very wary of strangers. If there were a spy around, I'd know it. Everyone would know it."

He turned to face her. She expected him to try to shift the focus of the conversation again. Instead he said, "We've uncovered German spies who were sent here six or seven years ago. They weren't strangers to the people who thought they knew them."

She studied his fine-boned face, with its long, straight nose, flaring cheekbones, and faintly cleft chin. But his eyes were now hooded and unreadable. She said, "You're suggesting the major might have been killed because he served as an enemy aircraft spotter for the Royal Observation Corps? But surely not. Not now, with the Normandy invasion well underway."

"I don't know why he was killed. But I would ask that you not speculate or repeat to anyone what you heard."

She knew a spurt of irritation. She wasn't going to get anything out of him, and he'd somehow managed to make her feel as if she were being unpatriotic simply by asking. "No; of course not," she said briskly and brushed past him to go sit on the major's tattered old horsehair sofa and yank on her muddy boots.

He stayed where he was, watching her. And she found herself wishing, inexplicably and infuriatingly, that she'd somehow found the time to darn her socks.

She came upon the shadow box when she was cutting back across the paddock.

Rather than heading straight home after leaving the cottage, she'd gone to sit near the edge of the cliff and watch the strengthening sun burn off the rest of the fog. She sat there for hours watching the gulls wheel against the sky, her thoughts lost in the past. It was only the sudden realization that her nana would be worrying about what might have happened to her that finally drove Rachel to push up from her perch and turn toward home.

The shadow box lay nestled in a tuft of grass, which may have been why she hadn't noticed it earlier that morning. Or perhaps she'd missed it because she was looking at the cottage and focusing on what she was going to say to the major.

Her heart beating suddenly fast, she swung around to stare back at the cottage. But Sergeant Gillingham and the ambulance driver had long since loaded the major's body into the requisitioned old baker's van and driven off toward Dr. Hayes's surgery. The two Scotland Yard men had lingered longer, searching for only they knew what. But they were gone now, too.

She hesitated another moment. Then, surprised to see her hand shaking, she reached to pick it up.

It was an old-fashioned shadow box that looked as if it dated back to the early years of the century, its frame decorated with scrolled carvings of ivy and roses picked out in gilt faintly tinted with pink and green. The latch was open but not broken, and the rosary was still there, still carefully pinned in place.

But the major's infamous seventeenth-century gold outer watchcase was gone, leaving only a round imprint in the faded blue velvet.

Chapter 4

Why the hell would someone with a house filled with priceless clocks and other art objects not lock his bloody doors?" Remus Stokes demanded over a late lunch of swill pie. "If you ask me, the old man must've been crackers."

"This isn't London," said Jude with a faint smile.

Stokes grunted and took another bite of his cold pie.

There were only three places in New Godwick to eat: the Black Horse Inn where they'd taken rooms, a somewhat seedy pub called the Mermaid, and Maria's Café. Technically there was a fourth option if you wanted to count the canteen run by Lady Bancroft in what had once been the church hall. Bancroft Court was the other "big house" in New Godwick, and like the Grange it had been requisitioned by the government at the beginning of the war. Its dispossessed chatelaine occupied herself by setting up the canteen and ruthlessly bullying the poor WVS girls assigned to her. Unfortunately her ladyship's French chef was not a party to the enterprise, and Jude had been advised by the unsavory odors wafting from its makeshift kitchen to avoid the premises.

Of the three remaining establishments, Maria's was undeniably the best. But Jude and Stokes were not here to enjoy the food. "Maria" was a black-clad Sicilian widow named Capello, and her son, Alberto Capello, was high on their list of suspects. As Jude watched, Alberto came out of the kitchen and stopped to whisper something into the ear of the pretty, blond-haired young waitress who laughed quietly.

"Think about this," said Stokes, leaning forward and dropping his voice. "That old major was worried enough about German spies sneaking ashore in the middle of the night that he slept with a loaded Webley by his bed. Yet he still didn't lock his bleedin' doors? Crackers, I tell you."

Jude watched Alberto Capello take a heavy tray loaded with dirty dishes from the waitress and disappear back into the kitchen. He was a slim, handsome man somewhere in his midtwenties with golden skin and a long, classical nose. When war first broke out, he'd been hauled in along with tens of thousands of other resident "aliens" and sent off to a concentration camp on the Isle of Man. The authorities kept him there for three years before finally deciding it was a less-than-generous thing to do to a refugee who'd fled to England to escape a nasty regime, and let him go.

But the War Office was beginning to reconsider its decision. They'd become aware of a mysterious series of radio transmissions from an area that—if you squinted at it right—sort of seemed to fan out in a rough half circle around New Godwick. Not only were the transmissions in Morse code, but the spy—if he actually existed—seemed to broadcast in his own private cypher. A cypher not even the experts at Bletchley Park had been able to crack.

Up until that morning, Jude had been inclined to think the transmissions were a hoax—the work of some schoolboy playing a dangerous game and laughing with his friends about his clever little prank. It was the only explanation that made sense: there was simply nothing around New Godwick for a saboteur or spy to target. Yes, the Grange and Bancroft Court had been requisitioned by the War Office, but the Court was being used as a driving school while the Grange was used to train army cooks. Not exactly high-priority targets. Kent's major airfields—Biggin Hill, Manston, Eastchurch—all lay far to the west. And Operation Fortitude, which had successfully fooled Hitler into thinking the

D-Day landings would take place at Calais rather than Normandy, had been run from Dover—and was over anyway. What was there around New Godwick that could possibly interest Hitler? Nothing.

The problem with that comfortable conviction was that someone had now murdered the local enemy aircraft spotter.

"We don't know that Crosby's death is connected to the radio transmissions," said Stokes, his thoughts obviously marching with Jude's. "We might still be looking for a tiresome schoolboy who somehow got his hands on a suitcase wireless and is using it to play tricks, just like you said before."

Jude shoved away the remains of his meal and folded his arms on the table in front of him. "And Crosby? Who killed him? And why?"

"Coulda been one of the pickers living out in the hop shacks." Stokes gave a reluctant grin. "They're from London. Maybe they heard the major didn't keep his doors locked like he should."

"A hop picker who knows how to throw a knife?"

"Or two hop pickers, like I said before. It's possible, isn't it? Well, isn't it?"

Jude shook his head as Alberto Capello came back through the swinging door, this time with his arms full of carefully balanced plates. For one intense instant his gaze met Jude's, then slid away.

But not quite fast enough. Not before Jude saw the unmistakable flare of fear in the Italian's eyes.

She shouldn't have picked up the shadow box.

This painful realization dawned on Rachel when she was halfway home. She should have left it where it had fallen and simply reported it. "Damn," she said out loud, because there was no one besides a sparrow and a black-and-white cow in the nearby field to hear. Too late now. She pondered her options and finally realized that whether she liked it or not, she was going to have to look up that unpleasant Scotland Yard inspector and give him the shadow box. But first she was going home to reassure Nana that her last surviving grandchild was still numbered amongst the living.

"Home" for Rachel these days was a small cottage tucked into a wild corner of the Grange's park. As she turned in the gates and nodded to the army sentry stationed there, she caught a glimpse of the Grange itself at the far end of the long, oak-lined drive. These days, she always experienced what she suspected was an unpatriotic welling of longing and homesickness whenever she saw it. Compared to most country houses, the Grange was fairly modest, a square sandstone block with tall Dutch gables and rows of mullioned windows that winked in the sunlight. The Townsends might be a tenacious family, but they'd never been particularly prosperous or adept at maneuvering the various dynastic squabbles that swept the nation. At one point they'd nearly died out in the early nineteenth century, until a son-in-law named Smith had been convinced to hyphenate and modify his own woefully plain surname in exchange for the inheritance. Now, with Ben's death…

But Rachel pushed that thought away.

Reaching the cottage's low stoop, she paused to kick off her boots so she wouldn't track mud inside. Once a gamekeeper's cottage, it was small—just five rooms including the lean-to kitchen—and crowded with all the things the three Townsend-Smythe women hadn't been able to bear to leave behind at the Grange. Now there were only two of them, Rachel and her grandmother, and the cottage always struck Rachel as both crowded and yet somehow empty at the same time.

Her rucksack was hanging on a hook outside the parlor door, and she paused to tuck the shadow box inside it before continuing through the kitchen and out the back door. She found her nana sitting there, as she'd known she would. A tall, elegant, white-haired woman in her seventies, she'd drawn her wheelchair up to the edge of the stone terrace and was stroking the white cat curled up in her lap.

"Ah, there you are, my dear," said Nana when Rachel went to wrap her arms around her grandmother's shoulders. "I was wondering."

Rachel kissed her cheek. "I know. Sorry."

Nana rested one gnarled hand over Rachel's. "I heard about the major."

"Already?" Rachel let go and came around to sit facing her on the low stone wall that bordered the terrace. "How?"

"From the butcher's boy, Jack. He'd just come from making a delivery to the Gillinghams, and you know what a chatterbox Dorothea Gillingham is. She says there's two men here from MI5—"

Rachel huffed a soft laugh. "Not MI5. Scotland Yard."

"Ah. Well, trust a boy to get that wrong. He claims they're looking for a German spy in the area."

Rachel suddenly lost all desire to laugh. "Did he say what this German spy is doing around here?"

"That he didn't seem to know." Nana reached out to take Rachel's hand in hers again. "I know what a great friend of yours the major was, dear. Are you all right?"

"Yes. Just…shocked, I guess."

Nana gave her hand a squeeze. "Marcus was here a while ago. Some of the cows are sick, and he wants to know if he should send for Dr. Archer. And one of those girls from the Land Army was looking for you as well, but she wouldn't say what it was about."

Before the war, the Grange's Home Farm had been under the direction of a steward. When the steward volunteered for the navy, Rachel's mother had taken over. And when her mother was killed in the same London air raid that had left her grandmother unable to walk, Rachel came home from her assignment in Dover to take on the task herself.

"I'll go see them now," she said, pushing up from the wall. "Shall I fix you some tea first?"

"I'll be right. You go on, then. But…" Nana hesitated, then

added, "You will be careful, won't you, dear? Just in case the butcher's boy is right?"

Rachel laughed and kissed her grandmother's cheek again. "I'll be careful. Promise."

The rich golden light of early evening was spilling across the fields by the time Rachel was finally free to haul her bicycle out of the shed, sling her rucksack over one shoulder, and ride into town.

She went first to the Black Horse Inn, where she'd been told the two Scotland Yard men were staying. They weren't there. Frustrated, she hesitated a moment, then pedaled out to the diminutive redbrick Georgian house on the outskirts of the village that belonged to an aged, retired schoolteacher named Alexander Nelson. He was in the front garden deadheading a blowsy pink rose and didn't look up when Rachel swung off her bicycle at the gate.

"Mr. Nelson?"

He turned slowly, for he was stooped and a bit trembly, with a ring of untidy gray hair and spectacles he wore pushed down on the end of a blobby nose. Once he'd been a teacher, but he was well into his eighties now and had spent the years since his retirement cultivating a reputation as the local historian. As such, he considered himself Rachel's rival, although she suspected his dislike of her dated back the better part of twenty years, to the time when she and Ben had pulled a prank on him that now made her uncomfortable remembering it. He scowled at the sight of her. "Miss Townsend-Smythe."

"You've heard about the major?" she asked, leaning her bicycle against the fence.

The old man took off his glasses and rubbed his watery eyes with a spread thumb and forefinger. "I doubt you'll find anyone in the village who hasn't heard by now. Terrible business, this. Terrible."

Rachel fiddled with the flap of her knapsack. "Did you ever

have much luck helping him trace the gold watch that went with that fancy old case of his?"

Mr. Nelson turned back to his rosebush and snipped off a couple of spent blooms before saying, "How did you know I was working with him on that?"

"He told me."

"Ah." *Snip, snip.* "Legend has it the last man to own the watch was from around here, you know. Lost his wife and three of his four children in freak accidents, and finally decided the watch was cursed and got rid of it."

Rachel nodded. She'd heard the tale from the major many times over the years. She'd sometimes suspected it was one of the main reasons he'd decided to take up residence in his wife's house at New Godwick—because of the village's link to the legendary watch that had fascinated him his entire life. "What was the man's name?"

"Osborne. Bertrand Osborne. He's buried in the churchyard."

"And did you ever find anything to suggest what happened to the watch?"

Mr. Nelson looked at her over the rims of his spectacles. "Why are you asking me about the watch?"

"Just curious," said Rachel as airily as she could manage.

Mr. Nelson grunted and went back to snipping spent blooms.

"So did you discover anything?" she asked again.

"Maybe. Maybe not."

She watched him snip at his rose and forced herself to smile, even though she was frustrated enough to want to upend his basket of spent blooms over his head. "That sounds a bit like you might have discovered something, Mr. Nelson."

He gave her a sly look. "Perhaps."

She tried a different approach. "So did it work? Getting rid of the watch, I mean. Did Bertrand Osborne's fourth child survive?"

"Oh, yes. He's still alive. Or at least he was the last I heard—although I suppose the Nazis could have got him with one of those new doodlebugs." He frowned at her. "Why are you so curious?"

"It just seems sad that the major never found it, that's all. After looking for it for so long."

The old man shrugged one shoulder. "Never could understand why he wanted to find it, myself. Who'd want to own a cursed watch?"

"Maybe someone who thinks he has nothing left to lose," said Rachel, going to retrieve her bicycle.

Mr. Nelson shook his head and looked oddly troubled. "Everyone living has something to lose."

Chapter 5

The simple headstone of Bertrand Osborne lay on the extreme southwestern edge of New Godwick's churchyard, about as far from the village's neoclassical church as it could possibly be and still be situated on hallowed ground.

"He wasn't buried beside his family?" Rachel asked the Reverend Francis Dingle, who had come upon her peering at the names on the old tombs and offered to show her Osborne's grave.

The reverend shook his head. He was a tall, bony man late in his middle years, with fading sandy hair and an expression of solemn sincerity that hid a voraciously inquisitive nature. "I'm told he was quite particular about where he wished to be laid to rest."

Rachel turned to look out over the churchyard. "Where is the rest of his family buried?"

"Over here."

The reverend led the way toward the church's east end, to an ornate, lichen-covered monument crowned by a statue of a weeping angel. "It's quite a tragic tale, you know," said the reverend as they drew up before it. "His wife drowned in a boating accident. Their eldest son died after being thrown by a bolting horse. The second son was killed by a falling branch in a storm. And their daughter perished in a fire."

Rachel felt a faint, unexpected shiver run up her spine. "So it's true; they did all die in accidents."

"Oh, yes. Only one survived. Peter, I believe is his name. I heard just the other day he's recently moved to Dover." The vicar frowned. "Or was it Folkestone?"

"You don't know which?"

The reverend shook his head. "Sorry. But I could find out, if you'd like."

"I would be interested to know, yes. Thank you."

The reverend gave her an expectant look, as if he were waiting for her to explain her sudden interest in the Osbornes. Instead, she cast a strategic glance up at the sky and said, "Oh, goodness; it'll be dark if I don't leave soon. Thanks ever so much for your help, Reverend."

His face fell with disappointment, but he nodded and called after her, "Best hurry."

She'd said it to avoid answering any more questions, but the danger from the gathering gloom was real. Thanks to the blackout, it could be deadly being caught on the winding country roads after dark.

As she wove through the weathered tombstones toward the gate where she'd left her bicycle, Rachel was saddened to realize just how many new graves there were scattered amongst the old: civilians killed in the bombings; military men brought home to die; family members too heartbroken by the loss of loved ones to go on. Even after five years of war, Rachel still had occasional flashes of unreality—that sudden, sweeping sense of *How can this be? How could my once safe, placid world have turned upside down in an instant?* The sensation was always accompanied by an aching nostalgia for an age of lost innocence and a world now vanished in the mists of time.

She'd almost reached the gate when she noticed a slender, fair-haired young woman laying a simple sheaf of yellow and white primroses at the grave of one of the children evacuated down from London at the beginning of the war, before the authorities realized Kent was not a safe place either. But the child hadn't been killed in a bombing run; she'd died of measles, crying inconsolably for her absent mother.

As Rachel drew closer, she recognized the woman as Pippa, the waitress from Maria's Café. Pippa MacAvoy was a Londoner herself and had evacuated down to Kent after losing her mother and elder sister in the bombing. Her sister's three-year-old little boy, Wills, was pushing a wooden car through the high grass at Pippa's feet. At Rachel's approach, Pippa looked up and gave her a wobbly smile.

"Did you know her?" asked Rachel, pausing beside the pathetically small tombstone inscribed simply, *Elizabeth Jones, 1935–1942*.

"No. I just find it so sad for her to be here alone without anyone who loves her. I try to come when I can." She bit her lower lip in a way that made her look both thoughtful and profoundly vulnerable. "I guess she doesn't know I'm here, and it doesn't really help anything, but…" Her voice trailed away, as if rather than explaining herself she had only succeeded in questioning her own motives.

"It helps," said Rachel, conscious of a painful welling in her chest. "I think it helps the spirit of the universe, the…the common chord of our shared humanity. There's too much that is horrible in our world right now. We all need to do our part to come down on the side of good and light."

"Yes, that's it," said Pippa, smiling sadly. "Thank you."

The last of the day was fading from the sky, and Rachel walked quickly to where she'd left her bicycle leaning against the churchyard's low stone wall. When she glanced back, Pippa was still standing beside the child's grave, her head bowed and her eyes squeezed shut in earnest prayer.

Jude Lowe was hot, dusty, and in serious need of a pint of ale. He and Stokes had spent the last five hours driving around eastern

Kent to personally inspect every blasted site pinpointed by headquarters as the location of one of that string of intercepted transmissions. They'd found nothing. Nix. *Nichts.*

Now he stood at the edge of a windswept cliff, his arms crossed at his chest as he stared out over a sunlit sea fading to a dark blue with the coming of evening. "See a pattern here?" he asked.

Stokes stared down at the crumpled, somewhat smudged paper that contained their list of sites, then turned to squint into the setting sun. "Do you?"

"Nope."

"Bloody hell."

Jude swung away from the cliff's edge. "Ready to call it a day?"

"Beyond ready."

Jude drove their War Office–issued Rover back toward the village while Stokes sat beside him, poring over their topographical map in the fading light. "I still don't see a bloody pattern." He muttered.

"You won't. Whoever is doing this is too clever for that."

Stokes shifted his attention to the list of the transmissions' coordinates, dates, and times. "All the transmissions have been in the early morning or evening."

"Of course they are. The only person in the entire village with a running car is that old doctor, which means our lad is using buses and trains to get around. Not only are buses and trains most frequent in the mornings and evenings, but he wouldn't attract as much attention traveling at those times."

Stokes thought about it a moment, then said, "That makes sense." He skewed around in the seat to face Jude. "You know, you're pretty good at this stuff. What are you planning to do when the war is over?"

Jude laughed. "Not join Scotland Yard." Yet even as he said it, he found himself thinking, *What are you going to do?* The ambitious future he'd once planned—pursuing a career at the stock exchange—now struck him as hopelessly dull and hollow.

Was the war doing this to everyone? he wondered. Addicting them to a life they desperately didn't want to continue and yet would in some way miss?

"Stop here," said Stokes, putting out a hand as Jude rolled into the village. "There's that German fellow, Sigmund Reinhardt. I want to talk to him again."

"He's Austrian," said Jude, pulling in close to the curb near where their quarry was just leaving the village shop. Sigmund Reinhardt was a thin, nervous man in his forties with a pale complexion, aquiline nose, and the air of a professor or musician. At the sight of them, he drew up, his slender frame quivering as if he were considering turning to walk rapidly in the opposite direction. But he stood his ground and waited stoically while the two men climbed out of the car and walked up to him.

They'd grilled Reinhardt once before, shortly after their arrival in the village. As one of New Godwick's two resident aliens—along with Alberto Capello—he was an obvious suspect.

"Gentlemen," he said now with a faint bow. He was not smiling, his gaze darting from Jude to Stokes and back again. "May I help you?" His English was very good, crisp and precise, with barely a trace of an accent.

Stokes planted his feet wide, hooked his thumbs in his waistband, and struck the attitude habitual to policemen for two hundred years or more. Jude personally found it both irritating and enough of a caricature to be almost comical. But that could simply be an innate, inherited prejudice: too many of Jude's ancestors had suffered from unpleasant encounters with law enforcement down through the centuries—one of the hazards, he supposed, of being descended from innkeepers, smugglers, and murderers.

"Where were you last night?" Stokes demanded, leaning into the Austrian.

"In my room. Asleep. Where else would I have been?"

"Alone?"

"Yes. Alone."

"I take it you've heard what happened to Major Crosby?"

The Austrian's jaw tightened hard enough to strain the sinews along the sides of his narrow, bony face. "I heard. I had nothing to do with that."

Stokes gave a patently false laugh. "Why should I believe you?"

When the Austrian simply remained silent and watchful, Stokes said, "You've been here in New Godwick since—when?"

"Well, if you ignore the two years I was a guest in one of His Majesty's concentration camps, I've been here since 1938, when the Nazis took over Austria. I watched what they did when they came to power in Germany, and I suspected Austria wouldn't be any different. Which of course it wasn't. They even used the same list of useful scapegoats: intellectuals, socialists, trade unionists, Jews..."

"And homophiles?"

Again, that strained flex of the Austrian's jaw. "Yes."

"Which category did you fall into?"

The man gave a low, unexpected laugh. "More than one." The amusement faded as Reinhardt shifted his gaze from Stokes to Jude, who had chosen to remain silent and watchful throughout the exchange. Reinhardt said, "What do you think? That I went out to the point to rob that old man? Why would I? I have money, you know."

"Oh?" said Stokes. "And how'd you get it out of Austria? I thought you had to abandon everything and pay a tax in order to leave."

The Austrian's chin lifted. "I sold what I could and bought rare postage stamps. They're small and easy to conceal."

"Clever," said Stokes grudgingly.

Reinhardt gave him a faintly ironic bow. "Thank you." Then his gaze shifted to Jude again. "May I go now?"

Jude nodded. "Just keep close to the village, will you?"

"I had no intention of doing elsewise," said Reinhardt with great dignity, and walked on.

After he had gone, Stokes said, "You think he's our bloke?"

"No."

"Why not?"

"Because why would a Jewish socialist homophile college professor want to work for Hitler?"

"You don't know he is who he says he is."

"I know," said Jude.

Stokes grunted. "So maybe Hitler is threatening someone he loves—someone he left behind in Vienna."

"It's possible."

"But you don't think so?"

Jude swiped one crooked arm across his hot, dusty face. "All I know is, I need a pint."

They were walking in the door of the Black Horse when Jude heard a woman calling his name—or rather, what she assumed was his name.

"Inspector? Inspector Lowe."

Jude threw a longing glance after Stokes, who had already disappeared into the malty-fragrant depths of the public room, and turned back to meet Miss Rachel Townsend-Smythe.

She was riding a beat-up, old blue bicycle and had an army rucksack slung over one shoulder. "I've been looking for you for hours," she said in a tone that suggested it was somehow his fault for not being available for her ladyship.

He resisted the urge to say, *I've been a tad busy chasing some bloody German spy around Kent*, and said instead, "Did you want me for something in particular?"

To his surprise, a faint touch of color rose in her cheeks. She really was a fine-looking woman, he thought, even wearing a baggy old sweater and with her windblown hair flying loose around her delicately boned face. "Could we—" She threw a quick glance at the inn behind him. "Walk with me a ways, if you would? I've something to show you."

"Of course."

She swung off her bicycle, and he turned to walk with her toward the green. It would be dark soon, and because of the blackout, there would be no streetlights, no glimpses of lamplight peeking through curtains that could provoke the local air raid warden in his or her tin hat to shout, "Put out that light!" But the evening was gloriously clear, with the first scattered stars just beginning to appear and a nearly full moon. With the moon shining on the rivers to form lighted pathways, any German bombers would have an easy time finding their targets tonight. And it occurred to Jude that there was something seriously wrong with a world in which you couldn't walk with a pretty girl on a moonlit evening without thinking about bombers.

She said, "I found something out at the point this morning, in the paddock by the lane. You and your partner had already gone by then, so I picked it up without thinking. I'm sorry if that disturbed any evidence or broke the chain of possession or some such thing, but here it is."

She was holding out a small wooden box with a framed glass lid—a shadow box, he realized—that she'd pulled from her beat-up rucksack.

"It belonged to the major," she said. "He used it to display a fantastically carved gold outer case that once held a legendary seventeenth-century pocket watch. It was by far his most prized possession, and now it's gone."

Jude took the box, which was a simple affair framed with a Victorian-looking scroll of ivy and roses picked out in tinted gilt. "I thought you said nothing was missing."

"I'd checked the locks on all the glass cabinets, and I know I would have noticed if any of the larger case clocks were gone. But he kept this on the wall near his chair. Unless you were specifically looking for it, I doubt anyone would notice it was gone."

Jude studied the curled rosary wound around a faint impression left in the fading blue velvet. "How valuable was it?"

"Quite. Not only was it solid gold and beautifully worked, but the watch it once protected—La Sirène—is famous."

"For what?"

"For its beauty and intricate workmanship, partially. But mainly because it's said to carry a powerful curse—"

"A curse," he said dryly.

"A curse," she repeated with a faint narrowing of her eyes. "There's a legend that the last man who owned the watch hid it somewhere around here. What if—what if someone found the watch and killed Major Crosby so he could steal the outer case that belonged with it? I was speaking to Mr. Nelson—he's our local historian—and something he said made me wonder if perhaps the major wasn't closer to finding the watch than I'd realized. I know he was excited about something the last few weeks, but he would never tell me what. He just kept saying, 'You'll see.'"

"You're suggesting he was killed because of a curse?"

Her eyes were now angry slits. "I didn't say I believe the curse is real. I'm simply telling you the legend attached to the case's watch. Why out of all the treasures in his house do you think the killer stole this one?" She jabbed her finger down on the glass cover of the shadow box as she said it.

"Perhaps he simply noticed the watchcase and took a fancy to it. It happens, you know."

"Well," she said with perfect politeness, although he noticed her nostrils quivering, "I must bow to your superior knowledge of such individuals." She turned her bike around with a clatter.

He frowned. "It's dark enough that you could get hit by a lorry on these winding country roads. Why don't you throw that in the back of the Rover and I'll drive you home?"

She scooted onto the bicycle's seat, her feet splayed beyond the pedals as she tossed her hair back out of her face. "Thank you, but that won't be necessary. The moon is quite sufficient." And with that, she pushed off and rode away down the lane.

Jude was still staring after her when Stokes came to stand in the inn's doorway.

"I thought you were right behind me," he called. "What happened?"

"This," said Jude, holding up the empty shadow box.

"What the hell is that?"

"A distraction, probably—although Miss Townsend-Smythe believes it is the key to Crosby's murder."

Stokes grunted. "That's because she doesn't know about the Nazi transmissions."

Jude frowned as he watched the slim figure disappear into the darkness. "No, she doesn't."

CHAPTER 6

EVERY MORNING EXCEPT ON Sundays, Mrs. Ida Tittlesnap walked up the hill from her thatched cottage to Mr. Alexander Nelson's tidy brick house to "do" for him. She was in her fifties, Ida, with a deep bosom, wide hips, and a head of curly, iron-gray hair that her Wilson used to say was as black as the night sky, when they were young and in love. Wilson was dead now, but while she missed his paycheck, she didn't miss him. The bloom had worn off that peach long before he was run over by a lorry one night on his way home from the pub at the beginning of the blackout. Fitting way for him to go, Ida always thought. She suspected he was so blotto he never knew what hit him.

It was hotter than usual that morning, and because she wasn't as slim as she'd once been, Ida found herself perspiring by the time she reached the historian's back door. She pressed down the latch and then turned to give the old door a good hard whack with her hip to open it. The thing was always sticking, and she told herself she ought to get her boy Jiggs to fix it. No point asking Mr. Nelson to do it, that was for sure. If a task didn't involve his roses or some musty old book, Mr. Nelson had no interest in it at all.

She dumped her bags on the kitchen table, surprised to see he hadn't yet had any breakfast or tea. He always left such a mess for her to clean up. "Aren't you up yet, Mr. Nelson?" she called.

Silence. Not that it surprised her, really, for the old gentleman was getting frustratingly hard of hearing. She put the kettle on, then went through the door to the passage. "Mr. Nelson," she called again. "You all right, then?"

A faint whisper of concern niggled at her. He was getting on in years, Mr. Nelson. What if he'd had a heart attack and was lying dead in his bed? Or dying and in need of help? Yet it didn't seem right, somehow, her going up to check. What if he was just having a lie-in?

She put her hand on the newel post and peered up the stairs. "Mr. Nelson?" She waited, then said, "Mr. Nelson, I'm coming up. If you're not decent, you'd best sing out right now."

She took the stairs slowly, both to give him time to answer and because stairs were hard on her knees these days. "Mr. Nelson? Are you there? Because I wouldn't want to—" She stumbled to a halt, one hand fluttering up to her face. "Oh dear Lord preserve us."

The old man's body lay facedown on the doctor's sheet-draped examination table. Jude stared at the strategically positioned purple slit in Alexander Nelson's bony white back and sighed.

"He was stabbed in the back," said Dr. Chester Hayes, as if announcing the solution to some grand mystery. "Got him right in the heart." Well into his seventies, Hayes was New Godwick's only physician, and had come out of retirement when so many of the kingdom's younger doctors went off to war.

"Does rather look like it, doesn't it?" said Jude, careful not to meet Stokes's gaze.

Dr. Hayes nodded sagely. "Don't see anything else could have killed him."

From the far side of the table, Stokes made an odd, strangling noise. "Think it was the same knife that killed Crosby?"

"Hope so. I'd hate to think we've two killers running around this village."

"How long would you say he's been dead?"

"Hmm. Not too long, I should think."

Jude gave up. "Well, thank you very much, Dr. Hayes. You will let us know if you should discover anything else?"

"Of course."

Outside the doctor's surgery, Jude paused on the top step, his eyes narrowing as he watched the butcher's boy making his rounds.

"Well, that wasn't exactly helpful, was it?" said Stokes, drawing up beside him. "I'm beginning to suspect we were wrong thinking Crosby's death had anything to do with those wireless transmissions. I mean, I can see our Nazi killing the major. But a retired schoolteacher? Doesn't make sense."

"I'm not so sure about that."

Stokes glanced over at him. "What does that mean?"

Jude settled his hat low on his forehead. "Yesterday morning, Miss Townsend-Smythe went out to Knowles Point and found Major Crosby dead on his kitchen floor. Then, just a few hours later, she stopped by to have a chat with Mr. Alexander Nelson. And now he's dead, too."

Stokes shook his head. "What are you suggesting?"

"I don't know what I'm suggesting. But I think I need to have another conversation with Miss Townsend-Smythe."

She was not easy to find.

Leaving Stokes to poke around the historian's house in the hopes of finding something helpful, Jude went first to the Grange, where he was directed by the sentry at the gate to a tiny cottage deep in the Grange's park that looked like something out of a German fairy tale—one of the scarier versions. A kindly, aged gentlewoman in a wheelchair told him she rather thought her granddaughter might be down by the cow barns.

He trudged through the cow barns, only to be sent out to a field where a troop of girls drafted into the Land Army were making hay. They thought he should try the orchards. When that failed, he went back to the Grimm's fairy-tale cottage, where the kindly gentlewoman told him Miss Townsend-Smythe had come back, only to go off again to look up something at the museum.

"Where's that?" he asked.

"Old Godwick."

"I thought that fell into the sea a hundred and fifty years ago."

"Most of it, but not quite all. Some of the abbey ruins are still there. It used to be a tourist attraction, you know, before the war."

"No, I didn't know."

"Mmm. That and the beach in the cove below." A white cat appeared from nowhere to rub up against her motionless legs, and she reached down a hand to pet it. "Of course, the beach has been closed since the beginning of the war. But I hear they've opened it for bathing this summer. The village children will be ever so pleased. Give them something else to do besides chasing after crashed fighter planes and blowing themselves up playing with ammunition salvaged from the firing ranges."

"And where is this cove?"

The cat leapt up into the old woman's lap, and she smiled at it before answering. "Just south of Knowles Point."

The remains of what had once been Old Godwick lay high on the cliffs above a broad, sunlit cove. The ancient abbey church was undeniably scenic, with two soaring west towers and a half-broken rose window that thrust up golden and stark against the distant blue sea. But the rest of the abbey was little more than a neglected jumble of tumbledown walls and vague mounds overrun with vegetation. The museum—located in what looked like an old tithe barn—had a big, crudely painted sign that read Closed. But the door stood ajar, and Jude went to peer inside.

Miss Townsend-Smythe was standing before a case of books on the far wall, her head tilted as if she were scanning the titles.

She was wearing coveralls and a man's work shirt, and had her hair pulled back with scarf. As his boot scraped the threshold, she gave a faint mew of surprise and turned. "You startled me."

He studied her pale, troubled face. "You heard about Alexander Nelson?"

She swallowed. "Yes."

He wandered the echoing, gloomy space, taking in the empty cases and fading imprints of vanished displays. "Where is everything?"

"Packed away for safekeeping in what is left of the old refectory's undercroft."

He nodded toward the shelves of books behind her. "Yet you left those out?"

"They're not irreplaceable. And I still occasionally use them. It's a balancing act, isn't it? For how long can we hide everything away and hope that someday the world will be safe again?"

"The world is never really safe. It's simply an illusion each generation creates for itself, only to be stunned when it all falls apart again—usually worse than the last time." He came to a halt before her, his gaze hard on her face.

"What?" she said, her lips parting as she stared up at him.

"I want you to tell me about this cursed watch."

They went for a walk along the cliffs overlooking the sea, with the wind buffeting their ears and the seagulls screeching overhead.

"It's called La Sirène," she said, "because of the beautifully worked mermaid or siren on its balance cock. According to the legend, the watch dates back to the last years of the seventeenth century, when a slave trader and buccaneer named Jean-Baptiste Du Casse helped the French fleet plunder the city of Cartagena. As a devout Catholic, the French admiral promised the city that the sanctity of its churches would be respected. But Du Casse was a Huguenot, not a Catholic, and after the admiral sailed away, he and his men indulged in a renewed orgy of rape, torture, and murder, and they didn't spare the churches. In fact, one of Du Casse's captains personally tortured the bishop into betraying where the basilica's treasures were hidden. As he lay dying, the bishop damned the pirates' souls forever more, and called upon God to lay a terrible curse upon their plunder."

"What sort of curse?"

She gave a wry smile. "I'm not sure the exact words were ever recorded."

"So what happened?"

"Yellow fever. Hurricanes. Shipwrecks. Dead wives and children. Lots of dead wives and children."

"And Du Casse?"

"He and his captain—a fellow by the name of Vautour—somehow made it back to the port of Saint-Domingue. And to show his defiance of the curse, Vautour had part of his share of the gold from the basilica melted down and made into a beautifully crafted watch engraved with the motto 'Je suis le seul maître de mon temps.'"

"'I am the only master of my time.' Cheeky. So what happened to him?"

"He died. Unpleasantly."

"And the watch?"

"Supposedly it wreaked a path of destruction on down through the ages. You'd think the curse would put people off. Instead it seems to have added to the watch's allure."

"Where is it now?"

"No one knows exactly. It was separated from its outer case early in the nineteenth century, and that case somehow ended up in Northumbria. That's where Major Crosby was originally from, you see—Northumbria. One of his great-uncles gave it to him when he was a boy and told him the watch's story. He was captivated by it, and spent the rest of his life looking for the watch. He told me it surfaced several times over the last century—once when there was a terrible plague in Edinburgh in the 1830s, and again in London with a string of gruesome murders some forty years later. At one point it belonged to a hot-air balloonist named Beecham, who had it with him when he took his daughter and grandson up in his balloon. They crashed and everyone was killed. I believe it then passed into the hands of a local man. But he suffered such terrible misfortunes that he got rid of it."

"So what's the link between Crosby and Alexander Nelson?"

"I think Mr. Nelson was helping the major trace the man's descendants."

Jude drew up at the edge of the cliff to stare out over the cove. It was a pretty place, with a long, gently curving crescent of broad, hard-packed sand that looked as if it had recently been cleared of the obstructions that had been thrown up along most of England's beaches during the invasion scare. But the massive concrete barriers laid down to discourage landing craft were still out in the water, supplementing the mounds of rock he had first thought were natural, then realized were actually clumps of fallen masonry from the now-vanished village.

"Haunting spot," he said.

She paused beside him. "The village was closer to the cliffs than the old abbey. But one day what's left of the abbey will go over, too."

"'Look on my works, ye Mighty, and despair,'" he quoted softly.

He was aware of her looking at him. "I didn't know Scotland Yard types admired Shelley."

"We can be versatile."

"Huh." She drew in a ragged breath. "I suppose it does help to put our current turmoil into perspective."

"Perhaps. Although meditating on an endless cycle of destruction and ruin isn't exactly cheery."

She gave a faint gurgle of laughter. "No." She was silent a moment, then said, "Is it possible Hitler could be interested in the watch? I've heard he has agents scouring Europe and North Africa for occult objects, and La Sirène is just the sort of thing that would appeal to him. That German spy you said is operating in the area—"

"I never said there's a German spy in the area."

"Not to me, no."

Jude turned to gaze back at the ruined abbey. "There was an abbey like this near the village where my father grew up, in Shropshire."

"Is that where you're from? Shropshire? So how did you come to be with Scotland Yard, Detective Inspector Lowe?"

"My father joined the army, married a vicar's daughter, and got himself killed in Kenya. His colonel felt responsible, and I guess paying my school fees soothed his conscience." It was an abbreviated explanation, of course, leaving out some of the stickier bits, but it served its purpose.

"And your arm?"

"That happened in North Africa."

He was aware of her looking at him. "You didn't answer my question about Hitler's possible interest in the watch."

He gave a deliberately negligent shrug and remained silent.

She put up a hand to hold back the hair that had blown loose from her scarf, but her gaze never left his face. "You're not really with Scotland Yard, are you?"

He managed a fairly credible laugh. "What else would I be with?"

"MI5."

He laughed again, although less credibly this time. A gull screeched overhead, raucous and haunting and drawing his attention to the sky. He said, "I don't think it's a good idea, you being out here all alone like this."

"Whyever not?"

"It's rather obvious, isn't it? There've been two murders in this village in two days, and you're connected to both victims. Will you let me drive you back to the Grange?"

He thought she would refuse.

She didn't.

⁂

They drove through a darkening countryside that smelled of fecund earth and sweetly ripening grain.

"If you look out there now," she said, her gaze on a grove of leafy, old-growth oaks flashing past. "If you look at the quiet fields and endless sea and chirping birds coming in to roost for the night, the world seems so peaceful, so beautiful and good. But it's not."

He glanced over at her. She had the window down, the breeze blowing her hair around her face. And something about the solemn cast of her features struck him as so vulnerable and troubled that he felt the urge to reach out to take her hand.

He did not.

She said, "Do you believe in God?"

He was silent for a moment, considering his answer. "I honestly don't know. As some sort of celestial manager? No. As a greater good to which we should all aspire? Perhaps. The problem is, as a species we seem to fail far too often. Spectacularly."

"I can't decide if that's reassuring or depressing."

He gave a soft huff of laughter. "Maybe both." Then he did take her hand. And rather than pull away, she held on to him.

Tightly.

⁂

"Did that nice MI5 man ever find you, my dear?" Nana asked when Rachel made it back to the cottage.

Rachel stooped to give her grandmother's cheek a kiss. "He insists he's Scotland Yard, Nana. But yes, he did find me."

"The reverend called while you were out."

Rachel was heading for the kitchen to put the kettle on, but that stopped her. She popped her head back around the doorframe. "Oh?"

"He asked me to tell you the gentleman you were inquiring after lives in Dover. Somewhere near the castle, he thinks." And then Rachel wondered what Nana saw on her face because her grandmother added, "That's important, is it?"

"It could be. I might catch the bus to Dover tomorrow, if you don't mind?"

"Of course not, darling. Why would I mind?"

Jude stood with one elbow propped on the mantel, Major Crosby's shadow box in his hands as he stared down at the empty hearth.

"You keep fiddling with that thing," said Stokes, looking up from where he was working on a report. "You aren't seriously giving credence to this whole 'cursed watch' thing, are you?"

Jude glanced over at him. "Hitler does have a well-known interest in occult objects."

"True. But it seems far-fetched to me."

"The idea of an unstable buffoon like Hitler managing to seize power in the first place is far-fetched," said Jude, setting the shadow box aside. "Yet it happened."

"It happened."

Chapter 7

The next morning, Rachel caught the early bus to Dover.

It was a trip she'd made often during those first years of the war, when she'd volunteered at the War Office and was assigned to work as an ambulance driver. Now as she watched the familiar villages and sun-dappled fields flicker past the bus's dusty windows, for one stolen moment out of time she felt herself slipping back to the days when Ben and her mother had both been alive, and Nana well and strong. Before news came of the sinking of the HMS *Thanet*. Before her mother and Nana made that fateful trip up to London that ended with her mother dead and Nana never able to walk again. Before so many had died and so much had been lost forever.

How had it happened? she wondered, her throat closing painfully with grief and despair. How had a country as cultured, civilized, and prosaically *sane* as Germany allowed itself to fall under the spell of a fast-talking charlatan who seduced them with empty promises and twisted their fears and anger into a lethal hatred directed toward society's most vulnerable members? *How?* She felt her eyes filming over and had to squeeze them shut before the tears spilled over to run down her cheeks.

By the time she opened them again, they'd reached the bomb-blasted outskirts of Dover, and ugly piles of dusty rubble had replaced the calm, timeless vistas of the countryside.

A few questions directed to the local authorities brought Rachel to a gaping hole where Peter Osborne's house should have stood. Fragments of masonry and blackened timbers lay jumbled together with still-identifiable objects like a twisted iron bed frame and what she realized was a fragment of a bathtub. The air was pungent with the stench of brick dust, burnt wood, and spilled sewage. She was still standing in the middle of the street and staring at the wreckage when a middle-aged woman in slippers and an apron came out of the house next door to pause on the stoop and call, "You all right there, love?"

Rachel dragged her gaze away from the shattered house. "I was looking for Mr. Peter Osborne."

"Oh, I'm that sorry, love," said the woman, wiping her hands on her apron as she hurried down the steps toward her. "Are you…" She hesitated, then corrected herself. "Were you related to him?"

Rachel shook her head. "No. He was from my village." She nodded to the bombed-out house. "When did this happen?"

"Just last night, it was."

"Was anyone else killed?"

"No one, thank the good Lord. If the Jerries had to hit one house on the block, it was right kind of them to pick the one that was empty."

"So Mr. Osborne wasn't killed?"

"Oh, the Germans didn't have nothing to do with that." She dropped her voice and leaned in closer, as if about to impart something so horrible it could only be spoken of in hushed tones. "Murdered, he was. Just four nights ago. Knifed dead in his bed. The authorities have no idea who did it. But I can tell you, I keep my doors locked these days, I do."

Rachel had the oddest sensation, as if the woman's voice were suddenly coming from a long way off.

The woman touched Rachel's arm. "You all right there, ducky? You don't look well. I don't know what I was thinking, breaking it to you like this in the middle of the street. Why don't you come in and sit a spell while I fix you a nice cup of tea?"

Rachel took the woman up on her offer.

Her name was Molly O'Malley, and she ushered Rachel into a kitchen with a gaping window and bits of fallen plaster that had been swept into a pile along with the shattered glass and some broken crockery. "Haven't quite got it all cleaned up yet," said Mrs. O'Malley, bustling about and putting the kettle on. "But you just have a seat there and let me cut you a nice slice of cake."

Rachel couldn't remember the last time she'd had a slice of proper, old-fashioned cake. "It's made with honey, of course," said Mrs. O'Malley, fussing with her teapot. "But my Charlie says it's ever so good."

Rachel knew real sugar when she tasted it, but she was polite enough to keep her mouth shut and simply enjoy the cake. Mrs. O'Malley obviously had connections to someone in the black market.

"So did you know Mr. Osborne well?" Rachel asked casually.

Mrs. O'Malley popped a knitted pink cozy over the teapot and came to settle in the chair opposite. "Not so well, no. He was a bit of a queer one, if you don't mind my saying so. Although I suppose it's no wonder, given all the tragedies I hear he had in his life. Like something out of a Dickens novel, it was. Blamed it all on a cursed watch he said his father used to have. Thought it sounded a bit like a Banbury tale, myself. But there's no denying he believed it."

Rachel paused with a forkful of cake raised halfway to her mouth. "Did he ever say what happened to it? The watch, I mean."

"Claimed his father hid it under an altar in some church crypt, if you can believe it. Said the watch was cursed because it was made of gold stolen from God, so the old man figured giving it back to God was the only way to contain the curse. Although when you think about what happened to poor Mr. Osborne in the end, it doesn't sound as if it worked, now does it?"

"He didn't say which church, did he?"

Mrs. O'Malley frowned. Rachel was afraid her questions had raised the woman's suspicions. But Molly O'Malley was obviously one of those people with such a bountiful curiosity about anyone and everyone that it never occurred to her to find Rachel's interest strange. "Hmm. Can't say he ever did, no." She pushed to her feet and went to collect a couple of cups and saucers. "I'll have to ask my Charlie. He might know. He was telling me just the other day that Mr. Osborne was talking about it. Seems some relative was visiting him and got him thinking on it."

"Did you see him? The relative, I mean."

"I didn't. But I think my Charlie did."

"Could you ask him for me and give me a ring if he did? Do you have a phone you could use?"

"Well, I suppose I could ask Mrs. York down at the corner shop if I could use hers." She went to fetch a bottle of milk from the icebox while Rachel scribbled down her number on a small notepad. "Now, how about another slice of cake with your tea?"

"Where were you that night? *Where*, damn it?" demanded Stokes, looming over the prisoner who sat shackled to a chair in the center of an otherwise empty concrete cell at the back of New Godwick's Victorian-era police station. The air was thick with the stench of urine, vomit, and fear that had seeped into the place down through the ages. Through the high, barred window, the sky was a patch of looming clouds.

"I tell you, I was home," whispered Alberto Capello, his shoulders hunched and his head bowed. A mixture of blood and mucus dribbled from his nose into his mouth and onto the floor below him.

"Let's try this again, shall we?" said Stokes. The Italian's head snapped sideways as Stokes backhanded him across the face. "Where were you?"

"Home."

Stokes hit him again. "You bloody fascist! You were seen leaving your mother's house."

Stokes drew back his hand again, and Jude said softly, "*Stokes.*"

Capello gave a strangled sob. "All right! All right, I'll tell you." He was breathing heavily, his body shuddering. "I went to see Lisa. Lisa Jensen."

Stokes and Jude both looked at Police Sergeant Gillingham, who stood with Jude in the cell's open doorway. "Who is she?" asked Stokes.

"A thatcher's wife. Her husband's with the army in Italy." Gillingham's nostrils flared with contempt as he glared at Capello. "You bloody bastard. I'd no idea she was such a whore."

Capello was crying openly now, the great, shuddering sobs of a broken man.

"We can check, you know," said Stokes, fisting one hand in the Italian's bloodstained shirtfront.

"Leave him," said Jude in disgust as he pushed away from the doorframe. "He's telling the truth, and you've just spent the last ten minutes beating an innocent man for the crime of being born in Italy."

"He lied to me," said Stokes, walking fast to catch up as Jude strode down the noisome corridor toward the outside door.

Jude swung to face him. "Of course he lied to you. He was protecting the reputation of a woman he loves. And now you've not only dragged her name through the mud, but you've effectively destroyed any self-respect that man had left."

Stokes set his jaw, his chest heaving with his angry breaths. "We're looking for a killer, in case you had forgotten. A killer who's also probably a Nazi."

"Oh, that's right; we're the good guys. I'm glad you reminded me," said Jude, and turned to walk off into the sea-scented storm.

CHAPTER 8

RACHEL STOOD BESIDE THE Osborne family's lichen-covered tomb in the churchyard of New Godwick, her head falling back as she stared up at the weeping angel outlined against the cloudy sky. Bertrand Osborne had buried his wife and three children here, beside the church's eastern end. But when it came time for his own death, he had insisted on being laid to rest as far from this point as possible. At first she'd assumed he must have sought to distance himself from his family out of guilt. But now she suspected it had more to do with what lay beside them in the crypt below.

Once, the crypt of St. Stephen's had been filled with moldering, cobweb-draped coffins dating back to the early decades of the nineteenth century. But a year into the war, Reverend Dingle had decided to clear the crypt and put it at the disposal of the villagers for use as an air-raid shelter. The vicar's congregation hadn't been particularly enthusiastic about the scheme—the thought of taking shelter in what was essentially a grave not having much appeal. But the reverend kept pushing for it, and Rachel had been one of those who'd finally volunteered to help move the old coffins to a quiet corner of the churchyard for burial. As far as she knew no one had ever used the crypt to shelter from a raid, but it was always left unlocked, just in case. And she had a vague memory of the simple stone altar that still stood at its eastern end.

A cool breeze kicked up, bringing with it the scent of the

coming storm, and Rachel gave a faint shiver. She would need to come back again in the morning, she decided. She turned and took two steps toward where she'd left her bicycle. But she knew she was being a coward, knew she was grasping for excuses to put it off. And so she drew up, sucked in a deep breath, and forced herself to walk to the south side of the nave where a vaulted stone staircase led down to the crypt.

The stair vault's old door opened with an ominous creak. Stale, foul air wafted out at her, tainted with the smell of dank stone and old death. There was no railing, so she had to skim one hand along the rough, damp stones to steady herself as she crept down the shadowy steps. At the base of the stairs, she paused, her heart thudding unpleasantly in her chest and her breath coming hard and fast. She told herself she should have brought a torch. She told herself she could still go home and come back tomorrow. But the truth was that between the light wells and the faint glow from the open door above, she would be able to see well enough if she just gave her eyes time to adjust to the gloom.

She stood still, willing her hands to stop shaking, and realized she could already pick out the shadowy features of the crypt—the double rows of stocky piers; the dusty old pews Reverend Dingle had moved down here "just in case, so people won't need to sit on the cold damp floor." At the far end stood an ancient stone altar that looked as if it had been brought here years ago from the Norman church at Old Godwick before it tumbled over the cliff into the sea. Once Rachel had asked her grandmother if the burials from the old crypt and churchyard had been moved, too, but she said she didn't know.

She found herself shamefully reluctant to leave the stair vault, so that she had to force herself to walk forward, the rasp of her breathing sounding unnaturally loud in the stillness. She realized she wasn't even certain what she wanted to find. As a museum curator, the thought of discovering something as beautiful and legendary as La Sirène filled her with excitement. Yet at the same time, the knowledge of the horrors it had supposedly wrought on down through the centuries filled her with a sense of dread she recognized as illogical even as she was forced to admit it was real. Then again, she reminded herself, her carefully reasoned guesswork could easily be wrong; the watch might not even be here. Or someone could already have discovered its hiding place and taken it.

She'd almost reached the east end when she heard the whisper of a step behind her, and Detective Inspector Lowe said, "What are you doing?"

She whirled around, one hand coming up to press against her chest in an automatic gesture that only increased her annoyance with herself. "Dear God. You frightened me half to death," she said. "How did you know I was here?"

"I saw you from across the churchyard."

"And followed me? Seriously?"

He walked toward her, his footsteps echoing in the empty space. "I thought we had agreed you were going to avoid putting yourself in danger."

"And precisely how am I putting myself in danger by visiting my village church?"

He drew up in front of her, his gaze searching her face in a way that made her wonder what he saw there. "If you don't think you're in danger, then why are you frightened?"

She gave an unexpected laugh. "I suppose because I've just discovered I'm more superstitious than I'd realized."

He cast a quick glance around the shadowy crypt. "So exactly what are you doing down here?"

"I think Bertrand Osborne might have hidden La Sirène in the crypt's altar."

He frowned. "Who is Bertrand Osbourne?"

"The local man I was telling you once owned the watch."

He turned to stare at the ancient altar tucked into the eastern end of the crypt. It was only now since her eyes had adjusted to the dark that Rachel realized its outline wasn't quite right. A section of the base had been torn apart.

"Looks like someone else had the same idea," he said, going to hunker down beside the scattered masonry.

Rachel went to stand beside him, conscious of a tingle of inexplicable fear running up her neck, as if she were in the presence of some great evil. "I wonder if he found it."

"He obviously found something."

She shook her head. "How can you tell?"

He held up a worn old box, its lid open to reveal an empty silk-lined interior embroidered in tarnished gold with the words "Je suis le seul maître de mon temps." The silk was frayed with age and had faded to a dull brown, but it still clearly showed the imprint of the object that had once nestled within it.

An imprint the precise size and shape of the long-lost La Sirène.

"Why didn't you tell me about this Bertrand Osborne before?" Jude asked Miss Townsend-Smythe over a pint in the Black Horse Inn's lounge bar. The voices and laughter from the public bar—an exclusively male preserve—formed a distant dull roar, but the lounge was virtually deserted.

"I did," she said, sipping a glass of cider. "The way I remember it, you weren't particularly interested."

Jude frowned. He had a vague memory of her talking about some tragedy-plagued local man who'd once owned the watch. But she was right; he'd written it off as just another segment in that long line of horrors supposedly wrought by the "curse" on down through the ages. "What made you think he'd hidden the watch in the village's crypt?"

"I discovered his only surviving son, Peter, recently moved to Dover. So this morning I went to see him. One of his neighbors told me a tale about his father hiding some cursed watch in a crypt's altar, and I figured it made sense that the old man had hidden it here in New Godwick." She glanced up as a middle-aged couple walked into the lounge bar and dropped her voice. "Peter Osborne himself is dead, by the way: someone murdered him several days ago. So you can add his name to your list of this killer's victims."

"*Damn*," said Jude under his breath.

He was aware of her studying him thoughtfully. She said, "This could all be the work of some murderous English collector who will stop at nothing to get his hands on the watch and its case. But that doesn't explain what you and your partner are doing here, or what I heard you say two days ago out at Knowles Farm Cottage."

He drained his pint and set it aside.

She said, "You're not going to tell me, are you?"

"No."

She pushed back her chair and was halfway up before he reached out a hand to stop her. "I can't tell you what I know, but I can tell you to be careful."

"Of *what*?"

When he simply stared back at her, she jerked her arm from his grasp and left him there, alone, with his pint.

The next morning, after the storm blew through, Jude walked out to the crumbling cliffs of what had once been Old Godwick. He stood for a time with his gaze on the ruined towers and broken rose window of the old abbey. He might not believe in curses or dark powers, but he knew that many did.

He kept thinking about what Rachel Townsend-Smythe had told him, that the village was a closed society in which any stranger would immediately be obvious. But that wasn't strictly true anymore. Thanks to the war, there were now many strangers in the surrounding district. It had been the practice before the war for East Enders to travel down to Kent for the hop harvest every autumn and then go home. But after the hop pick of '39, many had stayed. At the same time, both the Grange and Bancroft Court had been taken over by the War Office. And then there was the Land Army, the young women conscripted into service on farms to replace the men gone off to fight. Hell, he'd recently discovered that even Reverend Dingle had only arrived in the village six months after the war started.

The problem was, the War Office had only begun picking up wireless transmissions from this area some three weeks ago. And from what he and Stokes had been able to discover, no one new had been assigned to the district for several months.

So how long had this mysterious operative been in the area before he began sending his quick, coded messages? Six months? A year? Longer? And why had he suddenly begun contacting Hamburg? Because he'd finally traced both the watchcase and the watch itself? Did that explain the sequence in which the killer had struck—killing first Peter Osborne, then the major, and finally Alexander Nelson? And if the murders were all committed by the same man, then why had he killed Nelson? Because Nelson might somehow have been able to identify him?

Frustrated, Jude walked out to the edge of the cliff, his gaze on a pair of sand martins darting about their nest in the soft rock face. Standing here, staring out over a blue infinity of rolling waves, it was easy to forget that there was a hideous war going on out there. A half-forgotten line of verse kept running through his head... *The years of old stand in the sun and murmur of childhood and the dead.* What the hell was that from? He couldn't place it.

The sound of a car engine caught his attention, and he turned to watch the Rover bump and sway over the rutted track to the abbey. Stokes pulled up on the weedy sweep beside the ruined church, then got out and began to walk toward him.

"The War Office telephoned," Stokes called.

Jude stood still and let his partner come up to him. "And?"

"They picked up another transmission last night, from a couple miles south of here."

“Damn,” said Jude.

“They think they’ve finally cracked the code our boy is using. If they’re right, he’s asking to be picked up tonight at someplace designated as ‘rendezvous point two.’”

“Tonight?”

“Tonight.” Stokes hesitated, then said, “The code is in German.”

Jude gave a low, incredulous huff of laughter. “I’d have thought that was a given. He is communicating with Hamburg, after all.”

“They seem to think it’s a significant discovery.” Stokes stared out over the cove.

“What?” said Jude, watching him.

“They want us to bring in Reinhardt.”

Jude felt a surge of impotent frustration and fury. “It’s not Reinhardt.”

“They think it has to be. And they think if we put enough pressure on him, he’ll crack and admit it.”

“What kind of pressure?”

A faint line of color rode high on the Scotland Yard man’s cheeks. There was a tension, a wariness between the two men that hadn’t been there before yesterday afternoon and the incident with Alberto Capello at the village police station.

“Bloody hell,” swore Jude. “I’m not doing this.”

Stokes’s dark gaze met his. “We don’t have a choice.”

CHAPTER 9

THE LOCAL MAGISTRATE, SIR Hugh Bancroft, had telephoned that morning to tell Rachel that Major Crosby had left everything he owned to the abbey museum, with Rachel named as executor. The will wouldn't work its way through the legal system for a while yet, but Sir Hugh thought that under the circumstances it would be proper for her to pack away some of the more valuable items in the major's collection. "Just to keep them safe," he said.

And so she made the painful journey back out to Knowles Farm Cottage to draw up a rough inventory of the major's collection and prioritize what to store first. And because Sigmund Reinhardt had been a professor of art history in Vienna, she asked him to help her.

"I've always wanted to see this collection," said Reinhardt, pausing on the threshold of the double parlor crowded with display cabinets and cases filled with rare, beautiful, and wondrous objects.

She glanced back at him in surprise. "You mean you haven't?"

Reinhardt ducked his head to hide a sad smile. "The Nazis aren't the only ones who have problems with people like me."

People like me. Rachel felt a strange medley of emotions sluice through her. Which aspect of Sigmund Reinhardt's humanity had Major Crosby objected to? she wondered. Obviously it wasn't the Austrian's education, so what was it? His religion? His nationality? His socialism? His sexual orientation? It both shocked and shamed her to realize that she hadn't known this about the major—that he could judge people and find them lacking on the basis of such externals. She'd called him friend for more than twenty years, but she hadn't known about the dark smallness that lurked within him.

"That surprises you?" said Reinhardt, watching her.

"Yes. I'm sorry."

He shrugged and smiled faintly as he gazed around the room. "What an incredible treasure trove. Where would you like me to begin?"

They divided the room into sections and set about listing the contents of each case. But Rachel kept finding it difficult to focus on the task at hand, her mind drifting inevitably to the events of the last few days. At one point she went to stand beside the major's favorite fireside chair and stare at the empty spot on the wall where the shadow box had once hung. There was a small, very old book lying on the table beside his chair, a book she recognized as *A Perilous Journey to Rome* by Mary MacPherson. Rachel had actually gone out to the museum a couple of days ago looking for it, having forgotten that the major himself had recently asked to borrow it. When she picked it up, it opened to a page marked by a worn piece of ribbon, and she found herself staring at a chapter titled "La Sirène."

She glanced over at Sigmund Reinhardt. "How much do you know about Hitler's interest in the occult?"

He'd been inspecting a terra-cotta Etruscan statue of a horse, but at her question he looked up, his eyes narrowing. "I've heard it's not as intense as Himmler's or Bormann's. Why?"

"But his interest is real?"

"Oh, yes; it's real all right. After all, he recruited many of his top lieutenants—not just Bormann and Himmler but also men like Rosenberg and Hess—from the Thule Society and other Nordic cults. They say he keeps an extensive library on the subject in the private quarters of his bunker in Berlin—on everything from runes and astrology to reincarnation and ghosts."

"What about items reputed to have special powers?" she asked. "Does he actually collect them?"

Reinhardt was silent for a moment, his back to her as he carefully settled the Etruscan piece into its case. "He does, yes. Why do you ask?"

"Just wondering."

He turned to face her again. "It has something to do with the deaths of Crosby and Nelson, doesn't it? Is that why those two men were sent here from the War Office? Because Hitler has someone searching for some occult object? What?"

She shook her head. "Those men aren't from the War Office. They're Scotland Yard."

"The older one, perhaps. But not the tall, dark one—the one who's perpetually angry at the world because he's bright and educated, but it counts for nothing because he's the grandson of a simple tavern owner and he went to Cambridge on the strength of his intellect rather than on the power of an old family name."

Rachel stared at him. "How do you know that?"

Reinhardt picked up the pages of his inventory and made a quick notation. "I asked some friends in Cambridge about him."

Why? she wanted to ask. But then she thought about Reinhardt's background and Jude Lowe's reason for being here, and she understood.

The sound of an engine laboring up the rough drive from the lane drew their attention. "Who is it?" Rachel asked as Reinhardt went to stare out a side window.

"Our friends from London. Were you expecting them?"

"No." She heard the slam of car doors and went to stand beside the Austrian. "I wonder what they want?" Yet even as she said it, she realized she already knew.

"You'd best sit down," he told her.

"But—"

His tortured gaze met hers. "Trust me on this. Sit down, and no matter what happens, stay out of it. Please?"

Sigmund Reinhardt was locking one of the major's display cases when Jude and Stokes walked into the overstuffed front parlor. Jude cast one swift glance at the woman who sat stiff and straight-backed on a worn chair beside the empty hearth. But after that he was careful not to look at her again. He wished like hell she wasn't here to witness this, but there was nothing he could do about it now.

"Were you looking for me, gentlemen?" asked the Austrian, turning slowly to face them.

Stokes sauntered up to the former university professor with his exaggerated policeman's swagger. "How'd you figure that out, Herr Reinhardt?"

"Educated guess?" said the Austrian, right before Stokes backhanded him across the face.

Miss Townsend-Smythe came up out of her chair in a rush. "What are you doing?"

Stokes didn't even bother to glance at her. "You're under arrest," he told the Austrian.

She turned to Jude. "For what?"

Jude remained silent as Stokes slapped his handcuffs on the prisoner. "That's none of your business, ma'am."

"So we're taking lessons on tactics from the Gestapo these days, are we? You *hit him*. For no reason at all."

"We have our reasons," said Stokes.

Jude saw her hands clench into fists at her sides. Saw, too, when she forced herself to open and press them flat against her skirt. "You're wrong. He has nothing to do with what's been happening around here."

"Then he can prove it," said Stokes, jerking the Austrian toward the door.

For one moment, her gaze met Jude's. But all she said was, "How do you prove a negative?"

Sigmund Reinhardt sat on a metal chair in the center of a cold, empty cell, his head bowed and his shoulders slumped. *Bleak*, thought Jude, watching him. *Isn't that how all this started?*

Jude stood with his shoulders pressed against a far wall, his arms crossed at his chest. But Stokes paced the room, a kind of nervous energy roiling off him. And it came to Jude, watching him, that the Scotland Yard man was enjoying this. The thought made him vaguely sick to his stomach.

"So where's this rendezvous point they're supposed to be picking you up from tonight?" Stokes demanded.

"I don't know what you're talking about."

"Don't you? Where'd you hide the wireless?"

Reinhardt kept his gaze fixed on the foul drain at his feet. "I don't have a wireless."

Stokes swung around to grab a fistful of the man's hair, yanking back his head. "Where is it, damn you?"

Jude stared down at his own shoes, ashamed to be witnessing this, ashamed to be doing nothing to stop it, ashamed to be a part of it. They had searched the room the Austrian rented from a Mrs. Gibbs out by the crossroads. They'd torn it apart and found nothing—no wireless, no codebooks, no gold watch, no knife. Nothing.

"Where did you hide it?" Stokes demanded.

"I have no wireless."

Stokes let go of the man's hair. As Reinhardt's head slumped forward again, the Scotland Yard man brought up one knee to smash it into the Austrian's face.

Jude heard bone crunch.

"You need to try a different answer." Stokes grasped the man by the shoulders and slammed him back against the chair. "I don't think you understand the situation you're in. You have no rights here. I can lock you up forever. I can even kill you if I want, and no one will care. No one. Now, where's the bloody wireless?"

Reinhardt stared up at him. The Austrian's face was a mottled, swollen mess, with blood dripping from his shattered nose and one eye horribly distorted.

Stokes clenched his fist to hit him again.

"Stop it," said Jude, coming off the wall to snag his partner's arm. "Enough."

Stokes glanced over at him, his chest jerking with his heavy breathing, his face twisted into something ugly to see. "If you don't have the stomach for this, maybe you should leave the room."

He yanked his arm from Jude's grasp, and Jude let him. But as Stokes drew back his fist to hit Reinhardt again, the Austrian said, "No. Wait. Please. Listen to me."

"What?" demanded Stokes, not lowering his fist.

Reinhardt lifted one shoulder in an effort to swipe away some of the blood from his mouth. "I don't have a wireless—no wait," he said quickly when Stokes would have hit him again. "I'm not the person you're looking for, but I may know something."

"What?"

Reinhardt's tongue darted out to lick at his broken, bleeding lips. "It's something I overheard. It may be innocent—there may be a simple explanation, but—"

"What, damn you?"

He told them then, his voice a broken, hushed whisper from a broken man. Afterward, Jude fetched a basin of warm water and a cloth and tried to wash the blood from the man's face.

"Leave it," said the Austrian, jerking his head away.

Jude ignored him.

"What do you think?" said the Austrian, his gaze meeting Jude's and holding it. "That if you do this, it will in some small way atone for what you allowed to happen here today? Well, it won't. There is a darkness that exists within each of us, Mr. Lowe. All it takes is a seductive leader or the right circumstances to turn that darkness into evil. I have struggled all my life to stay on the side of goodness and light. What about you, Mr. Lowe? Do you even know which side you're on?"

CHAPTER 10

EARLY THAT EVENING THE sea turned rough, with great rolling swells that broke against the offshore rocks in the cove in great booming crashes that sent columns of spray high into the air. But the sky remained a clear, calm blue, and a rich golden light flooded the high cliffs.

After she'd checked the hop fields, dealt with a minor crisis in the damson orchards, and separated two Land Girls fighting over a scarf, Rachel was finally free to tuck the old French book into the pocket of her overalls and pedal her bicycle out to the abbey ruins. She was drawn there by a strange combination of the site's tragic history and its air of peace and solitude. But she still found her hands shaking as she opened the book to the marked chapter and began to read.

That night, a storm arose so suddenly and with such violence on the sea that it cast our ship onto a shore most desolate, and there we met a pirate who possessed a watch named for the mermaid etched within its wheels, wrought of the finest gold but carrying an evil curse…

Rachel found herself sitting forward, her fingers gripping the pages so tightly they turned white. She was far too much of an educated professional to believe in curses and dark powers. And yet…

She read on, skimming quickly through the Frenchwoman's tale. And then, near the end, her breath caught.

> *The old enchanter told him, "In truth, my words were that the spell would not be easily undone. But any spell or curse can be undone. To break the hold of this one requires your mermaid to pass through all four elements in turn—first water, then earth, then air, and finally fire."*

Closing the book, Rachel set the tattered volume on the stone step beside her and thrust her hands between her knees. The watch had already traveled over the sea when it was brought from Saint-Domingue to England. It had been buried deep in the earth after the Edinburgh plague, then passed into the hands of a hot-air balloonist who'd met his death in a horrible crash. All that remained was for La Sirène to go through fire, and then the curse would be—

Don't be ridiculous, she told herself sternly. *At this rate, you're going to start imagining you're seeing ghosts and leprechauns around every corner.* But her heart was still thudding uncomfortably, and she pushed up from the broken steps to walk through the saxifrage- and daisy-strewn meadows along the edge of the cliff.

Somewhere out at sea a storm must be brewing, she thought, watching the waves smash against the fallen remnants of the long-lost village that still lay offshore in the cove below. She turned her face into the salty wind, letting it stream her hair out behind her. In the first months after they'd learned of Ben's death, she had thought of the sea as her brother's grave and hated the sight of it for that reason. But at some indefinable point, she had begun to see the water as Ben—as if his essence had joined with the timeless oceans and now lapped the shores of his homeland to soothe Rachel's grief and fears with his eternal presence. Perhaps that was the real reason why she had come to the cove today, she realized: to seek guidance from Ben the way she had so often as a little girl. And perhaps, too, because the sea reminded her of the limits of study and education—of just how much in this world is unknown and unknowable.

The rattle of a falling pebble brought her head around, and she saw a young woman coming toward her along the cliff-top path. She had a towheaded little boy balanced on one hip, and she waved at Rachel.

"Pippa," called Rachel, turning to walk toward her. "Have you come to see the waves?"

Pippa broke into a broad smile as she looked out over the rough water. "Isn't it glorious?"

"We go for walk on beach," announced the little boy, wiggling with delight.

Rachel laughed. "Will you look for some seashells?"

Wills nodded. "Only, I forgot my pail."

Pippa's eyes narrowed as she studied the distant skyline. "Is there a storm coming, do you think?"

"Doesn't look like it, unless it's way offshore."

"With any luck it's hitting Germany," said Pippa, and Rachel saw something hard flicker across the woman's gently molded, sad features, as if she were looking across the water to the land that had taken her home, her family—everything except the little nephew she held clutched so tightly in her arms.

"That would at least keep the Luftwaffe away," said Rachel. "Although I don't think it stops doodlebugs."

"I suppose not." Pippa put up a hand to catch her flying hair. "I just heard on the radio that our troops should take Caen soon. They're saying that if we can retake France, Germany might surrender. But the vicar, he seems to think they'll fight till the bitter end—that Hitler is convinced he's the new Messiah and that there'll be some sort of divine intervention—a miracle—to save the day." She hesitated, then added. "Did you know he's German?"

"Reverend Dingle?" said Rachel, her voice coming out hollow. "He is?"

Pippa nodded. "Well, his mother was, at any rate. And he lived there for a time as a child." She shifted Wills's weight on her hip. "Must be hard on him, seeing two countries he loves tear each other apart like this."

"Yes," said Rachel, her throat suddenly so tight it hurt.

"Want go to beach," said Wills, stretching out his hand toward the sand below.

"Wills!" said his aunt.

Rachel laughed and ruffled the little boy's hair. "I guess all this talk means nothing to you, does it, little man?"

"Nothing, and yet everything," said Pippa.

Rachel could only meet her gaze and silently nod.

Lots of people in Britain had ties of some sort or another with Germany—even the royal family, Rachel reminded herself. She told herself the vicar's unknown heritage could mean nothing. And yet…

On her way back through New Godwick, she found herself pausing for a moment beside the lych-gate, her gaze on the simple church surrounded by the graves of the village's silent dead. Could a man of God really be operating as an agent for Hitler? she wondered. Could someone as seemingly kind and caring as Reverend Dingle ruthlessly kill three men? Simply to possess a cursed watch whose legendary powers might provide the Nazis' sinking regime with the help they needed to avert impending doom? It seemed a ridiculous notion—and yet not beyond the realm of possibility.

She positioned her right foot on the pedal and was about to push off again when the vicar himself came around the corner of the church and saw her. "Miss Townsend-Smythe," he called, waving. "Hold up a moment."

She paused.

"I had a telephone call this morning from a woman named

Mrs. O'Malley," he said, hurrying toward her. "Seems she lost your number and rang me in the hopes that I could get a message to you." He gave a rueful grin. "Let me see if I can get this right. She says she spoke to her husband, and he told her the relative who came to speak to Mr. Osborne was a woman—a woman with a child. But that's all he could recall about her." He paused and looked hopeful. "Does that make sense?"

"It does, yes. Thanks ever so much, Reverend."

She was aware of Reverend Dingle looking at her with that expectant expression of his, the one that was so effective at coaxing people to say more than they might otherwise have divulged. In the past Rachel had seen the reverend's inquisitiveness as nothing more than a personality quirk. Now she found herself wondering if it was, in truth, something considerably more sinister.

"Did you hear those Scotland Yard men roughed up Sigmund Reinhardt?" the reverend was saying. "His landlady, Mrs. Gibbs, tells me he's in such bad shape that she wanted to have Dr. Hayes in to look at him. But Reinhardt wouldn't hear of it."

"They've let him go?" Rachel said sharply.

"They have, yes."

Sigmund Reinhardt was sitting at a rusting iron table in Mrs. Gibbs's garden when Rachel came upon him. He had one hand raised to hold an ice pack to his face and a glass of what looked like brandy on the table beside him. His head was bowed, his eyes closed, so that Rachel thought he must be sleeping. She was about to leave him alone when he looked up and said, "Ah, Rachel. Come to see if I'm still alive, have you?"

"Dear God," she said, going to sink into a nearby chair. "I can't believe they did this to you."

"Can't you?" he said with a smile that pulled at his cut lip and turned the smile into a wince.

"I'm sorry."

"At least they let me go. For now." He threw a glance toward the shadows, where a constable stood watching him. Another man stood guard across the street.

Reinhardt set aside the ice pack, and Rachel gasped when she saw the rest of his face. "I think you ought to have Dr. Hayes take a look at you," she said.

"Probably." He laced the fingers of his hands together and rested them in his lap. He was not looking at her. "Do you know how I got them to stop beating me, Rachel? By turning their suspicions against someone else." He sucked in a ragged breath that shuddered his chest. "And I'm not certain I can continue to live with myself after that."

She shook her head, not understanding. "What do you mean?"

"They're convinced the killer is a German agent sent to the area to find some legendary seventeenth-century watch. And because I'm Austrian, they decided the agent must be me. Seems they deciphered a wireless transmission that makes them think the killer will be picked up tonight from someplace identified only as 'rendezvous point two.' I kept telling them I didn't know what they were talking about, that they had the wrong man. Only they wouldn't stop hitting me. So finally to make them stop I sent them after the only other person I know around here who speaks German." Tears were rolling down the Austrian's bruised, swollen cheeks. "I keep trying to come to grips with what I've done, but—I can't."

Rachel felt her heart break for him. "You told them about Reverend Dingle?"

Reinhardt looked confused. "Is he German? I didn't know that."

"But... If not the vicar, then who?"

"That poor young waitress at the café. Pippa—Pippa MacAvoy."

CHAPTER 11

PIPPA MACAVOY AND HER small nephew lived in a cozy flat tucked up under the eaves of the cottage that housed Maria's Café. But when Jude and Stokes arrived there after leaving the police station, it was to find the flat empty.

"Where'd she go?" Stokes demanded of the stony-faced Maria Capello.

The old widow stared back at them with flat black eyes. "She go out. An hour ago. Maybe more. She no say where she go. What you want with her?"

"Damn," swore Stokes, slapping his palm against the nearby wall. "She's gone off to this rendezvous point, and we don't know where the hell it is."

"Maybe," said Jude. "Or she could simply have taken the little boy for a walk."

Stokes swung toward the narrow stairs that led up to the flat above. "Let's have a look."

They wasted precious minutes tearing the homey little flat apart. Stokes turned drawers upside down; slit the mattress and armchair and pulled out their stuffing; he even yanked up a couple of loose floorboards.

And found nothing.

"Where's the bloody wireless?" demanded Stokes, swiping an arm across his now sweaty forehead.

"Not here, obviously," said Jude.

Stokes glowered at him. "That bloody Austrian must have lied to us, saying he heard her speak German to the little boy. He made it up."

"Maybe," said Jude. "Or maybe she's smart enough to keep anything incriminating hidden someplace else. Then again, she could simply know German for some reason that has nothing to do with Hitler and a cursed watch."

Stokes shook his head, his jaw hardening. "He lied. I'm going to pick the bastard up again, and this time he's going to tell me the truth."

Jude went to stand at the window looking out at the gloaming of the day. "Not with me."

"Fine. If you change your mind, you know where to find me. I'll leave you the car."

After Stokes had stomped back down the stairs, Jude paused in the center of the room. He thought about the quiet young woman, Pippa, coming home from an innocent walk with the little boy to find the havoc they'd wreaked in her life. He thought about her waiting for a lightweight airplane on some lonely stretch of moor, with La Sirène in her pocket and a dagger hidden somewhere on her person. Which was it? he wondered.

He was surprised to find that either possibility filled him with great sadness.

Leaving the cottage, he went to lean against the Rover on the far side of the lane and lit a cigarette. It wasn't a habit he indulged often—he didn't care what the doctors said; you could never convince him that poisoning your lungs with smoke was healthy. But there were times when it filled a need, and this was one of them.

He'd almost finished his cigarette when a woman on a beat-up bicycle appeared out of the gloom. He watched her brake outside Maria's Café, but she stayed on her bike and simply sat staring thoughtfully at the cottage.

"If you're looking for Pippa MacAvoy, she's not here," said Jude.

Rachel Townsend-Smythe swung her head to look at him,

and he knew by the widening of her eyes that she hadn't noticed him standing there. She said, "I saw Sigmund Reinhardt—saw what you did to him. Is that what we've become? An ugly reflection of all that we're supposed to be fighting against?"

He took a last drag on his cigarette and ground it beneath his heel. "What makes you think we haven't always been that way? We just don't usually take it as much to the extreme as our friends across the Channel."

"Reinhardt says he heard Pippa speaking German."

Jude pushed away from the car and walked toward her. "That's what he claims. But physical abuse is basically a form of torture. It can convince people to say all sorts of things that aren't true, just to make it stop."

She shook her head. "I don't think he made it up."

"Is that why you're here?"

She swung away to look at the cottage across the lane again, dark now in the gathering gloom, and he saw something quiver across her face. "He says you think the killer is planning to leave Britain tonight, but you don't know from where."

He searched her tense features. "What are you trying to tell me?"

She turned her head to meet his gaze. "I think I might know."

She refused to tell him what she knew, saying only that she would ride in the car with him and direct him where to go.

"All right. But we need to pick up Stokes and some constables first," he said, opening the door for her.

She hung back. "No. We go alone or not at all."

"You can't be serious," he said, leaning into her. "I'm flattered you have so much faith in my ability to stop a killer. But if this woman is who we think she is and her Führer is sending a crew to pick her up, there's a very good chance that without some sort of backup she might get away."

She met his gaze and held it. "I'm willing to take the risk."

"Are you? I thought Major Crosby was your friend."

"He was."

"Yet you would risk letting his killer go free?"

"Rather than see an innocent young woman brutalized the way you brutalized Sigmund Reinhardt? Yes."

He wanted to say, *That wasn't me*. But he knew that wasn't really the point.

"Don't you understand?" she said, her hands coming up pressed together as if she were praying. "We have to stand for something. Otherwise what are we fighting for? So we can say we won?"

He didn't have time to argue with her. "All right, damn it. Just get in the car."

She got in the car.

They drove through the gathering darkness, the winding country lane lit only by the waning moon and the faint slit of light that was allowed to show through his taped-over headlamps.

"Turn left," she said at the first crossroads. Then, "Next right. Now go straight."

After a while, Jude figured it out. "We're going to the abbey, aren't we?"

She neither confirmed nor denied it, but simply stared straight ahead, her arms wrapped across her chest as if she were cold, although he knew she was not.

He said, "What makes you so certain Pippa MacAvoy is the killer?"

"I'm not certain. That's why I'm here."

"But you know something else, don't you? Something we haven't learned yet."

She hesitated a moment, then said, "Peter Osborne—the man who was killed down in Dover—right before he died, a relative came to see him and asked him about the watch. I found out today that it was a woman. And she had a little boy with her."

He slammed on the brakes and swung to face her. "I think you should get out here."

She looked over at him, her eyes wide and her face pale in the moonlight. "No."

"Bloody hell," he swore and threw the car into first gear again.

The abbey ruins looked ethereal, almost wraithlike in the silvery light. Jude rolled the car to a stop beside the museum and said, "Will you at least stay here?"

She shook her head. "Even if Pippa is the killer, that little boy she has with her is innocent of everything."

"So you're—what? Determined to put your life at risk just to save his?"

"You think that's wrong?"

Rather than answer, he eased open the door and said, "Sound travels far at night, so get out as quietly as you can."

She could see better than he in the dark.

He realized that soon enough, as she followed him silently and sure-footedly while he blundered about and tripped trying to creep along the path that snaked down to the beach below. At one point, when he practically slid off a steep turn, she quietly went ahead of him, and he let her.

At first he thought that Pippa MacAvoy—if she were indeed their quarry—must be here at the cove to meet a dinghy sent ashore from a U-boat. But the rocks and concrete barriers in the water made that unlikely, even if the surf were calm tonight—which it most definitely was not. He could hear the waves breaking against the cliffs of the point and the tumbledown remnants of what had once been Old Godwick. It would be madness to try to get through that in a dinghy.

More likely was a small, lightweight aircraft that would come in to land on the long, gently curving beach, pick up its passenger, then head back out to sea again, flying low enough to elude British radar. Jude had a Webley .32 semiautomatic pistol in a shoulder holster beneath his leather flight jacket. It would stop a woman with a knife. But a plane? Not likely.

"Do you see her?" he asked quietly as they neared the base of the soft, sandy cliffs. The beach had looked empty from above, but he knew that meant nothing.

"No. Maybe she's already gone."

"Maybe. Or she could be waiting out of sight."

He was pondering how to go about searching the boulders at the base of the cliff for someone who surely already knew he was coming when he heard a woman's loud, ringing voice say, "Don't come any closer. I have a knife against the little boy's throat, and if you come near me, I swear I'll kill him."

They drew up. Jude said, "You expect me to believe you'd slit your own nephew's throat?"

"He's not my nephew," said the woman. "I don't know who he is. I found him as a baby screaming in the ruins of a bombed-out house in London."

Jude could see her now, standing beside the rocks near one end of the hard-packed sandy beach. Beside him, Rachel said, "And you just picked him up? As if he were nothing more than a stray kitten or puppy?"

She shrugged one shoulder. "His parents were dead. And a woman with a child always seems more vulnerable and less of a threat than a woman alone."

Jude felt a strange, icy sensation sluice through him. The cold-blooded calculation of it—the casual indifference—was horrible even to think about.

"Auntie Pippa?" said the boy in a small, frightened voice. "I want to go home."

"Soon, Wills," she said, pressing a kiss to the top of his head. But she kept the knife against his throat. To Jude she said, "Throw your gun into the sea."

He hesitated, and she said, "I know you have one. Do it now. And carefully—with your left hand."

He eased the Webley from its holster, drew back his hand, and sent the pistol spinning across the churning waves toward an outcropping of rock just offshore. He heard it land with a clatter, then nothing.

"Now back up," she said. "Both of you. That's right; keep backing."

He was aware of Rachel beside him, the briny wind blowing her hair about her face, her cheeks glistening with the spray thrown up by the wild waves hitting the offshore rocks. Reaching out, he took her cold, wet hand in his, and she clenched her fingers with his as they backed slowly toward the base of the cliff face.

"That's far enough," said the woman.

They drew up.

"Who are you?" said Rachel, her voice strong and clear.

The woman looked at her. "Does it matter?"

Rachel shook her head, as if struggling to understand this woman she'd thought she knew. "You killed all those men for a *watch*? A watch you think will save Hitler? It's cursed! It has brought nothing but misery and death to everyone who has owned it for the last three hundred years. Why would anyone want to own it?"

"Because it has power. Dark powers that can be harnessed to serve those who know how to use it."

"No. All it can do is tempt those vain enough to think they can control it into destroying both themselves and those around them."

The woman gave a low, unexpected laugh. "Perhaps. I suppose we'll know soon enough, won't we?"

Jude was aware of Rachel tensing, her head turning as she gazed out to sea. "I hear an airplane," she said quietly.

It took a moment before he heard it: the distinctive throb of a small German aircraft coming in low.

He knew from the lifting of Pippa MacAvoy's head that she heard it, too. She stood straight and tall at the edge of the surf, with the child she had stolen and cared for and taught to love her cradled in her arms while she watched the plane skim toward them across the cove.

Jude said, "Leave the boy."

She looked at him in surprise and shook her head.

"He's nothing to you," said Jude. "Leave him."

He saw it then. Saw the quiver of emotion that crossed her face, saw the faint but unmistakable way her arms tightened around the small body she held, and he knew. He knew that while her theft of the orphaned child might have been calculated, in the process of caring for him over the last two years, she had come to love him.

Rachel said, "Leave Wills. Please. You know what's going to happen to Germany in the months to come. Don't take him into that. Leave him. Give him a chance to live and grow up here, where he'll be safe."

The plane was banking now to come in to land: a twin-engined Gotha Go 242 assault glider, with jettisonable landing gear and retractable skids. Jude jerked Rachel down behind a pile of boulders at the base of the cliff as the Go 242 thumped down on the hard-packed sand, its hatch already open as it taxied toward where Pippa waited. She watched it swing around and then, at the last possible moment, she thrust the little boy away from her and ducked through the open hatch. The door slammed shut as, engines revving, the plane taxied down the beach again toward takeoff.

"Auntie Pippa!" screamed the child.

Jude felt Rachel pull her hand from his grasp.

"Wait!" he shouted, but she darted away from him anyway toward the sobbing boy.

Swearing loudly, he dashed into the cold, pounding surf, splashing toward the rocks where he'd thrown his gun. He could hear

Rachel cooing, "It's all right, baby; it's all right," as she scooped the screaming child up into her arms and held him tightly. "It's going to be all right, darling."

"*Auntie Pippa!*" sobbed the child, his arms stretching out toward the rising plane.

Jude skimmed his hands over the surf-washed rocks, felt cold metal, closed his hand over the wet gun. He brought up the dripping Webley, sighted on the retreating plane, and squeezed the trigger.

Click.

"Damn," he said, lowering the useless, waterlogged gun. *Damn, damn, damn.*

Rachel came to stand beside him, her wet hair plastered to her face, Wills clutched in her arms. Together they watched the small plane disappear into the night. For a time they could still hear the drone of its engines. Then that, too, was gone.

"She got away," said Rachel, her voice strained. "She killed three men, and she's not going to be made to pay for it."

"She's headed for Nazi Germany," said Jude, turning his back on the storm-swelled sea. "With a cursed watch in her pocket. I don't think she's going to get away with anything."

Rachel looked at him. "I thought you didn't believe in curses."

His heart was pounding, and he was shaking with adrenaline and reaction. He hooked an arm around her neck to draw her and the child close. "I don't. But if anyone ever deserved that watch, it's Hitler."

CHAPTER 12

Early May, 1945

JUDE LOWE SAT AT his desk in Whitehall, one splayed hand rubbing his forehead as he stared down at the series of black-and-white photographs spread across his desk. Five pretty, towheaded little girls lying dead in a row beside their brother. The burned body of a German shepherd dog. More burned bodies, this time of a man and a woman.

He looked up at the sergeant who had brought him the grisly images. "Are we certain the body of the man is Hitler?"

The sergeant nodded. "Hitler and Eva Braun."

Jude looked again at the picture of the dead Goebbels children, said, "Damn," and leaned back in his chair.

The sergeant said, "According to one of the blokes the Russians captured alive, Hitler was holding some gold pocket watch when he shot himself. Bloke said he was obsessed with it."

"Where's the watch now?" asked Jude sharply. So sharply he saw the sergeant's eyes widen.

"I guess it was burned with the bodies."

"*And, finally, fire,*" said Jude quietly.

"Sir?"

"Nothing, Sergeant," said Jude. "Thank you."

After the sergeant left, Jude stared at those blackened bodies for a long time. He kept waiting to feel something—elation, satisfaction, relief. But all he knew was a strange hollowness.

And a niggling wish he could see the charred remnants of that infamous gold watch in the photograph.

He left London early that evening, driving south through sunlit hop gardens now turning a fresh, riotous green.

He'd driven down to New Godwick often over the past year. With the war in Europe now essentially over, the last of the concrete barriers were being removed from along the roads, direction signs were back in place, and cars were becoming more plentiful. When he turned in through the gates of the Grange, the sentries were still there, but he could see a line of loaded lorries parked along the drive leading to the big house.

"Jude," he heard Rachel call, and glanced over to see her walking toward him across the park, a smile of welcome on her face and little Wills trotting behind her with a black and brown puppy.

He pulled off the drive and got out of the car. "What's all this?" he asked, nodding toward the trucks.

"The army's leaving," she said, coming up to him. "They say we should have the house back in another week."

"The war's not over yet," he said. "Not in the Pacific."

"No. But it will be soon. I guess they figure they won't be needing any more cooks."

He took her hand in his. "Hitler's dead. He killed himself."

Her smile faded as she sucked in a quick breath. "They're certain?"

Jude nodded. "The bodies were burned, but not so badly that they couldn't be identified." He hesitated, then said, "Supposedly he died holding a gold watch."

"Was it burned with him?"

"I honestly don't know."

She was silent for a moment, watching the little boy wrestle, laughing, with his puppy. They had tried to trace his original family, but it was looking increasingly unlikely that they would ever find them, and Rachel had grown to love the boy so much that a part of him was secretly relieved. She said, "I can't help wondering what happened to Pippa."

"I suspect we'll never know. The number of women and children dying in Germany right now is horrific."

"I'm glad Wills is here."

"Yes." He stared off across the park, to the Nissen huts that had housed the Women's Land Army. Soon they would be gone, too. The war had shattered so many of the barriers that once segmented their society, bulldozing boundaries between men and women as well as between classes and races. But the remnants of the old assumptions and habits were still there, and he suspected they would linger for a long time.

What had grown up between them had seemed possible when Rachel was living in a tiny gamekeeper's cottage and he was a wounded pilot assigned to MI5. But soon her father the general would be home, and she would be moving back into the big house to live the life of the lady of the manor. He might have a university degree, but he was still the spawn of innkeepers and smugglers. And worse.

He realized she was looking at him with a smile in her eyes. She said, "So will you ask me now? Or were you planning to wait until Japan falls, too?"

He gave a low, startled laugh. She was everything he wanted in a woman, fiercely brave, quietly noble and humane, formidably intelligent. It took his breath to realize that all he had to do was reach for her.

And so he did.

Acknowledgments

I'd like to thank, first of all, my fellow authors—Anna Lee Huber, Susanna Kearsley, and Christine Trent—for inviting me to be a part of this fascinating project. It's been a wonderful, amazing experience. My thanks also to my agent, Helen Breitwieser; to Kevan Lyon; to our editor, Deb Werksman; and to all the great people at Sourcebooks who made this possible.

About the Author

C. S. Harris is the *USA Today* bestselling author of more than twenty-five novels. She has sold over a million copies of her Sebastian St. Cyr historical mystery series and is also the author of the standalone historical *Good Time Coming*; a thriller series cowritten with former intelligence officer Steven Harris; and seven award-winning historical romances.